The Quest for Excalibur

Guinevere
Book Five

Fil Reid

© Copyright 2023 by Fil Reid
Text by Fil Reid
Cover by Dar Albert

Dragonblade Publishing, Inc. is an imprint of Kathryn Le Veque Novels, Inc.
P.O. Box 23
Moreno Valley, CA 92556
ceo@dragonbladepublishing.com

Produced in the United States of America

First Edition September 2023
Print Edition

Reproduction of any kind except where it pertains to short quotes in relation to advertising or promotion is strictly prohibited.

All Rights Reserved.

The characters and events portrayed in this book are fictitious. Any similarity to real persons, living or dead, is purely coincidental and not intended by the author.

ARE YOU SIGNED UP FOR DRAGONBLADE'S BLOG?

You'll get the latest news and information on exclusive giveaways, exclusive excerpts, coming releases, sales, free books, cover reveals and more.

Check out our complete list of authors, too!

No spam, no junk. That's a promise!

Sign Up Here

www.dragonbladepublishing.com

Dearest Reader;

Thank you for your support of a small press. At Dragonblade Publishing, we strive to bring you the highest quality Historical Romance from some of the best authors in the business. Without your support, there is no 'us', so we sincerely hope you adore these stories and find some new favorite authors along the way.

Happy Reading!

CEO, Dragonblade Publishing

Additional Dragonblade books by
Author Fil Reid

Guinevere Series
The Dragon Ring (Book 1)
The Bear's Heart (Book 2)
The Sword (Book 3)
Warrior Queen (Book 4)
The Quest for Excalibur (Book 5)

For Patrick, without whose constant support none of these books would have been written

Chapter One

OUTSIDE THE HALL, a fierce, wintry wind buffeted the vast thatched roof, but inside we were snug. Maia, my maid, had long since latched the wooden shutters on the few windows and hung heavy rugs over them to keep out any sneaking drafts. On the square of bare flagstones in the center of the chamber, a brazier of red-hot embers glowed, and on the walls, smoky torches in their iron brackets spread flickering semi-circles of light.

Seated at the table, with half-a-dozen candles illuminating my work and my stockinged feet buried for warmth in the thick wolf pelt that covered the flagstones, I chewed the wooden end of my pen, an object already misshapen from the attentions of my teeth. For comfort, two layers of sheepskin on my chair cushioned my bottom, and around my shoulders hung my fur-lined cloak. It being winter, my usual occupation held me in its thrall. Writing, especially in the Dark Ages, could be a chilly business.

Open on the table before me lay the book I'd commissioned from the only source capable of fulfilling such a specific order. Monks. Our nearest brothers kept the monastery at Ynys Witrin and had been taken aback by my request. Or rather, by my husband's order. As far as they were concerned, writing in books was their work, not that of a woman, no matter that the woman in question happened to be a queen. Their queen.

I'd insisted, and so had my husband, Arthur. As their king – the

High King of all Britain – had ordered it, they'd been forced to comply, albeit grudgingly. Now, here it lay in front of me at last, a mixture of the impatient pages I'd already written, that had been pried from my unwilling fingers, bound with great care, and no doubt read with salacious curiosity, and new empty ones, ready for me to fill.

My demand for blank pages had also offended them.

"Pages are written first," Abbot Jerome had declared, on his high horse and looking down his long nose at Arthur. "Only then are they sewn together and bound. No one ever has *empty* books."

Or they hadn't until I'd asked for one.

"And women do not bother themselves with reading and writing."

This last statement I knew to be untrue, as Arthur's sister, that devious witch Morgana, could certainly do both, although the abbot, a man of old-fashioned ways, didn't know that. He'd had to stifle his protests and have the book made. It had been delivered this morning, after a number of probably artificially induced delays.

My hand touched the leather-bound cover, the darkly stained calfskin smooth under my possessive fingers, caressing it as lovingly as I would have done a first edition of a rare book back in my old world – the twenty-first century. A lot of time and skill went into book manufacture, and the leather had been carefully worked and treated to last.

And last was something this book would have to do – last forever. It would be a thorough record of the history of the Dark Ages, a time when barely anything was written down.

Where I came from, only the work of one man from that era had survived, and who knew if he'd truly been the only one to commit pen to parchment? Others, monks all of them, might well have written books that had been lost to the ravages of time, books that might have told a different story.

The famous author of that single surviving tome went by the name of Gildas, a man who happened to be my friend. Right now, he and boldly came to lean on the table beside me, invading my personal space, as was his habit with everyone. "Can we go down the hill to the village?" he asked, dark eyes challenging. "Amloch told us he's having a bonfire at his house and asked if we could come. It's his naming day, and there'll be games and a suckling pig to roast." Scarcely a year older than Amhar, he stood a good head taller and was twice as wide with a disturbing look of his unpleasant uncle Cadwy about him, particularly in his overly fleshy lips.

"Good afternoon, children," I said, eyeing them up and down and taking note of their wind-blown, rosy cheeks. They all wore short cloaks over their thick winter tunics, and their booted feet had trailed mud across the thick rugs.

"Good afternoon, Mother," Amhar said, ever polite.

"G'd aft'noon, Mami," Archfedd mumbled, hopping from one foot to the other as though in need of the bucket in the corner.

I fixed Medraut with a hard stare.

He stared back defiantly, but I had more patience than he did, and won. "Good afternoon, Aunt Gwen." He had no difficulty making those four words sound surly and rude.

"Well," I said, studying their faces. "Firstly, Archfedd is too young to go with just you two. You know that. And secondly, it's late in the afternoon, and will be dark in no time at all. And that is *not* a good idea." I met Amhar's eyes, surprised to find relief in them. "So, no. You can stay within the fortress walls until supper. Perhaps if you can persuade Llacheu to take you, tomorrow *morning*, then I'll change my mind. But just you two boys – Archfedd should stay here."

Archfedd's face took on a mutinous expression, and she kicked her boot against the table leg.

Medraut stuck out his lower lip, more daring than she was. "It won't be his birthday celebration tomorrow morning. My uncle the *King* would let us go."

I sighed. "Not at this time of the day. And the King is not here.

While he's away, *I* am the one in charge."

A scowl settled on his heavy brows. "*Mother* would let me go."

Oh dear. How to deal with this. I had to remember that Medraut was still a child, even though he'd grown so large, and a child who must be missing his mother. Almost impossible, when all I could think whenever I looked at him was that he might one day bring death to my husband. If the legends I knew were correct.

"Your mother isn't here either," I said, frostiness creeping into my voice no matter how hard I tried to keep it out. "She left you in my care, so you're subject to my control, just as Amhar and Archfedd are. And I doubt very much that she would have let you go wandering about outside Din Cadan by yourself at this time on a winter's afternoon, with darkness not far off."

Undaunted, he tried again. "It's not wandering – it's a party. My *father* would have let me go. Let *us* go."

This I couldn't argue. Probably Theodoric would indeed have allowed his son to do just as he wished, even at only twelve years old, but Theodoric was not here. He was back at Caerleon, if he had any sense, and if he didn't, which seemed more than likely, he was riding out the winter storms in one of his ships in the middle of the Irish Sea.

I forced a smile. "You're probably right there, but I have the final say, and I don't like you arguing with me like this, Medraut. Look. Amhar and Archfedd don't look unhappy at my decision. They know they have to do as they're told." I glanced at my own two children. "Why don't all three of you go off and find Maia – she's been baking your favorite honey cakes. You can tell her from me you're all allowed two each. And tomorrow, you boys can take two to Amloch as a present. Off you go now. I have work to do and you're disturbing me."

Still grumbling to himself, but mollified by the offer of the honey cakes, Medraut departed with alacrity, probably worried I'd change my mind. Amhar and Archfedd hurried after him, the puppy bounding at their heels.

For a moment or two, I sat staring after them, distracted from my work. I couldn't say I missed Theodoric, to whom I'd never warmed, and in all likelihood Medraut didn't either, as he'd so infrequently seen his father, but I felt a pang of sadness for the boy.

His mother, Arthur's youngest sister Morgawse, had decided, after a good many years spent here in Din Cadan, that her place lay at her husband's side in the port where his fleet was based. Possibly due to Theo's predeliction for other women. This sudden determination didn't stretch as far as accompanying him to sea, of course, and in case he decided his only son should go with him on one of his almost piratical voyages, she'd elected to leave Medraut here in comparative safety.

"Training to become a warrior," she said to me as she kissed me goodbye nine months previously, "is a far safer option for my son than going off in one of those leaky boats my husband's so proud of. I know you'll keep him safe for me, and *I'll* keep his father away from him."

I had mixed feelings about this, understandably. Part of me wanted Medraut where I could keep an eye on him, but another part, perhaps the wiser part, had wanted him gone from Din Cadan and away from my children. A third, fatalistic part, suspected that whatever happened, Medraut was already treading the path to the fateful day of Camlann, and that nothing I did could avert it. So, I smiled sweetly at my sister-in-law and assured her that I'd care for her son as though he were my own. While inside I shuddered at the thought.

A shiver ran through me, as though someone had walked over my grave. Which they might well have, back in my old world, as I'd be dry old bones by then. I pushed the unwelcome thought away and returned to my book.

Each page held a lot of information. I'd crammed the writing in, leaving only small margins, and not wasted space on illuminations, even though the abbot had pressed me to include them. There'd been a lot to squeeze in from the notes I'd taken on the thin wooden tablets that served as my everyday writing surfaces.

I turned to the first smooth, virgin page. Even as a child I'd loved the feel of a new sheet of paper to write on, although then it had been in school notebooks, not the laboriously prepared vellum that now lay before me. Made of almost translucent calfskin, it provided the most satisfying and beautiful surface to write on, and the weight of responsibility sat heavily on my shoulders as I picked up my pen again and dipped the tip into my inkpot.

The pen was a piece of narrow wood, rounded like a modern pencil, with a curve of thin metal coiled about it. Dipping it into the ink loaded the spiral like a small cartridge and would allow me to write several words without redipping the pen. However, using it was a hard skill to master, and every word I wrote had to be done with slow and careful precision. Oh, for a nice word processing program on a laptop – how easy would that have made my task. And what a surprise for archaeologists.

But of course, I didn't have either program or laptop, so I had to make do with what lay before me and think myself lucky there was anything to write on at all.

At the top of the fresh blank page, I wrote a new title. *The Battle of Tryfrwyd*. In Latin. I could speak and understand it as though it were my native language, but more often our day-to-day conversations were in Brythonic Celtic. Something to do with how I'd got here enabled me to slip seamlessly from one language to the other. How odd that the words I wrote were not just Latin but probably early medieval Latin, and me quite unaware of my proficiency in it.

I dipped the pen into my ink pot and began to write.

Chapter Two

MY PEN SCRATCHED across the vellum. The monks had covered the pages with faint lines for me to follow, which kept my writing neat and straight, like the lined notebooks I'd had as a child.

The twelfth year of the reign of Arthur, called Pendragon, King of Dumnonia. The ninth year of his rule as High King of all Britain. Autumn came, and with it, fair weather. The corn stood thick and tall in the fields, and a plentiful hay crop had been brought in for winter. With the good weather, the Saxons of the east became brave and bold, perhaps seeking to seize our crops for their own winter provisions, for many of them are settled here, and never return to their homelands.

Their leader is one Aelle, uncle to Cerdic, king of Caer Guinntgwic, a town that lies some fifty miles east of Din Cadan, on the River Itchen. Cerdic attends the Council of Kings in Viroconium alongside the other British rulers, and has sworn fealty to the High King. Yet all must wonder where his true loyalties lie. His mother was Saxon born, a sister of Aelle. His father was a British king. He is a man with a foot in two camps.

This Aelle sailed his ships up the Tamesis River past the old city of Londinium where now no Briton dares set his foot. The Saxons hold much of the east, and Londinium is theirs. But they do not like to live in the ruins of the old Roman city. It is said they believe the wraiths of the past inhabitants still haunt the tumbled buildings, and they will not set foot inside the city walls for fear of what walks there. So, Londinium, "Caer Lundein" in our tongue, is a true ghost city, the ruins left for cur dogs and yowling cats, for specters and perhaps a few bands of the more desperate brigands.

The Saxons push continuously against our borders, edging westward at every opportunity. Already along the Tamesis, small settlements exist which past kings have tolerated, founded by the ancestors of those who till the fields there now. These were men invited into Britain by our departed Roman overlords, or perhaps by the Usurper, Vitelinus the Guorthegirn, himself. Yet even these have inched their way to greater territory, encroaching upon our native-born farmers, taking their women to wife, and this summer Aelle hoped to lead his men against Caer Celemion. This town, ruled by our ally, King Einion, has lately become a frontier fortress, lying as it does not far to the south of the great river. Strong stone walls encircle it, but these are long and difficult to defend.

Writing by hand for too long made my right arm ache, and this was a lengthy piece to commit to paper in one go, but I wanted to do it with the memory still fresh in my mind. I stretched and flexed my fingers. With this new narrative, I'd be almost up to date with my history, and I couldn't help but feel a little smug. It had been a marathon undertaking. My fingers a little less stiff now, I dipped my pen into the inkpot once more.

King Einion, due to the proximity of Saxon settlements, had already wisely undertaken to block some of the gateways in his town of Caer Celemion, the better to defend its walls. This town sits amid the forest and heathlands to the south of the Rivers Kennet and Tamesis, and to the west of the River Loddon, and was once known as Calleva to the Romans.

I chewed the blunt end of my pen again, as though doing so might help the creative flow, while composing what to write next. From over the partition wall came the sound of people chattering together in the hall as they pulled the trestle tables away from the sides in preparation for our evening meal. The scent of roasting meat wafted over, making my mouth water. No, I had to concentrate, or I'd never get this done.

Aelle brought ten keels with him, some crewed by his own men, some by reinforcements from their distant homelands, all hungry for the treasures he had promised. For gold from British churches and villas, for the taking of slaves, for our women, and for the blood of our brave warriors.

I was rather guessing this bit, but I considered poetic licence allowed me to assume what Aelle and his Saxon warriors had been thinking when they'd sailed up the River Thames on that golden, early autumn day.

Children's laughter carried over the partition. Amhar and Archfedd must have gone to help Maia prepare for the evening meal. Medraut would never have wanted to help, so perhaps he'd departed to find the company of some of the older boys he so liked. I hoped so. Amhar was altogether too easily led by his bossy cousin, and although Archfedd was nothing like her brother, she tended, at eight, to trail along hopefully in their wake.

I gathered my thoughts again and redipped my pen in the ink.

When Einion's scouts brought him news of how many keels had been drawn up on the riverbank near the mouth of the River Kennet, he lit beacon fires and sent a single man galloping to bring the news to the High King, at his stronghold of Din Cadan.

Drat it. Now I'd repeated myself in writing "bring the news." One thing I'd never make was a writer. And I could hardly go back and scrape away that whole sentence. It would just have to stay. If archaeologists discovered my book one day, they weren't going to be assessing it for its linguistic qualities, after all.

The most noble King Arthur –

Well, why not sing his praises? This was the sort of thing I imagined a writer would have put in an early medieval document, so why shouldn't I? I could hardly include any of the personal things I felt about him. That would have sounded too weird. And besides which, I liked being flowery.

– on hearing the request, immediately gathered his fiercest and boldest warriors and set off eastward into the territory of King Einion. Among these warriors he numbered his bravest men – Merlin, his wise advisor; Cei, his brother and seneschal; Bedwyr, knowledgeable in all things concerning healing; Gwalchmei, Prince of Guotodin; Anwyll the warrior; Morfran of Linnuis; and Drustans of Cornubia. Also with the king rode his own oldest

son, Llacheu, a young warrior of peerless bravery, beauty and great strength.

There, I'd given most of them a mention. I had to consider that this book might not make it through fifteen hundred years intact, and that only parts of it might survive, so at every opportunity I inserted as many details and names as I could. The other thing that might happen could be that it would just survive as a later copy, fragmented and meaningless if I didn't constantly name the people and describe them. With the benefit of hindsight, I was trying to cover every eventuality.

The mighty force of the King, his combrogi, joined with the men of Caer Celemion to give battle against the Saxon horde. Together, they marched north from Einion's town, through the forest to the shores of the River Tamesis where they met the Saxon raiders at a place called Tryfrwyd, a small settlement only a few miles to the east of the Kennet's mouth, where the River Loddon runs north into the great river.

Maia's voice carried over the wall, raised in admonition. "Amhar, Archfedd, that's enough. Time for your own supper. Leave Cottia and her daughters to their work. Reaghan, off you go to your mother."

More laughter. Their playmate was Cei's daughter, Reaghan, a solid redhead a year older than Archfedd. A choice of companion I much preferred to Medraut.

"Now." Maia sounded cross. "I shan't ask you again. This way." No doubt they'd been making a nuisance of themselves, made silly by too much sugar in the honey cakes. Hyperactivity in a time before anyone had ever heard of it. I smiled.

A distant door banged. Hopefully those two scamps were doing as they'd been told. Poor Maia. She loved them dearly, but sometimes they took advantage of that unquestioning love. I'd have to speak to them. Again.

I shifted a little and rubbed my feet together. However many precautions one took, no building in the Dark Ages could ever be draught-proof, and, down by my ankles, cold was percolating upwards. Maybe I'd ask Maia to stitch together a foot muff out of sheepskin. An attractive thought. She could wrap a hot stone and put it in there.

The day of the battle dawned bright and clear. As the Saxons approached, the mighty King Arthur, with his cavalry, held the high ground above the valley of the Loddon. The Saxons were on foot, as is their custom, horses not being carried on their ships. The High King charged, catching them between the higher ground and the river, trapped, as our brave British cavalry swept down upon them in the customary wedge formation, learned in the days of the Romans. Thus may a cavalry charge divide footsoldiers and defeat them more easily.

It was no use. I'd have to go and warm my hands over the brazier. Sitting still and writing in winter was not conducive to comfort. I'd be getting chilblains if I wasn't careful. I padded over to the brazier and held my hands over the glowing embers, basking in the heat. My skin began to glow.

From the room my children shared with Maia came the sound of their voices, telling her they didn't want cabbage again, followed by Maia reciting to them the reasons, learned from me, as to why they needed to eat green leafy vegetables every day. Not much variety in the Dark Ages in winter, so cabbage featured a lot in their diet. Mine too. There were a number of things you could do with it to add variety. However, unluckily for them, Maia thought just plain boiling it was best.

I smiled to myself as their protests faded. Did I have time to get this part of my book finished before it was time to eat? I'd try. Arthur was expected back in the next few days, so I needed to take advantage of his absence, and the opportunity to write.

The battle was long and fierce. Aelle is a brave leader and ferocious warrior. His men stood their ground as best they could, but the advantage of being on horseback eventually won the day for our British warriors. King Arthur and our valiant men beat the Saxons back bit by bit, until at last they reached the banks of the Tamesis River. Here, they found the Saxons' ships drawn up, and sent fire arrows into them. The Saxons fought like savage demons, using the river water to put out the fires the arrows started. Their men crowded onto the ships and pushed off into the wide river, and our archers continued to pelt them with fire arrows as they rowed away downstream toward Londinium. The day was won, and Aelle will think twice before returning. Our losses were small. King Einion welcomed the High King and his men into Caer Celemion with great rejoicing and a feast.

Was that enough? Reading it over, it didn't seem as though it was. Such a few words to convey what? Nothing about what a real battle was like. Putting it this way made it sound clinical and quick, as though my husband had easily put the enemy to flight.

It hadn't been like that. On that crisp autumn day with a bright blue sky overhead, a day when no one could have imagined anything awful happening, the little valley of the Loddon had become a bloodbath. And afterwards was always the worst. With the still smoldering Saxon ships hightailing it down the river, aided by the current, what was left behind where once had been a peaceful farming settlement was like something from my worst nightmare. I'd never get used to the aftermath of a battle, no matter how long I lived in the fifth century.

But I couldn't write that in my book. I didn't have the words for it, nor the stomach to recall it in such detail. Seeing it in my head was bad enough, but putting it on paper would have given the memory solid reality. And I didn't want that. History wouldn't need that. History needed dates, specific spots for battles, and names. Bare facts. And bare facts I would give them.

I blew on the page to dry the ink. Then, slipping on my boots, I went through the door into the Great Hall to take my place at the high table. Dinner was served.

Chapter Three

THE MORNING BROUGHT heavy rain, so Medraut and Amhar's trip down to the village never materialized, which pleased me. I couldn't get over my mistrust of Morgawse's son, no matter how hard I tried, and didn't want my boy going out of the fortress with him, even with Llacheu to watch over them.

Whether my mistrust had to do with the legends from my old world, or just Medraut's bossy, unkind personality, I couldn't make up my mind. Probably a bit of both. For some reason, though, Amhar liked him, admired him even. And thanks to Morgawse's departure to keep a much-needed eye on her husband, Medraut had been sleeping in my children's chamber, under Maia's supervision, forcing them ever closer together.

After a disgruntled argument, the boys trudged off to their lessons, shoulders slumped in resignation. No sooner had they departed, than my sister-in-law and best friend, Coventina, Cei's wife, braved the wind and rain to scuttle through the mud to the hall, accompanied by Reaghan, her nine-year-old.

Archfedd ran to her friend, and they embraced. "No boys today," Archfedd announced with glee. "They're doin' their lessons." The two girls giggled, and hurried to settle themselves to play with their dolls on the thick rugs that lay spread around the brazier.

In another world, these soft, pale-faced rag dolls would probably have been Barbies, but here, little girls like these were content with what they had. Maia had hand stitched the dolls for them a year or so ago, and, at my suggestion, added a varied selection of clothes, proving that the dressing and undressing of dolls amused little girls of any time period.

Coventina settled herself on a stool beside mine. A tall woman, with dark hair already streaked with gray, it took her a moment or two to find a comfortable position. Reaghan had been born by an improvised Caesarean-section that might have saved her mother's life but had left her with the constant pain of damaged nerve endings.

"That's better now." She heaved a sigh as she unfolded the sewing she'd brought, a contented smile on her homely face as she surveyed our two little daughters. "'Tis painin' me a bit today. I think 'tis the cold and damp of winter that do it."

For a moment I watched her, my brow furrowed. The lines about her eyes softened as her needle darted back and forth through the cloth. Heaving a sigh, I picked up my own sewing from where it lived on the table behind me, and viewed it with disfavor. I was supposed to be working on a shirt for Amhar, who was fast outgrowing the ones he had. Not my favorite pastime.

For a moment or two we worked in companionable silence. But not for long.

"Ouch!" I sucked my left forefinger, into which I'd just jabbed my needle, tasting blood. "It's no use. I don't feel like sewing today."

Maia, sitting stitching behind us, badly disguised a snort of laughter. Most of the clothes my children wore had been made by her, as by the time I finished anything, it often no longer fitted, and more than likely was decorated with splodges of my own blood. War-wounds, Coventina called them, knowing the constant battle I had with a needle.

Now she looked up with a smile from the beautiful embroidery she was working on a shirt for Reaghan. "Do you *ever* feel like sewing? There's not much else to do on a day like today. Not for us women."

I scowled. Dark Age winters could definitely drag – especially for women. With a pang of longing, I glanced across at the table where my book lay. I had to suppress the itch to open it and add some more to my history. How rude would that be when Coventina had come expressly to keep me company?

A sigh escaped me. "I'd like to be outside. Even if it's pouring with rain, it's got to be better than being cooped up in here with the brazier smoking like this."

With little draught to draw it through the thatch and out into the wet air, a heavy pall of woodsmoke hung in the high rafters. Not for the first time I wondered how difficult it would be to introduce a chimney into the great hall, as well as one here in our chamber. However, as working in a library wasn't much of a preparation for building chimneys, especially not in highly combustible thatched wooden buildings, maybe this wasn't one of my best ideas. I'd give that one a miss.

Coventina shook her head, laughing. "You do say some funny things. You'd catch your death out there. It's raining like a waterfall."

I grimaced and picked up my hated sewing again, the bleeding having stopped. The shirt already had liberal spots of blood from other stabbed digits decorating it, and I didn't want to add more.

Archfedd had dressed her doll in the pretty blue gown made from the scraps left over from her own – both made by Maia, of course. "The princess is marrying the prince," she said to Reaghan. "Like in Cind'rella." She stuck one of the doll's fat stuffed legs out. "See. She's got the glass slipper on."

Reaghan leaned forward to look, her small, freckled nose wrinkling. "No she hasn't. She's got a big fat foot like one of the Ugly Sisters. My doll's the princess. See." She paused, her face falling. "Only, we haven't got a prince for her to marry."

"That's such a lovely story you've taught them," Coventina said. "I don't know where you get them from. You have such an imagination.

Reaghan loves them." She smiled. "Her favorite's Rapunzel."

"I likes Snow White the best," Maia said, knowing she could speak her mind to both of us. "Because that ole witch what's mean to her reminds me of the Princess Morgana. Bet she do have a poisoned apple hid somewhere about herself."

Coventina and I chuckled.

Reaghan glanced up. "My princess is called Rapunzel. Look at her lovely long hair."

Her doll did indeed have a very long plait made of wool that had been dyed a vibrant yellow.

She jiggled the doll up and down. "Rapunzel, Rapunzel, let down your hair, that I may use it as a stair." She and Archfedd burst into fits of giggles.

The rain rattled on the wooden walls of the Hall, and I shivered. "Maybe you're right about the weather," I said, over the heads of the little girls. "But Arthur's most probably out in it, though, getting soaked to the skin. And Cei."

Coventina grimaced and nodded, her fingers working automatically, as though she had no need to look at what she was doing. No brown bloodstains on anything *she* sewed.

A sudden draught licked around my shoulders, and I shivered again. Arthur and his war band, almost certainly out in this, would be colder, though, and wet. Hopefully, they were already riding back from the south coast where they'd been called to less than a week ago.

Even though we now had a successful messaging service set up between the kingdoms, it irked that I still had no way of finding out my husband's whereabouts when he was gone from Din Cadan.

"Bloody Saxons, raiding in the winter," I muttered, under my breath so the girls wouldn't hear.

Coventina chuckled. "It weren't like this when they left. 'Twere a bright day as I recall. I daresay that'd be why the Saxons were troublin' the south coast. I'd guess they're as fond of pourin' rain and storms as we are."

"Bugger." I sucked a different digit this time, tasting the iron in my blood.

"Bugger," echoed Archfedd.

Botheration.

"That's not a word little girls are allowed to use," Coventina said, keeping her voice gentle. "So don't repeat it again, please."

Archfedd shot her a narrow-eyed, speculative look. She'd be saving that word up to use when we weren't within earshot, for sure. "I won't," she lied.

I was just about to try another stitch, when someone knocked on the hall door. Setting my sewing down in relief, I got to my feet.

Young Peredur of Gwent, cloaked and booted against the weather, stood dripping onto the rushes on the hall floor. A big grin split his face despite the rain running from his wet hair.

He bobbed a bow. "Milady, you've a visitor."

Raising my eyebrows, I shot a quick glance back at the others, glad for an excuse to get away from my haphazard sewing. "I'll just be in the hall." I stepped through the doorway and closed the door behind myself with a little more firmness than was strictly necessary. Phew. Maybe every time I sewed, I needed to organize someone to call me away.

This early in the day, gloom enveloped most of the usually brightly lit hall. Only a couple of torches burned in the iron wall brackets – just enough to illuminate the high table on its dais. In the body of the hall, close by the smoldering fire pit, a slight figure stood, holding his hands out to the glowing embers. A boy.

Instead of mounting the dais, as I would have done to receive a messenger from another kingdom, or a plaintiff come for judgement, I walked down the hall to where the boy stood huddled over the heat, his clothes dripping onto the thick carpet of rushes underfoot. Peredur followed close behind, but probably not from suspicion of the boy.

I stopped. "Hello?"

The boy straightened proudly, throwing the wet and ragged cloak that gave him the look of a peasant, back over his thin shoulders. I stared. Something about him seemed familiar. His brown hair hung in wet rats' tails, and anxious dark eyes looked back at me from a pale, rain-washed face, as though he were waiting for something. For recognition, perhaps. After a moment, he remembered himself and made a clumsy bow. "Milady."

"Do I know you?" I couldn't keep the curiosity out of my voice, sure I recognized him from somewhere.

A faint smile lit the boy's thin face and he nodded with vigor. A hand went to his tunic front, fumbling for something. When his hand emerged, he held it out, grubby palm uppermost. On his palm sat an oval gold brooch, a dragon embossed on it. The dragon emblem of Dumnonia.

Recognition dawned and I groped in my memory for his name. "Llaw... Llawfrodedd?" My voice rose in surprise. I'd never thought to see this boy again. "I remember you. The boy who found my horse for me at Breguoin, when I thought she was long gone – stolen by the man who knocked me out."

Llawfrodedd bowed again, with a little more panache, a smile lending his pinched features and red-with-cold nose the hint of a healthy glow. He straightened, puffing out his chest. "I did come 'ere to train to be a warrior, like you said. I did keep the brooch you gived me so's I could buy myself an 'orse and sword – jus' like you said. But our priest, he did say as not to buy un till I got here. Lest I were diddled out o' the brooch by dishonest men."

I couldn't help but return his open smile. "A good piece of advice, Llawfrodedd. There are many men out there who would have parted you from your gold and given you nothing in return but perhaps a lump on the head or even a dagger in the ribs." I paused, remembering the day I'd met this boy, in the aftermath of the bloody battle we'd saved his people from. "But how did you get here, if you have no horse? We're a long way from Breguoin, and this isn't the time of year for traveling."

The boy shivered. How stupid of me. He must be frozen, despite his proximity to the fire. "No, tell me your story later. Go with Peredur, to the house he shares with his friends, and see if they can find you something warm to wear. And food to eat. And something to drink. Only then may you return to the hall."

The boy, wide-eyed, bobbed another bow. "Thank'ee, Milady, for bein' so kind."

With a grin, Peredur flung a protective arm about his protégé's narrow shoulders, and led him off as instructed. He might well feel proprietorial, as it had been he who all those years ago had said to the boy that he should aim to one day become a warrior for the High King. Something he himself had only been aspiring to at the time.

With a smile, I went back to my chamber to tell Coventina and Maia about our new recruit.

Chapter Four

PEREDUR RETURNED WITH young Llawfrodedd in an hour. The clothes he and his friends had found the boy hung loosely about such a slight and skinny frame, emphasizing his extreme youth. But I'd long since learned that youth was no barrier to becoming a warrior in the Dark Ages.

On my invitation, Peredur brought the boy into my chamber, which served as far more than just a bedroom, being a place where Arthur often held meetings, where the children played, where I socialized with Coventina and the other women of the fortress, and of course, where I worked on my book whenever I had the time.

From just inside the door, Llawfrodedd stared around himself in awe, and for a moment I saw the room through his eyes. With rafters reaching into the lofty and gloomy thatched roof, and lit by the glow of the brazier and a few torches on the walls, it must have been the largest and best lit room he'd ever seen. Thick rugs festooned the flagstones and walls – furs, and a few heavily embroidered pieces that had arrived via Din Tagel's port from the distant Middle Sea, perhaps from as far afield as the country I'd call Turkey back in my old world.

Arthur's spare shields decorated one wall, each of them round and painted white with a ferocious black bear rearing up on them, their surfaces dented and pocked by the blows of the warriors he'd fought. My own shield, smaller, lighter, easier for me to handle, and painted blue with a gold ring emblazoned on its surface, hung beside them.

Between the shields, an array of the weapons Arthur had left behind when he'd ridden south had been attached: a couple of long spears, a lance, an unstrung bow and a quiver of finely fletched arrows. And my own sword, the object of my fierce pride.

Nudging the wall opposite the door stood our big, fur-covered bed, flanked by the two massive wooden chests that held mine and Arthur's clothing. On the far side of the brazier stood our table, its worn surface topped by my precious book.

I gestured to the chairs I'd placed ready at the table. "Peredur. Llawfrodedd. Welcome. Please sit down."

Coventina glanced up in curiosity from where she still sat sewing but didn't move, her industrious fingers stitching away at her embroidery. Reaghan kept her auburn head bent over her doll, but Archfedd watched the newcomer, her half-dressed doll discarded in her lap and her mouth slightly open.

I'd ordered a jug of hot spiced wine, and now I poured it into horn beakers. "Drink."

The boy picked his beaker up suspiciously and took a sniff. "'Tis wine? Like at communion?" His voice, on that difficult cusp where it was still breaking, held awe.

I nodded. "Try it. It's good." No such thing as sheltering kids from alcohol in this world.

Llawfrodedd's dark eyes opened wide, horrified. "Int it the blood o' Christ?"

Peredur sniggered a little impolitely.

I struggled not to do the same. "Oh." I paused. "No. That's only *communion* wine. This is different." Was it? I scrabbled about trying to think why it would be different. "The priest blesses special wine to turn it into communion wine. This hasn't been blessed. It's not Christ's blood. It's just wine."

He regarded me out of eyes that told me by their look of doubt that he wasn't sure whether I was telling the truth. I smiled, and took a swig of the wine, and so did Peredur. Llawfrodedd, eyes still wide, took a tentative sip, as though he feared he might burn in hell for so doing. A little smile ventured onto his face. "'Tis much better than the wine we did have for communion back home. That were like vinegar."

I laughed. "This is a king's house. Only the best wine here." I paused. "Now, tell me about your journey."

His was a sad tale. I'd underestimated his parents, who, poor as they were, had not tried to take the brooch away from him once I'd left with Arthur and his army, even when hard times had hit them and the boy had offered it. No, they'd insisted it was his, given to him by the Ring Maiden, and that one day he should do with it as we'd suggested so casually – buy himself a horse and sword and become a warrior. Something that would improve his position in life from unimportant peasant to respected warrior. Social mobility of the Dark Age kind.

He couldn't tell me his age, but by counting back the seven years to the Battle of Breguoin and remembering how small he'd been then, I guessed him to be about fourteen now. No more, surely, although undersized and skinny from a peasant diet.

His mother had died three years ago, he thought, birthing her eighth child. He didn't know the details, but from the mess he'd had to help his father clear up, it sounded like a post partum haemorrhage. The baby had died too, within days, as they'd had no milk to give her. A sad story probably repeated frequently in this time period.

While he talked, Archfedd got to her feet and came to stand beside the table, her doll hanging loosely from her hand, pressing her small, warm body against my side and gazing at the boy out of wide brown eyes. In another world I might have shielded her from his story, but not in this one. This was a world where death lurked in every corner.

"Then this summer my da were workin' for Arlin, our town blacksmith, makin' swords what the king had ordered. My da were glad o' the work. I were helpin' too. The more the better, Arlin said. Lots o' swords to make."

My ears pricked. Lots of swords? For the king? A king who must be Cadwy, in Viroconium. The king who seven years ago had sworn not to oppose Arthur any longer. The king with whom Arthur had formed something he liked to think of as an alliance? I'd have to think about that one later. And tell Arthur.

The boy hesitated, clasping and unclasping his still grubby hands where they rested on the table. Peredur put a supportive arm across his shoulders, and Archfedd sidled closer, gazing up in a mixture of fascination and sympathy.

"There were a big fire, and my da were burnt somethin' bad, all down one side." The boy swallowed. "We did carry him back home, and the Priest did come and see to him, but it weren't no good." His voice faltered. "He – he did die, he did." He shook his head, studying his hands. "Weren't a good death, neither." He fell silent.

We all sat and waited, not hurrying him. At last, he raised his head, eyes glistening with unshed tears. "With his dyin' breath, he told me to follow me heart an' come here to find you – the queen what give me this." He held out the brooch. "To bring this back to you, the Ring Maiden. So's I could become a warrior an' better meself."

"Do you have no other family?" I asked, keeping my voice as gentle as I could. "No brothers or sisters? No grandparents?"

He shook his head. "Our neighbors did take my only sister. She's five years old, so I couldn't bring her wi' me. They'll be kind to her, I don't doubt. They don't have no girls o' their own, and the wife, she did badly want one. The Priest did say 'twas for the best."

I nodded. Such was life in the Dark Ages. No welfare state or social workers to make sure a child was well cared for. I hoped his neighbors hadn't seen his little sister as a useful drudge for their household. And Llawfrodedd, considered at fourteen to be an adult, had been cast adrift into the world, parentless and alone. I reached out and covered his bony hands with one of mine. "And you *shall* become a warrior. I'll make sure of that."

Archfedd reached up and added hers to mine. She, a child who had never known want, beamed a five-hundred-watt smile at the boy who had nothing. "My mami'll be kind to you, boy. I promise."

His dark eyes shone with tears. "Thank you, Milady. And you too, Princess. I can pay my way. I have the brooch, still, to pay for my sword an' horse."

I shook my head. "You won't need it. If you become one of my husband's warriors, then a horse and sword will be provided. But first, you must learn everything there is to know about being a warrior. You'll live here in the fortress with the other boys your age, and you'll have lessons every day. Not just in fighting. There's more to becoming a warrior than just swordsmanship."

Archfedd nodded sagely at the boy. "That's right. You can learn all about it with my brother and his friends." Her small, sweet face, suddenly serious, gazed at him with all the confidence her position had instilled in her.

Chapter Five

"HE'S HAVING WEAPONS made?" Arthur said. "You're sure of this?"

I nodded. "From the horse's mouth, so to speak. Llawfrodedd's father was killed helping forge the swords Cadwy ordered."

Arthur had been back scarcely an hour, and we were standing in our chamber facing one another, with him still in his wet armor and cloak, dark hair plastered to his face and six days growth of beard shadowing his jaw. I'd thought it best to tell him straightaway about the news Llawfrodedd had so unwittingly divulged.

My husband shook his head. "It could be he just needs new weapons..."

I compressed my lips and made no comment. Let him reach his own conclusions. I'd spent last night lying awake considering the reasons why a fellow king might be arming himself in what sounded like a hurry. You only needed extra swords if you intended to have extra warriors, and every king had a goodly number of them already. They had to, otherwise they'd never have survived with the threats that hemmed us on every side.

Arthur sank onto one of the wooden chairs beside the table, his hand rasping across his bristly chin. "We have an agreement of non-hostility that's lasted six years or more. There has to be a reason for this – a plausible explanation."

I stayed silent, watching him. At thirty-five, my husband still had the appearance of youth about him, muted a little by the few lines around his eyes and mouth. No hint of gray marred his thick mane of almost black hair, and his only sign of stiffness was from where he'd been wounded in the thigh over eight years ago. After more than a week on the march, he looked, and smelled, much in need of a bath and a change of clothes.

"Well," he said, heaving a deep sigh. "Too late now to stop him. If the swordsmiths were laboring for him this autumn, then he'll have all the weapons he needs by now. What does he think he's doing? Arming his peasantry? His townspeople?" His voice rose in incredulity. "I need word from my spies in Viroconium."

I put a hand on his arm. "We've no way of knowing, and your spies might not even be of any help. But you're soaked. Let's get you out of these things. You'll catch your death if you don't get dry."

He raised his eyes to look into my face, and gave me a rueful smile. "Ever the mother hen. I've been in these wet clothes for the last three days, so I don't see what difference it'll make." He sighed. "But all right. You win. I'll take them off."

I smiled. "I could tell that from the smell of you."

Rising, he discarded his sodden cloak in a heap at his feet, then unbuckled the heavy leather belt that held his sword.

My gaze lingered for a moment on the plain hilt and the worn, dark-leather grip as, with more care than he'd had for his cloak, he laid sword and belt on the table. This was the sword he'd drawn from the stone nine years before, in the forum at Viroconium. The sword I suspected his brother, Cadwy, had never forgiven him for taking. He'd made his peace with Cadwy two years after that, after the latter's botched attempt at assassination during the Council of Kings. Back then I'd not been sure the peace would last, and now it seemed it might not have.

I helped him out of the heavy mail shirt and laid that on the table as well, careful to keep the wet items away from my precious book.

His padded tunic came off next, leaving him in his damp undershirt and leather braccae.

I wrinkled my nose at the stink of sweat and horses, but it didn't offend me nearly as much as it once would have. "I ordered the bath house made ready, thinking you'd all need a soak in hot water."

Our bath house was nothing like its Roman antecedent, being just a small building provided with wooden bath tubs that laboring servants had to fill with hot water, but it was better than nothing.

He grinned, the boyish look I loved returning. "Thank you. If I didn't have to share with my men, I'd have you come as well, to scrub my aching back for me."

That brought a chuckle. "I think your men might object if I invaded the bath-house when it's in use, even though I've seen them naked before." On the march, they often bathed in rivers, and I'd grown used to their lack of modesty. "Come back here when you're clean and warm, and I'll rub your back. That's a promise."

I rummaged in his clothes chest to find him a clean shirt, braccae and tunic, and made a neat pile of them. He fastened a fresh cloak against the rain, tucked the clean clothing under it to keep it dry, and left.

His going left a palpable hole in the room. His was such a vital presence that when he'd been with me and had gone, I felt as though a part of the life of the room had departed with him. I picked up his mail shirt and hung it on its regular hook. He could oil it later, or get a boy to do it for him, to stop it from rusting. Amhar might be pleased to help with that. Gathering his discarded cloak, I hung it over the back of two chairs as close to the brazier as I dared, and it began at once to steam.

Back at the table, I studied his sword for a moment or two. Innocuous and bland, it lay like any other sword, and I'd seen plenty of them in my time. I even had my own, hanging on the wall. The question that had so often puzzled me rose again in my heart. Could this plain, warrior's sword be the famous Excalibur? Arthur had drawn it from the stone where Merlin had set it, proving himself to be the true High King, and, facing the scrutiny of all the other kings, had repeated the feat in front of them.

No one had ever attempted to bestow on this plain warrior's sword any kind of name – other than 'the sword of destiny' which wasn't a name that had survived to the twenty-first century. I touched the hilt with the tips of my fingers. The brown leather hand grip had worn smooth with use, blackened a little from the hands that regularly held it and weren't always clean.

Excalibur. A name to conjure with. But maybe this sword wasn't it. More than one sword legend had attached itself to Arthur's name – not just the story of the fabled sword in the stone, but also that of the Lady of the Lake, and her strange weapon. As far as I could remember, the name Excalibur applied to the one supplied by the mysterious watery hand. I smiled. It seemed unlikely we were ever going to see *that* happen.

I shook my head at myself for even considering some magical creature with the capability of breathing under water might stick out an arm to offer her sword to Arthur. Plain silly. And yet…

My ruminations on the sword legends were rudely interrupted as the door from the children's room burst open, and Amhar and Medraut catapulted into the room. Were my children incapable of coming through a door any other way?

"Father's home!" Amhar announced, possibly in case I hadn't noticed, his face alight with excitement. "We were in our lessons and didn't hear him come back. Peredur told us."

For once, Medraut was hanging back, a diffidence in his eyes I didn't often see. I had to feel sorry for him. He was only twelve, after all, and practically parentless now, but luckier than Llawfrodedd, who'd had no one to care for him. Medraut did at least have his extended family, and we were nothing if not rich and influential. He was never going to be abandoned to manage on his own, however far away his real parents wandered.

I smiled at the boys. "He is indeed. In the bath house right now, getting clean and hopefully having a shave." I wagged my finger. "Let this be a lesson to you boys – we ladies do not like men with beards."

"Eww," Medraut exclaimed, back to his usual self. "I don't want to know that, thank you very much. I'm never kissing a girl. They're gross."

Amhar pulled a similarly disgusted expression. "Me neither." He rubbed his baby-soft chin. "If I grow a beard, then maybe I'll never have to."

I chuckled. It felt like only the other day his half-brother Llacheu had been saying just the same things. Now eighteen, however, he'd changed his tune. I'd spotted him more than once with the very pretty Ariana, daughter of Anwyll, heads together as though no one else in the world mattered.

I'd been considering asking Arthur if he'd noticed. A father to son talk might well be needed here, before something serious happened between them. They *were* teenagers, after all. Memories of young Drustans at much the same age, and his illicit liaison with Princess Essylt of Linnuis, surfaced.

"Can we eat with you and Father tonight?" Amhar asked. "Instead of with Maia and Archfedd? She's such a baby still, and me and Medraut are nearly old enough to be warriors."

How I hated it when he reminded me of that. Even seven years on from the Battle of the City of the Legion, I still couldn't bear to think of how Cei and Coventina's son, Rhiwallon, had died in his first year as a warrior. Barely fourteen years old, a Saxon warrior had disembowelled him. Arthur and I never spoke of it, but it didn't take any sixth sense on my part to tell me he'd not forgotten his own part in the boy's death, and never would. To end the suffering of his brother's son, he'd had to slide a knife under the boy's ribs and into his heart.

I shivered at the memory and forced myself back into the present. "You'll have to ask your father. But Archfedd will be jealous if he says yes."

"Who cares?" sneered Medraut. "She's only a girl and doesn't matter."

Little shit. Only not so little now – my nephew could easily have been mistaken for a boy several years his senior.

Amhar's brow furrowed. He loved his little sister dearly, but Medraut was a big influence on him. Too big, in my opinion, but we were stuck with him now his mother had decided his father posed a danger. Unless we dispatched him off to live with his Uncle Cadwy, and that alternative didn't bear thinking of. At least while he remained here, I could keep an eye on him with the help of Merlin, in whom I'd confided my fears.

"Girls matter very much," I said to Medraut. "As you'll find out one day. And it's best to always treat them properly."

He gave me a disbelieving look. "But they're useless. They can't fight, or climb trees or ride properly."

Arrogant little sod. "Of course they can do all of those things," I retorted, stung, but keeping my voice level. "It's just men won't let them." I pointed to where my own sword hung on the wall near Arthur's weapons. "You know very well that's my sword hanging there. And that I know how to use it."

"Mother killed a man," Amhar said, his grubby face glowing with pride. Something Medraut's mother had never done – to my knowledge.

"Just the one," I said. "And it was to save someone's life."

Medraut shifted his weight, looking awkward. "But you're diff'rent. You're the Ring Maiden. Everyone knows that. I mean ord'nary girls can't do stuff. Girls like Archfedd. She's jus' going to grow up and marry some prince. What does she need to learn to fight and ride for?"

By his side Amhar stood watching, mouth slightly open, perhaps a little shocked by Medraut's boldness, his eyes flicking back and forth between me and his cocky cousin.

I sighed. "Perhaps Archfedd won't want to just become someone's wife. Perhaps she'll want to become a warrior princess, or even to write books, like me. No one has to do what is expected of them, Medraut. We all have free will."

"Isn't that heresy?" Amhar asked, his voice small and low.

I frowned. "Has that village priest been up here again? Today?"

Both boys nodded.

"Teaching you that you don't have free will?"

Two more nods.

Medraut volunteered more information. "He said as free will was wrong. He said as in the past we British had practised something bad called…" He sought for the word. "P-Pelagianism, and it was all wrong. We have to believe in pre… pre-ordained lives. That we can't change anything. That we're born wicked."

Well, if I was right, Medraut certainly might have been.

I smiled. "That's not precisely what Pelagianism means." *Stupid uneducated priest.* "It means that we're born innocent and we have the power to reach salvation ourselves. Babies are not born sinful."

"Are *you* a Pelagian, Mother?" Amhar asked, eyes round.

This conversation was not going in a direction I felt comfortable with, nor at ease in discussing as I didn't know enough about it. I shook my head. "No, I'm not." I'd have liked to have said I'd been baptized into the Church of England by my parents, but I held my tongue. "I have my own beliefs that I don't wish to share with you boys right now."

Medraut scowled as though this had been something he really wanted to probe. "Do you worship the old gods then?" he asked. "Keelia's daughter, Kala, told me you came here from Annwfn – from fairyland. Right out of the hill at Ynys Witrin. Where old Gwyn ap

Nudd lives. The fairy king."

Amhar nodded. "She did too. She said you was a fairy. That your father was Gwynn ap Nudd hisself." He paused. "She said that made me fairy-born an' that the fairies might come and try to snatch me back, at night, when I'm asleep. Is that true?" His voice wavered with uncertainty.

I kept my face straight. Bloody Kala with her garbled stories. Everyone at Din Cadan knew I came from Ynys Witrin, the island in the middle of the marshes that would one day become Glastonbury.

Stories abounded about my origins, not just here in Din Cadan, but elsewhere, none of which were true. I set my hands one on each boy's shoulder, Medraut's solid and well covered, Amhar's slight and bony. "I do *not* worship the old gods, and my father was *not* Gwynn ap Nudd. Both my parents are long dead and were perfectly human just like you. However, I *was* with the monks at Ynys Witrin."

Briefly.

"Nothing more than that. And you are not fairy-born, Amhar." I squeezed his shoulder. "You can rest assured I shall be having words with young Kala."

Chapter Six

ARTHUR AGREED TO the boys dining with us in the hall that night, mollifying Archfedd by letting her spend the night with Reaghan, in Coventina's house, under her maid Keelia's watchful eye. To Archfedd, this was a much more enjoyable way to pass the evening than having to sit at the high table in the hot and smoky hall on her best behavior.

Maia dressed the two boys in their finest tunics for the occasion, and when Arthur and I walked through to the hall, they followed us in solemn procession and took their seats to my right. Cei and Coventina had their usual places to Arthur's left, with Merlin on the far side of the boys, ready to help me keep them in check.

In the twelve years I'd known Merlin, he'd not changed a jot. Standing an inch or so shorter than my husband, he had a long, narrow face and clever, dark-brown eyes that missed nothing – unless it had to do with women.

Still miraculously youthful in appearance, the only time I'd ever seen him look anything near his true age was when he'd been moping after Morgana eight years past. Since then, although not precisely happy, he'd seemed settled in his routine of teaching the boys Latin, statesmanship, reckoning, geography and history.

After Christmas, I planned to ask him to include Archfedd in the lessons. At eight, she was old enough, and could already read as well as Amhar, so why not? After all, he'd taught Arthur's sisters, Morgana and Morgawse, alongside their brothers when they'd been children.

Din Cadan's magnificent great hall spread so wide it needed two rows of stout wooden pillars, now decked with flaring torches, to help support the roof and divide it into three aisles. The servants had pulled forward the long trestle tables, and men and women now crowded along the bench seats, crammed in shoulder to shoulder and already carousing with one another over horn beakers of mulled cider.

Halfway along the central aisle, the hearth fire glowed in its stone-lined pit. A sweating servant labored there to slice collops of meat off the roasting carcass of the deer that had been tenderizing in one of the barns these past four days. The scent of cooked meat mingled with the tang of woodsmoke and the not so alluring smell of over a hundred unwashed bodies, but I was used to that now. The scents of the hall were the familiar smells of home.

More servants piled the tables with platters of food – meat, vegetables, pies and bread, much of it smothered in some kind of rich sauce. Beside me, Amhar's eyes glittered with relish as one of the servants slid a large helping of meat onto his plate, then ladled leeks and sauce beside it. In their nursery, where they usually ate with Maia, the children's fare was much less varied. Too much cabbage, according to Archfedd.

"Can I have wine?" Medraut asked, as the servant carrying it approached. He held out his goblet, a far more ornate affair than the horn cups used by most of the people in the body of the hall, expectancy written across his autocratic face.

"Watered," I said, at exactly the same time as Merlin, and we both laughed.

Medraut's expression descended into that of a sulky child as the servant dished out equal measures of water and wine.

"They're growing up fast," Merlin said to me over the boys' heads as they smugly toasted one another in watered wine. "Before we know it, they'll be leading men themselves."

I forced a smile. Although Merlin had brought me here from my old world, he had very little idea of what I'd given up when I chose to remain. Did he imagine the world I'd left behind to be like this one? A conglomeration of small kingdoms where boys grew up to become warriors or farmers, blacksmiths or priests? I had no intention of correcting him. I'd long ago learned to keep what I knew of the future to myself.

"Give them time to still be children," I said, a little more curtly than I'd intended. "Let them enjoy it."

He raised a quizzical eyebrow and didn't answer that remark.

I picked up my own goblet of unwatered wine and took a sip. Good stuff. Only the best for the king's table, probably brought in from the Middle Sea via Din Tagel's small and rocky port. Like the silk for my underwear, the olive oil we burned in our small clay lamps, and many of our other luxury goods. All thanks to men like Captain Xander – the captain of one of the merchant ships brave enough to venture through the Straits of Gibraltar into the dangerous Atlantic to trade their exotic goods for our prized tin ingots.

Our entertainment for the evening began – three traveling tumblers who'd been here a week already but not yet outstayed their welcome. Two men, and a young woman. Her, lissome as a willow wand and wearing very few clothes, which probably accounted for the popularity of their troupe.

All three of them cartwheeled up and down the central aisle as a warmup, then walked on their hands to loud applause from their tipsy audience.

"Look at her."

"Show us yer tits, darlin'."

"Come'n'dance over here, an' I'll show you a good time."

The shouts became more ribald, and I glanced at the two boys, but they were too busy eating, the delights of this particular female form ignored. Although, was that Medraut, always the more precocioius, taking a sneaky peek?

The girl stood on one man's shoulders, then somersaulted from him to land lightly as a piece of thistledown, balancing on her hands on the other's shoulders. Another cheer went up, mainly because her skimpy skirts had flopped down to reveal her equally skimpy underwear.

Medraut gave Amhar a nudge and leaned closer to whisper, loud enough for me to catch his words. "Cor. Look at her. I c'n see her pants."

Amhar's snigger made me smile. If all they were bothered about was seeing a girl's underwear, then that was fine with me. Just like small boys in my old world – laughing if you climbed a tree and they got a look at your knickers.

On the table closest to us, young Llacheu sat beside pretty little Ariana, Anwyll's oldest daughter. However, despite having been enthralled by Ariana's charms since the summer, he now had his eyes fixed hungrily on the almost double-jointed antics of the girl tumbler. Something Ariana, not a stupid girl, hadn't missed. Her face had been growing longer and angrier as the night progressed. Trouble brewing there.

As Llacheu had matured, his likeness to his father had become less striking, but he'd nevertheless grown into a handsome young man, popular with the unwed teenage girls in the fortress, and probably some of the married ones as well.

I leaned toward Arthur. "I'm thinking it might be time to see Llacheu married," I shouted into his ear, an act necessitated by the level of noise inside the hot hall.

He turned to face me, eyes widening. "He's only eighteen."

"Exactly." I inclined my head toward my stepson. "And very popular with the girls already."

Arthur grinned. "That's my boy."

How very typical of the father of a teenage boy, here in the Dark

Ages, and in the twenty-first century as well. Of men in general. Until they realized their daughters were prey for the sons of other men.

I sighed. "Have you not noticed that even though he's been seeing Ariana since the summer, for the last seven days he's only had eyes for that ridiculously bendy tumbling girl. Making a fool of Ariana and on track for making an enemy of her father. Of course, being eighteen, he'll probably only have one thing on his mind. For both of them."

Arthur's eyes twinkled. "Why not? I'd met his mother at that age. In fact, he'd already been born."

Men. "That may be so, but was *her* father one of your warriors?"

He shook his head. "No. She was a servant from one of the farms at the foot of the hill. I think her father was dead. I never met him, nor her mother. She was glad to escape the drudgery and come to live up here with me."

I couldn't help it. A tiny nub of jealousy rose, as I pictured Arthur as a boy Llacheu's age, tucked up cosily with this son's mother and his baby, long before he met me.

I pushed aside this intrusive thought. "Exactly my point. Ariana has both father *and* mother, and I doubt they intend her to become any warrior's mistress. Not even *your* son's. Marriage is what they'll be after for her – preferably before she relinquishes her virginity." If she hadn't already.

The cogs visibly clicked into place in his head. "Oh."

"Yes. Oh. He either needs somewhere... someone... to work off his frustrations with, and that girl acrobat might be the one, or he needs to be married and do it legally and not risk offending one of your best warriors."

Although I felt certain Llacheu had already discovered the pleasures of a woman's body, Ariana, and her father, required my protection.

Arthur's brow furrowed. There were indeed women within the walls of Din Cadan whose husbands had died, and who now made ends meet by servicing the unmarried warriors of the fort, and some of the married ones as well. The thought of sending Llacheu off to visit one of them probably appealed as little to Arthur as it did to me. "Marriage, then," he said. "I'll speak with Anwyll."

I suppressed my laughter. "Better speak to Llacheu first. He may have changed his mind about Ariana now he's set eyes on the way that girl can bend herself almost double."

A mischievous grin split Arthur's face. "A girl who can get into those positions does have her attractions…"

Underneath the table I slapped his leg. "Be happy with what you've got – if you want to keep it."

He grinned wider still, leaning in close so he could whisper-shout in my ear. "Why would I want a peasant when I have a queen at home?"

I chuckled, and let my lips brush his in a kiss. "Just you remember that."

"Eww," exclaimed Amhar from beside me. "That's gross."

Chapter Seven

SNOW ARRIVED SOON after Christmas. It fell heavily for weeks, draping the countryside in a freezing veil of white that should have been pretty, but in reality, brought deadly danger in a time with no rescue services on standby.

Any animals out grazing faced death from either being buried in drifts, or lack of food, or both. Farmers struggled out daily in search of livestock in distress, unable to bring them all into shelter. The deer in the forest went short too, stripping the branches of the holly bushes bare and gnawing the bark from the trees – the only things left for them to eat.

We couldn't hunt. We couldn't even get out of the fortress, and no one could get in. Living on top of a steep hill had its drawbacks; both roads down the hillside had frozen to a slippery death-trap reminiscent of a toboggan run. So we had no news from Arthur's spies in Viroconium regarding Cadwy's increase in arms production.

Our once ample supply of firewood began to run low as we struggled to keep warm. Arthur had as many families as possible move into the Great Hall to conserve what heat we could produce, one fire being so much better than many. And all those people in one building created some heat of their own.

Coventina and Cei brought their bed into our chamber, as did Maia and the children, to keep warm by our brazier. Reaghan, full of excitement at the adventure, snuggled down at night in one bed with

Archfedd and Maia, while the two boys slept top to toe in the other.

For the children, of course, the snow began as exciting and novel. We'd had snow in previous years, of course, but nothing like this, persisting week after week. Along with the other fortress children, they made snowmen every day, and had snowball fights that went on for hours, running through the maze of passageways between the buildings, pelting one another at every opportunity. And they made toboggans out of bits of wood or old flour sacks and slid down the steep slope to the main gates at speeds that brought a knot of fear to my chest.

The long icicles hanging from the blackened, snow-encrusted thatch of every house tempted the boys to target practice, and, once knocked off, they could be used as swords or daggers until they melted in small mittened hands.

But with the passing of the weeks, and Arthur's sensible conservation of our supplies – we had to rely on the livestock kept within the walls – enthusiasm waned, and boredom set in.

"Why can't we ride out?" moaned Medraut, as he sat with his chin in his hands by the brazier in our chamber, the chessboard I'd had made for the boys on a low table between him and his cousin.

Amhar heaved a sigh. "Father promised he'd take us hunting this winter. And now all we get to do is sit inside." He gave the board a shove and some of the pieces fell over. "And play chess all day long."

"Chess teaches you strategy," I remarked, with a quick glance up from where I'd been trying to work on my book at the table. Not that I'd managed more than five lines all afternoon.

Coventina smiled. "You could go over your lessons." She was helping Reaghan with the finer intricacies of stitching a long embroidered belt the little girl had been working on all winter.

"Pfft," Medraut exclaimed. "That would be even worse. I don't know why Merlin thinks we have to know *Roman* history."

"In Latin, too," added Amhar. "It's *so* boring."

"Everyone who's anyone knows how to speak Latin," Coventina said, a woman who'd had to learn it from scratch herself once she married Cei.

"To *speak* it," Medraut scoffed. "Not write it and read it."

Amhar nodded, ever keen to back up his cousin.

"I like reading Latin," Archfedd piped up from where she sat cross-legged on the floor with Reaghan, dressing her ragdoll. "And I like reading all those stories from long ago. *I'd* like to go to Rome one day. It sounds wonderful. All those big buildings made of *stone*. Merlin's told me all about them."

Had he now? Curiosity kindled in me. How could Merlin know about the "big buildings" unless he'd been there himself at some point? I filed that away to ask him about when I could get him alone. An unlikely possibility at the moment, with the hall chock full of warriors and their families.

The side door to our chamber opened and Arthur and Cei came in on a blast of colder air. Muffled from head to toe in furs against the cold, they closely resembled a pair of yeti. Not that they'd have known what that was.

"Papa!" cried Archfedd, leaping to her feet, her doll forgotten.

Arthur held up a restraining hand, stamping his feet on the rush mat by the door to dislodge the snow from his boots. "Let me get out of these clothes first. I've got icicles in my hair."

"Can I see?" Amhar asked, getting to his feet. "Real icicles?"

"I've got some up my nose," Cei said, chuckling. "It's cold enough out there to freeze my b—"

"Cei." Coventina, anticipating what was coming next, held up her hand as well. "Children present."

"I know what bollocks are," Medraut said, loud and clear.

Archfedd's head swiveled so she could stare at him. "I don't. What are they?"

Amhar snorted in derision. "They're—"

"Silence, all of you," Arthur boomed, his voice filling the suddenly much smaller space of the chamber. "Polite language, please. Ladies present. This is not the barracks room."

"I wish it was," Medraut muttered. "Might be more fun." For some time, now, he'd been itching to move his sleeping quarters to the barracks so he could be with the older boys he so liked.

Arthur and Cei began taking off their outer clothes and hanging them on the hooks near the door, shaking off the snow as they did so.

"Nothing going on out there," Cei said, as he hung up the thick sheepskin jacket he'd been wearing. "Quiet as the grave. And dark with it." He rubbed his ginger eyebrows to rid them of crusted snow. "Still snowing."

Arthur came to stand by the brazier, holding red hands out. "Snow as far as the eye can see."

"Can I come with you tomorrow night, when you do your rounds?" Medraut asked. "I'd like to see the snow in the dark."

Arthur shrugged. "If you wrap up warm. It's bitter, and tonight there's a wind making it worse, whipping the loose snow up off the ground and making a storm out of it." He wiped a hand across his forehead where his own eyebrow snow was beginning to melt and run into his eyes.

Archfedd, who'd followed him to the fire, tugged his sleeve. "Can I come too?"

He looked down at her, a gentle smile softening his face. "If it's not too windy. You're still so little the wind might pick you up and carry you off, and I don't want that. Who knows where my little chick might end up?"

"Annwfn's gates," Medraut said, giving her a spiteful, narrow-eyed look. "The fairies'd snatch you for sure before anyone could rescue you."

Archfedd's lower lip began to jut. Forestalling the threat of tears, Arthur swept her up in his arms and carried her to the table where he sat down next to me, cuddling her on his knee. "Don't you worry, my little chick. I'll keep you safe."

Beaming, she threw her arms around his neck and planted a damp kiss on his bristly cheek. "I love you, Papa."

Setting down my pen, I smiled at the picture they made. If I could have captured this moment in my book, I would have, but there were no cameras here, and I'd never had any skill at drawing. My heart swelled with love: for the tall, handsome man I'd given up my old life to be with; for the little girl nestling on his knee; for big, bluff Cei adding logs to the brazier to try to keep the cold from creeping inside the chamber; for my handsome little son, still sulking over his game of chess; for my kind friend Coventina, keeping her sorrow for the loss of her own son locked in her broken heart; even for young Medraut, who, now free from being spoiled by his mother, might gradually be improving.

Arthur's dark hair fell forward across his face as he bent over Archfedd's lighter chestnut curls, his strong arm holding her close, and I felt a sudden upsurge of longing for him I knew I couldn't slake, sharing our room with so many as we were. I'd have to wait to feel his naked body against mine for some other reason than to keep warm. A little sigh of anticipation escaped my lips, and with a shake of my head, I picked up my pen again, not really in the right mood for writing.

⟫⟫⟫⟩✕⟨⟪⟪⟪

THE SPRING THAW came gradually, leaving deep, icy drifts still lurking in sheltered spots, capable of supporting a man's or even a horse's weight. As soon as the snow on the road down from the main gates had almost gone, our men rode out hunting. Not that they found a lot to hunt. The deer were thin, and the canny old boars had hidden themselves deep inside the forest, leaving only their cloven hoofprints behind them in the morass of mud brought about by the melting snow.

Much to their delight, Medraut and Amhar were allowed to hunt for the first time, riding off on their ponies like the proud little princes they were. Heads held high, spears clutched tightly in their hands, they'd dressed in their drabbest cloaks to give them some camouflage amongst the grays and browns of the winter forest's clothing.

Standing just outside the Hall with Coventina and Reaghan, Archfedd and I waved them off. Boden and his junior huntsmen had ridden on ahead on their stocky little garrons, cracking their whips to keep the pack of hungry hounds, all slavering with excitement, under control and with their noses to the ground. With the hounds this hungry, it was to be hoped the farmers down below on the plain had their livestock shut away.

Amhar waved a cheery hand at me as he trotted past, but Medraut didn't even turn his head. The two boys vanished into the crowd of hunt followers streaming out through the wide-open gates and heading down the hill toward the muddy plain.

"I wish I could go," Reaghan said, hanging on to her mother's hand. "It looks such fun." Both girls could ride astride, as I did. Archfedd had inherited little Seren when Amhar had moved on to a bigger pony, and Reaghan had a pretty little roan, called Melys.

Coventina shook her head. "Hunting's not for girls."

"It can be," I said. "I've been, but I didn't like it. I don't think you girls would either. The death of a beautiful wild animal isn't nice to see." This, and being kidnapped by the late King Melwas on my way back from the hunt, had put me off for life. Not unreasonably.

"I've seen the pigs killed," Reaghan said. "I won't mind seeing a stag or boar killed." She scratched her head. "B'cause I like to eat meat, I'd like the chance to hunt for it, as well."

A logical argument. I glanced at Archfedd.

My daughter shook her head. She'd had the benefit of as many bedtime stories about animals as I could remember from my days as a librarian – *The Animals of Farthing Wood, Wind in the Willows, The Jungle Book, Born Free* even, not that she knew what a lion really looked like. My children had a full set of carved animals for their wooden ark, including animals they were unlikely ever to see, and which, from the inaccuracies of the carvings, the craftsmen had little idea of either, despite me having drawn the animals out on slivers of wood. "I'd like a baby deer as a pet," she said firmly. "Not to kill and eat."

Chapter Eight

BEFORE THE HUNTING party returned that evening, we had visitors. The sun had emerged from behind the clouds, and halfway through the afternoon I took the girls to the wall-walk to see if we could spot the hunt returning. Happy to be out of doors for once, they ran up and down between the guards on duty, shouting with laughter as they dodged each other around the smiling men's legs.

Reaghan spotted the visitors first. We were almost at the main gates, where towers rose to a wide wooden gatehouse spanning the entrance. The roadway up from the plain was just visible where it emerged from between the massive embankments that ringed the hilltop. "What's that?" Peering between the wooden crenellations, she pointed a mittened hand. "That's not one of our wagons."

Archfedd squeezed herself in beside her, and I leaned over the top of them. Along the wall and from the crenellations on top of the gate, a row of similarly curious faces peered over at the new arrivals. After a winter with no visitors, any newcomer interested us all.

Lurching up the trackway, still precarious from patches of ice, came a wagon covered with stretched skins that gave it the look of an American pioneer vehicle on its way across the prairie. Two shaggy horses strained under its weight, puffing their cloudy breath into the late afternoon's still wintry air.

A small, dark man occupied the front seat, a fellow of perhaps early-middle-age with a nose made rosy-red by the cold. He'd wrapped his scrawny body in a long cloak and had a floppy cap jammed down over his head. Mittened hands clutched the horses' reins tightly.

The wagon ground to a halt a short distance from the gates, which were closed, and one of the guards leaning over the parapet at the top shouted down to the little man. "Who goes there?"

The little man wobbled to his feet on the unsteady front platform of the wagon and doffed his floppy hat with a flourish, revealing his shiny, hair-free and pointy-like-an-egg pate. He made a flamboyant bow, holding the hat out to one side. "Ruan the Rhymer at your service," he announced in a deep and melodious voice, as though this was a name we should all recognize. "Come to entertain your lordships."

"Just you?" called the guard, sounding unimpressed. I had to stifle my welling laughter.

"Not at all, milord," Ruan called back, sitting down again, probably for his own safety, and making the wagon rock. "Ruan does not travel anywhere alone." He twitched the leather curtain behind him, and two female faces emerged, one about his age, with gray in her untidy dark hair, and the other much younger, with unruly chestnut curls and the sort of face that said, *come hither, young man*. I'd seen her sort before.

The girl slipped out from behind the curtain and settled on the bench next to Ruan. Considering how cold it still was, she appeared scantily dressed, in a low-cut red gown that barely reached below her knees and short red boots over dark woolen stockings.

She'd draped a simple, woven shawl about her shoulders, but now, with a degree of practised artfulness, let it slip to show the generous curves of her body. With a toss of her head, she gazed up at the guards on the gatehouse, an insolent, but decidedly inviting, look in her wide brown eyes.

When they'd rolled up their tongues from somewhere down by their boots, they managed to get down and open the gate to let the wagon inside. Every wall guard for forty yards each way hurried to watch the Rhymer's entrance into the fortress.

"If he's a Rhymer," Reaghan said, oblivious to the effect the girl was having on the men. "I wonder what stories he'll tell. New ones we haven't heard before, I hope."

I caught the girls' hands. "Let's go and find out then, shall we?"

By the time we'd all climbed down the treacherous steps to the mud below, the wagon had creaked its way up the winding road to the top of the slope and come to a halt in front of the stable buildings. Ruan and the girl had climbed down from the seat and were standing on the dirty cobbles looking around themselves as a crowd of interested inhabitants gathered to stare at them.

I joined the crowd, still holding the girls' hands.

Ruan helped the older woman down from the back of the wagon. She had a wooden pipe in her hand, not unlike the recorder I'd learned to play, badly, at school, and this she promptly put to her lips. Music sprang out of it, twisting into the chilly air, haunting and ethereal, a lot better than anything I'd ever produced.

And yet I couldn't find it in myself to like it. Why not? We'd had enough performers visit the fortress in the past, but none had made me feel the foreboding that had seized my insides. I was being stupid. I shook myself and watched along with everyone else.

Now without her shawl, and bare armed despite the cold, the girl tossed her head again, no doubt because she knew it to be alluring. In time with the music, she began to gyrate for the crowd in a wild, earthy dance like nothing I'd ever seen before. She stamped her red-booted feet on the cobbles, twirled and pirouetted, letting her arms make shapes in the air almost reminiscent of ballet, but far more animalistic.

As the pipe music rose to a crescendo, her long chestnut hair flew, until, with sudden abruptness, the music stopped and the girl stood motionless, transformed into a statue of a dancer. Her curls hung forward in a tangled veil over her face, and her long fingers extended eloquently. Only the sound of heavy breathing broke the silence.

A ripple of clapping began, joined by a few whistles and catcalls. Notably from the men rather than the women. I wouldn't have wanted to lay odds on most of the wives here suspecting their husbands of liking what they'd just seen a bit too much.

The girl shook her head, righting her curls, and a wide smile split her face. Not such a good idea – her teeth had grown overcrowded and crooked, and spoiled her beauty. But of course, the men weren't looking at her teeth.

"I wish I could dance like that," Reaghan said, her voice wistful. A sturdy child, like her mother, she'd never have the willowy, elegant physique of this wild girl. Not that her mother would have wanted her to, of course.

Ruan bowed to his audience. "If we can unhitch our horses in a corner somewhere, and beg food and cider from you, we'll entertain you all again this evening, in your hall." His pronunciation sounded good, but I detected a certain forced nature to the way he spoke, as though he were an actor reciting a speech.

Goff the blacksmith, who'd emerged from his forge to watch, indicated the space where he often parked wagons or carts that needed repairs to their ironwork. "You can park it here if'n you like. 'Tis a warm spot aside o' my forge."

Ruan bowed again. He was a little too free with his obeisances for my liking. "And is there room for my tired horses, Bran and Branwen, in your stables? They'd appreciate a feed of oats and a bite of hay, outta the cold wind and the snow. Hard workers, both o' them." Yes, when not expounding to an audience, his speech slipped a little.

Eoghan, the retired, one-armed warrior in charge of the stables, stepped forward from amongst the audience who'd watched the show. Eyeing the girl up and down with a lascivious leer, he nodded at Ruan. "Aye, bring 'em in when you're ready. I've room." He looked back at the girl. "An' you can tell me what yer girl's name is, too."

Ruan grinned. "Why, she's Hafren, and she ain't my girl. She's her own girl, 'tis sure." He nodded at the older woman. "And this be Heledd, though I see plain that you're more interested in my dancer than my musician." He gave a little knowing chuckle, probably having seen it all before.

Ribald laughter echoed from the men in the crowd, who'd not wandered off as the women and children had, but had hung around to spectate these newcomers. They moved in closer to get a better look at Hafren. As more than half of them were happily married, their wives would not be pleased.

I gave Archfedd and Reaghan's hands a tug. "Come on, back to the Hall and something to eat for you two, I think."

"Do I have to go back to my house?" Reaghan asked. "Can't I stay with Archfedd again tonight?"

Cei and Coventina had moved back to their own home, now our supplies of wood were no longer under threat of running out, but Reaghan had still not joined them.

I shrugged. "We'd better see what your mother says."

⋙✦⋘

"WHO ARE THOSE people I saw by the stables?" Arthur asked, standing naked in the middle of our chamber, halfway through changing out of his mud-splattered hunting garb and into something more respectable for the evening meal in the Hall.

From my position sitting on the bed, I had a pleasing view of his rear, lean and muscled as ever, one thigh still slightly thinner than the other, thanks to the nasty wound he'd received nine years ago. I was so busy ogling my handsome husband in the buff, I quite forgot to answer.

"I said, who are those people in the wagon?" he repeated, huffing, but not getting any further on with his dressing.

I jumped. "Oh, yes. Ruan the Rhymer and his two women – a musician and a dancer. By the looks of her, what I'd call an *exotic* dancer."

He pulled on clean, dark blue braccae. "I saw the girl when I was unsaddling my horse – she'll be the dancer, I imagine." He paused. "Definitely exotic."

From over the wall in the hall came the sounds of preparation for the evening meal. Many of the warriors and their wives would be there – possibly more men than usual thanks to the promise of further dancing by such an attractive, and underdressed, girl.

As he picked up his clean shirt, a chuckle shook him. "Llacheu's already spotted her. As have his friends. They all hung around outside the stables instead of going back to their houses to change their muddy clothes." He chuckled again. "Like bees around a flower in summer."

Arthur's attempt at a father to son talk with Llacheu a few months ago had not gone to plan. Llacheu had shied away from the suggestion of marriage like a horse from fire.

"None of my friends are married," he snapped at his father, anger bubbling close beneath the surface. "And I refuse to be the first to get tied down. If Ariana doesn't want me, I'll be going down the hill to have some fun with the village girls, like all my friends do." As far as he was concerned, it seemed, Ariana and her father could go take a hike. And so could his father.

This was the first time they'd ever argued, and Arthur had come away from it rather shellshocked. Considering Llacheu was eighteen, I'd only been surprised they'd not clashed before. But Llacheu had been living in one of the barracks houses with his friends for the past few years, so there'd not been much opportunity for angry words. Until now.

"Uh oh," I'd said, when Arthur recounted the results of his parental chat to me, and left it at that, heartily glad Amhar was still so young.

Arthur pulled his tunic on over his tempting torso and fastened a tooled leather belt around his waist. "What it is to be young and in love, eh?"

I laughed. "You make us sound like an old married couple."

He came over to the bed, standing over me. "Well, we are, aren't we?"

I had to put my head back to gaze up into his eyes, his face plunged into shadow by the light of the clay oil lamps behind him. "You think?" I put my hands on his narrow hips.

With an irrepressible grin, he dropped his hands onto my shoulders and pushed me back on the bed. "D'you feel old?" He followed me down, leaning over and keeping his weight off me, curls of his dark hair hanging over his face. "I do, sometimes, when I look at Llacheu and see he's a man grown already." His hand ran up my body raising goose-pimples of delight.

I sucked my lips in, trying not to laugh. "When you do this to me, I feel about seventeen myself," I whispered.

He laughed, and I joined in. "That's the answer I wanted to hear." He kissed me quickly on the lips, then straightened up. "Come along, they'll be waiting for us."

I took his proffered hand and let him pull me to my feet. Then together, we walked into the Great Hall.

⁂

THE MEAL WAS half over when Ruan the Rhymer left his two women standing by the Hall doors and walked up the central aisle with his lyre in his hand. He'd donned a tunic of rich red wool, hung about with long festoons of gold ribbon, his performance costume, and as he walked, his matching red slippers scuffed up the dust from the strewn reeds.

The hubbub of noise rising to the rafters continued unabated as the small man took his place on a low stool beside the glowing hearth. Seemingly oblivious to the fact that he'd been ignored, the musician carefully plucked a few notes from his instrument, head bent, as though nothing else mattered.

On the far side of Arthur, Cei lumbered to his feet with some difficulty as he'd been drinking heavily all evening, a habit he'd fallen into since his son's death. "Silence," he bellowed, glaring around the hall at the revellers from beneath his heavy ginger brows.

Not a man to disobey.

Silence fell.

Cei nodded to Ruan. The musician plucked a few more individual notes, pure and clear in the fug of the hall, seeming to cut through the heavy air. Then he smiled to himself as though satisfied, and set free a rivulet of music that rippled around the silent hall, climbing the stout wooden pillars, twisting about the rafters, settling in the hearts of every listener. As his clever fingers danced across the strings, the air hummed with sweet sound, and every eye fixed on him. The men might like exotic dancers, but a storyteller was to everyone's taste.

He chose the Dream of Macsen Wledig. What did it matter that everyone knew it well, even me? Every storyteller had a slightly different version. This man with his entrancing music was the equivalent of a good film on the television, on Netflix maybe. The story he told was an old one, of how a Roman general dreamed of a beautiful island, our island, then came here, married a British princess, and went back to Rome to conquer the eternal city.

"Macsen Wledig was emperor of Rome, a comelier, a better and a wiser emperor than any that had gone before him," began Ruan. "One day he held a council and said to his fellow kings, 'I desire to hunt on the morrow.' And the next day he set forth with his combrogi until he came to the valley of the river that flows toward Rome, where he hunted until the sun was high in the sky and the heat was great. And sleep came upon the Emperor. His attendants set up their shields around him upon the shafts of their spears to shade him from the sun, with his own gold shield beneath his head. And Macsen slept."

Macsen's story closely mirrored that of Arthur's own great-grandfather – Constantine III, who'd done much the same a scant thirty years later. Both had been proclaimed as Emperor by the legions in Britain, both had gone off overseas, to Gaul, or further, never to return.

The song, more a recital accompanied by music, finally came to an end, finishing with the cutting out of the tongues of the Armorican women lest they corrupted the British language. Lovely touch. Perfect for children. The silence in the room was complete. Ruan's chin rested on his chest, the firelight flickering across his naked scalp and turning it to bronze. His fingers fell from his lyre, slack and spent. The only noise came from the crackling of the flames.

Heledd's joyful pipe music burst into the silence, and the girl, Hafren, cartwheeled down the aisle, narrowly missing immolating herself in the hearth fire, and revealing to everyone her startling and complete lack of underwear. A few gasps of shock arose from the women present, but not from the men. In front of the high table, she sprang to her feet, flashing a dazzling smile straight at Arthur, bold, brassy, and inviting.

I bristled with indignation, and purposefully laid my left hand over Arthur's where it rested on the table, like a dog peeing up against a tree to mark its territory.

Hands off.

I wasn't so distracted, though, not to notice how from his seat amongst his friends in the body of the hall, Llacheu was watching Hafren open-mouthed, with admiration, and lust, written clearly across his face. That same uneasy sense of foreboding returned; the strong instinct that this was an infatuation that shouldn't be encouraged; that anyway, it was my husband the girl was ogling, not his youthful son.

Heledd, the older woman, had followed the girl down the Hall, the pipe producing more of the wild, ethereal music we'd heard earlier. If I hadn't known better, I might have thought it fairy music. But I didn't believe in fairies.

Young Hafren's booted feet began to dance, her hands to weave shapes in the air, her hair to fly, as she leapt and spun, whirled and stamped. Heledd's pipe music rose into the rafters and twisted through them just as Ruan's had, but in a wild, abandoned way – in sharp contrast to her husband's almost mournful tune.

From the fire, Ruan watched his two women out of narrowed, satisfied eyes, the lyre resting across his knees.

I glanced at Arthur. A smile played about his lips as he watched the girl dance, and the fingers of his free hand tapped a rhythm on the tabletop. I tightened the grip I had on his other hand, and he turned and looked at me, eyes twinkling. "I think there's magic in that music and the dance she does. I feel sorry for any man she sets her sights on."

I nodded, my eyes sliding sideways toward her, certain that the man she'd set her eyes on was Arthur.

Chapter Nine

"Milord, tis most kind of you t'allow us space to set up our 'umble camp."

The dancing girl, Hafren stood in front of us, or should I say in front of Arthur, in her skimpy, too-short red gown, cut so low her breasts were almost leaping out of it. They must have been freezing.

Up close, as long as she didn't open her mouth and show us those dreadful teeth, she was prettier still, with the wide, dark eyes of a fawn, the full, red lips of a selfie-pouter who's had lip implants, and the clear, if a little grubby, skin of a baby. Her abundant brown curls hung down her back in disarray, and right now she was batting her far-too-long lashes at my husband right under my nose.

Bitch.

Arthur and I had halted just outside the stables, accompanied by all the children. Merlin, Llacheu, and Cei stood to my left, ready to accompany us when we took the girls for the ride they'd missed out on the day before, as they were too young to hunt.

Llacheu was staring in open-mouthed fascination at Hafren, lust reeking from every over-sexed teenage pore.

If it had just been him she seemed intent on flirting with, I'd have ignored it, but here she was, posturing provocatively at my husband.

Arthur smiled at her, as susceptible as the next man to a pretty face and come-hither eyes. "You're most welcome. We value good entertainers here. I trust my people have made you feel welcome."

Hafren sidled closer, hands on hips, thrusting those breasts invitingly in Arthur's direction. If she breathed any deeper, they'd be popping out, which would probably be too much for Llacheu, who was fidgeting restlessly as though his braccae had suddenly become uncomfortable. Men.

I itched to give her a shove and force her back two steps. No, make that half a dozen, or maybe hard enough so she fell on her arse in the mud. Only then she'd be displaying her knickerless state. She'd edged far too close to Arthur, gazing up at him out of her doe eyes, her breasts rising and falling tantalizingly. Pert breasts that had never had to feed a baby.

"They have indeed made us welcome," she purred up at him, inching even closer and turning her shoulder toward me. "I did not know how warm a welcome the King o' Dumnonia would give us. If'n I'd'a known, I'd have aksed Ruan to come here all the sooner." Flutter, flutter went those eyelids.

Ruan, standing behind her, cap in hand, fidgeted, shifting his weight from one foot to the other, and clenching and unclenching his hands on the cap. "We did come as fast as we could," he mumbled, his speaking voice degenerating even further from the one he used for reciting his tales. "Snow did hold us up sore bad in Caer Gloui."

Hafren shot him a sharp frown from suddenly hostile eyes, and he fell silent. With a coy smile, she stretched out a hand as if to touch my husband's tunic front, her poise recovered, and the flare of anger hidden.

I clenched my fists, aware that a queen should ignore such insults but wishing with every fiber of my body to be able to punch her on the nose and rearrange that pretty face a bit for her. Maybe with a log.

Archfedd saved me the embarrassment that would have caused. She stepped between Hafren and Arthur and tugged her father's sleeve, staring up at him with a determined frown on her small face. "Papa. I thought you were comin' to help me an' Reaghan catch our ponies?"

Hafren stepped back, a knowing little smile on her face, as Arthur, with an almost imperceptible shake of his head as though to free himself from her influence, made her a slight bow and bent to our daughter. "Just so. Excuse me, duty calls." And he turned away.

Everyone else did too, leaving Hafren standing in the mud, watching Arthur's straight back as he walked off with the girls. I moved toward the stable entrance, as Alezan, my horse, was already in there, but I paused before going inside, my gaze on Hafren as she watched my husband. Was that raw hunger in her eyes, or maybe something else?

"You don't trust her, do you?"

I glanced around. Merlin had come to stand beside me, also watching Hafren.

"Not one bit," I spat, through gritted teeth. "She's got a cheek. Standing there flirting with Arthur right under my nose."

Merlin nodded. "That's not quite why I don't trust her."

I focused on him instead of her. "What d'you mean?"

He pursed his lips. "Didn't you listen to what she said? What she called Arthur?"

I frowned, struggling to remember. I'd been a bit too busy looking daggers at her and controlling my urge to sock her one.

Merlin leaned closer and lowered his voice. "She called him King of Dumnonia."

It took a minute for the significance of that to sink in. "Not the High King?"

He nodded. "Why would she do that? Everyone knows he's High King. Even if she didn't when she arrived here, which is unlikely, she'd have found it out soon enough. And yet, she seeks to flatter but doesn't use his proper title."

"I don't understand."

He glanced her way again, but she'd hitched her skirts up to show off her white thighs, to the delight of the watching men, and was climbing into the back of Ruan's wagon. "Who doesn't see Arthur as High King? Who wouldn't want to give him that title? Think."

Of course. My husband had more than a few enemies who resented him holding the High Kingship at such an early age. I nodded. "Cadwy. Caw of Alt Clut. Morgana, maybe. Someone who doesn't like him. Hates him, maybe, for having that title and the power that goes with it. Someone who refuses to acknowledge him as High King." I paused. "Somehow I don't think it would be Cadwy though – he and Arthur shook on their agreement."

Merlin shrugged. "And yet Cadwy is arming men. The boy Llawfrodedd told us this. And we still don't know why."

"That doesn't mean he intends to break the agreement. He might be arming against the threat of more Irish raids. Why would he even want to go against Arthur? It would be foolish of him to cause internal strife when our enemies surround us."

"You'd think." Merlin rubbed a hand across his stubbly jaw. "Men, and kings in particular, don't always have the wisest judgement."

I glanced again at the wagon, but no sign remained of its inhabitants. "But what could that girl have to do with any of my husband's enemies? A traveling dancer, and probably a woman of loose morals at that. What could she or her companions have to do with Arthur's enemies? She's unimportant. Poor."

Medraut and Amhar came toward us, leading their muddy ponies in from the paddocks and laughing together.

Merlin grimaced. "Who else is there? I don't think it would be Caw. He's too far off, up beyond the Wall and the Caledonian Forest. And we still have his son down here, as hostage."

We did indeed. But eight years on, Gildas, now a monk at Ynys Witrin, would not be wanting to return to his father's court, and surely Caw had found another son to replace him in his affections?

I bit my lip. "That only leaves... Morgana."

He nodded, and turned to the boys.

With one last glance toward the wagon, I went inside to find Alezan, my heart troubled by what he'd just suggested.

Arthur joined me five minutes later, having supervised the girls tying up their ponies in two of the stalls. He slipped in beside his big bay horse, Taran, a present from King Garbaniawn of Ebrauc, after his old horse, the beautiful Llamrei, had been killed at the Battle of the City of the Legion. He brushed in silence for a few minutes, whistling tunelessly between his teeth. I continued grooming Alezan, who'd begun to molt.

When I moved to start her other side, I found him leaning on the wooden partition, chin on his folded arms, a loose curl of his dark hair flopping over his eyes and making him look even more devastatingly attractive than usual. No wonder Hafren couldn't take her eyes off him. Power *and* good looks. He raised an eyebrow at me. "What's wrong?"

"Nothing," I said, bending over to brush Alezan's girth area.

He sighed. "You're not much good at lying."

I straightened up, glancing down the row of stalls to where Merlin and Cei were chatting as they readied their own horses. "All right. I'm pissed off. I don't like that girl, Hafren, and I don't trust her." The words came out in a rush, discontented and sharp.

His eyebrows shot up. "Don't *trust* her?" He rubbed his nose, a twinkle in his eyes. "What's she done? Are you sure you're not annoyed because she was flirting with me?"

I leaned my weight against Alezan's warm flank and frowned. "Well, yes, that's part of it. I'll freely admit I don't like her doing that. But even before she did, I sensed something in her – something bad. Right off, as soon as I met her when they arrived here in Din Cadan. Something I didn't trust. I've got a bad feeling about her." I paused. "Not the other two, I don't think. Just her."

His grin went a long way to dismissing my fears. "You've no need to worry. She can flirt all she likes, but I only have eyes for one woman." He reached out a hand and tapped me on the nose with his dirty forefinger. "This one right here. Get Alezan saddled, and let's be off. The children'll have their ponies ready before us at this rate."

I managed a smile, but for some reason his disregard for my worries didn't quite put me at ease. I couldn't rid myself of the uneasy feeling that something was brewing. Maybe I did have the Sight, after all, or maybe it was just women's intuition. I gave myself a shake and lifted my saddle and bridle from the end of the partition where they lived.

With our horses saddled, we led them out into the cobbled yard, where the children were already mounted up, the girls on their small ponies, Medraut on his chestnut and Amhar on Saeth, Llacheu's old black cob. Llacheu himself had moved up to a proper warhorse three years ago, which although it wasn't appreciably bigger than Saeth, was better trained. A warhorse served as an extra weapon for a warrior. Saeth was enough for a boy in training, but not for a warrior.

We adults mounted and settled ourselves comfortably in our saddles. Nothing like the sort of saddle I'd learned to ride on, these were four horned, much like Roman cavalry saddles. The horns came in useful for hooking on your shield and weapons to carry to war, as well as bedrolls and sundry baggage, although we had nothing extra to carry with us this morning.

The leather curtain at the back of Hafren's wagon moved, catching my eye. Was that her sly face peeking out at us? At me, this time, not Arthur?

I turned my back on her and jog-trotted the few paces to catch Alezan up with Arthur's horse as we set off.

At the foot of the slope, the fortress gates swung open to allow our party through, and we clattered down the cobbled road between the huge defensive embankments, skirting the patches of rapidly melting snow.

The wide plain stretched away, the colors of winter still upon it, dull grays and browns, patchworked with the soiled white of stubbornly resistant snowdrifts. Spring had just begun to touch a few of the trees in the forest with the faintest blush of green. Give it a week or two, and no more snow, and that fresh green would be everywhere. My heart swelled with delight at the thought. I loved the birth of spring after the long death that was winter.

On the farmsteads that populated the plain, the small, square fields remained too wet to work, but the farmers and their families had taken advantage of the drier weather to start repairing field walls and filling in potholes in the muddy roads. Dust clouds hanging in the air outside some of the barns told us they must be threshing the last of the winter's wheat, and house doors stood wide open, indicating the housewives had begun their spring cleaning, for want of anything else to do.

We rode eastwards, as to the west the lower-lying land had been made soggy and impassable by the amount of melting snow. The two girls' ponies had to jog-trot to keep up with our larger horses, and behind Arthur and me the two boys fell into an argument about whose pony was the faster.

Cei and Merlin brought their horses in beside us.

Alezan laid her ears back in bad temper, as even at her now advanced age, she didn't like other horses coming too near.

"Now we're not within the fortress," Merlin said. "What are you planning to do about Cadwy's weapons caches?"

Arthur glanced back at the boys, who were badgering Llacheu to race with them. "We don't know yet what he wants those weapons for. Now the weather's turned, we'll be hearing from my spies if anything untoward is going on. We'll soon find out if he's been mustering more troops or buying Saxon foederati." He shrugged. "But until then, I have to go on the pact of non-aggression he made with me, and believe he meant it."

Cei shook his head. "You're a fool to trust him. There's not a reliable bone in his body."

Arthur sighed. "But if I don't trust him, what then? For the good of Britain, I have to. We need to present a united front against our enemies, or we'll be lost. And I have to lead by example. If I show distrust of my own brother, the king who should be closest to me, how can I expect the other kings to trust one another? Or me?"

Merlin caught my eye. "What about you, Gwen? Do you trust Cadwy?"

I frowned, unhappy at being put on the spot. But I'd been present when Arthur and Cadwy had made their pact. I'd seen Cadwy's face when they'd clasped hands. "If Arthur thinks we should trust him, then trust him we should," I said, hoping I was right.

Cei let out a disgruntled snort.

Ahead of us, a flock of sheep bolted across the plain, alarmed by our approach.

"Can we have a race?" Medraut asked, squeezing his pony between Taran and Alezan, his jaw jutting in belligerence. "Can we? Please? We haven't had a proper gallop for *such* a long time." His voice, which was already breaking, rose an octave. He cleared his throat, cheeks flushing.

Archfedd must have overheard. "Yes, please," she squealed, eyes alight with excitement. "I want to race too." She patted Seren's already sweaty neck.

"And me," echoed Reaghan. "Melys is so fast she's going to beat Medraut and Amhar's ponies."

Amhar snorted with derision. "You think? Saeth is the fastest here. She's not called Arrow for nothing."

Llacheu, on his dun warhorse, laughed out loud. "You'll not beat me, little brother."

"So, can we race? Can we?" persisted Medraut, staring up at Arthur out of determined eyes. His frowning, thick-set brows reminded me uncomfortably of his uncle Cadwy.

Arthur glanced at Cei and Merlin, a smile lighting his face. Cei shrugged, and Merlin pulled the sort of expression that said it was up to Arthur.

"Pleeease." Amhar's attempt at wheedling made me chuckle. Saeth, dancing sideways, had picked up her rider's excitement.

"All of us?" asked Llacheu, a frown on his face as he eyed the two girls.

"All of us," Arthur said, the smile becoming a grin. He enjoyed a good, carefree gallop as much as any rider.

I smiled. "You're all ridiculously optimistic if you think any horse here can beat Alezan."

Medraut's face fell, turning pouty. "I'd forgotten about her. Can we have a head start?"

Arthur shook his head. "No head starts. All out war. See that line of trees over there?" He pointed. The trees lay a good mile away. "First one there's the winner. Ready?"

Medraut dug his heels into his pony's sides, and it sprang forward. Amhar gave a shout of fury and urged Saeth after his cousin. For just a moment, Alezan danced excitedly under my tight hold as I met Arthur's eyes, full of the same boyish excitement as his children's.

I didn't wait. Giving Alezan her head, I let her bound from walk to gallop like a racehorse, as I crouched over her neck. Beside me, Arthur, Cei and Merlin did the same, switching their reins back and forth across their horses' shoulders like whips.

However, even though I had the fastest horse here, I had no desire to beat my children. Not that I thought they should always win, but because I wasn't all that competitive and wanted to keep an eye on the two girls.

I needn't have bothered; both of them were hammering their galloping ponies' sides with flapping legs, balanced in that loose, natural way children have, only their bottoms in contact with their ponies' backs, like Pony Club mounted games riders in my old world. Melys and Seren's short legs thundered across the close-cropped turf as they hurtled after the three boys.

A mile on a fast horse takes barely two minutes to cover. A minute and a half into the race, and three quarters of the way to the clump of trees, Arthur was keeping pace on my left and letting the boys hold onto their lead.

I glanced over my shoulder at the girls, now trailing behind us but still pounding their ponies' sides with their heels, both of them every bit as good as any boy. And as I did so, I felt my saddle lurch precariously to the right. I swung back to face the front, unsure what was going on. And my saddle slid heart-stoppingly to the left instead.

Whoa. What was happening?

In a knee-jerk reaction, I leaned back into my right stirrup. The saddle swivelled that way instead, loose as though the girth wasn't done up tightly enough. Or wasn't done up at all.

But I'd done it up myself – really tight. I wasn't an idiot. Checked it, too.

My throat constricted. I heaved on Alezan's reins, but that only made the saddle move more, sliding forward this time, and I had nothing to brace myself against. Fighting to balance it, I leaned left again, toward Arthur.

Could the girth have come undone?

It felt as though I were astride a greasy barrel. The only thing keeping my saddle on must be the breast strap. But if it hadn't been there, I might have been able to somehow rid myself of the slipping saddle, as I'd seen the Household Cavalry do in their display at the Horse of the Year Show, and ride bareback.

Arthur must have caught my movement out of the corner of his eye. He turned his head, the wind blowing his hair back. For a brief, heart-stopping moment, our eyes met. Then my saddle lurched toward him again. Only my balance was keeping it and me on Alezan's slippery back. I gave up trying to slow her down and buried my fingers in her flying mane, hanging on in desperation.

The words of my old riding school instructor echoed in my head. *Always wear a hard hat, just in case.* But I had no hard hat, and the wind of our speed was whistling in my ears and yanking the long braid of my hair out behind me.

If you look down, you'll fall down. I fought not to look.

I lost.

Galloping hooves. Muddy ground whizzing past in a blur of speed.

Galloping hooves. I raised my eyes to meet Arthur's again. Mine must have been wide with terror because his were too. "My saddle," I shouted, as I tipped further his way. He leaned precariously toward Alezan's head, stretching to grab her bridle and slow her down. The saddle slid. I reached out my hand in one imploring gesture, the other still clutching Alezan's mane, tangled in the long hairs.

Arthur lunged for me instead of the bridle. Our fingertips touched. The saddle slid down Alezan's side, and I went with it.

"Gwen!" His shout of panic was the last thing I heard, our horses' pounding hooves in front of my face, the last thing I saw.

Chapter Ten

CRYING. SOMEONE CRYING. Eyelids glued shut, leaden, sore. Breathing difficult. A burning sensation in my nose. Cheeks stinging. My head booming as though it would explode.

The crying stopped. Silence instead, and soft, cushiony darkness. I drifted away on a cloud of nothingness.

Floating. For a long time. For an eternity.

Whispering. Wordless whispering hissing in the dark.

Someone had weighed down my eyelids. They wouldn't open. Had they placed coins on them because I was dead? I struggled against the marshmallow darkness.

The weights fell away. My eyelids creaked open. Bright lights flashed and my eyes throbbed with pain. I closed them again as my heartbeat filled my head, pounding loud as a beaten drum. I sank into oblivion, content to be nothing, no one.

I floated for a long time. Or no time at all.

Whispering again. A low, throaty giggle. Light in the darkness. Two people standing in the shadows, arms around one another, laughing. One of them tall and unmistakable. Arthur, holding a stranger in his arms, hungry mouth on her throat, eager hands exploring her lissome body. The woman's softly provocative giggles filled my head, rising ever louder. In slow motion, she gazed at me over Arthur's head out of triumphant doe eyes, a grin splitting her face open wide. She had uneven, crooked teeth.

No!

On a silent scream, I fell into a bottomless well, spinning out of control with bright lights flashing all about me, like some horrible fairground ride. I screwed my eyes tight closed but couldn't shut out the lights.

After another eternity, the bottom came up and hit me hard. Not water. Not the bottom of a well at all. Grass, tickling my skin. Tall reeds rustled in a breeze and the sound of bird song filled the air. A sedge warbler's distinctive chirring call. The smell of mud and cold air strong in my burning nostrils.

I opened my eyes.

Cool, misty daylight. A lakeside. Distant, shadowy trees fringing a dark expanse of peaty water. Windblown ripples breaking up the mirrored surface, silvering in the pale light. The warbler calling again. I strained my eyes to spot him as though finding he was real meant everything.

And failed.

I pushed myself upright, the damp ground soft beneath my fingers.

I'd somehow landed on a grassy bank, with reeds growing tall about the water to left and right, and a view across to those distant trees.

Moving my head, I found the pain had gone.

A flat-bottomed boat nestled amongst the reeds, its worn planks silvery with age. Waiting for me. Was this the River Styx? Was I really dead? On my way to the otherworld? *No.* Since when was the River Styx a lake with lilies growing on it?

However, instinct told me the boat was meant for me.

In the blink of an eye and without moving, I found myself sitting in the boat, my bare feet resting on the weathered boards. Slowly, it nosed out of the reeds, gliding across the water as though drawn by some invisible power. I sat motionless, unresisting, letting the boat carry me to the center of the lake.

Lilies thickly dappled the water, their flat green pads jostling for position, and their flowers open in pristine white cups. The boat slowed and stopped. Silence. The unseen warbler had ceased his song, the breeze had given up shaking the reeds, and even the sounds of the water had died.

Beside the boat, the surface stirred, drawing my eyes like a magnet. I couldn't have looked away even if I'd wanted to. The lily pads gently parted. Beneath the dark, peaty water, a pale shape coalesced before my eyes, half hidden by the depths.

"She brings it for you." A child's voice spoke, soft, commanding, knowing.

With an enormous effort, I dragged my eyes away from the water. The child was seated in the prow of the boat. Small, scarcely eight years old, with long dark hair hanging loose to her waist. I stared.

Merlin's clever eyes stared back at me.

"Nimuë." Her name came on a breath, as though I'd known it all my life. I had.

Pale face, porcelain skin, small bare feet, long-fingered hands resting on knees covered by a simple shift. So much in her of Merlin, so little of her mother.

She glanced over her shoulder as though fearing someone might overhear, then leaned toward me. "Do not believe your dreams," she whispered, her voice low and melodic. "You are the Ring Maiden. You must take him to the sword and fulfill the prophecy." She pointed. "Set Excalibur in his hands."

Entranced, I followed her finger. The ethereal shape rising from the depths had drawn closer. The water rippled. The shining tip of a sword broke the surface, rising out of the darkness. Higher, higher, until the hand that held it emerged as well, water running off in rivulets. Right beside my boat.

Unsure what to do, I turned back to Nimuë.

The front of the little boat was empty.

Beside me, within touching distance, the sword glimmered like a fairy blade, drinking all the misty light, soaking it up, until all else was darkness. I reached out my hand and took it.

⇶⇷

"Gwen? Gwen?" A voice I ought to know.

I opened sticky eyes a crack. "Arthur?"

A fuzzy shape filled my vision. I blinked and another shape replaced it. "Gwen? Miss Fry?" A different voice.

"The sword," I mumbled, my mouth parchment dry.

"What's she talking about?"

"She's confused."

I tried to wet my papery lips but failed. "Water…"

Flashing lights. Blurry flashing lights. And pain.

"Don't knock her. Be careful."

Bumping. Was I being carried? On some kind of stretcher?

"D'you want to come with her?"

"Yes."

"In you get then."

Bang. I screwed my eyes shut.

"Let's give her some intravenous paracetamol."

Paracetamol?

Distant rumbling. Movement. Bouncing. Smooth again. My fingers clutched the softness of a blanket.

A siren.

What?

"Here, sip this." Someone gently pushed a straw into my mouth, and I sucked water, cool and refreshing, lubricating the dryness.

I spat the straw out. "Arthur?" My voice sounded croaky and wrong.

"Are you Arthur?" A gruff voice, deep and resonant.

"No. I'm Nathan." A pause. "Nathan Wilton, Gwen's boyfriend."

No!

I wanted to scream, but sound wouldn't come. Or maybe it did. Hands took hold of me, pushing me down. I thrashed, fighting back, as somewhere far off wild animal noises rose.

"We'll have to sedate her. Sir, can you stay seated. She's clearly frightened of you. Gwen, I'm just going to give you a little scratch on your arm. Hold her still. There." A pause. "Radio ahead and make sure the police are waiting for us."

"I didn't touch her. I swear. I found her like this in the tower."

"Save that for the police, sir."

A woman laughing.

"Do not believe your dreams."

Darkness.

>>>*<<<

I AWOKE IN a hospital bed. Whiteness everywhere. Cool crisp sheets, lots of pillows. Alone.

A nurse in blue scrubs came over. "Good, you're awake." She lifted my wrist and took my pulse. "Everything's getting back to normal. That was a heck of a bang you took on your head. How are you feeling now?"

I swallowed thick spit. "Thirsty." Croaky voice still.

She smiled. Young and pretty with her blonde hair in a high ponytail, she had kindness stamped through her like a stick of seaside rock. "Here you are. Let's sit you up a bit, then you can drink properly."

After she'd adjusted my bed and helped me sit up straighter, she handed me a plastic beaker of water. "Small sips. It might make you vomit."

I ignored her and took a big gulp. *Chlorinated water. Yuck.*

I pulled a disgusted face. "Where am I?"

"West Mendip Hospital, Glastonbury. Guinevere Ward."

My eyes flew wide. How very ironic. Memory flooded back. I plonked the beaker on the table beside the bed. "I shouldn't be here. This is wrong."

She put a gentle hand on my shoulder, pushing me back against the mountain of pillows. "Yes, you should. The police will be coming to talk to you in a while. To find out who did this to you. Just lie still, please. Bed rest for you."

I bit my bottom lip and lay still. How on earth had I got here? And hadn't I heard *Nathan*'s voice? A voice I could scarcely recall after twelve years' absence. And yet, he hadn't sounded surprised to see me after all that time. I struggled to piece together the jigsaw in my aching head, and failed.

The nurse went away. I finished the water in the beaker, despite its taste, and refilled it from the jug. Several times. Then I lay back and closed my eyes, surprised by the weakness in my limbs. My exploring fingers found a bandage circling my head. One of the horses must have kicked me, or maybe I'd hit my head on a rock.

Time crawled.

From where I lay, I had a good view of the nurses' station and the clock on the wall over it. Half past five. In the afternoon? Electric street lighting filtered through the drawn blinds on the windows. Dark already. Winter.

I closed my tired eyes, but a girl-child with long dark hair and Merlin's eyes haunted me, pointing a pale hand into bottomless water. "Do not believe your dreams." And a woman's triumphant laughter plagued my half-waking moments.

"Miss Fry?"

I blinked awake, heart hammering with relief at being free of that laughter.

A policeman stood before me. Young, with short cropped blonde hair and a cherubic face. Spots covered his chin and forehead.

I managed a smile. "Yes?"

"I need to ask you a few questions. If you don't mind."

"Where's Nathan?" Did I even want to see him after all these years? And on top of that, why would he want to see me? Might he still think of me as his girlfriend? How weird was that? I had so many questions.

"In the Relatives' Room. We're not letting him see you until we've ascertained the facts and found out what you know. And who did this to you."

I frowned. "You don't think *he* did this, do you?"

The policeman pulled a skeptical face.

I shook my head, which hurt. "Well, he didn't."

He took out his notebook. "Do you know who did, then?"

I nodded, which hurt more. "My horse."

He raised a quizzical eyebrow. "Your horse? On top of Glastonbury Tor? *Really?*"

On top of the Tor? I licked my lips, uncertain how to respond. "Ye-es." It didn't come out as brimming with conviction.

Silence fell between us. His pencil scratched across the page of his notebook for a moment or two before he looked up again. "So. You're saying it wasn't your boyfriend?"

"I am."

"You're sure? You have a lot of bruising. Not just your head. It looks like someone's taken a baseball bat to you." He paused, leaning forward with a mixture of compassion and earnestness on his spotty face. "You can tell me anything you like. We can keep you safe. Find you a women's refuge. You don't have to ever see him again. Just tell us what happened."

I heaved a resigned sigh. "I'm telling you the truth. It wasn't Nathan. He'd never hurt me."

He closed his notebook. "Very well. I'm not sure I believe you though. I'll file my report." He began to turn away, but paused. "If you should change your mind, here's a card for an organization that helps battered women."

After a long pause, I took the card, laying it on the table beside my empty water jug. "Thank you."

Five minutes later, Nathan appeared, face flustered with worry. "Gwen, are you all right?" He was gabbling, possibly with shock at having been a suspect. At still being one. "When I found you, for one awful moment I thought you were dead. What happened?" He shook his head. "Those bloody policemen thought I'd done this to you." He sat down on the single chair beside the bed. "Fucking cheek of it."

He must be very upset as he rarely swore, and almost never using the f-word.

I stared, taking in the man I'd left behind all those years ago. Tall, with dead-straight brown hair that flopped heavily forward over hazel eyes, he'd not changed a bit in the twelve years since I'd last seen him. "Hello, Nathan."

The worried frown melted away. "Hello." He gave himself a little shake. "Sorry about the rant."

I smiled. Once upon a time I'd loved this man. Or I'd thought I did. Was it possible he'd never stopped loving me? How else had he been here to find me? Twelve years after he'd lost me.

I licked my still dry lips. I needed some lip salve in the warm dry atmosphere of the hospital. "How... how did you find me?"

He reached out a hand and covered mine, his palm soft. "When you didn't come back, I got worried and decided to go up the Tor myself to find you. Good thing I did. You could've lain there all night. Died of cold. Not many people go up there in winter."

Wait a minute? *What* was he saying?

I struggled again with those awkward jigsaw puzzle pieces. Was this...? Could this be the *same* day I'd gone up the Tor to scatter my father's ashes? Cold fear clenched its fist around my heart, its icy fingers creeping through my body. Had all my years in the Dark Ages been somehow wiped away? *"Do not believe your dreams."*

He must have seen my expression change. "Steady on. It's all right. You didn't catch your death. I was there to find you. And call an ambulance. You're okay. Just a nasty bump on your head and a lot of bruises. You'll be back to normal in no time." He squeezed my hand.

Normal? I wanted to scream. Was anything ever going to be normal again?

A woman's laughter, loud and triumphant, echoed through my head. Not a dream this time. The laughter was as real as Nathan's words. My head swung around, searching for the source. Quiet patients dozing in other beds, nurses working, an auxiliary carrying a covered bedpan. I blinked, but nothing changed. "I think I need to get some sleep." The words came out stilted and tense.

Nathan's eyebrows rose, but he stood up. "Okay. Visiting time's nearly over anyway. I'll come back in the morning to collect you. They said you have to stay in overnight." He bent and kissed me on the forehead, with warm, wet lips. Then he left.

I wiped the feel of his kiss off my skin.

Then I lay back, exhausted, as tears trickled down my cheeks, despair welling up from the bottom of my broken heart to fill my body. Could I have dreamed the last twelve years?

Oh Arthur, where are you?

Chapter Eleven

A LITTLE AFTER six, an auxiliary brought me some kind of unrecognizable stew served with over-cooked vegetables and mashed potato that had hard, undercooked lumps in it. Sponge pudding and custard with a thick skin on it followed for dessert. When had I last been in hospital? To have my appendix out, aged twelve. I'd forgotten how bad hospital food could be. Then a cup of strong tea. Nectar. How many times in the last twelve years had I longed for a nice cup of tea?

I lay considering my position while the lady in the next bed watched *Antiques Roadshow* with earphones on. Television. I stole a sneaky glance, marveling at how much I hadn't missed it.

Forget the TV. Much more important was working out how I'd got back here. I shoved aside my first horrified thought that I'd dreamed my time in the Dark Ages, as my bruises gave the lie to that. Hadn't I been riding across the plain below Din Cadan with my family and fallen off my horse? Had that fall somehow returned me to my old world? It didn't make sense.

The certainty that I hadn't imagined the years I'd been away pressed in on me. Yet, here I was, on what appeared to be the very day I'd left, battered and bruised and confined to a hospital bed – a twenty-first-century hospital bed. I hadn't acquired these bruises from rolling down a grassy hillside. And anyway, Nathan had found me *inside* the tower.

"Do not believe your dreams."

A feeling of terrifying urgency enveloped me as I watched the clock's hands tick around in infuriating slow motion, counting off the minutes I'd been back in my old world, turning them into hours. I had to get away before those hours became days. I had to get back to where I was meant to be. Somehow, the conviction that the longer I spent here, the harder it would be to return to my chosen life swept over me like a rising tide.

The nurses were bustling about with a new admission to the empty bed opposite mine. One of them shot a glance at me and I looked away, uneasy under her curious gaze, conscious they regarded me as a bit of a mystery. That they thought my boyfriend had beaten me up.

I gathered my wandering thoughts. If I'd got back here the same way I'd left this world, then magic must have played a part. And this time not benevolent magic. That triumphant laughter I'd heard echoed in my head again, like a tune you hear then can't get rid of. A woman's laughter. Hafren's? I conjured up her face and the acquisitive looks she'd given Arthur, and balled my fists. No. Whatever she was, she didn't have the power to do this to me. But someone else did.

Oh, Merlin, I need your help.

Nathan would be back in the morning with my clean clothes. He'd want to take me to the place I'd once considered home, miles from here. Miles from the only possible way back to the man I loved… and my children.

A lump rose to my throat as I thought of Arthur, Amhar and Archfedd, and my stomach churned at the almost insurmountable gulf of centuries stretching between us. A plan. I had to make a plan: find a way to get back, find out what power had banished me back here. And find out *who* had done it. That someone had done this on purpose, I had no doubt.

When no one was looking, I slipped out of bed and peeked into my bedside cabinet. Walking boots and coat. No clothes, though. They'd probably been filthy. Nathan must have taken them. Damn it. I needed clothes now.

What was that lump in my coat pocket? Aha. My cell phone. That might come in useful. I pressed my thumb to the bottom button. It burst into bright life showing 85% battery. Not bad. A message, time 9:34, from Nathan, waited to be answered. *Where are you? I'm getting worried.*

I bit my lip. I couldn't let him turn up tomorrow morning and take me back to my old life – working in the library, living in that neat little house with all the modern conveniences I no longer missed. I didn't need them. I didn't need *him*. What I needed, above all else, was Arthur and my children.

The ache in my heart was physical. I couldn't sit here and let this happen. I couldn't passively accept what someone else had decreed for me. I wasn't that woman any longer. I was a warrior queen, not a librarian.

I glanced at the nurses, busy at their large desk under that ticking clock. Instinct told me a stopwatch was running, counting down the time I had to act. That the window on the Tor, now it had been opened once again, would shut forever if I wasn't quick. That the person who'd sent me back here would make sure of that. Very soon.

I had to get away from here.

Did I have phone signal? Yes. Four bars. Great. With fingers unaccustomed to technology, I fumbled to the web browser. What had the nurse called this hospital? I did a search. West Mendip. Maps next. Satellite view. There it was. Now, where was the Tor and my doorway to the past?

I gripped the phone and stared down at my fingers, not seeing the screen at all.

The ring. I'd need the ring.

My fingers were bare.

My heart began to thump painfully hard against my ribs, and my hands on the phone shook so much, I dropped it onto the covers on the bed. No ring meant no magic. How had I got back here without it? Where was it? I never took it off. How would the doorway on the Tor open without it? Real, unreasoning terror crawled up my spine, desperation parching my mouth.

Arthur's face hovered in front of my eyes, with Amhar's and Archfedd's, their mouths moving, but making no sound. Were they calling my name?

I had to think straight.

With an enormous effort, I stilled my shaking hands and, reaching over, pressed the button to call a nurse.

A different one this time. Older, grumpier, dyed red hair in a neat bun. "Yes, is there something wrong?" She sounded fed up and jaded.

I held out my hand. "My ring's gone. D'you know if someone took it off while I was… unconscious?"

She frowned. "Can't this wait until the morning?"

I shook my head, gripping the bedcovers with my other hand. "No. It can't. It's a very special ring. I won't be able to sleep without it." I hoped my eyes were pleading.

She sighed and plodded back to the nurses' station. Crossing my fingers and holding my breath, I watched her as she talked to a second nurse. They bent over something I couldn't see – perhaps a drawer. I waited, heart thudding.

The first nurse came plodding back. "What does this ring of yours look like, then?"

She had something in her hand, in a small plastic bag.

"Gold, with a dragon embossed on it."

She raised her eyebrows. "Unusual. That's why I asked you. Here." She held out the bag. "Apparently, they took it off you in the ambulance in case your fingers swelled. We had it locked safely in a drawer. I'm not sure you should be putting it back on just yet though – there could still be swelling."

I managed a smile, taking the bag with trembling fingers. Without a second look, she walked away, and I pried open the ziplock on the bag and took out my ring. For a moment I let it lay on my palm, savoring the warmth of the gold, before slipping it back into place on my not-at-all swollen finger. With a deep possessive sigh, I wrapped my other hand around it and held both hands tight against my chest.

Enough of that. Urgency pressed in on me. Back to the map on my phone.

I found the Tor. My finger, no longer shaking, but determined, traced the road I'd have to take, and I committed to memory the turns and junctions. Country lanes for the most part, which would most likely be narrow and unlit at night. I used the app to estimate the distance. A little over a mile and a half. I could do that, even battered and bruised. I *was* a warrior queen, after all. And it had to be tonight, before time stretched out and separated me from my home and my loved ones forever.

I put the phone on silent.

The lights went out at nine, except the one by the nurses' station – enough to faintly illuminate the side-ward I was in.

The clock hands crept slowly round.

At half past nine, when the one nurse on duty, the grumpy red head, went off to answer someone's call for help, I slipped out of bed. Making sure my delightful, open-at-the-back hospital gown was covering my backside, I retrieved my coat and boots, and set off to find the toilets.

Odd that the thing that struck me most forcibly would turn out to be the toilets. Lit glaringly, with shining porcelain basins all white and clean and actually flushing. I stopped on the threshold to stare, wide-eyed, as though I'd never seen a toilet before. A stark comparison with the bucket in the corner of my chamber at Din Cadan. Waste not, want not. I used the facilities and flushed with a strange sort of pleasure. In fact, I flushed twice, the second time for pure fun.

Comfortable now, I stepped out into the corridor, still carrying my coat and boots. Difficult to make an escape dressed in a flappy hospital gown. I needed more substantial clothing.

Opposite the toilets stood a door marked Staff Only. Worth a look.

The staff changing room. Down the center ran a rack with back-to-back bench seats and a row of high coat pegs. I sat down for a moment, legs weak, and looked about. A row of lockers – all locked, of course. They'd store their own clothes in them while they worked. Impossible to get into, but in a corner stood a sizeable bin – for dirty washing. Getting up, I padded over and lifted the lid. Used scrubs. Not really dirty – just not possible to wear twice in case of infection.

Beggars can't be choosers etc. I had no qualms about wearing someone else's dirty washing.

I rummaged through and found a set that fitted. In went my flappy, bum-revealing hospital gown and on went the scrubs. Much better.

Now what? I touched my head. I'd have to get rid of this bandage. A dead giveaway that I wasn't a nurse. In front of the small wall mirror, I carefully unwound the bandage. Not so bad. A jagged, neatly stitched cut across a swelling on my forehead. A hefty bump on the back of my head. A half-closed black eye and bruised cheek on the same side. Grazes. I'd live. I'd seen far worse. Odd to see my own face accurately reflected back at me after so long without a decent mirror. Did I look older? No way of telling in this state. No gray hairs yet though.

I bent and pulled on my boots, double knotting the laces. My coat had dried mud on it from my fall down the hill twelve years ago… no, this morning… so I brushed it off. The same coat I'd abandoned in Din Cadan. For a moment I held it in front of myself, staring, trying to work out how it could be in two places at once, and failing. Then I slipped it on over the scrubs and went to the door.

The corridor stretched away in both directions, empty. I stepped out as if I had every right to be doing so, and set off for the exit. No one looked at me as the sliding doors in reception opened, and I escaped into the night, unchallenged.

Chapter Twelve

COLD NIGHT AIR hit me like a wall, almost taking my breath away after the warmth of the hospital and making me wish for something more substantial than scrubs. I stood on the steps under the overhang, trying to match the map in my head with the reality in front of me. How much easier would navigating the open countryside of the Dark Ages have been? Although the marshes around Ynys Witrin might have covered this particular spot.

I glanced at the parked cars and turned up my nose. A horse would have been handy.

The lights in the car park showed me the way to the road. Now turn left.

I half-walked, half-ran along the pavement, trying not to draw attention. At least the streetlights helped. A couple of cars passed me, and when they'd gone, I crossed the road to where the pavement continued.

The fear that someone would discover my absence plagued me, and I couldn't help but snatch glances over my shoulder as I went, half-expecting to see nurses running down the road in hot pursuit.

No nurses appeared, thank goodness.

Before long, the pavement and streetlamps ran out, as the road narrowed into a country lane, looming dark and uninviting. I hesitated, nervous, not used to roads and traffic anymore. A car might hit me in the dark. The driver wouldn't see me until it was too late. A few faint lights shone from houses on my left, but that was all.

I had to take the risk. If I heard a car coming, I could flatten myself in the hedgerow. With a determined step, I recommenced my journey.

Luckily, half a waxing moon hung in the sky, illuminating my way. Was that a farmyard, close by the road? Prickly hedges pressed to the tarmac on both sides.

No cars though. Thank goodness, as there was nowhere to get out of their way.

I hurried on, leaving the fields and hedges behind, and found a housing estate with more streetlights to all too briefly illuminate my way. A nice safe pavement to walk on. I stopped for a breather, hands on knees, chest heaving, which hurt, and got out my phone to check the map.

A car crawled past, the lights sweeping over me, and for a moment I froze, afraid without reason that it was Nathan come to look for me. That maybe the hospital had rung him when they'd found me gone, and he'd set out to track me. But the driver kept going, indifferent.

I straightened up and followed the car, half-running along the pavement, chased by the urgency of my quest. Certain that time was paramount, and if I didn't hurry, it would be too late, and I'd never get back to where I belonged.

This had to be the very edge of Glastonbury, on a lane that skirted to the north of the town. Going the right way, at least. But it felt like more than the mile and a half I'd measured.

Oh, Arthur. I'm coming. Wait for me.

What was that? A road sign pointing left said Wick Hollow. No pavement, but I didn't care. Narrow, dark, overgrown. My booted footsteps clattered on the tarmac, and the wind soughed in the bare branches of the trees making them whisper together conspiratorially. But within minutes I was in open country, with fields to either side, and just the odd tree here and there with its branches silhouetted against the moon.

I'm coming.

I had to stop to catch my breath. It rasped in my lungs and my ribs ached. Not broken, but badly bruised. Despite the cold, sweat soaked my stolen scrubs, and the rhythm of my heart pounded in my ears, ticking away at the time I had. Urgency pressed down on me. Breath scarcely regained, I set off again.

Ahead, the dark mound of the Tor showed as a darker hump against the blue-black of the sky, the lonely, ruined tower crowning it. I upped my pace, feeling like Cinderella at the ball, racing back because she'd forgotten the time, her pumpkin carriage already returning to its vegetable state. Did I have till midnight, like her? Would all be lost if I didn't get there in time?

The lights of a car approaching from behind swept across the sky. Instinct had me climbing over a rickety five-bar gate into the nearest field. I crouched in the mud behind the hedge, fighting to still my heaving breath. Was I being paranoid?

The sound of the engine drew nearer, not traveling fast. I peeped out between the straggling hawthorn branches. A police car crawled past, the driver, window down, peering into my field. I crouched lower and closed my eyes, lest he catch a reflection in them.

Who else could he be looking for but me?

The car kept going.

I stayed still. Now what? Not the road, that was for sure. He might come back or lie in wait for me up ahead. I fished my phone out of my coat pocket. Eight missed calls from Nathan. Ignoring them, I studied the map again, satellite view. A junction lay ahead, at which I needed to turn left, and where the policeman might wait. Stowing the phone away again, I started down the field side of the hedge in the same direction as the police car, my eyes fixed on the hump of the Tor looming ever closer in the darkness. So near and yet so far.

I'm coming.

At the thankfully unguarded road junction, I found no handy gate and had to fight my way through the hedge to get out of the field, ending up scratched and bleeding. Someone had kindly put a bench on the corner, so I sat on it for a moment, pulling twigs and dead leaves out of my hair.

Did I dare walk along the lane until I reached the official, concrete path to the summit? What if the police car came back this way? They must think I'd be returning here because this was where I'd been found.

The friendly moon hid behind a patch of cloud, plunging my world into greater darkness. I'd have to risk it. Two hundred metres, maybe, according to the map. I could do it. That distance could be run in half a minute, if you were fit.

Unfortunately, with bruised ribs, I wasn't at my best.

I ran, ignoring my aching body, ignoring my gasping lungs, ignoring the throbbing in my head. But maybe I was only staggering.

Just before the parking layby, I scrambled over a wooden five-bar gate into the small field that was sometimes used for overflow parking. At right-angles, another gate blocked my way to the summit. I had no time to waste.

Struggling to control my heaving breath, I clambered over the second gate and stood for a moment, listening.

Nothing.

Gathering my courage, I stepped out onto the pale, concrete path that ran beside the hedge and turned right toward the Tor in a shambling run.

I'd made it fifty yards up the path when the deceitful moon peeped from behind her cloud. A shout rang out behind me, and a powerful torch beam sent my shadow leaping up the path toward the Tor. "Hey, you. Miss Fry! Where d'you think you're going? Stop!"

I slid to a halt and spun around. The police car must have been parked by the main gate, sitting in the dark and waiting to see if I'd turn up. Now, the officer stood by the kissing gate, a dark shape made almost invisible by the powerful torch he had fixed on me like a spotlight.

I didn't wait. I ran. They say in books that fear lends you wings. It's true.

He probably hadn't been expecting that, which gave me a good head start. Maybe he had to go back and lock his car. Hopefully, he wasn't as fit as I was after twelve years of living in the Dark Ages. Probably he thought that if I ran up the hill I'd have nowhere left to go.

I didn't look back. My feet pounded on the concrete track, the tall trees looming over the fence at the foot of the hill drawing closer. The bright torch beam swerved wildly across them, illuminating the hillside behind and plunging the rest of the night into impenetrable blackness.

If only he'd put that bloody torch out. It was ruining my night vision. I almost fell up the couple of steps to the gate under the trees, staggering with a grunt of pain. The shadows of waving branches wove across the ground, dancing with the light of that stupid policeman's torch.

I flung open the gate and started up the hill. Steps. Of course, steps up the steepest parts. My breath rasped in my chest as I galloped up them, praying I wouldn't slip and fall. I could barely see, but at least the trees now protected me from the worst of the torchlight.

Adrenaline fueled those wings of fear. On my right, the hill rose ever steeper, the main path winding up like a switchback road, with small earth-cut steps leading straight up the steep, grassy hillside in a shortcut. I'd never gone up that way before, but tonight was definitely the time to start. I scrambled on my hands and knees, grabbing tussocks of grass to steady myself, the torchlight picking me out like a fly on a windscreen.

I didn't stop. He must have been close behind me now, also scrabbling up these makeshift steps. Why had I never noticed the steepness of the Tor before?

The steps gave out. I was on the last steep rise to the summit, staggering now on legs like spaghetti, the tower within my reach. My chest rose and fell as I gulped in air to oxygen starved lungs and muscles.

"Stop!" His shout sounded far too close.

I forced my exhausted legs to struggle on.

"Miss Fry! Stop!" Pause. "What're you doing?" Pause. "I only want to help you." He sounded as out of breath as I was.

My hands touched the cold stone of the tower, the ring on my finger catching the moonlight. My heart leapt in exultation. Leaning on the solid wall, I looked over my shoulder. "Keep back." So exhausted I could hardly speak. "Don't come anywhere near me."

The wind had died to nothing. No sounds carried from the town or roads. We could have been in another world. Only the rasping of our labored breathing broke that silence.

"Miss Fry," he gasped. "You need to be in hospital. Half the force is out looking for you. You're safe now."

He stood twenty yards from me, illuminated by the moonlight, the torch beam lowered to a yellow circle on the grass. Early thirties, thinning brown hair, pale eyes.

I held my hand up, gesturing him back. "Don't come any nearer." I had no breath to say anything else.

Bending over, he put his hands on his knees. "I bloody well can't. What the hell did you want to run all the way up here for?"

I glanced at the tower, the open archway dark, yet welcoming, and took a step closer to it. "I have to go back."

He peered up at me from his bent position. "And I've got a bloody stitch now. Go back where? What d'you mean?" Probably he thought he had me. That I couldn't get away. That the urgency of his mission had vanished.

Another step. I was standing in the doorway, half in his world, half... where? In mine? What if it didn't work? What if I stepped into the tower with the ring on my finger and nothing happened? What if this policeman took me back down the hill to Nathan, and I had to go on with the life I'd left behind twelve years ago? Back in the library. It would kill me.

"Do not believe your dreams."

"I don't belong here," I whispered, my voice carrying in the sudden stillness.

What if I never saw Arthur and my children again? My heart ached for them with a deep primal need, a desperation, a pain I'd never get over. Tears formed in my eyes and ran down my cheeks, and I choked on a sob.

"Of course you do," the policeman said, his voice gentle, gaining strength as he got his breath back. Most likely he thought he was humoring a mental patient. "You don't have to see your boyfriend. We'll find someone for you to talk to. About the way you feel. Don't worry about that. You don't need to do anything drastic."

Oh God, he thought I was suicidal.

I shook my head. "I'm sorry. That wouldn't help. I have to go. Say goodbye to Nathan for me."

He stretched out his hands toward me, mouth open, but I didn't hear the words.

I stepped back into the tower and darkness enfolded me like a welcome warm blanket.

Chapter Thirteen

I SWAM THROUGH a heavy, cloying darkness toward a tiny pinprick of light that flickered far off in the distance. Focusing all my being, I struggled in desperation as the shackling lead weights of my old life, and something else less tangible and more terrifying, dragged at me.

Kicking out, I fought my way forward, determined not to give in, no matter how much easier it might have been to just sink back into that other world.

The light ahead flickered brighter, calling to me, drawing me on, while dark shadowy things with no shape nor form swirled about me, whispering in my ears. *"Arthur doesn't want you any longer." "You belong with Nathan." "Let go." "Stay with us."*

No! I refused to give in to them.

The light ahead brightened and grew, blossoming like the shimmering sun viewed from deep underwater. One more kick would free me, take me home.

"He doesn't want you. He doesn't want you. He has Hafren. She's younger than you and more beautiful." A hissing voice echoed inside my head, coiling its way into my mind like a canker to smother common sense.

My legs ceased to kick, and the light began to recede.

Doubt seeded itself in my brain and in my heart. What if this were true? What if my dream was real? What if he did want a younger woman?

"Give up. Go back. Back to where you belong. This isn't your world." A

hissing woman's voice. A voice I knew.

Morgana.

No! I kicked out with my legs, arms outstretched, the ring on my finger leaving a trail like a sparkler on bonfire night, and the hissing voice rose in a wordless scream. I tumbled forward, down and down and down.

I landed on my back with a jolt, and my eyes flew open. I was no longer in the tower on the Tor.

"Gwen?" A gentle, anxious voice. A voice I knew and loved. A man's. Not the policeman. Not Nathan.

The brilliant light had been replaced by the soft glow of candlelight, and the tangy scent of woodsmoke tickled my nostrils. I blinked, and the world came into focus. Arthur's face hovered over mine, handsome, unshaven, haggard, but beautiful. Loved.

I burst into tears.

His hand touched my face, warm and alive... and real. I cried harder. Tears of relief, of love, of thankfulness cascaded down my cheeks as his rough thumb caressed my skin.

"Don't cry," he whispered. "Don't cry. You're all right. Thank God." He bent closer and kissed my forehead. "Thank all the gods." The side of the bed sagged. He must be sitting on the edge.

My gaze focused on his dark eyes, flecked with gold, that I'd feared I'd never see again. Tears sparkled on his thick lashes.

He swiped his free hand across his face, wiping away the tears and cleared his throat. His Adam's apple bobbed as he swallowed.

We had only a moment to stare into one another's eyes before Coventina's face appeared behind Arthur's, smiling through tears of her own. "Let me dry your eyes," she said, her voice low and gentle, a voice for the sickroom. "No need to cry. We've all been doing enough of that."

She dabbed my eyes with a soft cloth, her hands shaking a little, and stepped back.

I couldn't take my eyes off Arthur. How close had I come to losing him? And how had this happened to me? With an immense effort, I tried to lift arms that felt too heavy to raise. "Arthur." The words came out croaky and rough.

He gathered me up, holding me close against his body in a warm embrace, his bristly cheek against mine. "My love."

With an enormous effort, I put my leaden arms around him and hung on as though I never wanted to let him go. Which I didn't. My fingers crooked in the linen of his undershirt, hanging on like cats' claws. I breathed him in, the smell of horses, woodsmoke, sweat, all perfume in my nostrils. And he held me back just as tightly, pressing my body against his, so close I felt his pounding heart had cleaved to mine.

How long we clung to each other like that, I had no idea. But at last, Coventina coughed discreetly. "I think Gwen should rest."

Very tenderly, Arthur loosened his hold and laid me down on the pillows. Not moving from his perch on the edge of our bed, he covered my hands with his, and held on. Perhaps he, too, had feared us parted forever.

I heaved a sigh of relief that hurt my ribs, and winced. His hold on my hands tightened. He glanced at Coventina. "Poppy syrup?"

"No," I whispered, terror washing over me at the thought of sleep, and the dreaming that might bring. "I'm fine. It's just a twinge." I shifted a little in an effort to get more comfortable, wishing for the painkillers they'd given me in the hospital. "I need a drink." Still croaky. "What happened?"

Coventina proffered a horn beaker, and Arthur supported me while I sipped the water. I still had the tender lump on the back of my head, so probably the cut on my forehead as well. If Bedwyr hadn't stitched it neatly, I'd end up looking like Harry Potter.

He lowered my head to the pillow again, and Coventina stepped back, her attitude all broody hen.

"Your girth broke," Arthur said, his brow furrowing as his grip on my hands tightened. "At a gallop. You fell." His voice faltered. "I'm so sorry. I couldn't catch you in time." It cracked. "I–I thought you were dead. That I'd lost you."

I managed a smile. "I thought I was too." I couldn't get above a grating whisper, despite the drink.

"You've been unconscious for three days," Coventina said, twisting her hands in the apron she wore. "Bedwyr wasn't sure you'd waken up."

Arthur shot her a heavy frown.

I touched my head. Bandages. "Did I get kicked?"

Arthur nodded. "You fell beneath the hooves of our horses. They couldn't help but kick you. When I got to you…" His voice broke again, and he wiped his eyes. "When I got to you, you were face down. I-I hardly dared to turn you over." He swallowed. "You were barely breathing. Merlin found your pulse."

Tears trickled down my cheeks and he wiped them away with his fingers.

He had to visibly pull himself together. "I sent Llacheu galloping back to the fortress, and he brought a wagon down with Bedwyr. We put you in it and carried you back. You've been lying here ever since." He gripped my hands so hard it hurt. "I was so afraid you'd not wake up."

Coventina backed away. "I'll tell Merlin and Cei she's awake," she murmured. The door banged as she went out.

I licked my lips. Still dry. "*How* long did Coventina say?" My mind felt numb and foggy, unable to retain things.

The candlelight danced over Arthur's tired face. "Three days." Dark shadows ringed his eyes. Had he slept since the accident?

I turned one hand over to interlace our fingers. "I was afraid, too. Afraid I wasn't coming back."

His Adam's apple bobbed again. "I don't know what I'd do without you."

The unwelcome memory of my dream, of him kissing Hafren, surfaced, and I must have flinched because his eyebrows knitted in another frown. "What is it? Where does it hurt? What can I do?"

I shook my head, which did hurt. "I had a horrible dream while I was unconscious." Small underestimation. I shivered.

But I couldn't tell him.

He smiled. "You're safe now. No dreams can harm you."

But was he right? More memories filtered back. The girl in the boat whom I'd thought was Nimuë, the pale ethereal creature under the lily pads, the sword, shedding incandescent water droplets as it rose from the lake's surface, and the girl's words, etched into my mind. *"Take him to the sword. Fulfill the prophecy. Set Excalibur in his hands."* Fevered imagination, surely? Delirium peopling my dreams with the legends I knew? Maybe even wishful thinking. How was I supposed to tell if what I'd seen hadn't been some kind of dream?

But what about that triumphant laughter? Had I only imagined it? And those hissing, furious words as I'd struggled through the darkness back to Arthur. Who'd spoken them? Who hadn't wanted me to return?

Morgana, of course.

I closed my eyes for a moment, seeing again the solid reality of the hospital, the darkness of those country lanes, the chasing policeman.

I shook my head. No dream-like quality had clung to it, no random leaps from one place to another. Everything I'd seen, felt, smelled, touched, had all been too horribly real. Reality and dream wound themselves together in my head like the ribbons on a maypole, and for a moment I screwed my eyes shut, trying to block out the memories.

How could she have done it?

"What is it?" Arthur's thumb caressed the back of my hand, his voice laced with anxiety. "Tell me what's wrong. Let me help."

I swallowed what little spit I had and spoke the words I knew without a doubt were true. "This was more than an ordinary accident." I gazed up into his tired, red-rimmed eyes. "Magic took me away from you, and tried to prevent me from getting back."

He shook his head, disbelieving, and his forehead furrowed with concern. "What d'you mean? How? There's only Merlin here with magic, and he would never have done that to you."

I shifted my grip and caught hold of his hands in both of mine, holding them tight. "What about Morgana?"

His eyes narrowed. "She's miles away." But uncertainty tinged his voice.

I had to keep going, had to make him understand. "No. She may not be as far away as you think. You can't be sure. And even if she is, maybe she can do things from afar. Who knows? I wouldn't put anything past her..." Where my strength was coming from, I had no idea.

He frowned, perhaps not wanting to believe his sister capable of such malice. "But she only has the Sight. Not the sort of magic you're talking about. She doesn't have the power to harm you. It doesn't work that way. That sort of magic isn't real..." The uncertainty remained.

What sort of magic did he think had brought me here in the first place?

I had to convince him. The danger that had threatened me still remained, menacing all of us.

I squeezed his hands. "She could. I know she could." I pushed myself more upright in the bed. "Ask Hafren. She's somehow involved. I know it. I–I saw her in my dream." My eyes drilled into his. "And I saw Nimuë as well."

For a moment, Nimuë's childish face with Merlin's clever, knowing eyes gazed at me. Was she evil like her mother, or had Merlin protected her by whatever it was he'd done that night seven years ago in her nursery? Morgana had been incandescent with fury as she watched, bound and helpless, as those weird and terrifying shadows climbed the walls of that dark room.

I swallowed again, my mouth even drier. "Nimuë was there. *For me.* Not against me. I'm certain." I willed him to believe me. "I think she drove her mother's magic away and replaced it with her own."

Until I said it, I hadn't known. But now the truth shone like a beacon in the dark. I gripped Arthur's hands harder still. "I need to speak to Merlin."

I sensed the struggle going on in Arthur's head; the conflict between his common sense telling him that what I said couldn't possibly be true, and the ingrained Dark Age belief in omens, magic, foretelling the future, and evil spirits. A belief he'd deliberately turned his back on and claimed not to give credence to. I'd done the same myself, but now I knew differently.

"The blow to your head's confused you..."

I shook my head and wished I hadn't, because it felt as though my brain was rattling loose inside my skull. "No. It hasn't. I've never felt clearer headed. I need to speak with Merlin." I kept my gaze fixed on his.

For a moment, he wavered, gazing back into my eyes as though he could draw out my story through them. Then, with reluctance, he released my hands and stood up, hovering for a moment by the bed as though still uncertain.

"Merlin," I repeated, my voice strengthening along with my growing determination.

He left the room, and I lay back on my pillows, staring up toward the shadowy rafters above my head, exhausted, every bump and scrape pressing in on me, making me aware of how sore my body was. Oh, for some lovely codeine. I closed my eyes.

Time ticked by.

The slight creak of the door opening disturbed me. Merlin padded across the room on booted feet and halted beside the bed. I waved a hand at where Arthur had been sitting. "Please. Sit."

Wary, he perched on the edge, a little further off than Arthur had been, those clever dark eyes of his fixed on me, brow furrowed. The eyes he'd passed on to Nimuë. "You wanted to see me."

I held his gaze. "Morgana stole me away and tried to send me back."

His eyes narrowed. "What d'you mean?"

"Just that. She sent me back to my old world." I paused, watching his reaction.

His eyes widened. "Go on…"

"I was there. Back in my old world on the exact same day you brought me here. Someone… found me." Best not to mention Nathan and confuse matters any further. "He took me to a hospital – a place to treat my injuries. The ones I got here, not the ones I got from rolling down the hill. The ones from falling off Alezan and being kicked." I paused. "That was how I knew everything was wrong."

His frown deepened, and his gaze sharpened. "How can that be?"

"I hoped you could tell me that."

He shook his head. "I've no idea." A pause. "What did you see?"

I told him, describing everything I'd seen and heard, from Arthur kissing Hafren, to Nimuë in the boat, the sword, the message, the ambulance and hospital, my flight – the policeman… the laughter. I made sure I told him about that laughter.

For a long time after I'd finished, he sat in silence, staring at his hands where they rested in his lap. I closed my eyes, so exhausted sleep beckoned, but determined not to give in. Afraid to give in. Afraid I'd be snatched away again if I slept. Afraid of how strong her power might be.

"Someone sabotaged your girth."

My eyes flicked open. I nodded. "I suspected as much. I keep my saddle in good order. When I last cleaned it, I'd have seen if any stitching needed redoing. It didn't."

Merlin nodded. "Not one of our people. None of them would wish harm to their Queen, the luck of Arthur." He shook his head. "The only strangers in Din Cadan are Ruan and his two women."

"It was Hafren. The dancing girl."

"You can't know."

I shook my head, and regretted it again. "But I *do* know. She's a witch. Like Morgana. Nowhere near as powerful, but a witch, nonetheless. She has to be in Morgana's pay."

Tiredness pressed down on me, but I had to keep going and fight off sleep. "Her wagon's right beside the stables. She had every opportunity to damage my saddle. Not hard for her to find out which one it was. Everyone knows Alezan, and we all keep our saddles on the ends of the partition walls."

I had to stop to take a breath. My aching ribs made talking difficult. "Maybe Morgana's waiting close by. Maybe she doesn't have to. I think, no, I know, she sent Hafren to us. She's always hated me." I paused again. "And it has to do with the sword Nimuë showed me. I'm certain. Morgana didn't want me to see it."

"If it's her, then she's waited a long time for this."

I nodded. "Because of the sword? Excalibur?"

He shrugged. "We'll probably never know."

I'd make it my mission to find out, once I was better. "Where is Hafren now?"

"All three of them are in the lockup. Have been since we got you back here and examined your saddle." He paused. "We'll need to keep them in there. The other two may well be in league with her." He shook his head. "She may be guilty of the sabotage, but it can't have been Hafren who sent you back to your old world. If she were that powerful, I'd know, and I sensed nothing different about her."

A little smile escaped me. "Like you sensed Morgana was lying to you when she said she loved you?"

He returned the smile, ruefully. "You're right. I'm blind where Morgana is concerned. Maybe I'm losing my touch. But not with others. I'd have known if Hafren had any power worth speaking of. I always do."

I reached out a hand and took one of his. "But I'm back now, and we've had warning. I'm certain Nimuë tried to help me, to keep her mother away, but she's a child and she's not strong enough yet. I think she tried to stop her mother sending me back, but she couldn't. But she did manage to show me what Arthur has to do next. He has to find Excalibur. I have to help him do it. Maybe that was what Morgana didn't want me to do. Why she tried to send me back."

His brow furrowed again. "What is this name – Excalibur? Not one I've heard before."

My smile widened just a little at his ignorance. It wasn't often I could feel smug that I knew something he didn't. "Oh, the sword in the stone was one thing, but Excalibur is quite another. You put a warrior's sword in that stone for Arthur to take, a plain, ordinary sword made magical by your hand... and my words. Perfect for what was needed then. But Excalibur is different. You'll see." Why tell him everything? Let him find out for himself.

He sat in silence for a minute, head bent, and my rebellious eyelids drooped. Eventually, he looked up again, eyes glittering in the candlelight. "You need protection, I can see." A pause, while he sucked his lips. Then he heaved a deep sigh. "I need to do for you what I did for my daughter."

I'd always wanted to know what he'd done for his baby daughter that night in Viroconium when Arthur and I had retreated out of the doors, chased by the nameless shadowy shapes he'd conjured. A shiver ran down my spine.

"Lie down and close your eyes," Merlin said.

Chapter Fourteen

I WAS ABLE to leave my bed in the morning to walk stiffly through the Great Hall and out into the spring sunshine. The children clamored around me, excited to have me back to the mother they knew. They weren't used to seeing me lying in bed and hadn't liked it.

Llacheu came running up from the barracks house he shared with his friends, and flung his arms around me, oblivious to my wince. "Gwen," he mumbled, inarticulate as only a teenage boy can be where emotion is concerned. The top of my head only reached his nose nowadays. I hugged him in return, so glad to be back where I belonged.

Cei joined us. "Ruan and his women are still shut in the lockup. I doubt they can get up to much mischief from in there."

Hopefully, he was right.

I glanced downhill toward the fortress walls, where the crude hut we called the lockup sat. Low roofed so prisoners couldn't stand up straight, earth floored and with no latrine. They'd have had to use the floor as a toilet and then lie down on it. Was that fair on Ruan and Heledd? Might they be in league with Hafren? They'd deny it, of course, so we might never know.

But my sense of fairness rose to the fore, and I turned to Arthur. "I think we should have Ruan out and question him."

"My own thoughts exactly." He gave Cei a nod, and his brother set off down the slope with a determined stride.

Five minutes later, Arthur and I were seated on our thrones in the Great Hall, with Merlin standing in the shadows behind us, like a guard dog. The doors banged open and Cei and Drustans marched Ruan in, much the worse for wear. Four days worth of gray stubble covered his chin, he stank, and his clothes were filthy. Underneath the dirt on his terrified face, purple bruises were beginning to yellow. The warriors who'd taken him had not been gentle, it seemed. They were all very fond of me.

Cei frog-marched the little man up the central aisle, holding him by the scruff of his neck, so high his feet barely scraped the ground. When they halted, Cei released his hold. Ruan's legs collapsed under him, leaving him in a pathetic heap in the rushes. From where he stood guarding the door, Drustans grinned in malicious satisfaction.

"Get up," Arthur snapped, all regal king. He'd gone back into our chamber and put on his gold circlet crown. Ruan couldn't have missed it.

I shifted in my seat in an effort to get more comfortable, glad of the kind person who'd put a few cushions on it.

The little man pushed himself to his feet, and stood, clasping his hands in front of him, eyes downcast as though he feared to meet either Arthur's or my gaze.

"Head up," Cei grunted, giving him a kick in the shins. "Look your king in the eye."

Ruan lifted his head. His moist bottom lip trembled. A dewdrop dangled from the tip of his nose and his eyes were red. He'd been crying. Well, so had I. My concern for him only went so far.

Arthur regarded him in silence for seconds that stretched out. I did the same, searching for any sign of guilt. Nothing. I resisted the temptation to glance back at Merlin for his opinion. That would have to wait.

Arthur's strong hands, resting on the arms of his throne, twitched. He tapped his fingers, a sure sign he was annoyed.

Ruan's anxious eyes fixed on them. He wrung his hands, and fresh tears ran down his dirty, bruised cheeks.

"Well," Arthur said, when the silence had reduced Ruan to a quivering jelly of terror. "What do you have to say for yourself?"

Ruan's mouth opened and closed a few times, he drew a breath as though about to speak, then his eyes slid sideways toward Cei's towering presence, and he shut his mouth again instead.

Merlin stepped forward out of the shadows, bent and whispered in Arthur's ear, his eyes fixed on Ruan as he did so. The poor man looked ready to wet himself with fear.

Arthur nodded, and Merlin stepped back.

You could have heard the proverbial pin drop. I waited.

Leaning a little forward in his throne, Arthur spoke. "How long has the girl, Hafren, been working with you?"

Ruan's eyes shot wide open. He clearly hadn't been expecting that question. Maybe he and Heledd had been ignorant of her involvement with Morgana. A crumb of sympathy rose in me. Only a crumb, though.

The little man's mouth opened, shut again, then opened. A trail of drool ran down his chin. "She come to us this spring... Milord King." Gone was the voice for reciting poetry and songs. Instead, he sounded small and scared and abject. A mouse of a man, wringing his hands before us.

"How long?"

Ruan gulped. "'Bout two month back, when we were spending the snow time in Viroconium."

My breath hissed out between my teeth. He'd condemned Hafren with that one sentence.

Arthur's eyes narrowed. "Why did you take her on?"

Ruan, distrust emanating from every pore, let his gaze slide sideways toward where Merlin stood, half hidden in the shadows. He licked his lips, a little more confident now he probably thought he could see where the questioning was going. "Our normal girl, she got attacked one night and chucked off the walls."

His voice rose in confidence. "She broke her leg an' her arm, Milord, lucky to be alive she were. She couldn't dance like that, now could she?"

His eyes looked an appeal. "We had to find another, an' quick, what with the season startin'. Hafren was in the inn when our girl got tooken. She came forward and offered her services. We watched her dance and knowed as she'd be a good draw." He paused. "Prettier than the other, too."

Arthur glanced at me. I gave him the smallest of nods. How convenient that their original girl had been so badly damaged she could no longer dance. I gritted my teeth.

Arthur looked back at Ruan. "And what made you decide to come here, to Din Cadan? We're a long way from Viroconium, and the weather's been bad for traveling." His words rang out clear and ominous in the silence of the hall. Cei's hand slid toward his belt, where his dagger hung, as though he feared Ruan might foolishly decide it a good idea to attack the king.

Ruan licked his lips, his hands never still. "She-she said as that she'd heard we could earn a good livin' here in your Hall… Milord. She said as it was a good place to come to, for traveling rhymers like us. For a dancer like her…" His voice trailed off, and he wiped the back of his hand across his snotty nose, sniffing loudly.

"And Heledd?" Arthur asked. "Tell me about her. She's been with you how long?"

Ruan wrung his hands some more. "Twenty years, Milord. She's my wife, she is."

So, if Ruan were innocent, Heledd most likely had nothing to do with Hafren's plan either. With the plan Morgana had asked her to carry out. In fact, it didn't seem likely either of these people had any idea what Hafren had intended. How had Morgana persuaded her to act? Perhaps by suggesting Hafren could take my vacated place. Hafren looked the sort of girl who might think that possible.

Arthur waved a dismissive hand. "You may go." He got to his feet. "Take your wife and your wagon and leave Din Cadan, and never come back. And my advice to you is never to return to Viroconium, either. Now, leave."

Ruan ran. Clearly, he couldn't wait to get out of our fortress. The doors banged shut behind him.

Cei called out to Drustans. "Better go and give him back his wife. But don't let that hussy of theirs out. She stays put." The door banged again behind Drustans as he left.

Merlin stepped forward out of the shadows. "Viroconium. The plot thickens."

It did indeed.

"How handy that their own dancing girl was incapacitated," Arthur said, repeating my own thoughts. "It seems you both were right. Morgana did have a hand in this."

"What will you do with the girl?" I asked, standing up as well.

Arthur and Merlin exchanged glances. "She's a witch, in league with a witch," Arthur said.

Merlin nodded. "She can't be allowed to live."

Had I really expected anything different? But freshly back from a world with perhaps more mercy than this one, I quailed at their cold judgement.

I frowned, my gaze traveling from Arthur's face to Merlin's. "Isn't that a bit hypocritical?" I fixed my eyes back on Arthur. "Your own sister is a witch, and you do nothing. And yet you're ready to condemn this girl to death? Just because she's poor and has no other worth."

"She tried to murder you," Arthur said, voice coldly calm. "I'm not condemning her for her magic, if indeed she has any at all. I'm condemning her for what she tried to do to you – my queen." He paused, reaching out a hand to take mine. "The woman I love."

Why was I arguing for this girl's life? Maybe because I came from a world where execution no longer existed. But he had it right. She'd meant to kill me. But it hadn't been her own idea. Morgana had asked her to. Did I want to be merciful? Would she have been to me, with her sly flirty looks at my husband and her evident ambition to replace me?

"But she didn't succeed, did she?" I said. "I'm here. Alive."

"Her intent was to kill," Merlin said, his voice icy cold.

Arthur tightened his grip on my hand. "What would you have me do with her then? Pardon her and send her on her way, back to my sister? So together they can hatch another plot? Another way to harm us?" His eyes flashed with anger. "Or maybe we should just go on keeping her in the lockup indefinitely? Or cut off her hand as we do to common thieves? Or brand her and send her on her way?" He caught my arm. "She intended to take you from me, Gwen. And I won't tolerate that. I love you too much."

The ground under my feet shifted like quicksand. "Can't we lock her up for a while in a prison?" A silly question. When had I ever seen a prison here?

Merlin shook his head. "She's in our prison right now. We have nowhere else to keep her. Surely you don't want us to keep her there forever?"

I stared at their implacable faces, knowing they were right. Where could we send her? What sort of punishment existed other than death or mutilation? Could I stand by and let them execute her for doing as Morgana had instructed? She'd been a pawn in that woman's hands, even if she had fancied stealing my husband for herself.

"Nuns," I said, inspiration seizing me. "Send her to a convent. Like Cadwy's mother."

Two sets of eyes opened wide to stare at me. "To the nuns?" echoed Merlin.

"Lucky nuns," Arthur said, a chuckle suddenly in his voice.

"There are nuns, aren't there?" I asked, not quite so sure of myself.

Arthur nodded. "There are. A few convents of them, here and there. You're right when you say Cadwy's mother was sent to one when my father put her aside to marry my mother." He paused. "If you're certain you don't want us to put an end to her, that is?"

I compressed my lips and nodded. "She meant to kill me, but she didn't succeed. She was Morgana's tool in this, I'm sure. Shut her up in a convent. For life. That'll be punishment enough for a girl like her – shut away from men forever. Perhaps she'll learn humility and goodness."

A grin spread over Arthur's face. "I doubt that very much. But you're right. Just retribution."

Cei nodded. "She won't be practising her wiles on anyone again."

Lucky nuns indeed.

Chapter Fifteen

MY BRUISES FADED, the stitched cut on my forehead healed in the shape of a crescent moon, and spring morphed into early summer. Arthur, despite his claims that he had to trust Cadwy, despatched more spies to Viroconium to check up on what his brother was up to with all this feverish arms-making. Which made me wonder how many spies Cadwy himself might have here in Din Cadan.

The kings might come together at the Council of Kings without hostility, but that didn't mean they weren't constantly plotting against one another. As High King, Arthur was likely to be the one most plotted against, and he and Merlin had a network of spies across every kingdom. Very MI5 and James Bond.

With the fine weather, the boys and their friends were out every day practising sword fighting, or charging on horseback with their short lances at the wooden targets. Their every spare moment seemed to be spent on horseback, if not within the walls, then outside them. They liked nothing better than galloping across the grazing lands and annoying the shepherds and their flocks. It disconcerted me how they were growing up much faster than I'd have liked.

A few new recruits to our army arrived from other kingdoms, lanky boys and young men in the first flush of their youth, eager to join the High King's famous army. Arthur spent long hours training them, leaving me to ride out with Archfedd and Reaghan, often accompanied by Merlin. We always took an escort with us, sometimes including a few of the boys in training to give them experience at the duties warriors had to undertake.

From time to time this included young Llawfrodedd, the boy from Breguoin. He'd filled out on good food, grown taller, gained muscle from his training, and no longer resembled a skinny stalk of grass. Archfedd particularly liked riding with him, as he talked to her as though she, too, were a boy, showing none of the scorn Medraut felt for her, and that too frequently Amhar copied.

"When I'm older," she said to Llawfrodedd as we ambled through the forest edge on a winding path above the lower lying marshlands. "I'm going to learn sword fighting like my mami."

Llawfrodedd put his hand on his own sword where it hung at his hip, a possession he was proud of. They were riding just in front of me where I could easily overhear their conversation. "'Tis a useful skill for anyone."

"Mami killed a man all by herself," Archfedd said, flicking her long plait back over her shoulder. "Mami rides into battle like my papa."

As he had his head turned toward my daughter, I couldn't miss Llawfrodedd's toothy smile. "I did hear as she killed a dozen men all by herself."

Archfedd's laugh tinkled through the mild air. "Silly. That's just a fireside story. It was only one. She told me so."

Llawfrodedd grinned. "Folks do like to think as it were a dozen though. She be the luck of Arthur. They all do know that."

"You do talk funny." Archfedd giggled. "She *is* the luck of Arthur. That's how you say that."

"She *is* the luck of Arthur," Llawfrodedd repeated, taking care with his enunciation of the words, trying to iron out his rural accent and copy Archfedd's intonation.

I smiled to myself. Although now nearly fifteen and old enough to be included in the army, the boy's quiet, gentle nature shone out of him, and he possessed none of the bluster and bravado of some of the others. Perhaps his peasant upbringing had instilled in him an appreciation of what he now had, that boys like Medraut just took for granted.

"That's better," my canny daughter said. "And I've just had a good idea. If I teach you how to speak properly, then you can teach me how to fight with a sword. Is that a deal?"

I suppressed my laughter. Who was I to stop her? Swordswomanship might well be a skill that would one day come in handy for her, as it had for me. Every girl should be able to defend herself. Maybe I should suggest to Arthur that all girls of the fort were taught alongside their brothers. I chuckled to myself as I pictured his incredulous expression.

"Deal." Llawfrodedd spat onto his grubby palm then held his hand out.

For a moment Archfedd looked down at his hand in wonder. Then she put her reins into one hand, spat in her own palm, and took it. "Deal."

I kept a bit of an eye on her swordfighting lessons to begin with, but I needn't have bothered. Llawfrodedd was a careful teacher. He found her a small wooden practice sword, and used a similar one himself. She was a fast learner.

Her lessons didn't go unnoticed though.

"I see Archfedd is intent on emulating her mother," Merlin said to me one afternoon as I strolled along the wall-walk in the warm sun. He'd climbed up the steps near the gate to stride purposefully toward me.

I smiled and nodded. "And surpassing me."

He hooked his arm through mine. "But she's not who I came up here to talk to you about." He steered me around until I was walking back the way I'd come, away from the gatehouse. "I came to talk to you about Medraut."

My heart sank. I'd seen very little of my nephew lately, with the long days and the training he and the other boys were doing. He and Amhar had taken to eating with the young warriors at the tables at the foot of the Hall. Too grown up by half.

"What about him?" I asked.

The breeze blew Merlin's long loose hair out behind him. "He seems to be gathering a faction."

I bit my lip. "I feared as much."

Overhead, a female sparrowhawk swooped toward a pigeon. A flurry of feathers and she headed toward one of the fenceposts around the horse pens. Her plucking post. Such was nature. And so do boys cease to be the children we'd like to have them stay, and turn into men before our eyes. Unavoidable nature.

Merlin frowned. "I see it when I'm teaching. He has a group of what you or I might call friends, but they're not quite that. They're more like his followers. A little afraid of him. Awed into subjection. He's a big lad, and he has a way with him that inspires obedience if not affection or admiration." He shook his head. "No, that's not quite right. They do admire him for his daring, his ruthlessness. But they have no affection for him."

"He's only twelve."

"Old enough and looks older."

We walked a few more paces to where we wouldn't be overheard by the guards along the wall-walk. I pulled him to a halt. "And Amhar?"

"In his faction."

Amhar was such an easily led child. I feared for him if he ever became a king like his father. I feared for him as well because I'd never heard, in any of the legends from my old world, that Arthur had left a living heir. And I feared for him most because of how he'd been thrust together with Medraut.

"Can we break it up?"

Merlin leaned against the parapet wall, eyes screwed up against the sunlight. "We could try."

I faced him, hands on hips. "Tell me how."

Chapter Sixteen

THAT NIGHT IN our chamber, I put Merlin's suggestion to Arthur. He was a little drunk from having imbibed too much wine at dinner, and intent on getting me out of my gown, something he was very bad at when tipsy due to all the laces that needed undoing. Especially when he was in a hurry. But experience told me this would be a good time to get my own way.

"I've been thinking about Medraut," I began, as he fumbled about behind me, swearing under his breath.

"I've been thinking about you," he said. "All evening."

Like I hadn't noticed. I smiled to myself, a warm tingle percolating down through my body to settle in my groin. "He's bored kicking about the fortress with the other boys. He's head and shoulders above them intellectually. We should give him some responsibility." I'd have said fast-track him, but that would probably have been a phrase Arthur wouldn't have understood.

My dress loosened as he got the laces partially undone. "Damn it," he muttered.

Determined not to be side-tracked, tempting as his ardor was, I persevered. He was so busy at the moment, that last thing at night like this was the only time I had him to myself, and I wanted him as much as he wanted me. But a spot of manipulation had to come first. "We could send him to one of the smaller forts. To learn from the warriors stationed there. It would do him good to be away from where he's spent his childhood."

The laces finally surrendered, and Arthur's hands slipped inside my dress, hot on my skin. A shiver of excitement ran through me at his touch. As it always did. The temptation to give in to desire and discuss Medraut another time grew ever greater.

"Merlin says he's ready for it," I persisted, turning round in his arms to face him and resting my hands on his shoulders. He was at his most beguiling, hair tousled, eyes brimming with desire, his handsome face inches from my own.

He bent his head and kissed my neck, his hot, demanding mouth sending more shivers coursing through me. I couldn't help myself where he was concerned. Even after twelve years, his touch still kindled a flame inside me, making me weak at the knees and putty in his hands. He had more than his fair share of the Pendragon charm, whatever that was. Magic perhaps, allure for certain. In my old world it would have been called sex appeal.

He slid my gown off my shoulders, and his kisses ran down my throat toward my breasts. Then lower. Weak at the knees, and decidedly weak of will as his tongue teased me, I abandoned trying to have a sensible discussion, and gave in.

Some time later I lay naked in his arms, sweat cooling on my body and my cheek against his chest, the hairs tickling my nose. The steady beating of his heart sounded in my ear, as his chest rose and fell with a gentle, reassuring rhythm. Life. How often when we lay like this did I rejoice that he still lived? The burden of having his death to think of weighed me down so much sometimes that I almost forgot the joy of living. Maybe that was why I found so much enjoyment in sex with him – that eternal affirmation of life. Which brought me back to the question of his nephew.

I twisted a little so I could look into his face. "We haven't resolved the problem of Medraut yet." I gave him a little poke with a finger. "You distracted me before we could reach a decision."

He opened his eyes and yawned. "Do we have to right now? I was almost asleep."

This time, with nothing to distract me, I wasn't going to give up. "Yes, we do. I think he needs to be away from here. Somewhere fresh and new. But not with his mother."

I had no qualms about sending a twelve-year-old to live with a bunch of strange warriors. I'd got over that when we'd done something similar to Gildas – only we'd sent him to a bunch of monks. As luck would have it, a move that had turned out well for him. Pity the monk who tried to cross *that* young man.

Arthur yawned again. "All right. I'll listen. But don't blame me if I nod off."

I pinched him. "You're not allowed to."

"Ouch. Get on with it then."

I licked my lips. "Merlin and I have noticed he's outstripped his peers. Merlin thinks he needs to be somewhere else for a year or two." I'd already decided to lay everything at Merlin's door. "To learn from people other than us. Perhaps to find out life isn't always easy." I played with the hairs on Arthur's chest. "He needs a bit of adversity in his life. He's so big and clever that everything here's too easy for him. And no one will ever cross him because he's your nephew. He needs to be somewhere his blood doesn't count. Where he's treated as just one of the men."

Arthur shifted a little, the arm around me tightening. "If that's what you and Merlin think. He's certainly a big lad – more than ready to fight. I've taught the boys he's with, and he's by far the best with a sword. Gifted, you might say. An instinctive fighter." He chuckled. "He fights like me."

Ominous words. I pushed them to the back of my mind in haste. It didn't do to dwell on something like that. Or I'd be out there pouring poison in a cup for the boy.

I'd watched Medraut fighting as well. Made it my priority, in fact.

He certainly was a good swordsman for a boy his age. Better than Amhar, that was for sure. If ever there was a boy more suited to the life of a scholar, it was Amhar. But no one was going to suggest that to him. He was his father's heir. Destined to be king one day. But Archfedd had more kingliness in her little finger than my son had in his entire body. I held my tongue on that subject.

"Where could we send him?" I asked, still playing with the hairs on his chest.

He sighed. "I don't know. Do we have to decide that now?"

As far away as possible.

Satisfaction settling over me, I snuggled closer. "No. We can do that in the morning."

"Good." He kissed the top of my head. "Now let me go to sleep."

⸻

MEDRAUT TOOK THE news of his posting to some faraway, as-yet unnamed fortress with surprising equanimity.

"Because you think I'm better than the others?" he asked, standing squarely in front of Arthur by the fire in the Hall. I'd accompanied my husband purely to see what our nephew's reaction would be.

Arthur smiled. "More mature is how I'd put it. Ready for something new. And you're my nephew. The other boys will get there too, though, have no fear. They just need more time than you do."

A smile that could only have been described as sly slid over Medraut's face. At twelve he already stood as tall as me, but whereas Llacheu had been willow slim at that age, Medraut had all the promise of ending up looking like his hefty uncle Cadwy. His voice had already lowered, and acne had begun to appear on his face. Whereas Amhar still remained a little boy, Medraut stood on the threshold of manhood already.

"Will I be in charge of *men*?"

"Not for the foreseeable future," Arthur said. "You may be big, and the nephew of the king, but that won't replace experience. You need to be a follower before you can become a leader. I'm sending three of your friends with you. The four of you will work together under the fort's commander, and he'll report back to me."

"Where am I going?" Medraut asked, a surly frown beginning to form. Clearly, he thought he ought to be in charge of wherever we were sending him.

"Dinas Brent." Arthur stared down at him, a frown on his face as well. "A small and insignificant fortress on our western coast, close to the sea. It's been abandoned now for some time, but I'm sending a contingent of warriors and workmen to reinstate it."

He paused. Was he thinking about how it had come to be so abandoned? "At present all it houses is a beacon fire to give us advance warning of raiders coming up the Sabrina Sea. A squadron of men based there in a proper fort will give us added protection. You will be amongst them."

Dinas Brent was where the traitor Melwas had been based. I shivered. He'd kidnapped me before Amhar was born, and I'd feared I'd never escape his clutches with my nose intact, or even alive. Abbot Jerome had brokered my release in return for Arthur's pledge not to punish Melwas and his men. When later he'd taken the poor beggar children of Caer Baddan and thrown the ones he didn't want, the ones he considered not useful, into the marshes around his hilltop fortress, Arthur had gleefully punished him for that, instead. But we'd all known what he'd really been punishing him for.

Even here, in Din Cadan, the people told stories of the haunted marshes around Dinas Brent, where you could hear the drowned children crying at night, and, if you were unlucky, see their pale, sad faces beneath the waters. A shiver of foreboding swept over me at the thought that we were sending Medraut to the former den of such a wicked man.

"May I go now, to tell my friends?" Medraut asked, impatience in his voice. This was news to be shared and boasted about.

Arthur nodded. "Choose three to take with you."

And Medraut was gone.

I turned back to Arthur. "You're refortifying *Dinas Brent*?"

He sat down on one of the trestle tables, his feet on the bench seat. "Needs must. It's been more than eleven years. I can't go on leaving such a pivotal position unoccupied."

"Yes, but you know what the people say about it."

He frowned. "Idle gossip. I don't believe in ghosts."

I shivered again. "I'd like to say I don't, but I've learned how foolish it is to dismiss things I know nothing about. I didn't believe in magic until I came here. And yet somehow this ring," I held up my hand to show him where the ring sat on my finger. "This actual ring transported me here and allowed me to speak your language. *That's* magic. So I don't dismiss things like ghosts out of hand any longer. I'm open to believing things I'd never have believed before."

He snorted with derision, but it wasn't an entirely confident snort. "Melwas and his victims are long gone. They can't harm us now."

I thought of Bretta's curse. I'd never told him what she'd said to me. *I curse you, Queen of Dumnonia, and I curse your husband and your son. You and yours shall know the loss I feel.*

She'd been grieving the loss of her brothers and sisters, slain by Melwas and his men, and I'd just given birth to Amhar. I'd understood her vindictive sorrow. It had been my idea to force Melwas to do something about the poor children of Caer Baddan – but not in the way he'd done it. She'd blamed me for the children's deaths. Rightly, perhaps.

Back in my old world the curse of a grieving teenager would have been disregarded, but here, in the superstitious Dark Ages, the fear that her words carried weight had never left me. Melwas could indeed still harm us.

I shook my head. "That place is evil. Should we be sending a child there? An impressionable child?" The thought that we were sending not just any child there reared up in my mind, but I couldn't tell him that. "Isn't there somewhere else we could send him? Somewhere safer?" And I didn't mean physically safer.

Arthur shook his head. "I've made my mind up. I was sending men to refortify it anyway. Those boys can go with them. Morfran of Linuis will command them. It'll be a good responsible posting for him, and he'll take no nonsense from boys. Medraut's no longer a child. He can work hard there along with the other boys he'll choose, and the men under Morfran's command."

"He's twelve." My voice rose in protest. Why was I trying to protect him when I'd just thought about lacing his drink with poison? The vagaries of the human mind.

"Nearly a man."

"Not in my opinion."

"He's as big as some of the much older boys. He's ready for this."

I fumed, frustrated that my plan had taken a turn for the worse. "I know. I want him to go. But maybe not to Dinas Brent." I couldn't get the fear out of my head that the evil of the place would influence Medraut, that Arthur was sending him somewhere that would mold him into the man I feared him destined to become.

Arthur held up his hand. "Enough. This isn't open for discussion. I've made my decision, and this is what's going to happen. The matter's closed."

I folded my arms across my chest, my lips making a thin line of resignation. What had I set in motion? It seemed that no matter what I did the road to Camlann kept on unrolling before my eyes like some sort of fateful Yellow Brick Road. Could I even have made matters worse? The nugget of fear that constantly inhabited my stomach blossomed, and my heart began to thunder.

Chapter Seventeen

As we were only delivering Medraut and the three boys he'd chosen as his companions to Dinas Brent, Arthur decided not to take a large force with him. With *us*. I'd persuaded him to let me come too. It was quite some time since I'd journeyed far from Din Cadan, and I had a morbid interest in seeing what remained of the fortress I'd been imprisoned in all those years ago.

Amhar wanted to come as well, but Arthur put his foot down about that, and I reinforced his decision, a little more tactfully. Medraut had tried to choose Amhar as one of his allotted companions, but Arthur calmly told him no, that as his heir, Amhar had to stay at Din Cadan and learn statesmanship and how to one day become a good king.

He hadn't seen the look of furious jealousy in Medraut's eyes as he turned away, but I had, and it chilled me to the core.

All of this caused a scene when Amhar found out he wasn't even to be allowed to escort his cousin to his new home.

"Why can't I come too?" Amhar demanded, beligerence, possibly fueled by some expert behind-the-scenes prompting from Medraut, oozing from every pore. Fortunately for him, this happened in the privacy of our private chamber. "I'm nearly as old as he is. And one day I'll be king. He's my friend, and he wants me to come."

"Because I don't want you to," Arthur said, leaning back against the table with his arms folded across his chest, while Amhar stood in front of him, willow thin, face flushed with fury and fists balled at his sides.

"That's not a good reason," Amhar retorted, his voice rising in frustration. "Mother's going. I can fight as well as she can." He shot me an angry glance. "Better."

Arthur's brows lowered in the start of a frown, which should have warned our son. "There'll be no fighting. We're not riding into enemy territory. We're just visiting one of my forts. And your mother is an adult and will not be a hindrance to me."

Small lie. When had I ever not been a hindrance?

Amhar made to stamp his foot, his leg twitching. I knew him well enough to guess his intent, and stifled a smile. Luckily, he thought better of crossing his father even further. "But I want to see where Medraut's being posted." Now he sounded downright sulky.

"Well, you can't," Arthur snapped. "And that's all there is to it. Merlin wants you here, working at your lessons. Medraut is older than you and ahead of you in everything. You need to do some catching up before you'll be ready for a posting."

I frowned. If I had my way, he'd never be sent to a remote frontier fortress, especially not one where he'd be with Medraut and out of my supervision and care. But I'd have to cross that bridge when I came to it.

Amhar's dark eyes filled with a mixture of fury and unhappiness, tears sparkling in their corners. "But, Father, that's so unfair!" His voice rose to a plaintive whine. A child's protest.

"Unfairness is something you need to learn to deal with," Arthur said, pushing himself off the table and straightening up. "Life is never fair, so you'd better get used to it. Now, get out of here before I decide to punish your rudeness with a beating. Go on. Back to sword practice which is where you're meant to be right now."

When he wanted to, Arthur had a very intimidating presence. Although tall, he wasn't a big man, but he had about him an aura of strength, of animal power that could be interpreted as threatening. It exuded from him now in waves.

"Yes, sir," Amhar muttered, and fled.

"Thank you," I said when he'd gone, banging the door behind him in temper. Merlin and I had decided that Amhar should not be allowed to go with his cousin. The sooner they were parted, the better. But I'd asked Merlin, who knew my reasons, to suggest it to Arthur. However, Arthur didn't seem to have handled it in quite the tactful way I'd been hoping for. Implying Amhar wasn't as good as Medraut might not have been the best thing to say, under the circumstances.

Amhar sulked like the child he was for the next few days, while Medraut strutted around the fortress like a young cockerel, boasting to any who would listen that he'd been singled out for special treatment and been allowed to choose the boys who'd share the honor with him. Amhar, looking more and more dejected, skulked on the periphery of the little group of chosen ones who were to accompany his cousin.

"I'm glad he's going," Llacheu said to me, on Medraut's final day as we sat on the fence watching the boys practise their sword fighting. "He's an arse."

Eighteen now, and very much a young man and not a boy, he closely resembled his father in almost every way, apart from the fact that he'd had his dark curly hair cut so short by Coventina I could only describe it as a buzz cut. His excuse had been that it was too hot for long hair now summer had arrived. It gave him an edgy look of toughness that his lovely curls had hidden.

I grinned at him. "You may well be right about that." I loved Llacheu like my own, and seeing him now, such a well-rounded adult, brought a glow of pride to my heart.

He swung his long legs. "Amhar's in a right bad mood about it, though."

I nodded. "He wanted to go too."

Out on the practice field, Amhar swung his wooden sword with gusto, paired up with a boy half a head taller than he was. Wham. The sword struck his opponent's simple shield a mighty blow. He wasn't bad at sword fighting – just younger and not so strong as his big cousin. He would have a long, lithe horseman's build, like Llacheu and his father, not the solid squareness of Medraut. Although Arthur had never allowed his own lack of bulk to affect his fighting skills.

"And I'm glad Amhar's *not* going." Llacheu glanced across the fortress toward the gatehouse where a laden wagon of hay was lumbering in. "I don't like the way Medraut is with him."

Their cousin was hammering his own sword against the shield of a boy I thought might be Iestyn, a good three years older than Medraut but not much taller.

Boys can be secretive. Maybe Llacheu saw more than I did. More than Merlin had seen. I raised my eyebrows in invitation for him to go on.

"Medraut thinks he can boss all the other boys about," Llacheu said, kicking the fence with his heels. "No, that's wrong. He doesn't think it. He knows it. You'll notice he's chosen only older boys to go with him?"

I nodded. "Owyn, Cahal and Iestyn."

"Well, that's because he can boss them about, and he likes being able to do that with older boys. In fact, he's the leader amongst all the boys, and those three're his chief heavies. He always makes Amhar do what he wants: running errands, fighting who he says, and they put the pressure on. He gets these older boys, who're all keen to get in his good books, to be mean to Amhar, to beat him on the practice field. And Amhar puts up with it because he wants nothing more than to be Medraut's favorite, because Medraut is the leader. D'you think those bruises he gets are by chance?"

"What?" How could I not have seen this? I closed my mouth which had dropped open. "Why didn't you say something earlier? Before now? Why hasn't Amhar said anything to me?"

Llacheu shook his head. "What goes on between the boys usually goes no further. They don't tell on each other, and we older warriors don't tell on them. Most say it toughens them up. And it's an unwritten rule not to snitch. But as Medraut's leaving... I thought I could tell you."

"I'm glad you did." I struggled to keep my voice level. Anger welled up, hot and vivid. Anger that an unwritten rule like this even existed, preventing vulnerable boys from telling anyone in authority they were being bullied. Anger that Llacheu had seen fit to keep this to himself. Anger that he'd kept this rule because perhaps he too had once suffered at the hands of older boys. Anger that my child had been bullied under my nose, and I'd been too stupid to notice. I spoke through gritted teeth. "I'll have to speak to Arthur about this."

Llacheu shook his head. "No point. He won't do anything. It probably happened to him when he was a boy. It certainly happened to me. What hurts you makes you stronger."

I frowned. Llacheu had it right – it had indeed happened to Arthur. His own brother, ten years the elder, had been the one bullying him, the one threatening his actual life, so much so that Merlin had feared the child Arthur would end up dead. Suddenly, this world seemed one devoid of rules and laws, where an older brother could decide to rid himself of a younger one, where boys could freely bully and intimidate those weaker than themselves. A bit English public school, really.

I jumped down from the fence. "But I don't want Amhar made stronger that way." My voice rose. "I want him safe and unhurt."

Llacheu slid down as well. "He's Father's heir. You can't stop him becoming a warrior, you know. And you don't want him turning out soft, like a girl." His voice was gentle, and his brown eyes, slanting a little as his mother's did, held sympathy. How much did he guess about the way I felt? How much did he know? Gossip about me had rustled around the fortress from the moment I'd arrived, and most people knew I'd come from some place very different to this.

I sucked in my lower lip, and shook my head. "But I can keep him mine until then."

He snorted. "You think? He's not been yours for some time. He wants nothing more than to be like his cousin. Medraut has a hold over him that I don't like. This separation might break that, but I doubt it. Medraut needs to be away from Amhar as long as possible."

I looked back at the practice ground where the boys had downed swords for a breather. Wooden weapons were heavier than metal ones and served a dual purpose. They built up muscles and avoided severe injury. I'd thought all Amhar's bruises had been caused in practice. Now it seemed I'd been wrong. Llacheu's words brought an icy chill to my heart. Had I lost Amhar already, without ever noticing it happening?

Chapter Eighteen

WE TOOK A route roughly northwest the next morning, riding out across the still dewy plain under a cloudless blue sky with the summer sun beating down on our backs despite the early hour. Behind us followed the men of Morfran's command, leading packhorses laden with the tools they'd need to restore Dinas Brent to some semblance of working order. Bringing up the rear came a small contingent of other warriors acting as escort. Never wise to go unprepared.

Medraut and his three friends rode knee-to-knee just behind Arthur, Merlin and me. Their laughter and continual banter made them sound for all the world like normal boys, not the bullies and thugs Llacheu had described.

When we set off, the four boys had been self-conscious in their first armor – over-large mail shirts and helmets of boiled leather covered with interlinking metal plates, but they'd soon grown blasé and cocky, and every so often one of them would draw his sword and wave it about, the blade catching the sunlight, or unhook his helmet from his saddle horn and put it on. Their claims of the feats they'd accomplish as warriors grew more exaggerated by the minute.

Arthur must have seen my sour face as Medraut boasted of how he'd cut Pict heads off and stick them on spikes outside some unnamed fortress he'd one day command. Again.

He grinned. "Ignore them. They're just boys finding their feet in a man's world."

If only that were true. I managed a smile, but riding this close to the boys didn't make for comforting listening. "They're cocky little bastards," I said, keeping my voice down low so they shouldn't overhear. "Don't you ever get fed up with boys' boasts?"

This made him laugh, and Merlin, who'd been riding a horse's length ahead took a pull on his reins and brought his horse in beside us.

"Boys," Arthur said by way of explanation. "They're annoying Gwen."

Merlin glanced back at the boys, three of whom were now tossing Cahal's helmet between them with shouts of laughter while he struggled to retrieve it.

"It's not boys in general," I said, giving Merlin a meaningful glare. "It's *these* particular boys."

Arthur shook his head. "We were all boys once." He grinned again. "Well, not you. But Merlin and I were, and no doubt our elders all thought we were as bad as you think these four are."

I doubted that very much.

"Best to ignore their empty boasting," Merlin said softly, his eyes meeting mine. "We'll be rid of them soon enough."

Not soon enough for me.

Arthur kicked Taran on to catch up with Neb, our guide from the lake village who was to take us through the marshes, and I glanced back once more at the boys.

A gentle breeze ruffled their short hair, cropped for the first time in their lives, and they could easily have been a group of cheerful schoolboys off to their first sports match. They'd put aside their wooden practice swords, and proper metal weapons now hung on their swordbelts. Dressed and armed like that, they had a look of children caught wearing their parents' clothing, even Medraut, with his sharply knowing eyes.

Merlin leaned toward me, keeping his voice low. "Hard to think of him as dangerous."

I glanced at Arthur's back. "When Medraut's like this, acting like any other boy, I suppose that's true."

Merlin pulled a rueful face. "Only we know it's not, don't we?"

I peered over my shoulder again. Cahal had regained his helmet and stuck it on his head where he probably thought it safe, and Medraut was holding forth in a loud voice as his friends hung on his words, their eyes full of admiration. Only Cahal's held a hint of resentment. "We certainly do."

<hr />

Well past mid-day, we spotted the hill of Dinas Brent. It rose steeply out of the flat western horizon, the only hill between us and the sea, surrounded by its own midge-ridden sea of marshland. Small, at first, and probably still four or five miles distant, it slowly grew larger and rose higher as we approached.

Farmland clung to the lower slopes of the hill. Twelve years ago, Arthur's men had put every building to the torch in a fit of furious, long-simmered vengeance, but the people must have come creeping back. Small, reed-thatched huts clustered the lowest land, just above the edge of the marsh, and sheep grazed the steep hillside. From the top, a thin column of smoke rose into the warm summer air.

The people working in the fields, rightly wary, spotted us from afar, and, like ants, hurried to cluster together, clutching their hoes and wooden staves, their children hiding behind their legs, as though their action might protect them if we meant them harm.

We crossed the raised causeway through the marsh under their hostile, frightened gaze, the sound of their children's crying carrying to us on the light breeze. Were they the same people Arthur had thrown out when he'd burned Melwas's hall to ashes? Or had a different group of people come to repopulate the lonely hill? By the look of them, they knew who Arthur was and didn't much care for him.

Yet, technically, they were his people. The thought that some of his subjects didn't like him seemed strange. But if you were a poor peasant toiling on your little patch of land, what good would *any* king be to you? Would you care if one fell and another took his place? Probably not. You'd see them as all the same – living off tribute from your hard toil in their fine halls, while you grubbed about in the dirt and lived hand-to-mouth.

"Look at their faces," Medraut's loud, sneering voice carried to me over the rattle of bits and chainmail. "Dirty peasants, the lot of them. I wonder if there are any decent girls amongst them."

Iestyn laughed every bit as nastily. "I'm having that one over there. See her peeking over that wall. She's not so dirty as the rest."

More laughter. They were teenage boys, after all, so was it little wonder they looked at girls this way? But nevertheless, my skin crawled at the way they'd said this.

My hands tightened on Alezan's reins. Mixing with older boys couldn't be good for Medraut, not if it was giving him this attitude to women at such an early age. Most of it would be bravado, but the way they'd spoken had left a bad taste in my mouth.

I glanced back at Llacheu, riding beside his friend Drem. Both of them were girl mad, or should that be sex mad, to the point where Drem had recently been forced to marry the girl he'd impregnated, at the tip of her father's sword. So far, Llacheu had managed to escape what he clearly saw as the shackles of marriage. But neither of them, as far as I knew, had ever spoken about a girl this way, not even any of the young women of the fortress who sold their favors to keep themselves and their children fed.

I could smile about Llacheu's and Drem's exploits, but Medraut and Iestyn's words only made me cringe. The thought that one day they might talk about Archfedd and Reaghan in this way sent a cold finger of fear down my back.

The narrow, hillside path in the sunken lane we'd taken flattened out, presenting us at last with the high, grassy banks of the fortress, still topped by the few charred stumps that were all that remained of Melwas's palisade wall. Probably the farmers had carted the rest away for firewood. We rode through the gap where the gatehouse had once stood into the grassy interior.

Dinas Brent was a much smaller fortress than Din Cadan, and the hall it had once boasted had been mean in comparison with ours. Now, only blackened and jagged wooden teeth remained. To one side of the ruin stood a single house, a new-build – little more than the sort of rude hut the villagers inhabited. The smoke twisting up from its freshly thatched roof must have been what we'd seen from afar.

In front of the hut, at a safe distance, stood the heaped beacon fire, waiting to be lit in time of peril. And sheltering from the prevailing westerly wind against the ramparts, our outpost keepers had erected a lean-to for their horses, who were at this moment grazing loose, but with heads raised and ears pricked as they viewed us new arrivals.

A couple of the warriors, who'd been watching our progress up the hill from the top of the ramparts by the gateway, slithered down the grassy slope and came loping over to us. "Milord Arthur." They touched their foreheads and bowed, the curt, economical bow of soldiers. From the far side, where the ramparts faced seawards, a third warrior waved his hand, but didn't come to greet us. Keeping watch on the Sabrina estuary for pirate ships. How useful would he find a telescope?

Arthur swung down from the saddle. "Elgin, Duer, well met." He clasped forearms with each man. "I've brought reinforcements so you can start rebuilding this fortress, and a company commander." Morfran dismounted to greet the two warriors, and they saluted him with respect. There'd be no trouble here.

Arthur waved an arm to encompass the decrepit walls. "It's time a new palisade rose here, and a few better houses than that one. When the winter winds blow, you'll find it in the sea and half-way to Dyfed."

Elgin, a grizzled warrior with a large bald patch nestling amongst his thickly curling hair, laughed out loud. "Aye, you're right at that, Milord." He surveyed the men we'd brought. "But you didn't need to bring me all yer army." He grinned at me. "Though we'll be happy to have yer luck with us."

Arthur's turn to laugh. "Half the men are for you to keep. Half to ride home with me. And I can assure you my wife will be of that party. But first, we'll stay a while and get you started. With the weather so fine, we've no objection to camping out while we work." He beckoned Medraut and his friends to come closer. "I've also brought you four green boys to forge into men. I thought it best to get them away from the fortress where they've spent their childhoods. Here they can start afresh and be treated as men, not boys."

Elgin surveyed the four boys, who were all much the same size and build – sturdy as Medraut, and well-muscled from their daily sword practice, but surly of face. An unlovely group.

He grinned. "Aye, we can lick this lot into shape until they're worthy o' bein' called men. No problem." He looked back at Arthur. "Now, a horn of cider for you, I think, Milord."

※※※

THE CAMP WE made on the summit of Dinas Brent was slightly more comfortable than a marching camp. Unbeknownst to me, Arthur had ordered a tent brought with us on the pack ponies – for him and me. The rest of the men were consigned to sleeping in the open, which would be fine as long as the weather held.

After we'd sat around the cookfire and eaten a hearty stew of meat and root vegetables, cooked in beer and thickened with coarse flour to the sort of consistency you could scoop up on hunks of bread, Arthur and I retired to our tent.

It was made of leather and big enough for me to stand upright at the apex, if not for Arthur, but like the men we had to sleep on the ground. I unrolled my bedding with singular lack of enthusiasm for the fact that we'd be spending longer here than I'd expected. It had nothing to do with the camping out part, but rather was due to the unquiet memories I had of this place.

Even though the sun had sunk beneath the distant Welsh mountains to the northwest, the evening remained warm, and Arthur tied back the flaps of the tent to let fresh air in. We still had our privacy though, as the tent pointed toward the ramparts and our men had rolled out their bedding behind us, around the dwindling campfire.

I kicked off my boots and slipped out of my braccae. I'd discarded my tunic along with my hot mail shirt as soon as we'd arrived, in preference for my thinner undershirt, but even that was hot and sticky. However, no way was I getting naked in a tent surrounded by soldiers. I lay down on top of my bed roll and watched Arthur stripping off. He seemed to have no qualms about nakedness, but then, he was a man.

He lay down on his side, facing me, his face just a shadow.

Outside someone was singing a mournful song – one I knew – the sad ballad of Gwawl, last of the giants, and how he'd wandered the world searching for his people. The melancholy of it seemed to fit the way I felt about Dinas Brent and its ghostly inheritance.

I shuffled closer to Arthur and he lifted an arm so I could snuggle against him. He smelled of sweat, horses and woodsmoke. I draped my arm across his body.

His chest rose as he inhaled deeply. "Been a while since we camped out under the stars like this."

My cheek pressed against his chest, the drum of his heart loud in my ear. "It has." I paused. "But do we need to stay so long? I know it's summer and the weather is good, but I'd rather be at home with the children." Reluctance to put into words how I felt about the ghosts I suspected clung on here prevented me from being honest with him.

He pulled me closer, and his free hand slid up under my loose shirt, the fingertips grazing my skin and sending shivers through my body, despite my apprehension. "Just a few days, to get them started. I was rather looking forward to some physical work. It's a long time since I've built anything." His fingers reached my breasts.

Exactly what physical work did he have in mind right now?

"We've brought them men, so they should have no trouble accomplishing the work before winter sets in," I whispered, hooking my leg over his and sliding my hand down his belly. "Do you really want to stay here so long when we could be at home in our own bed... indulging in more of... this?"

His hand cupped one of my breasts and his head turned to mine, moving closer. "What's to stop us indulging right now?" His voice had lowered, the huskiness in it betraying the lust snaking through his body. My hand discovered him primed and ready.

I let my lips brush his. "Forty men asleep only yards away. Or maybe forty men who are *not* asleep only yards away. Listening."

He snorted. "What do I care?"

I removed my hand. "You might not, but I do." I kissed him, lightly this time, determined to have my way. "I'll not be the entertainment for the evening, not even for you." Disentangling myself from his embrace, I rolled away and turned my back on him.

A THREE-QUARTER MOON shone in through the entrance to our tent, low in the sky, half hidden behind a cloud. Somewhere, outside in the wide beyond, a vixen called, wild and abandoned and primal. Was that what had wakened me?

The moonlight spilling through the entrance showed me Arthur sleeping on his back, one arm flung up over his head, the other across his naked belly. He'd pulled a blanket up to cover his legs but a bare foot protruded.

The fox called again. Wide awake now, the need for a pee settled in my groin, more insistent by the moment. I'd have to get up and find somewhere private to relieve myself.

Taking care not to disturb Arthur, I crawled out of the tent and stood up, stretching my aching body. Why was it every time I slept on the ground, I chose the bumpiest bit possible?

On the far side of our tent, the embers of the fire glowed faintly red, and the humps of sleeping soldiers showed like rows of chrysalises, every man wrapped in his own cocoon. An owl swooped on silent wings, and over on the western rampart I spotted the silhouette of the man chosen to keep the night's watch.

Now the need to pee was reaching crisis point, so, avoiding the lookout, I headed toward the entrance on bare feet, intent on using the encircling bank to shelter me as I peed. We'd set up our camp nearer the entrance than the western bank so it wasn't far. I slipped through the wide gap in the rampart and squatted down to do what needed to be done.

Once finished, and much more comfortable, I got to my feet, but something stopped me from hastening back to the tent. The marshes lay spread out before me in the moonlight, stretching as far as the dark rise of the distant Mendip hills. A few lights showed, scattered across the darkness, and here and there the waters glimmered with the moon's soft reflection.

Beautiful.

The owl swept over me again, screeching its night-time call, eery and lonely and somehow other-worldly.

Standing here where her family had died, how could I not think of poor, bereaved Bretta? Where had Melwas's men thrown those children into the marshes? Had they dragged them down this very track, either alive and struggling or stiff and dead? The thought of someone doing that to my children brought a lump to my throat and tears to my eyes. Tears for children I'd never met, but for whom I felt responsible.

I'd never been a particularly religious person, but standing in the moonlit dark, alone on the hillside, I muttered a heartfelt prayer that all these children should find peace and not be tied here, haunting their marshy graveyard.

I must have stood there a while, because in the east the sky began to lighten, staining the clouds pink and gold, and a pre-dawn chill descended, dew settling on the grass and on my shirt. Cold seeped up my legs from my bare feet, and a shiver brought me to myself. On frozen feet I headed back to the tent.

Chapter Nineteen

WHEN WE LEFT, three days later, Medraut and his friends showed no regrets at being abandoned at Dinas Brent, despite the primitive living situation. Boys of that age, in fact warriors of any age, don't care about such things as baths and proper toilets. Only fighting seems to matter to them.

Morfran, beaming with pride at his first proper command, bade us farewell just outside the gateway. "I'll be as hard on them as you would be, Milord," he promised, standing by Arthur's stirrup. "They'll not have a spare moment for getting into trouble."

This last was because I'd passed onto him what I'd overheard the boys saying about the girls in the farm settlements. Haha. Good luck to them if they tried to get down there for some illicit pleasure. Not that I thought their boasting had been any more than youthful showing off to one another.

Arthur patted Taran's gleaming bay shoulder. "I'll expect to see them molded into obedient warriors by this time next year then."

A badly disguised snort of obvious derision shot out of Merlin.

Arthur threw him a quizzical look. "Why not? They're big strong lads."

"It's the 'obedient' I was quibbling," Merlin said. "Don't forget, I've taught them. Medraut has a way about him of a boy who intends to give the orders, not follow them."

Too true.

Arthur shrugged. "We'll see. A year or two here should knock them into shape. Even Medraut, I hope." He turned back to Morfran. "No special treatment for my nephew."

Morfran nodded. "I'll see he toes the line."

Good luck to him on that one.

>>>*<<<

WE REACHED DIN Cadan late in the afternoon after a long journey home via the foothills of the Mendips. Tired and grubby, I rode up the dusty road to the gates beside Arthur, happy to be home again.

We'd scarcely had time to dismount by the stables before Archfedd came trotting down to greet us, her brow furrowed and her lower lip wobbling in dejection. I handed Alezan's reins to a servant, and bent down to her level. "What's wrong?"

She threw herself into my arms with all the dramatic flair of a hammy stage actress. "Amhar's gone to live in the barracks," she wailed, tears now streaming down her face. "He said I was just a baby, and he wasn't going to live with a baby anymore."

I wrapped my arms around her, meeting Arthur's gaze over the top of her head.

"We'll see about that," he muttered, and turned to Llacheu who was just dismounting. "Can you go and tell your brother I want to see him in the Hall? Now."

Llacheu shot me a worried glance before hurrying off toward the barracks houses where the older boys slept and often ate. No doubt there'd been four spaces come up free thanks to Medraut and his friends' departure. Anger that Amhar had done this behind our backs – behind my back – flared, and I hugged Archfedd all the tighter.

Arthur passed his horse's reins to another servant. "Give her to me." He held out his arms. I disentangled Archfedd from my hold, and Arthur picked her up, holding her on his hip, even though she'd grown a bit too big for that lately. "Come on. We'll go up to the Hall and wait for your brother to arrive. I can't wait to hear what he has to say about this."

Cei, waiting solemn faced outside the hall doors, followed us inside without a word.

Arthur set Archfedd down on one of the tables and turned to his brother. "What's been going on in my absence?"

Cei folded his arms across his chest in classic defensive pose. "Nothing."

I sat down on the table beside Archfedd with my arm around her shoulders. She wiped her teary eyes on her sleeve and snorted to clear her nose.

"So, what," Arthur said, enunciating his words with precision, "is my daughter crying about?"

Cei sighed, but I could sense his awkwardness. "I suppose it's my fault," he said, after a moment. "When he asked me, I said Amhar could move into one of the empty beds in the boys' barracks house. He was upset he hadn't been allowed to go with you to Dinas Brent. I thought it would do him good. Bolster his confidence."

My son? Sleeping in the barracks with the rough boys who'd been bullying him? Well, maybe not all of them, as the worst ones had probably gone with Medraut. But in all likelihood, those that remained would be nearly as bad, and glad to take over the roles vacated by Medraut and his cronies. A horrible vision of Amhar being battered daily by older, bigger boys rose before my eyes. I held Archfedd closer to me, glad she wasn't another boy.

Arthur pursed his lips and drew a deep breath. "Why does his confidence need bolstering, pray?"

Cei glanced at me, clearly uneasy, his gaze sliding down to rest on Archfedd's tear-stained face. I took the hint and jumped down off the table, pulling Archfedd with me. "Come along. We'll go and find Maia and see if she has some honey cakes for you." I took her slightly sweaty hand in mine and gave her a pull.

She sniffed long and loud, threw Cei an angry glare, but let me lead her to the door into our chamber. As luck would have it, Maia was in there tidying.

I thrust Archfedd at her. "Honey cakes and a cuddle, please."

Without waiting for an answer, I slipped back through the door into the Hall. I wanted to be privy to this conversation. Arthur and Cei had moved to the dais where the high table stood, and Merlin had sidled into the hall and taken up his customary place in the shadows, watching.

"Well?" Arthur said, his voice icily cold. "I'm waiting."

I'd never seen Cei so reluctant. He shifted his weight from one foot to the other, one hand fidgeting with the opposite sleeve. Whatever it was, he clearly didn't want to put it into words.

Arthur, on the other hand, was the picture of affronted rage, his dark brows furrowed and his whole body rigid with anger. If looks could have killed, Cei would have been lying dead at his brother's feet. I hoped I'd never be on the receiving end of this fury.

"He thinks you don't love him," Cei said, at last.

"What?" The word shot out of Arthur.

"You wanted the truth," Cei snapped, angry now, as well, and even more on the defensive. "I asked him what was wrong, after you'd left. He told me you'd said he wasn't good enough to go. That Medraut was, and he wasn't." He paused, his own ginger brows lowering to match Arthur's. "I tried to explain to him why Medraut was being sent away, but he wouldn't believe me. He didn't want to."

He paused again, his eyes sliding sideways to meet mine. "Whatever I said, he was convinced he had something to prove to you – to both of you. To gain your love, and more importantly your respect. I couldn't convince him otherwise."

My stomach twisted with anguish as I stared into Cei's beseeching eyes.

Merlin emerged from the shadows. "You couldn't have done anything else."

Arthur's angry gaze switched to his friend, his shoulders rising and falling as though he'd been running. "He's my son. I'll say where he sleeps, and no one else."

"He's just a boy," Merlin said. "He doesn't understand like an adult would. He's jealous of Medraut, and he thinks you don't love him."

Good for Merlin. He knew all about Medraut and his destiny, because I'd seen fit to confide in him, and now the secret must be burning a hole in his soul. He couldn't tell Arthur any more than I could about why we so feared what Medraut would become. And he couldn't warn Amhar how dangerous his friendship was. In case we were wrong.

Only he and I shared this secret, and it had to stay that way. Who knew whether everything we'd done so far hadn't brought Medraut and Arthur closer to their Camlann despite our desperation to avoid just that?

But I'd been right about Arthur's lack of tact in dealing with Amhar. Too late now. The damage had been done.

An angry scowl settled over Arthur's face. "Of course I bloody love him. He's my son. He's nearly a year younger than Medraut, but looks younger still. Of course he's not ready to go somewhere like Dinas Brent. And even if he were, I wouldn't send him there." He walked as far as the smoldering hearth fire, swung on his heel and strode back to halt in front of Cei and Merlin.

Cei stood stiff and still. "I told him the very same thing. But he didn't believe me. He thinks you prefer Medraut because he's bigger, cleverer, stronger."

Arthur's fists balled by his sides. "How could he be so stupid?"

"Easily," I said. "You weren't exactly tactful in what you said to him."

He spun around to stare at me.

I stood my ground. "It isn't easy being a parent. A father. Your words can be misinterpreted by a child all too easily. And that's all he is. Whatever he thinks he might be, he's just a child, and you gave him the impression you thought Medraut was better than he was."

Arthur opened his mouth, perhaps to deny this accusation, then snapped it shut again.

"You need to tell him all that yourself," Cei said, his voice low. "He asked me if he could go to live in the barracks because he wants the position Medraut's vacated. He wants the other boys to follow him the way their fathers follow you." A grim smile crept across his face. "He wants to be like you."

I bit my lip. Instinct and knowledge of my child told me this was unlikely to happen. For several reasons, not least the fact that those boys had followed Medraut because they feared him. No one feared Amhar, and I didn't want them to start doing so. But also because Amhar just wasn't like his father in the ways that would count. He was softer, gentler, more thoughtful. And I loved him for it. Archfedd had more of Arthur in her than he did, but she was a girl, and could never inherit the throne.

The hall doors swung open and Llacheu came in, followed by Amhar. When Llacheu had been a child I'd seen in him so much of the boy Arthur must once have been, but with Amhar it was different. Superficially he was like both Llacheu and his father, but there the resemblance ended. His soft features and limpid brown eyes held nothing of his older brother's determination, courage and strength.

If I'd been asked to describe him, I'd have said he was a dreamer, one of those people content to wash along on the tide of life, not someone who'd want to seize the tiller and direct the ship. Unlike Medraut, who'd have knocked the helmsman aside and stolen his place, which was precisely why he wasn't here any longer.

Amhar halted in front of his father, slender as a reed, his hands clasped behind his back. He swallowed. Llacheu stepped back a couple of respectful paces. The torchlight flickered over the faces of father and son.

Arthur gazed down at Amhar in silence. Was he lost for words? He never was with his men.

Go on, tell him.

"I hear you've moved into one of the barracks houses," Arthur said, voice formal and stiff, as though he were fighting to keep his feelings in check. Why were men so useless at emotional stuff?

Amhar nodded. "I have." The voice of a child, reedy and thin as the boy himself. He paused, then added, "Father." He stood ramrod straight, tense as a bowstring. The taut air twanged between them.

Arthur licked his lips. "Do you like it there?"

Amhar nodded.

I itched to speak, to guide them, but this was something Arthur needed to do alone. In another world, *my* world, it would have been for both parents to sort out, but here in the Dark Ages, I had to let Arthur take the lead. And it was his own mess needing to be sorted.

Arthur's gaze never wavered from our son's determined face. "Your sister misses you."

Amhar nodded again. "I know. I'm sorry, but I'm nearly a man now, and it was time to join the other boys." His voice trembled, and I saw him dig his nails into the palms of his hands.

Bloody tell him you love him and want him to come home.

Arthur heaved in a deep breath. "Very well."

Amhar's eyes slid sideways to meet mine, sparkling with unshed tears. Whatever he'd been hoping for, this wasn't it.

I couldn't stand by and watch any longer. "Come home, Amhar," I said, reaching out to touch his arm. "You're too young to be with the other boys yet. I want you here in the Hall with us, where you belong."

He pulled his arm away. "I'm not a baby anymore, Mother." The tears brimmed over and ran down his cheeks, giving the lie to that statement. He brushed them away with a hasty hand. No boy on the brink of warriorhood can afford to cry. "I'm as good as the other boys. As Med—"

"You're not as old as Medraut," Arthur cut in, too late. "Your mother's right. If she wants you here, then you must do as she says."

Merlin made to lift his hand, then let it drop, as if resigned to what was about to unfold.

Eyes flashing, Amhar rounded on his father. "I said I'm not a baby, Father. I don't want to be treated like one. I want to be treated like the other boys." He hesitated, gulping in air. "Like Medraut."

Llacheu took a step forward, opened his mouth, then shut it like a trap as he met my gaze. I shook my head at him.

Arthur floundered. "What're you talking about? We treat all you boys the same."

Their shadows leapt up the walls, grotesque and distorted.

"No, you don't," Amhar threw back at him, the tears staining his cheeks unheeded now. "You treat Medraut better than any of them. Better than me. You treat him like a prince. And *I'm* the prince, not him. He gets sent off to a posting like a proper warrior, and I don't. They all *laughed* at me. Medraut and the other boys say it's because I'm not—"

His voice broke off, his mouth a round O of horror, eyes wide with fear at what he'd said. What he'd *almost* said.

Merlin took a step forward, but Arthur held up a restraining hand.

As the silence lengthened, Arthur seemed to grow taller, more forbidding. "Not what?" His voice echoed around the empty hall, and his shadow loomed, threatening, over all of us.

Chapter Twenty

STANDING FACING HIS father, a small, slight figure overshadowed by a giant, Amhar floundered.

His mouth opening and closing like a goldfish, he took a step back and stumbled, landing on his backside in the rushes close to Merlin.

After a pause, Merlin held out a hand. "The other boys talk rubbish because they're jealous. Ignore them. Now go and wipe your eyes and blow your nose so you can return to your barracks with some dignity."

The silent seconds ticked past before Amhar took the offered hand and let Merlin yank him to his feet.

"Go," Arthur said, glowering down at him.

Amhar fled.

Behind him, the torches seemed to have dimmed and the hall to have grown darker still.

As soon as the door banged shut behind Amhar, Arthur turned to Llacheu, his face dark with fury. "What is it the other boys say to him?"

Llacheu's eyes moved shiftily from my face to Merlin's and back again. He plainly knew exactly what the boys were saying, but didn't want to tell us.

"Tell me," Arthur said, the menace in his voice like a blow.

"It's just stupid boys joking together," Llacheu said, making a valiant effort to dispel the tension still zinging around the Hall.

"I don't care if you think it's just boys joking," Arthur said. "It clearly means something to Amhar, so spit it out."

Llacheu's cheeks, that had flushed with heat, now paled. "I-I can't say it," he muttered. "Not in front of Gwen."

"That's all right," I said, in a hurry to reassure him. "I've heard everything in my time. You won't offend me."

"I think I will," Llacheu muttered, eyes dropping to study his boots. "You won't like it."

"For God's sake, spit it out," Arthur snapped. "What are those boys saying about my son?"

Llacheu glanced as though for support to Merlin, whose face was as puzzled as mine. Then he swallowed. "They say… they say Amhar's not your son."

My hand went to my mouth to stifle the cry of horror. Not this again. Not after all these years. And how had anyone found out? What could have made these boys repeat this lie to Amhar? No one knew of this base calumny but Arthur and me. Not even Merlin, whose eyes had gone wide with shock. How could a rumor like this have started amongst our son's friends? If you could even call them that. Friends don't say things like that about you. They don't repeat salacious lies.

Arthur's face darkened with rage, but he didn't move. Instead, he aimed a furious glare at Merlin, as if this were all his fault. "I want all the boys from Amhar's barracks here. Straight away. I'm getting to the bottom of this before it spreads."

Before it spreads? It sounded to me as though it already had, and the damage had been done. Did Amhar believe it? Was that the reason for his behavior?

Merlin hurried out of the hall, and Llacheu bolted after him, leaving us standing alone, marooned like ship-wrecked sailors.

I went to Arthur and took his hand, but he didn't respond, his fingers slack in mine, as he stared down the Hall toward the doors.

"Be careful what you say," I whispered, as though afraid the lurking shadows had ears. As though somehow, whatever we said in private might become public property through no fault of our own.

As it already had.

The suspicion rose in my heart that Arthur had confided in someone, back in those days twelve years ago when he'd believed the terrible lies of that dying traitor, Melwas. I hadn't told a soul, so, if the story was out, then surely it must be his fault. I released his hand as though stung.

We waited in a prickly silence for the boys to arrive.

There were eight of them. Each barracks slept twelve boys or young warriors, and Medraut's going had left four spaces, one of which was now Amhar's. They entered the hall nervously, most likely having picked up on the gravity of their situation from Merlin and Llacheu's demeanor, and clustered in a group at the foot of the dais, hands clasped respectfully behind their backs as they'd been taught.

Most of them were a year or two older than Amhar, some from local farms and villages, one or two from the few villas that still remained – noblemen's sons. All equal now in the barracks room. They made untidy, hurried bows to their king.

Arthur surveyed their anxious, guarded faces from his position on the dais, towering over them but staying silent. Time ticked by. The boys shuffled uncomfortably, sneaking peeks at each other but saying nothing, their expressions revealing their uncertainty.

At last, Arthur spoke. "I will not have baseless rumors repeated in this fortress." His gaze ran over each boy's face. "Not here in my hall, amongst my people, nor in the barracks houses. If I hear once more of rumormongering amongst you boys, then whoever is responsible will be first beaten, then, after a spell in the lockup, demoted to pig boy – for life."

An indrawn gasp from every boy hissed up to the rafters, their eyes wide with fear and fixed on Arthur. Caring for the pigs was a job undertaken only by the lowliest of people – usually a slave. And Arthur was a man of his word.

"Do you understand?"

"Yes, Milord."

"Yes, Milord."

Their nodding replies echoed after their gasp of fear, twisting upwards like the smoke from the fire. More hasty bowing followed.

Arthur glowered at them from under his dark brows. "Let this be a warning to you. The only one you'll get. I don't believe in second chances."

They hurriedly bobbed a third bow, en masse.

"Now, get out of my sight, before I decide you all need beating."

The little group reversed back up the aisle toward the doors, perhaps mesmerized by their king's angry glare, then ran.

Arthur looked across at Merlin. "I've ended it, but I want to know how this rumor started. I'll leave it to you to speak to the other boys and young warriors. Give them the same warning. Question them as hard as you wish."

Merlin glanced at me. "I'll do my best to find out. Llacheu can help me."

I nodded, lost for words, but with a nub of ice formed already in my heart. Someone needed to reassure Amhar that this wasn't true.

LLACHEU TURNED OUT to be the better sleuth. After all, he'd had practice when I'd once asked him and Rhiwallon to spy on Merlin. He traced the origin of the rumor back to one of the older boys, Brien. Three years younger than Llacheu, he already had a penchant for the ladies that knew no bounds, and had been loudly boasting, to any boy who'd listen, of a raunchy encounter with Hafren before she'd ended in the lockup.

All avenues of enquiry led back to him, and thence to Hafren. On questioning, by Llacheu and Merlin using methods I didn't want to hear the details of, Brien revealed she'd whispered it to him during their brief liaison in one of the barns. She'd told him to tell the other boys that Amhar wasn't a prince and shouldn't be treated as such, which Brien, with ever an eye to his own standing with Medraut, had passed on with relish. And of course, Medraut had seized upon the gossip with unholy glee.

As Hafren had by now been wearing suitable sack cloth and slaving for some far-off nuns for quite a while, we couldn't ask her where she'd come by her information. It wasn't hard to guess, though. Morgana.

That bloody woman. Not content to send some lackey to try to kill me and then make an attempt to banish me back to my old world, she'd also found a way to undermine the relationship Arthur and I had with our son. Though how she'd found out about Melwas's groundless claim, I had no idea. I rejected my initial suspicion that Arthur had blabbed to someone about it, as he certainly wouldn't have chosen *her* as his confidant.

There was nothing for it. Even though it was the last thing I wanted to talk about, I had to come clean to Merlin. This took some plucking up of courage.

When Arthur was busy holding court in the Hall, I sent a message asking Merlin to come and see me in my chamber.

I'd already taken a seat at the table, mainly because my legs had come over weak and wobbly with fear, when he came in through the side entrance.

I'd have to get it off my chest straightaway, before I chickened out.

"Melwas told Arthur that Amhar was his," I managed, through almost gritted teeth. "Just before he died." I didn't look at him. I couldn't. "He-he tried to imply I'd lain with him... willingly."

God, this was so hard to say, to rake up again after all these years just when I'd thought I'd never have to visit it again.

Merlin's mouth was hanging open. He shut it with a clack of his teeth. "It was a lie, of course?"

Was that a *question*? Did he maybe think it could have been *true*? Inside me, anger boiled toward the surface, like magma under a volcano, waiting to erupt.

"Of course it's a lie," I snapped. "Do you think Arthur would have brought up that shit's child for eleven years?"

Merlin sat down heavily in the chair opposite mine.

"But that's not the point any longer," I said, in a hurry to diffuse the tension arcing through the room. "Arthur knows Amhar's his. The problem here is that only he and I knew what Melwas had said. And neither of us has told anyone." I raised my eyes to his. "So how could Morgana have found out, and told Hafren to spread it around Din Cadan? It must have been her. I can't see who else it could have been."

Merlin swallowed. "I can't see that Morgana could have," he said, shaking his head. "You've both kept this to yourselves extremely well." His eyes searched mine. "I had no idea. And if Arthur had been going to tell anyone, it would probably have been me. Or maybe Cei. Usually, I know everything that goes on within these walls."

"Magic," I said, still more than a little shocked at myself for considering it as a possible answer to my question. "She has the Sight. She's used it on me before. She read my mind, I'm certain, long ago before Amhar was even born. Made me think Medraut might be Arthur's son by incest. I couldn't help but have it in my head because it was a story I knew. She couldn't have thought it up for herself. She just couldn't. Somehow, she must have hooked it out of my memories and used it against me."

"You think?"

I nodded. "In my time, it's all part of the legend most people believe about Arthur. But it's from a much later date – a story added in just to spice up the legend, by people hundreds of years from now. People with nasty minds."

I faltered, not liking even the saying of this. "The story is that Arthur grew up apart from Morgawse and… and slept with her unwittingly. Not knowing she was his sister. After which Medraut was born. *You* know the story. I've told you before. But I had it in my head when I was looking at Medraut as a baby, because Medraut looked so like Arthur. Morgana must have known… read my mind perhaps… and used it against me. I'm sure she did. Certain, in fact. And it nearly worked."

Merlin leaned forward, elbows resting on the table. "And you think she's done the same with this? Plucked a thought… a memory… from inside your head and turned it against you? Even from so far away?"

I nodded again. "I do. I think she's behind this. No. I *know* she is. She must have told Hafren to spread it here. It only took one whisper into the ear of a gullible boy, a boy who wanted to endear himself to Medraut, no doubt. And Medraut was more than willing to use it against Amhar. He's jealous of him. He wants his place in Arthur's heart, and in the succession. I know it."

"You may well be right." He rubbed his chin. "Morgana's nothing if not resourceful."

I met his gaze. "I want her stopped. I've had enough. This needs to end."

Chapter Twenty-One

AMHAR REMAINED IN the barracks, surly and unresponsive, Brien the troublemaker was demoted to looking after the pigs, and Arthur remained aloof and bad-tempered. News came from the spies in Viroconium that Cadwy was training extra troops recruited from the farms around the city, but so far hadn't displayed any martial intentions.

This didn't make Arthur any sweeter tempered, and he could often be found out on the training field, hammering with a heavy wooden sword at any poor warrior brave enough to offer himself up as an opponent. Each night he came to our bed exhausted and silent.

Fed up with my menfolk, I tried to comfort Archfedd, but she stayed upset with her brother and lonely with only Maia for company in the evenings. She had Reaghan during the day, of course. Merlin was teaching both girls now, although Arthur had forbidden them to learn alongside the boys. Instead, Merlin came to my chamber for an hour or two every morning, and the girls sat studiously at the table, brows furrowed over history and Latin, and sometimes reckoning.

I was interested to note that Archfedd, despite being two years younger than Reaghan, surpassed her friend in aptitude, and had she but known it, her brother too.

After a few weeks, we had news, brought by one of the frequent messengers that arrived from all over Dumnonia and sometimes from further afield. Medraut and his friends were working hard and doing well at Dinas Brent, and a new fortress had already begun to rise, phoenix-like, from the ashes of the old.

Not that this gave me any pleasure. The knowledge that Medraut had willfully used the rumor about Amhar against him had once and for all removed any vestige of sympathy I might have retained for that boy. Thank goodness he lived far enough away not to hurt Amhar anymore.

Unusually for this time of year, we received no news about coastal raiders. This was the season when the sea was kindest, and they were usually the most active. Yet, this year, we had nothing.

Arthur used the unexpected free time to organize our warriors to work on improvements to our defenses, and to break and train replacement war horses, always an ongoing occupation. When the men had any spare time from their building work, they spent it in training not just themselves but also the younger, upcoming warriors, and the boys, Amhar included.

I used the time much the same way – to improve my sword skills, aided by Merlin and Llacheu. And Archfedd threw herself into educating Llawfrodedd in return for him teaching her to fight. It amused me to see them sitting at the table in our chamber of an afternoon, the lanky fifteen-year-old beside the chubby eight-year-old, heads bent over a writing tablet while she taught him to read.

"It's easy once you know how," she said, with all the nonchalance of someone for whom all learning came easily. "And my mami says everyone should be able to read things for themselves and not rely on scholars to do it for them." She beamed at her large pupil. "She says we can all be scholars. You'll see."

He beamed back at her, but I detected an air of doubt when she told him he could be a scholar.

For myself, despite the daily sword fighting, I had plenty of time to think. And my thoughts each day returned to the time I'd been unconscious after my accident, and what I'd seen. Or rather, the sword that Nimuë had *shown* me. If it had even been real. More and more now, with the passage of time, I felt inclined to see it as a fevered dream brought on by the blow to my head.

But all the same, I'd still not mentioned it to Arthur. Merlin remained the only one I'd shared it with.

"I can't tell him," I said, voicing my fears to Merlin, as we stood on the wall-walk gazing out over the plain toward the marshes surrounding distant, mist-swathed Ynys Witrin. "I don't quite believe it myself. It feels like it was just my imagination. That because I *know* the legend of the Lady of the Lake, and because Morgana called her daughter Nimuë, I dreamed it all."

He shot me a knowing look that told me he didn't believe me for one minute. Since my accident, I'd recounted the legend in more detail, and together we'd considered whether any of it could have been based on truth of any sort. But he had magic, and so did Morgana, and Nimuë had probably inherited a double dose. Could she really have been there, inside my head? Or could she have physically transported me to a magical lake to show me where the sword lay? I just didn't know.

I managed a weak smile and heaved a sigh. "What else can I think? It can never come true."

He remained silent, eyes fixed on mine.

I shook my head. "I know you made the sword in the stone story come true, but that was at least *sort* of possible. A woman under the water holding up a sword just isn't." I chuckled. "She'd have to be bloody good at holding her breath."

He raised an eyebrow.

"Oh, for goodness' sake. Excalibur is something made up by medieval romance writers, not a real sword." I gripped the weathered wooden battlements, watching a kite wheel across the sky, its mewing call plaintive. "I've thought about it a lot now, and I refuse to believe any of that could be true. It was some kind of trick my brain played on me while I was unconscious."

He inclined his head. "Whatever you say."

I scowled. "I can see you don't believe me."

He shook his head. "It's not that I don't believe you. It's that I think you've interpreted it wrongly."

"How? It was just like one of the legends my father used to read to me at bedtime. It couldn't have been real. For a start the boat moved by itself with no one rowing."

"Maybe it was symbolic."

I bristled. "Symbolic of what? The more I think about it, the more I know it was just my imagination. That it couldn't have been anything else."

Keep telling yourself that.

He shrugged. "I think you should tell Arthur about it."

A breeze blew bits of loose hair across my face, and I put up a hand to brush them behind my ears. "You know I can't tell him things like that. Things about the future. He once told me he didn't want to know."

Merlin leaned on the battlements. "You mean *you think* you can't tell him. That's something quite different."

I stiffened. "Is it? You think I don't get the urge to come clean to him over and over again? That it's not been on the tip of my tongue countless times to spill everything I know? That I don't wonder that if I tell him, together we can change the future... my past? The history I know? Or think I know." I shook my head. "That maybe Camlann doesn't have to happen, or maybe it's unavoidable and nothing any of us can do will stop it from coming about. Do you think he'd want to know if that were the case?" I paused. "Would *you* want to know when you were going to die and by whose hand?"

The bubbling song of a skylark carried on the breeze. The sound of summer. And the laughter of children playing hide and seek wafted down from within the clustered buildings on the hilltop. Maybe one of them was Archfedd.

"You love him, don't you?"

"You need to ask that?"

He smiled. "Then you must trust him. Sometimes, you behave as though you don't."

I stared at him. "But I do. With my life. With my children. With everything."

"Not enough to tell him your secrets. Secrets you seem happy to tell me."

I swung away from him, anger coursing through me, my fingers entwining themselves. Unfair of him to say this – to accuse me. And not true. I longed to tell Arthur my secrets, yearned to have nothing hidden from him. To finally be honest.

"It's different with you." I bit my lip. "You understand. I don't think he will." I paused. "I don't think he can."

"Try him. I'm not saying tell him about Camlann. Tell him of your dream, at least. Somehow, I don't think it was your imagination, nor caused by your fall. I have a feeling it's important."

I narrowed my eyes. Suspicion that he'd used his Sight to spy on what lay ahead arose. "Have you been looking?"

He grimaced. "I might have been."

"But he already has a sword. Why would he need another?"

"I think this sword, that you call Excalibur, is something special. Something different. Twelve years ago, you told me about a legend from your time. To bring it about, I took an ordinary sword, any sword, and thrust it into that stone in the forum at Viroconium. Arthur was the only one who could draw it, and by doing so he proved his right to the High Kingship, which was what I intended. But that was all it was. A means to an end. People are easy to manipulate."

He paused and rubbed his hand across his chin. His bristles rasped. "You're right. I have looked. But when I use the Sight to look for this sword you've told me about, it's not Arthur's hand I see on it." The air had gone very still. No sound echoed from the hilltop houses. Even the children had fallen silent. "I see the hand of someone long dead."

Now I was interested. "Whose hand?"

"An emperor's hand."

My eyes widened. "His great-grandfather's? Constantine's?" The man who'd led the final British legions into Gaul at the end of the Roman occupation and never returned. Could Excalibur have been his sword?

Merlin shook his head, brows furrowed. "Somehow, I think not. My vision isn't clear enough. When I look, I see purple, the color of rank within the Roman Empire, and I see a crown of golden laurel leaves on someone's head. The wearer's not young, but he's a warrior emperor, of that I *am* certain. His hand rests on the hilt of a sword. A splendid sword." He let the hint of a smile creep across his face. "Perhaps it's your Excalibur?"

"Who else could that be, then, but Constantine?"

That small smile played about Merlin's lips. A knowing smile. Was there something he wasn't telling me?

I reached out and took hold of his hand, my fingers tight and demanding. "Tell me who you think it was."

"Macsen. Macsen Wledig."

Of course. I'd heard the fairytale of Prince Macsen told around the hearth fire many times. *The Dream of Macsen Wledig.* "He was a *real* person?" Memories tickled my brain, elusive and out of reach. The story had seemed too far-fetched to be true.

Merlin nodded.

I struggled to remember if my father had ever mentioned that name, and failed. If he had, then I'd forgotten. Its familiarity was from hearing the story told by the hearth, of a winter's evening.

"Who was he then? Are you saying the sword in my dream is his? That Nimuë showed me his actual sword? That it's in a lake somewhere? And I have to give it to Arthur?"

Merlin gripped my hand back, the breeze blowing his long hair across his face. He swiped it away. "Before Constantine, there was Macsen. Unlike Constantine, he wasn't British born, but he served here with the legions. As an officer of rank, and nephew of the famous general Count Theodosius, he married a princess of Gwynedd, Elen."

This sounded as though it had an element of truth about it, unlike the fanciful story as told by bards.

"He declared himself Emperor here in Britain, and, like Constantine, went overseas, leaving his wife and some of his children here in Britain. For a few years, he succeeded, until he attacked Rome and was defeated and executed."

"Do you mean he's *Magnus Maximus*?" I'd heard of him, for sure.

Merlin nodded. "The name the legions gave him. To us he was Prince Macsen."

Of course. Why I hadn't spotted the similarity before, I didn't know. Too long spent here in the Dark Ages.

"And you think the sword in my dream might be his sword?"

"I see a hand on the sword, an imperial hand, and not the hand of Constantine."

I swallowed. "How can you be sure?" Magnus Maximus was just a name to me. All I knew was what I'd heard around the fireside, and what Merlin had just recounted, and I couldn't count on any of that being true.

Merlin's lips curled in a smile. "Let me show you."

Chapter Twenty-Two

I STARED INTO Merlin's young-old brown eyes, wide and clever, but not safe. What did he mean? How could he show me? On an impulse of curiosity, I nodded.

"Give me both your hands."

He held his hands out to me and after a moment's hesitation, I set my own in his.

"Now, close your eyes."

I did as he said. The breeze soughed in the branches of the trees at the hillfoot, the kite mewed high above us, the children's laughter sounded again. His hands, warm and strong, gripped mine, and every sound faded.

A man in armor I recognized as Roman stood on a battlefield, all around him the dying and the dead. Middle-aged, his face bore lines etched deeply by the cares of life. A dirty bandage wrapped his wrist and hand. Before him kneeled another, much younger man. Long red cloaks hung from their shoulders over elaborately worked breastplates, and the older man wore a plumed helmet, its chinstraps hanging loose.

"My Lord Emperor, you must flee," the younger man beseeched, his hand clutching his master's cloak.

With a sad shake of his head, the older warrior drew his sword from its scabbard and held it out, the blade shimmering with light, to the kneeling soldier. "Lucius, my friend, I cannot flee the Fates." His deep voice rumbled, like distant surf on a pebble beach. "But you must. For I have one last thing to ask of you. Take my sword to my wife and children."

"My Lord?"

Something on the Emperor's blood-stained finger caught the light. A ring.

My eyes fixed on his hand. A golden dragon romped, embossed on the wide golden head of the ring. My dragon. *My ring.*

"Take it."

The younger man reached for the sword with reluctance, his stubbly cheeks tear-stained, eyes anguished. Filthy fingers closed around the hilt. "My Lord, I will not rest until this sword lies in the hands of your wife." His head bowed in supplication.

The dragon ring winked at me in the raw daylight, as the Emperor laid a hand on the young soldier's bare, short-cropped head in benediction. Withdrawing his hand, the Emperor fumbled at the ring with awkward, bandaged fingers as the young man rose wearily to his feet, and slid the sword into the scabbard by his side.

The Emperor, his own cheeks wet with tears, held out the ring, gripped between finger and thumb. "Take this as well. It was my wife's."

It fell into the soldier's open hand, and the young man turned it over, so the dragon rested uppermost on the filthy palm.

An overwhelming urge to reach out and snatch it washed over me, but the vision vanished. My eyes flicked open.

I was back on the wall-walk again, with Merlin still holding my hands and the dragon ring on my finger glinting in the afternoon sunlight.

My breath came hard and fast. "Was that sword *Excalibur?*"

"I don't know, but I think so. This is the clearest I've seen him. All I can tell you is that every time I look, I see this sword gripped in that hand. That hand with that ring. This ring." He indicated the ring on my hand. "And I believe that what I'm seeing, what I've just shown you, is Macsen's defeat by the Emperor Theodosius. I think he knew execution awaited him and wanted to send his sword back to Britain. Perhaps it was a British-made sword – even linked to the Princess Elen, his wife."

Since I'd arrived here in what was my past, I'd seen enough of the supernatural to believe what Merlin had just told me – shown me – far more than I was inclined to believe my own dream. I didn't doubt that he'd seen this man and this sword... that I'd seen the man and sword myself... but what his vision meant, I had no idea. "But if he was executed miles away – in Rome or somewhere like that – did that young soldier bring it all the way back here? To a lake in Britain?"

Merlin shrugged. "Someone brought it back, I'm sure. And, as it's never been found, then perhaps they hid it. In the lake you saw... were shown. And now, maybe, it's meant for Arthur's hand. According to your dream, Nimuë seems to think it is." His eyes changed, softening as he spoke her name, and my heart ached for him. She was the same age as Archfedd, and must be growing fast into a young woman.

I touched his hand. "And Morgana too. I had the feeling Nimuë was determined I should see the sword, and that her mother didn't want me to."

He frowned. Thinking of his daughter must, of necessity, mean he'd have to think of her mother and how she'd come to be conceived. And that would hurt.

I shook my head, steering the conversation away from Morgana. "But underwater? For over a century? It would rust to nothing, surely?"

"Perhaps. Perhaps not. But you owe it to Arthur to look. They call the sword I embedded in that rock *the sword of destiny*, but it isn't. This one is."

"Nimuë told me I had to give it to Arthur..."

"I think it must be vital to him."

I hesitated. "Then I'll have to tell him. I'll choose the time myself, though."

"Don't wait too long," Merlin said. "I have a feeling time presses hard on us, and that sword has a part to play."

⟫⟪

WITH THE MIDSUMMER festivities behind us, the corn began to ripen in fields that resembled a patchwork quilt of colors from green through to golden, taking in the blue of flax and the pale tawny of hayfields cut and cleared. Wagons lumbered up the hill bringing in the tribute from the farms – loads of hay, vegetables, and meat on the hoof ready for butchering. Summer was a time of plenty.

A week after my conversation with Merlin, I dreamed of Nimuë again.

I'd been working all day with the green young horses we'd brought up from the grazing lands, and had come in hot and tired, but satisfied that the horses were coming on nicely. I'd picked out a rangy mare I thought would suit Amhar now he was finally growing, and spent some time working with her on foot, looking forward to the moment when I'd tell him she was his. Tomorrow, we'd be backing her. Maybe I could let Amhar play a part and be the first to test her with his weight. A good idea. I could get Arthur to tell him he could do that, in an attempt to repair the broken links between them.

Sleep took me the moment my head hit the pillow, and nothing Arthur could have done would have kept me awake, even if he hadn't been as tired as me.

In the deep of the night, something jerked me out of my slumbers. For a moment I lay still, heart hammering, sweat springing out all over my body, sensing the urgency of whatever it was that had disturbed my sleep. Then I opened my eyes. Moonlight streaming through our unshuttered window spotlit a small, solitary figure standing six feet from our bed, bathing her from head to toe in an ethereal glow.

I'd have known her anywhere. A thin sleeping shift covered her slight body, and her small, pale feet were bare. Long dark hair so like her mother's hung to her waist, but the eyes that regarded me solemnly from shadowed sockets were Merlin's.

Was she a ghost? Had she died in far off Viroconium and come to haunt me? I blinked and pushed myself upright in bed, but her image didn't waver. And surely an image was all it could be. She couldn't really be here, in my chamber at night, over a hundred and fifty miles from her home.

I stared, mesmerized.

For a minute that lasted an eternity, we regarded one another. Then the apparition glanced over her shoulder as though expecting an interruption. When she turned back to face me, her solemn expression had vanished, replaced, instead, by anxious fear.

She leaned toward me. *"Take him to the sword."* Her lips never moved, but her words hissed around the quiet chamber. *"Fulfil the prophecy. Set Excalibur in his hands."* Her voice held sweetness and urgency, mingled with that cold fear. A child's clear treble, and yet the voice of something older than the world I knew.

"What do you mean?" I asked. "How can I take him somewhere I don't know? Tell me?"

But her image was fading. Through her shimmering body, I saw the cold brazier, the table, the closed door to the hall.

"Don't go," I cried. "Tell me where I have to take him. I don't know where to go."

Her image rippled, like a reflection in water. Eyes now stretched wide with fear, she held up her hand and pointed. Northwest. Toward Ynys Witrin.

"Don't go!" I shouted the last words, reaching out my hands toward her as her image dissipated like smoke in the wind.

"Gwen." Hands shook me and my eyes flew open. I grabbed wildly, trying to snatch Nimuë back into reality, and found solid flesh. Arthur was leaning over me in the dim light of early morning, his face barely visible in the gloom. "Wake up, you were having a nightmare. Wake up."

I blinked.

He heaved a deep sigh. "I'm not going anywhere."

Of course. He thought I meant him. "I'm all right now," I whispered as I nestled against his warm body, his arm tight around me. "I had a dream." It was now or never. "Like the one I had after my accident."

He drew me a little closer. "You were shouting. You woke me up."

For a moment I saw Nimuë's slender figure again, this time in my mind's eye, with her arm extended and her slender finger pointing. "There's something we have to do," I whispered, my cheek against his chest. "Something you and I have to do together."

Chapter Twenty-Three

WITH THE DAM broken, the words came spilling out. I couldn't stop them. I told Arthur everything I'd seen in my dream and what Merlin had shared with me. I finished by telling him what Merlin suspected might be the truth about the sword. Arthur listened attentively, making no comment until I'd finished, and the pale light of dawn was creeping through our open window.

In the shadowy half-light it was hard to make out his expression as we lay facing one another in bed, but his voice held scepticism. "Underwater?" he asked, at last. "I'd believe this more if only the promised sword were in a dry place." He paused. "But anyway, the tale of Macsen is from generations ago. I don't even *know* how ancient the story is."

A smile curved his lips, and I had a sudden impulse to lean forward and kiss him.

His smile broadened. "A sword hidden underwater for that long will have rusted to nothing." His warm breath tickled my cheek. "I think the story I was told is that my great grandfather, Constantine, married one of Macsen's daughters, so I suppose he could be my ancestor. But that's just a legend, and I doubt very much if it's true."

I seized upon this. "That would make him your..." I paused to work it out in my head. "...your great great grandfather. Maybe Constantine's marriage to Macsen's daughter strengthened his own claim to be emperor?"

He chuckled. "Like I said. It's just a legend. I don't even know the woman's name. No one does. My father didn't, and she would have been his own grandmother. She died long before he or my uncle Ambrosius were born. I'm sorry. It can't be true."

"But don't you see?" I whispered, as though afraid someone somewhere might be listening. Morgana, perhaps. *Evil, eavesdropping cow.* "If he *was* your great great grandfather, then this is properly your sword. I mean, *you* should be inheriting it. It's not a random sword – it's a *family* sword." I paused. "A sword meant for you – and that's why Nimuë wants you to have it." I shivered as though someone, Morgana maybe, had walked over my grave. "And why Morgana *doesn't* want you to have it. Why she tried to prevent Nimuë from showing me."

He chuckled again. "Another thing to rile Cadwy with, I suppose. If he got wind of this, he'd be claiming it as the older brother. If Morgana's child knows of this, I'd like to know why my sister's not sent Cadwy running off to find it."

I sat bolt upright in bed, the covers falling back from my nakedness. "That's it. She doesn't know. Nimuë is hiding this from her mother. Don't forget, she's Merlin's child as well."

For a moment, I was back in that gloomy chamber with Morgana bound to her bench seat, her furious eyes bulging above the gag, while Merlin wove spells over his little daughter's head. Eery shadows leapt up the walls, sending Arthur and me running for safety outside in the courtyard.

I seized Arthur's hand in mine. "Whatever he did to protect Nimuë when she was a baby, it must have worked. She knows the sword's meant for you. She was frightened she'd be caught, but she sent me those messages – showed me what we have to do and where we have to do it. We have to find the sword. We have to find Excalibur before Morgana realizes what we're doing."

"It's not safe," Merlin protested late that evening, when Arthur unwisely revealed our plan. "You need to take guards with you." A servant was extinguishing the torches in the hall one by one, and most of the warriors were heading back to their houses with their wives.

Arthur, standing with me beside the high table, frowned. "Nonsense. We've fast horses and we'll both be armed. And we've had no trouble with raiders all summer. Why should we now?"

Merlin's face reddened. He rarely showed anger, but now he clearly wanted to. "What about brigands?"

Arthur's face began to redden as well. He'd had a lot to drink and his own anger bubbled not far from the surface. "What brigands? We've had no reports of *them*, either. It's safe, I tell you." My fingers tightened on his arm.

Merlin turned to Cei, who'd been wisely sneaking away. "Tell him," he blustered. "Tell him it's not safe. And ask him where he's going."

Looking shifty, probably because he'd been privy to the plan since this morning, Cei hesitated. Behind him, a few of our newest recruits were unrolling their beds on the floor close to the walls, chattering together in low voices. "I daren't try and tell him what to do," Cei grunted, maybe aiming for diplomacy. "He's my king."

"And your brother," snapped Merlin. He turned back to Arthur. "Let Cei and me come with you, then, wherever it is you're going. Four is better than two."

Arthur shook his head. "No. This is something Gwen and I need to do by ourselves. We're going alone."

※

And so here we were, as the sun peeked over the distant horizon, sneaking out of Din Cadan before most people were up. Although I wouldn't have put it past Merlin to have had us watched and followed – to have followed us himself, even, at a discreet distance. Hence the early morning departure, with dew sparkling on every leaf like scattered diamonds.

The sleepy guards on the gate gave us surprised looks, jerking themselves to attention at sight of their king, but they knew better than to question his vagaries. We'd be well beyond the village before anyone but them noticed we'd gone.

To be on the safe side, though, we urged our horses into a canter as soon as their hooves touched the short grass of the grazing grounds. A rough track skirted the edge of the village and headed toward the more substantial road to Ynys Witrin. Because it was toward that misty island that Nimuë had pointed her pale finger.

As we reached the forest, I brought Alezan in beside Taran, reins tight to prevent her snapping. Arthur brought Taran down to a walk, and we rode knee to knee through the thickening woodland. A deer paused on the path ahead, turned to stare at us for a moment, then bolted, vanishing into the verdant gloom with a flash of her white scut. And somewhere a woodpecker tapped, paused, then tapped again, searching for grubs in a dead tree.

I cast a sly look at my husband. I had half an idea that he'd decided to humor me and have the fun of a rarely-come-by sortie without accompanying guards. But the other half of me hoped he'd agreed to come because something had told him my dreams might be true.

"Merlin might guess where we're heading," I said. "We shouldn't dawdle."

"You're right." He gathered his reins and Taran broke into a trot. Alezan needed no urging. In a moment we were bent over our horse's necks, cantering along the forest track, with low, leafy branches sweeping across our backs.

By the time we reached Nial's lake village, sweat lathered our horses' coats.

We rode through the sparse trees of the forest edge and down the gentle slope to the water. Thirty yards out over the lake, the village sat on its wooden platform, supported by the network of pilings that covered the detritus of its past incarnations.

A rickety and narrow walkway stretched across the dark water, if anything, even less inviting than on the day I'd first seen it. Smoke curled skyward from the thatched rooftops of the village houses. And out beyond the platform, on the wide expanse of silvery water, mist, like draped chiffon, drifted in from the marshes, veiling the distant banks of reeds and the braided river channels.

Even though the hour was still early, Nial must have had lookouts posted, as any wise village elder would. As we jog-trotted into the cluster of barns and sheds that made up the landward part of the village, he emerged from one of the barns, a long piece of dried grass dangling from his lips and a grin on his face.

"Arthur. Milady Guinevere." The seed head on the grass danced as he spoke, and he bobbed a bow.

A small, wizened man even when I'd first met him, the years had only served to enhance his likeness to some woodland sprite, incising deep lines across his face, and gnarling his hands like knotted roots. His skin had burnt to a deep brown that might have been summer sun, or dirt, and his hair had thinned to a sparse fringe around a bald patch that had all but taken over his head. He grinned, revealing gaps where he'd lost teeth.

Arthur swung down from the saddle and held out his hand. "Nial. Well met."

Nial took his hand, and they shook like the old friends they were. "Arthur." No milording for a man who'd known Arthur as a callow youth.

I slid down from Alezan, glad to have my feet on the ground after our fast ride. "Nial. It's good to see you looking so well."

He bobbed another bow to me. "Can't complain. And 'tis good to see you both as well. Bin a while since you rode this way." His eyes strayed past me. "D'you not have guards with you terday?"

Arthur shook his head. "Just us. We're on a very particular journey. We need your help. A boat across to the island would be useful."

Nial bobbed a third bow, perhaps in affirmation. "O' course, o' course. I'll tek you m'self. It'll be like old times. You, me, a boat an' a fishin' rod."

Arthur laughed. "You'll be the one with the rod, I'm afraid. The queen and I have a different mission in mind, tempting though the thought of fishing is."

Nial chuckled. "When did you not have somethin' on yer mind?"

He shouted a quick "hoi" and a couple of younger men emerged a little shyly from the small barn. "Tek the king's horses for him, an' see they's rubbed down well. You know what to do." He turned back to us. "You know the way."

I did indeed. And didn't like it. I shot a worried glance at Nial's small and skinny frame, and those of the two men who were leading away our horses. All of them half Arthur's size. That walkway had a distinct look about it of only being strong enough to support scrawny village dwellers – and them only one at a time. But needs must. And as it stood on wooden legs, surely the water couldn't be deep. Not that I fancied a dip in the murky depths. After all, where did the toilet waste of the village go? I took a deep breath and stepped onto the walkway.

Every time I came here it had been the same. That bloody walkway, which looked wide from on the land, once embarked on shrank to barely the width of my body. Or so it seemed. The only way to do this was to hurry, so I fairly galloped across it, convinced that at any moment bits of it might collapse – like a dodgy Indiana Jones rope bridge.

Arthur strode across it without a fear in the world – of course. I had to wonder sometimes if he lacked the imagination to be afraid of some things, or was just plain braver than me. Probably a bit of both.

Despite the early hour, the village teemed with activity. In the central open space, surrounded on all sides by the roughly constructed houses, the women, as small, sun-browned and withered as their men, sat gutting fish, their husband's nets put aside. Their older children were busy stringing the gutted fish on frames ready to go into the smoke house.

The rank stink of fish clung to everything, and underfoot scales glittered on the wooden boards. A couple of buckets of entrails sat between the women, fast filling as they worked, and a few mangy cats stalked about, eyeing the racks of fish and meowing hungrily.

The women's blank, incurious eyes followed us as we passed through their workspace, and the grubby, half-naked toddlers playing amongst the buckets of fish froze, mouths hanging open, staring.

We squeezed between two of the thatched houses to reach the little landing stage at the back of the village, where a low platform led down to a cluster of flat-bottomed boats. With a grin, Nial offered a rough and callused hand, and I stepped into the boat, which rocked alarmingly until I sat down on the narrow seat across the middle. With a hand gripping each gunnel, I felt a little steadier. Until Arthur stepped lightly in beside me and set the boat rocking again.

Bloody well sit down.

He did, in the bows, and Nial, after untying the mooring rope, hopped onto the stern with a long pole in his hands and pushed us off.

We drifted out into the gentle current, and the mist crept in from the marshes to shroud the village behind us. Only the dark rooftops showed above the soft whiteness. Bare feet gripping the rough wood, Nial propelled the boat onward with his long pole. We could have been taking a trip in a punt in Oxford, were it not for the cool dampness the descending mist had brought.

Arthur leaned back in the bows, the mist beading droplets of moisture in his dark hair like seed pearls. I sat bolt upright in the center, trying not to think about how deep the water beneath us might be, or about our transport's possible watertightness, or lack of it.

Thick weed trailed beneath the water's surface in long green tresses, drifting in the current, and beyond the mist a male bittern boomed, an unseen ghost of the marsh. Glimpsed briefly to our right, a heron strutted in the reeds, tall and almost prehistoric in appearance. And over to our left a moorhen sped for cover.

I kept my tight grip on the thin wooden sides of the boat, knuckles white, glad for Nial's guiding presence. I'd never have been able to navigate the intricacies of these braided channels, between the endless ephemeral islands of reeds and marsh grasses.

Wielded by Nial's experienced hands, the pole made scarcely any noise, and the mist seemed to mute all other sound, just the gentle lapping of the water breaking the silence.

Arthur broke that silence. "Nial? I need to ask you a question." His voice sounded loud, out of place and intrusive, as though an alien creature had invaded the marshes. A creature used to giving orders. I wanted to tell him to be quiet.

Our guide inclined his head, never taking his eyes off the river. "Ask away, Arthur." Somehow, his voice, soft and a little rough, felt a part of the misty marshlands.

Arthur lowered his voice. "Have you ever heard tell of a place on the island where offerings were made to the old gods?"

My ears pricked.

Nial spared him a quick, reflective glance. "Aye, I have that." His eyes reverted to the river's course, as he navigated between two stands of rushes.

In the bows Arthur remained leaning back, the picture of relaxation, as though the answer to his question mattered nothing to him. "Where would that be, then?" Almost a whisper this time, as though out beyond the mist eavesdroppers lurked.

Nial shrugged thin shoulders. "I couldn't tell you, I'm afraid. I don't know where it were. 'Tis only a story, now, told to children by their mamis of a night to scare 'em. We's Christians now."

Like I believed that. Christianity lay in only a thin veneer over Britain, and the peasants paid lip service, preferring instead to turn to the old gods in times of need. Even the nobility didn't always seem convinced of who or what they should be propitiating.

Arthur's gaze followed a flight of ducks as they rose over the mist. "I'm not meaning human sacrifice. I'm meaning things like swords."

Nial chuckled. "'Tis all the same to me. And probably to them that come before us. I'd think they put 'em all in the same spot, if they thought t'was a spot the gods would favor. Swords and sacrificed people the same."

The whispering water rippled with our going, dark and devoid of light. If I fell in, it would swallow me forever, taking me as a human sacrifice. I tore my gaze away with an effort and glanced over my shoulder at Nial.

He shook his head in apology. "I still don't know where it were done. I'm sorry." His sharp eyes flicked from Arthur's face to mine, then fixed on the river ahead.

Arthur waited a while before he posed his next question. "Is there anyone on the island who might know?"

Up ahead, the monks' wharf, its short bank shored up with solid wooden stakes and planking, materialized out of the mist. Nial shot Arthur another quick glance, then steered the boat toward it. "Ask at the village. There might be one there as knows. I do doubt as anyone in the abbey would. Too pagan for their liking." He chuckled again as the boat's nose touched the side, perhaps at the thought of the reaction we'd get if we tried asking Abbot Jerome about pagan sacrifices. The boat rocked again as Arthur got to his feet and leapt ashore with the rope.

I waited, still holding tight to the sides, until they had it secured fore and aft, then let Arthur hand me out, which set it rocking even more. A relief to have solid ground beneath my feet at last.

How strange that the mist seemed to swathe only the marshes, and not the island's cultivated slopes. I glanced up. Above the treetops the familiar hump of the Tor dominated the skyline. Unbidden, my mind went to the small stone circle on the summit. The way back to my old world.

Chapter Twenty-Four

NIAL TUGGED HIS forelock. "I'll sit an' fish fer my supper while you're about yer mission, then." He winked at Arthur and hoicked his rod out of the bottom of the boat where it had been lying in a puddle of murky water. We left him baiting his hook with something he'd found in his pocket that I didn't want a closer look at, but which might have explained the continuing odor of fish that had followed us across the water.

"We'll go to the village," Arthur said, taking my hand. "If there's anywhere on this island where our ancestors made offerings of their weapons, then one of the older villagers might know where to find it."

I'd gathered that much, but couldn't help an uneasy feeling of foreboding in my gut. A large part of me shied away from returning to the primitive cluster of huts I'd seen on my first day in this world. They hadn't been all that friendly then, and they might well not be now. In fact, at least one of them had wanted to lynch me. Best if I held my tongue about that.

"What makes you think the sword would be with other offerings?" I asked as we walked.

"I don't particularly. But it's a place to start." He gestured around himself. "This island's pretty big, and the girl in your vision wasn't all that specific, was she? In fact, she could have meant anywhere in this general direction." He chuckled. "Even as far as the sea and beyond."

Was he just humoring me?

We threaded our way between the silvery trunks of a small and stunted wood, sunlight filtering through the leafy branches to dapple our path. A sow and her litter of half-grown piglets ran squealing away from us, and overhead a blackbird called a warning.

Arthur seemed familiar with where the village lay. Without hesitation, he headed north, taking a winding path through the abbey's orchards and along the long ridge of high land that pointed south into the wetlands. Only small, unripe fruit on the trees at present, but come autumn, there'd be a fine crop for cider making.

Where the land spread out around the foot of the Tor, and the path we followed would have led us west toward the abbey, he took a well-worn track to the east that ran between oaks, chestnuts and ashes, all heavy with foliage.

"Are you sure this is a wise idea?" I asked, as the squat, thatched houses of the village appeared between the trees, and the scent of woodsmoke, pigs, and middens drifted toward us on the warm air. "They didn't like me much when I first met them."

He tightened his grip on my hand. "Nonsense, you're their queen now. And yes, we do have to ask. Asking will be the best thing to do." He smiled, and I still had that feeling of being humored. "You saw the sword in water and heard what Nial said."

With growing reluctance, I let him lead me out of the woodland and into the center of the group of houses. Nothing much had changed. The middens might have grown larger and smellier, and the roofs perhaps a little more blackened and less waterproof, but ostensibly the village seemed much the same as I remembered from that frightening first day in the Dark Ages. A lifetime ago.

Every house opened onto the communal central area, much as the houses in the Lake Village did, only here this area spread larger as they occupied dry land. Rickety doors, hung on leather hinges, stood open wide in the summer's heat, and outside almost every dwelling a woman sat at her loom, many of them with children playing in the dirt at their feet.

As we stepped out of the trees and into their view, hands stilled, and adults and children stared at us out of hostile, watchful faces. Thick plaits hung down the women's backs, and their barefoot children wore only grubby shifts. Not one of them looked clean. No sign of their menfolk and that aggressive giant who'd been their headman, whose name I'd forgotten.

The women squinted at Arthur in the bright sunlight, their children edging closer to them, to hook wary fingers in their mother's clothing.

Although Arthur had dressed with his customary lack of anything ornamental, preferring instead a dark blue tunic and leather braccae, everything about him spoke of his regal bloodline: his height, his well-dressed, well-nourished appearance, his cleanliness, and his bearing. And the thick, dragon-finialed gold torc about his neck rather gave the game away.

A good forty pairs of eyes stared, unblinking. They'd probably never seen their king before, and despite having no crown and not wearing armor or helmet, nor carrying a shield, he made a splendid sight.

Suspicious eyes ran over my boy's attire, and at least one of the women made the hasty sign against the evil eye. Much as they'd done on the day I'd first met them. Another crossed herself. They were hedging all bets here.

One of the older women, her almost white hair in a scrawny plait, turned and called something unintelligible into the hut behind her, her voice a coarse bark. A name, perhaps.

After a moment or two, the curtain across the low door twitched, and a man emerged. Short and solid, with no neck to speak of, and clad in only a grimy, knee-length tunic, he closely resembled a bull. His heavy, almost neanderthal brows furrowed, and he stepped in front of the woman who'd called him. Hands on hips, he spread his sandaled feet as his gaze took in the sword at Arthur's side. He wasn't the man I remembered as being in charge.

"Milord," he muttered, gruffly, after a moment's clear assessment of whether he owed this to us or not.

Arthur regarded him with more than a hint of frost. "Is that all you owe your king?"

The man's eyes widened, the women shifted uneasily as one, and I stood up straighter, endeavoring to appear more queenly in my boy's clothes and probably failing.

After a pregnant pause, the man made a clumsy bow. "I'm right sorry, Milord King. I did not know you." He straightened up. "And dint expect to see our king in this our 'umble village."

Arthur let his expression soften, and seeing that, I allowed myself to relax a little, as well.

"Your name?" Arthur asked.

"Turi, Milord." He tugged his scanty forelock in a tardy show of respect. "You be right welcome to our village. I be the headman here." He bowed again, lower this time, perhaps trying to make up for his people's surly, silent welcome. *Lack* of welcome.

"You can stop bowing, Turi," Arthur said, his smile slipping into a grin. "I get enough of that at Din Cadan. I'm here to ask for your help in an important matter." He paused, presumably to let that sink in.

Turi's eyes sharpened.

Arthur gave him a nod, man to man now, not king to peasant. "I have need of direction to a certain spot on this island. Nial from the Lake Village told me to come here and ask you. He said there might be one amongst you who could help."

Turi's face brightened. Not that it did much for his looks, which remained a cross between an angry bulldog and a belligerent wild boar. Having been commanded not to bow, he tugged his forelock in deference again instead. "I'll be glad to help you in any way I can, Milord." He gestured around himself at his women. "So will all of us, though most o' the men be at the abbey, workin' for the abbot. 'Tis our tribute that they pay. Tribute by work."

So why had he been inside his hut instead of working with them? Not the time or place to enquire about possible corruption amongst village leaders, though, so I contented myself with pressing my lips together and frowning at him.

He ignored me.

"Good," Arthur said, sounding satisfied.

Not an eye wavered. Even the children stayed motionless, although some of them had managed to close their mouths.

Arthur encompassed them all with his gaze, and spoke loud and clearly. "I need to know where the ancients, your ancestors, made their sacrifices to the old gods. Before the monks brought Christianity to you." He paused. "Is there one amongst you who can tell me?"

A communal indrawn hiss of breath sounded from the listening women, and a baby lying on a grubby blanket on the ground began to wail. Turi's face blanched beneath the tan and dirt. His mouth opened and closed a few times. Clearly this wasn't the request he'd been expecting.

At last, he found his voice. "Old Mother Nia – she were the keeper o' secrets," he managed. "But she been dead these five year now."

The would-be lyncher? Her wrinkled face and mad eyes had etched themselves with clarity onto my brain twelve years ago, and I'd not forget her in a hurry.

"Did she pass the knowledge on to anyone?" Arthur asked. In an age where records rarely made it to paper, word-of-mouth counted for everything.

Turi scratched his bristly, pepper-and-salt beard. "We don't talk much about it now," he said, crossing himself. "Not now we's Christians."

Were they? Really? Working for monks did not make them believers in the monks' God, in my experience.

"Her grandson be the keeper now, by ancient right. She did bring him up from a nipper after his mother and father did die o' the sweatin' sickness. She've passed him the secrets she had from her own ma, I b'leive." He crossed himself a little too flamboyantly for sincerity. "But we never speaks ter him about 'em. Like she did, he keeps wot he knows ter hisself. You'll have ter ask him fer yerselves."

A whisper of rustled agreement ran between the women. Some of them had caught hold of the nearest children to hold them against themselves, as though they feared some sort of retribution from the old gods, worshipped no doubt in secret, whilst giving lip-service to the monks and their new deity in the abbey church.

"Please send for this boy immediately," Arthur said, in a voice not accustomed to asking twice.

Turi tugged his forelock again. "Right away, Milord." He turned to one of the older children, who'd been gazing wide-eyed at us from behind a loom. "Run ter the abbey fields, and fetch Con. Quick now. You're not to keep the king waitin'."

Con?

Didn't I know that name? Twelve years had passed but I'd never forgotten the boy I'd met on my first day here. Could this be him, all grown up? Surely not. A common name anyone could have.

With the boy dispatched, Turi and the women sprang into action. The looms were pushed to one side, the children shooed away to play elsewhere, although in reality they only went so far as to hide behind the huts and peek out at us, big-eyed and curious.

Two not very trustsworthy looking seats were fetched out for us to sit on.

"Will you be seated, Milord?" Turi asked, all obsequious retainer now.

Arthur took the offered seat as though it had been given by another king, bowing gracefully to the two women who brought them, and sitting down as though on his magnificent throne at the Council of

Kings. I perched on the edge of the second seat, wary of fully committing my weight to it.

Another woman fetched beakers of strong, earthy cider, and a fourth brought honey cakes, which, to my surprise, were delicious, despite my misgivings about the cleanliness of their preparation.

"These are the best I've ever tasted," Arthur declared with surprising tact for him, as he took a second cake. "You'll have to come and work for me in the Great Hall at Din Cadan." He beamed at the woman, whose face flushed scarlet with delight. Through the dirt. No doubt she'd be telling everyone how much the king had liked her baking for years to come. The equivalent of the Royal Warrant in my old world.

Nibbling mine with much less enthusiam, I was only hoping we wouldn't get e-coli or salmonella poisoning or even botulism. The only forms of food poisoning I could think of on the spur of the moment.

We didn't have long to wait. The little messenger boy came racing back with Con loping behind him. A tall, dark-haired young man with wide eyes and an open honest face. Something about him struck a chord the moment I laid eyes on him. Was I right? Could this hefty lad be the little shepherd boy I remembered?

He slithered to a halt in front of us and made a hurried bow. As he straightened up, our eyes met. My memories slid into place. Of course. It *was* him. The young man's features still held an echo of the boy's.

"Con?" I said. "Don't you remember me?"

He must have been about twenty by now, long and lanky as a younger boy still, but with the promise of thickening out to make a strong man. Dark stubble shadowed his chin and upper lip, and heavy black brows framed wide brown eyes. He stared, and I could almost hear the cogs of his brain whirring into place. "You be that girl I did find on the hillside that time," he said, almost as though he didn't believe his memory. "In them funny clothes. The one that we did take to the abbot." His gaze went to my hand on the beaker of cider. To my ring. "The one wi' the dragon ring."

I nodded. "I am she." I held out the hand with the ring on it. "And here is my ring, still on my finger."

Impatient, Arthur frowned. "She is your queen now, boy. Show my wife due respect."

Con shifted awkwardly and bowed again, deeper this time. When he came up, he kept his eyes lowered, as though not wanting to look at either of us now he knew who we were.

Men's voices sounded. They were returning through the trees, no doubt curious to see their king and queen who'd so unexpectedly come to visit. Quietly, they shuffled into the crowd now gathered about us, bobbing self-conscious bows one after another as they arrived.

Arthur fixed Con with a firm stare. "We have come to question you, boy."

"Milord. Milady," Con mumbled, remembering himself and bowing again, but still keeping his eyes on his dirty bare feet.

"Enough of that," Arthur snapped, a little impatient, I suspected. "Stop all this bowing. One's enough. We've come here today seeking information." He nodded at Turi then turned back to Con. "Did your grandmother ever show you where the ancients made their sacrifices to the old gods? Your headman swears you know."

Con's head shot up and his eyes widened, some kind of recognition kindling deep down in them. He glanced at Turi, who gave him an encouraging nod. The boy licked his lips. "Aye, she did that." He hesitated. "Milord."

Whatever I'd seen in his eyes flickered again – was it exultation, pride? Some grain of knowledge that perhaps he wanted to share. Was there more to this than just surprise at our request? Was he, in fact, surprised at all?

Arthur set down his beaker. "Then you will take us there."

Con's face had paled under the tan and dirt. He licked his lips again, his tongue darting around them several times. "As you wish, Milord."

That knowing, almost exultant look returned, as his gaze slid from Arthur's face to mine, and back again. A little shiver slithered down my spine.

Chapter Twenty-Five

"This way, Milord," Con muttered, addressing his feet. He'd dropped his eyes the moment they'd met mine, perhaps to disguise the expression in them. Too late. I'd seen it. Did I trust him? Might this be some kind of elaborate trap? No, it couldn't be. No one could have predicted we'd arrive today. Something else must be at the root of the boy's excitement. Something I couldn't even guess at.

He indicated the track through the woods that surrounded his village – the track Arthur and I had arrived by.

Arthur rose from his makeshift throne and waved a regal hand. "Lead on."

Con set off along the track, his natural long stride hampered by constant furtive glances over his shoulder, as though he expected us to perhaps vanish in a puff of smoke, or stop following him. Or maybe he hoped we would.

His behavior reminded me of when he'd found me, covered in mud and disorientated from my tumble back in time, and led me to his village. Every time he peeked over his shoulder at Arthur, his eyes slid involuntarily to me, then zipped away at speed. That feeling of there being something more to him persisted. Had Arthur noticed?

The sun had risen high in the sky by now, burning off most of the marsh mists that so often hid this mysterious isle from the outside world. No wonder stories about magic had seeded themselves here, linking this hilly protruberance back through time to Gwynn ap Nudd himself, lord of the Otherworld.

A little shiver ran down my spine at the thought of how far I'd come since the day I'd found myself here, lost in time, and how hard, back then, it had been to believe it. Right now, I felt ready to accept anything that came my way – including, perhaps, an underwater woman holding up an ancient emperor's sword for my husband to take.

No. Scotch that one. I did *not* believe we'd be seeing her.

Arthur took hold of my hand as we walked, and I felt grateful for the warm contact with his skin. The rough calluses on his palms, and the firmness of his grip anchored me in reality and pushed the idea of this magical isle to a distance I could manage.

"The boy seems to know the way," he whispered, leaning close to my ear as we walked.

I nodded, keeping my gaze fixed on Con's lanky frame as he strode in front of us. Slightly better dressed than the last time I'd seen him, he wore a dirty, mud-colored tunic over braccae that reached to just below his knees, and went bare-footed. A knife, the hilt bound with twine, nestled in a plain scabbard on his belt, and around his throat a necklace of wooden beads completed his ensemble. His dark hair hung loose and unkempt about his shoulders.

"We'll be giving the abbey a miss, I think," Arthur said, as it came into view. A few monks were working in the gardens close by the cluster of thatched buildings, but the small, square fields were empty, as our arrival must have denuded them of the lay workers. No doubt the men would return… eventually.

"Milord, Milady. This way if yer please." Con indicated a narrow path that skirted the fields, making its way along the most distant edge of the apple orchards. Beside the abbey buildings, the monks downed tools to stand and watch us pass, squinting against the brightness of the light.

Even from here I could make out the curious expressions on their faces. Was Gildas one of them? He was much the same age as Con now, a man grown, but I hadn't seen him for some while. The last news I'd had, he was working in the copying house, laboriously writing out manuscripts, something far more suited to his nature than slaving in a garden. He'd complained, of course. When did he ever not complain? He wanted to be writing his own compositions, not copying out the work of others.

We left the apple orchards and abbey behind, passing through open grazing lands where sheep dotted the slopes. Here and there a few cattle waded belly-deep in the mud at the marsh edge, where the choicest morsels grew, and the whine of insects filled the air. With an impatient hand, I swiped away the flies that circled my head.

At last, Con brought us to a finger of dry land that stretched out between two narrow inlets of rush-fringed water. He halted. "'Tis 'ere," he announced, turning to look at us out of wary, knowing eyes. "This side." He indicated the left tip of the small peninsula.

Arthur narrowed his eyes. This place looked no different to any other. "Are you certain?"

The boy nodded. "I should know it well. Old Mother did bring me here 'nough times to show me where the ancients worshipped." He wiped a hand across his nose. "When I were a boy an' then again when she did see her own end comin'."

It looked just like the rest of the island. Grass, cropped short by sheep and peppered with their droppings, lay under our feet, and scrubby willow and alder trees dotted the sloping ground. Nearer the water, the reeds and rushes began as the land softened. Beyond the reed beds, water glinted, and beyond that, distant marshy islands lay, still festooned with shreds of mist. It didn't resemble the open, lily-infested water I'd seen in my dream at all.

"Well?" Arthur asked, turning to fix me with an enquiring gaze. Behind him, Con fidgeted, his large bony hands picking at loose threads in the sleeve of his tunic.

"I don't know," I mumbled, avoiding meeting his eyes and staring around. "Nowhere here looks anything like what I saw."

Further out, small reedy islands rose just a few feet above the water, not big enough for habitation, but enough to reduce the visible waterway to just a few braided channels.

I shook my head. "I don't think this can be the right place."

Arthur turned back to Con. "Any boats kept here?"

For answer, Con trotted down the slope to where the reeds grew thickest and picked up a frayed rope from the grass. He gave it a tug, and the reeds parted as the nose of a boat pushed between their stalks. "She be mine," he said. "For fishin'. I do keep her here 'cause 'tis a spot no one do dare to come. On account o' the ghosties."

She so resembled the boat in my dream I had to do a double take. But then, so had Nial's boat. Flat-bottomed, old, nestling in reeds like some enormous water bird.

Inspiration came. "Are there any open stretches of water near here?" I asked, stepping closer to the boy. "With water lilies?"

He took his bottom lip between his teeth for a moment, staring into my eyes. Did he want to ask me another question? I could almost hear it on his lips.

But no. He gave himself a shake, and wrinkled his nose. "There might be." The feeling that he was keeping some secret hidden away deep down in his heart rose again, but no instinct warned me of threatening danger. Whatever it was he knew, it didn't frighten me. More a feeling of an underlying current of excitement running through him, as of someone who was finally drawing close to what they've long desired or waited for.

However... not *another* trip in a boat. Mentally girding up my loins, I turned back to Arthur. "Then that's where we have to go."

He nodded. "Can you take us there, boy?"

With a nod, Con pulled the boat in closer, and held the prow while Arthur handed me into it. A moment later, Arthur settled beside me, and Con moved to the flat stern, long pole in hand.

With infinite care, he poled the boat out of the rushes and into the narrow, reed-fringed channel, showing an expertise to match Nial's. The plain little workboat skimmed across the water as though winged, causing scarcely a ripple to disturb the dark surface. At the edge of the reeds, the moorhen and coot watched us with equanimity, as though once in Con's boat, we'd become part of their world, and they didn't fear us.

After only a few minutes, the channel widened to open water, and there before us stretched the water lilies of my dream. Flat green pads, round as illustrations from a children's story, covered the water, the creamy cups of the flowers sitting on them like porcelain sculptures.

The pool was large, the distant shores still hung with mist where trees had snagged and held it, bestowing on them the look of a mystical fairyland. Perhaps not too far from the truth, if my dream and Nimuë's messages were to be believed.

I seized Arthur's hand as excitement coursed through me. "This is it. The place in my dream. We're here."

He stared across the wide expanse of lilies. "But where? It's huge. How do we know where to look?"

Very true. My shoulders sagged with little hope that an arm was about to appear to order holding the sword we wanted. Things like that only happened in story books. "Maybe we should start in the middle?"

Without comment, but with that same knowing, half-triumphant look in his eyes, Con poled us out between the lily stalks, the pole disappearing further as the water deepened.

Not liking the idea of how much water now lay below us, I gripped the sides of the boat as sweat sprang out on my skin. But we were here now, and it would be foolish to turn back just because of my fears. I stayed silent, trying to dig my fingers into the rough wood.

Arthur held up a hand. "Here. Stop."

We were in the center of both lake and lily pads.

Con stopped poling, holding the boat still with the pole anchored in the mud that must lie below us. The boat bobbed quietly in the still, dark water, and far off a warbler chirred. The lily pads, parted by our arrival, closed in around us again, as a gentle breeze stirred the rushes at the water's edge making them whisper like gossipy old women. A duck and ducklings swam for cover on the far bank, where willows overhung the water.

I stared across the quiet pool. Not quite large enough to be called a lake. My eyes studied the banks of reeds and rushes, with their furry heads bobbing in the breeze. I followed the line of willows that leaned their drooping branches far out over the water, until the tips trailed in their reflections.

Wait. Was that a figure, standing in the dappled shadow of the willows?

I blinked and looked again. Nothing.

Con glanced at me, but stayed silent. He'd seen. I could feel it in the trembling air. He knew.

Leaning over the side of the boat, Arthur parted the lilies, pushing them to the sides and peering into the peaty water. Taking my courage in both hands, I did the same on the other side while Con watched us, still silent, inscrutable as a cat.

The long stalks of the lilies vanished down into the murky water, twisting away in a wild plait of nature, twining about each other like thick snakes. Dangerous.

Something, some sixth sense perhaps, made me lift my head from my investigation. There, on the bank in that patch of shadow. Someone standing motionless, watching. A small figure. I narrowed my eyes and stared, but the harder I looked, the harder it was to see, the shadows and the water's reflection shimmering like a mirage. Nothing.

"What be you lookin' for?" Con finally asked, but the feeling he already knew came strongly to me.

I glanced up at him, narrowing my eyes and trying to see inside his head. No point in hiding it if he already knew. And if he didn't know, and we found it, we could hardly conceal it from him. "A sword." I watched for his reaction while Arthur continued to peer into the water, wet now to above the elbows.

Con's eyes widened, and he sat down hard on the seat at the back of his boat, one hand luckily remembering to hold onto the pole where it stood up like some weird art installation. Was that relief as well as exultation and a touch of fear on his face?

"You know, don't you?" I said.

Chapter Twenty-Six

ARTHUR STRAIGHTENED UP and abandoned his watery search. He fixed a regal stare on the boy, enough to quail the bravest warrior. "What is it you know? Best to tell us now and avoid my wrath." His eyebrows had lowered to a threatening frown.

The stare had little effect on the boy. Perhaps he knew of something even greater than the wrath of a king.

He lifted his chin, and suddenly the wary peasant fell away from him, and a veil of nobility settled in its place. "She told me you'd come one day, if not fer me, then fer whoever come after me," he said, voice clear and proud, almost as though he were reciting a speech he'd had long prepared. "She told me to watch out for you, in case it would be me that had to show you."

"What?" Arthur's chin came up. He sat up taller. "*Who* said this to you, boy?"

"My old granny. She what were called Old Mother by everyone, on account of her age, 'cause she were th'oldest in our village – oldest in the world, I'd wager. But she were *mine*. Not theirn. Mebbe she weren't rightly my granny, like, but my granny's granny."

I wiped my wet hands on my tunic. "Your grandmother told you we'd come... for the sword?" My eyes must have been wider than his. Not for a moment had I thought he'd know anything about it, despite the strange looks he'd been giving us. "How could she have known?" A thought flashed into my head. "Did she... did she have the *Sight*, maybe? Do *you* have it?"

I met Arthur's gaze.

Con shook his head. "Doan ask me. I jest listened to what she telled me. The secrets she knowed. They're *my* secrets now." That last sentence came out possessively, as though he might be unwilling to part with them, wanting to keep them hugged tight to himself. Maybe in memory of his granny's granny. The mad old bat who'd wanted to string me up.

"Tell us what you know, boy," Arthur said, a little more gently now, but more demanding than I'd have been. "And make it quick."

"Yes, you can tell us. Your grandmother would have wanted you to," I added, laying a calming hand on Con's knee. "This is the time she warned you would come. We're here for the sword. The time is right. You need to help us find it."

Con's gaze slid from Arthur's face to mine, and back again. "My granny, she were older than old. She did say as she remembered the legions, marchin' away wi' the old emperor." His eyes lost their focus, and a smile slid over his face. Perhaps in his mind's eye he saw his granny. "An' when she got so old an' thought she were going to die, she chose me to take on her secrets. She'd brung me here first when I were just a little lad, an' now she showed me where the sword were hid." He paused. It gave his words a good dramatic effect. "*His* sword."

His sword? Who did Con think "he" was? Had his granny known?

"So you know where the sword is?" My voice rose.

His head bobbed in assent.

I let out my breath. Why hadn't we just asked him in the first place? Although, how were we to have guessed that he knew? That this was one of his secrets.

Arthur shot me a quick glance. "There really *is* a sword?"

Had he not believed me then? Had I been right, and he'd been humoring me? Indignation, and a touch of smugness that I'd been correct, sent heat rising to my cheeks.

"Aye, there is that," Con said. "*She* showed me where it were." He fixed his eyes on me. Somehow the feeling that he wasn't talking about his granny surfaced, and that he wanted me to know. Had Nimuë visited this boy as well as me?

"Do you know where the sword came from?" I asked, struggling to keep my voice level. "Was it thrown in here, where old swords used to be thrown, perhaps as another tribute?"

Confidence radiated from Con now. "No. It weren't tribute. It were hid. Granny did say as her own mother showed her where it were hid, when she were old enough to know. Told her to keep it safe. That one day someone'd come for it. The man it were meant for." His eyes flicked toward Arthur again.

"How did she know where it was?" Arthur asked. "Did she know who hid it?"

The wind rose, rustling in the stunted trees on the far side of the water. Did I see that small figure again, just for a moment? Was there a second, taller figure by its side?

Con licked his lips. "Her own mother did put it there, Granny telled me. T'were her ma what hid it. For *him*."

Arthur's hands gripped the side of the boat, knuckles whitening.

My breath caught in my throat. "Who did she hide it for, Con?"

"Prince Macsen," Con said, with all the flair of a magician revealing his greatest trick. "She did hide it for the Prince."

Silence filled the air around us. Even the rustling in the treetops had died to nothing. Just the slap of water on the hull disturbed us. Who was the woman who'd hidden this sword for a man who'd died so far away? What had she to do with him? How had it gone from the hands of the young soldier I'd seen to those of a peasant woman on a mystical isle in far off Britain? Had he brought it here and given it to this woman? And had she then hidden it? Why had it not gone to the mysterious Princess Elen, Macsen's wife?

Arthur had gone very still, eyes fixed on Con's face. "You are telling us the truth?"

A touch of defiance colored the boy's expression. "I am that. Tellin' you what my granny telled me. Word fer word."

I just wanted to make sure I had it right. "Your great-great-grandmother's own mother hid this sword for Prince Macsen?"

Con scowled. "I telled you, dint I? Thass what I said. Thass all I knows."

But was it?

Arthur straightened up. "Then show me where the sword lies hidden, for I am the man it's meant for. I am the heir of Macsen Wledig."

Con pointed. "By them trees. Unner the water."

I followed his finger toward the spot where I'd seen that shadowy watching figure. A shiver ran down my spine. Without thinking, I made the sign against the evil eye I'd so often seen the women of the fortress make. For good measure, I crossed myself as well. But whatever this was, it wasn't Christian.

"Then take us there," Arthur said, eyes alight with excitement.

Con got to his feet and, using the pole, propelled us between the lily pads, bringing the boat to a halt ten yards from the overhanging willows with a clear view of the bank. No one stood in the shadows.

Resting the pole along the length of the boat, Con parted the lilies and peered into the water. "'Tis down there. Wrapped up 'gainst the water. My granny did say as when the right man searches for it, he'll find it no problem. She did say as if his hand were the right one, the sword'd find it."

Arthur's fingers were on his belt buckle, already undoing it. "Then I'll find it," he said. "Or it'll find me. It's meant for me, I know it." He tossed his sword belt into the bottom of the boat, and yanked his tunic over his head.

"You're going to dive for it?" I asked. Stupid question really. How else was he going to get it? No sword-holding hand of an aquatic woman had reared out of the water to help him: that was just the stuff of legends… and dreams.

I peered at the mess of tangled lily stalks beneath the water, and my heart did a leap of fear. Suppose we were wrong and this sword wasn't for him? Suppose Nimuë had lured Arthur here to drown him, bidden by her evil mother? Did I trust those lilies not to ensnare him if the magic of this place rejected his quest?

"Of course." He pulled his undershirt off. "It's not deep water. It'll be lying in the mud at the bottom." He grinned, as though excited by the challenge. "If we're right, fate will guide my hands."

I glanced at Con, who'd sat down again. Blank-faced, he watched Arthur pull his boots off. How could this be safe? My fear that it might be some trick that Con was part of surfaced again.

Arthur was pulling off his braccae now. I put a restraining hand on his arm. "Be careful. Morgana might have had a hand in this."

He shook his head, naked now, clothes in a heap on the thwart of the rocking boat. I'd quite forgotten to be afraid of it doing that. "Not her. This is the sword of Macsen Wledig, and now it's going to be my sword. You watch."

He planted a hard kiss on my lips and slid over the side of the boat into the water. "Whoa. Bloody chilly." He laughed up at me, more an excited boy than a man of five and thirty. Then, before I could think of a reason to stop him, he took a deep breath, upended and dived beneath the lily pads, feet kicking out.

He was gone. The ripples from where he'd dived dispersed. The lily pads floated back to cover the space where he'd vanished. Silence descended. As if he'd never been here.

I stared at Con, and he stared back. All sorts of things flashed through my head. Might he be in Morgana's pay? Like Hafren. Was he party to a deception, a pawn in the hands of the powerful? Had fate made a pawn of me too? My brain churned so much I couldn't decide.

Under the willows, the shadows seemed to shift as though someone standing there had moved, and another shiver ran through me. Was this magic, or something else? Ghosts? The hairs along my skin prickled upright.

Time ticked by far too slowly. The hot sun on the back of my neck burned into my skin, the dark water shimmered, and insects whined as they skimmed the surface. My hands resting on the boat's edge drummed an anxious tattoo.

Where was Arthur? Too long had passed. This wasn't right. For how long could he hold his breath? A sudden vision of him trapped, entangled in the lilies' grasping stalks with Morgana laughing in triumph, came to me, and I made to stand up, with no idea what I'd do.

The boat rocked, and Con shot out a hand to push me down.

Right beside the boat, the surface of the water broke and the lilies parted. Arthur's head appeared, mouth gasping for breath, hair slick to his face. He seized the side of the boat with one hand and hung on for a moment, gulping air.

I heaved a deep breath myself, realizing with a start that I'd been holding it, and reached out to cover his hand with mine. How cold it was.

For a moment he raised his eyes to meet mine, triumph blazing in them. Then he spat water from his mouth, and raised his other hand out of the water. In it he held a long, soggy shape, wrapped in wet cloth. Unmistakably a sword.

"Oh my God, you found it," I gasped, leaning toward him, hands outstretched.

He shoved the wrapped sword into my arms, then heaved himself in over the stern, flopping onto the boards, water running everywhere. The boat rocked wildly again, but I didn't care. He hadn't drowned.

Con sat holding the pole and watching, the light of triumph burning in his brown eyes as well, as though he'd just witnessed something he'd never thought to see. Perhaps he'd thought his old granny had spun him a tale, or that even if it were true, it would never happen during his custodianship of the secret.

Without bothering to get dressed, Arthur sat up and wiped his wet hair out of his eyes, then took his hard-won prize. Layers of some kind of oiled cloth had made a fat sausage of the sword, bound with many ties, but the shape was clear. Grabbing his knife from his discarded swordbelt, Arthur slid it into the layers of ancient cloth, slicing through them. They fell away.

Pulling the last layers from off the sword, he laid it, long and deadly and perfect, across his bare thighs. The oiled cloth had preserved its integrity and no hint of rust or any other kind of degradation marred its beauty. Perhaps something more had helped to keep it pristine in its watery grave for over a century, waiting for the right man to give it rebirth. Who knew?

No ordinary warrior's blade this, but a weapon fit for an emperor. The glimmering damascene blade caught every beam of sunlight and shone as though a star had fallen to earth. Was the ornate pommel made of real gold? The cross-guard, wider than normal, boasted an intricate patterning to the tips, and the grip was of worked red leather, ridged to give a firmer hold, and with no sign of damage after its long submersion.

"I never dared t'think it might be real," Con whispered, mesmerized. "That it'd happen while I were keeper."

Arthur set his hand on the grip, lifted elated eyes to mine, and raised the sword. Across the patterning on the blade, that rippled like watered silk, the light shifted and danced.

Mesmerized as much as Con, I couldn't take my eyes off it.

Lifting it above his head, Arthur pointed the tip toward the wide blue sky. "Excalibur is mine."

Over on the bank behind him I caught a movement. Were those two figures watching us again? Or had I just imagined it? No. Nothing there. Or whatever it was had gone, perhaps satisfied that we had the sword at last.

Chapter Twenty-Seven

NO HASTE ATTACHED itself to our return. Joining me in an awed silence, Arthur pulled his clothes on again, unable to tear his eyes away from the sword where it lay on the thwarts of the boat, as Con poled us back to firm ground.

Our guide nosed the boat into the reeds again, until it bumped against dry land, then he ran lightly along its length and leapt ashore with the mooring rope. A hefty tug brought us close enough that I didn't have to get my feet wet when I stepped ashore.

With the little boat well-hidden in the reeds, we walked back across the island in silence, Con following. Arthur held the sword reverently in both hands, unable to wipe the look of satisfaction from his face.

This time we didn't skirt the abbey, but stopped at the collection of thatched buildings that sat around a square, well-kept courtyard. A young monk, who'd been busy with a birch broom, came hurrying across the pristine cobbles when Arthur hailed him.

Arthur didn't beat about the bush. "We're here to see the Abbot."

The monk raised wide eyes from where he'd been staring at the naked blade in Arthur's hands, his chin wobbling in what could only have been consternation. Unlikely they were often visited by warriors holding drawn swords.

"Milord." His voice came out in a squeak.

"Now," Arthur growled, scowling at him.

The terrified young man scuttled away, leaving his broom discarded on the cobbles.

A couple of minutes later, an older and calmer monk returned. Without removing his hands from his sleeves, he made a low bow to Arthur. "Milord King. Milady the Queen. Please come this way."

We followed him to the abbot's spartan office, a room I hadn't been in for a couple of years, not since Gildas had left the novitiate behind and become a fully fledged monk. Visits to young monks by women, even queens, were frowned upon. Maybe it had been the sight of a woman, as well as a drawn sword, that had helped to terrify the young monk.

Abbot Jerome rose from behind his large wooden desk – an object almost modern in conception – to make his bow. "Milord King. Milady the Queen."

His unruly bush of dark hair remained almost untouched by gray, with scarcely a peppering to hint at his advancing age. As he straightened from his bow, his sharp, intelligent eyes went straightaway to the blade in Arthur's hands, and his bushy eyebrows rose toward his hairline. He gestured to the two chairs positioned in front of his desk and took the one behind it for himself.

Having settled himself comfortably, he steepled his hands and looked Arthur in the eye, steadfastly ignoring the elephant in the room. "To what do I owe the honor of this visit?"

Arthur laid the sword on the table. "I'm here to show you this."

Jerome sat motionless for a long moment, gaze fixed on the beautiful sword laying before him on the tabletop. Then he shifted his weight and leaned forward to peer more closely at it. "I see a sword before me." He raised his eyes and looked at Arthur. "A sword of exquisite workmanship." He tilted his head to one side, the hint of a frown creasing his forehead. "And yet on your arrival, I remarked that you already have a sword hanging by your side." He paused. "So what is this one?"

"The sword of Macsen Wledig," Arthur said, with a touch of bravado.

Jerome pursed his lips and inhaled a long breath. "Aha." He drew out both syllables.

Despite the season, and the time of day, Jerome's office was poorly lit by two narrow slit windows in the outer wall, and yet the sword on the table seemed to glow with an inner fire. But that was probably wishful thinking on my part.

"Where did you find it?" Jerome asked, his voice clipped and economical. "If I may presume to ask?"

Arthur smiled. "Here, on Ynys Witrin. Hidden since Prince Macsen's death a century or more ago."

Jerome's eyes went to Arthur's straggly wet hair, still clinging to his head in dark curls. "Beneath the water, I see." Nothing got past his watchful eyes.

Arthur got to his feet, and, reaching for the scabbard on his hip, drew out that sword. The sword he'd drawn from the stone all those years ago. With care, he laid it on the table beside Macsen's sword, his fingers resting for a moment on the dowdy hilt. It looked like what it was – a plain warrior's sword, workmanlike, ordinary. "This is the sword from the stone in the forum at Viroconium. The sword that proclaimed me as High King."

He ran a finger along the sharp, well-oiled blade. "It's served me well, but now I have the sword of my ancestor, the sword of an Emperor." His hand moved to touch the shimmering damascene blade. "A king needs but one sword. This one has fulfilled its purpose. I've come here today to ask you to keep the sword in the stone safe for me. To stow it with your treasures and allow no one else to take it. To guard it with your lives."

He sat down.

"Me?" Jerome's voice rose in surprise, his clever eyes flicking from sword to king, then back again.

Arthur nodded. "Possession of this sword won me the High Kingship of Britain. No one else must ever find it. It will be safer here than at Din Cadan. I ask you to keep it hidden." A smile touched the corners of his mouth, lightening his expression. "Perhaps not quite as hidden as this one was though." He glanced at me and the smile broadened.

Then he returned his gaze to Jerome's impassive face. "No other hand may touch the sword from the stone but mine. I entrust it to you, Jerome, to guard with your own life and the lives of all your monks."

Jerome bowed his head. "An unusual request, but you are my king. I will carry out your orders. The sword shall remain hidden here where none will think to find it."

"Good. I thank you for that." Arthur extended his hand and the two men clasped forearms for a moment across the desk. Then Arthur got to his feet and picked up Excalibur from where it lay on Jerome's table, glowing in the feeble window light. He stared at it for a moment before sliding it into the empty scabbard at his side.

The old sword lay on the table, a little dull and plain after the beauty of Excalibur. Arthur brushed his fingertips over its blade, as though in sad farewell. His Adam's apple bobbed. "I'll leave it with you and trust to your discretion. I thank you again, Father Abbot." He nodded his head in the slightest of bows. "Until we meet again."

Back in the courtyard, we rejoined Con, who'd been sitting quietly on the mounting block in the sunshine, chewing on a blade of dried grass.

Arthur halted in front of him, and the boy scrambled to his feet, the nobility I'd seen earlier vanished. He was all peasant lad again.

"Thank you, Con, for your part in this day's work," Arthur said, his hand resting on the sword's beautiful hilt where it now peeked from his scabbard. "You are a good guardian of secrets, just as your grandmother clearly was, and I would like to reward you. If you wish,

I can find you a farm nearer to Din Cadan, and a good strong girl to be your wife. You would be able to grow fields of wheat and raise sheep and cattle on good land. And children."

Con, gone shy and self-conscious again, studied his grubby bare feet. "Thankee kindly, Milord, but I doan b'long there. I b'long here, wi' my people. Wi' my granny's people. I makes a good livin' here by fishin', and wi' me few sheep, an' there be a girl I has my eye on. I'll stay here if 'tis all the same wi' you."

Arthur nodded as though he understood. "Very well, but at least let me send you some more sheep. No, don't protest. I insist. My seneschal will have them brought to the island for you."

Con bobbed a bow, eyes remaining down. "Thankee, Milord."

Having sent Con back through the woods to his village, Arthur and I walked back hand-in-hand to the monks' wharf. Nial was sitting in the hot sun on the wooden jetty, bare brown feet dangling in the water, a rush basket of wriggling silvery-gray eels beside him.

"Good haul," Arthur said, dropping down to sit on the jetty. "Takes me back to my boyhood."

Nial grinned, his whole face crinkling with pleasure, as withered as an ancient apple. "Aye, I remember well the boy you were back then. Allus after me to take you out in my boat. You an' that gurt big brother o' yourn." He chuckled. "Be he still that gurt?"

Arthur laughed back. "Bigger still. Hard to find a horse strong enough to bear his weight."

"I'd best not tek him in my boat then, lessen he sinks it." More laughter, from both of them. They could have been two friends in any time, sitting with a fishing rod beside a river, instead of a king and his lowly subject.

I stood behind them, staring out across the peaceful waters at the small islands, the banks of rushes and the stunted trees, now clear of all but the last shreds of mist. A heron took off and flew across the sky, the beat of its wings ponderous and prehistoric. Amongst the rushes, small waterfowl bobbed in and out, and twenty yards away a fish leapt.

At Arthur's side the hilt of his new sword drew the light, as though greedy after its long incarceration. Deep inside me a tiny nub of anxiety hatched and grew. A sword is a strange chimeric thing – part beautiful object to be admired and cherished, part dangerous weapon and life-taker. And Arthur didn't need it for its beauty. He needed it for its baser function. If this was indeed the time he needed Excalibur, then Camlann must be drawing closer.

I swallowed down my fears and stepped nearer, my fingers brushing his hair.

"I could sit here all day," he said, his voice soft and dreamy. "And never fight another battle."

Chapter Twenty-Eight

"**Y**OU MUST PRESENT the sword in the Hall tonight," Merlin said, eyes alight with excitement as we three stood in the royal chamber. "Everyone needs to see this. And we'll need to let the other kings know you have it."

"Must?" Arthur said, one eyebrow raised.

Merlin frowned. "Should. Stop being pedantic. This is the sword you were destined to bear. The sword that will vanquish Aelle and his Saxons forever. The men need to see it."

Arthur laid the sword on the table, where the candlelight flickered over the blade making it appear to ripple like water. "There's no doubt about it. It's a magnificent blade. I've never seen such workmanship." He looked up and grinned at his old friend. "And it has a name, as any legendary sword should. Excalibur."

I held my tongue. I doubted very much that Magnus Maximus had called this sword Excalibur. Could it be that the only reason it had that name was because I knew it from legend? That Nimuë, like her mother, had snatched that name from somewhere inside my head? If so, then I'd done it again. Made history out of a legend. Now this sword was named after itself, just as I was. Confusing.

Merlin ran a fingertip along the blade and the light seemed to move before his touch. Did it recognize the magic in him? The same magic Nimuë possessed. "A good name for a truly beautiful sword. And a deadly one."

Arthur smiled. "As a sword should be." But his eyes held no mirth. Was he remembering the men he'd killed with his other sword, and the many men who'd died fighting by his side? Was he thinking of the men lying in his future, whose blood this new sword would drink? I remembered his reflective words as we'd sat on the dock at Ynys Witrin. Could a warrior king like him ever find peace, or was he destined to fight until the day he died?

The door from the hall banged open, and Llacheu almost catapulted into the room, eyes alight with excitement. "You've got it?" he blurted out. "The sword of Macsen Wledig?"

As one we turned to face him.

"How do you know?" Arthur demanded, more than a little on the defensive.

Llacheu halted in front of his father. "Tulac had it from one of the hall servants. They overheard you talking." He was panting.

"No secrets from servants," Merlin said, grimacing. "It'll be all around the fortress before tonight."

"In less than an hour, you mean." Arthur sighed. "That rather forces my hand." He stood aside. "Here it is."

Llacheu stepped up to the table and stared, wide-eyed, down at the magnificent sword for a long moment, his shoulders rising and falling with his fast breathing. At last, he spoke. "The sword of an emperor." He turned to his father. "*The* emperor." He must have learned his lessons in Roman history from Merlin well. "Does this mean *you'll* be an emperor, too?"

Arthur laughed uneasily. "I have no military ambitions beyond Britain. I'm a patriot, not an empire builder. Prince Macsen left this sword for someone, for his heir, and that's turned out to be me. But that doesn't mean I'll be following in his footsteps, nor those of Constantine." He glanced at Merlin. "Both were foolish to follow their too greedy ambitions and take their warriors overseas. It only brought them failure." He touched the blade. "I aim to use this sword for defense, not attack. This is the sword that will save the kingdoms of Britain from our enemies."

Prophetic words. A shiver ran down my back. I'd helped him to this sword, and with it likely set him firmly on the road to Camlann's bloody end.

>>><<<

WORD ABOUT THE sword had indeed flown around the fortress. Every warrior, with his wife and grown sons, and many of the tradesmen – among them the blacksmiths, wheelwrights, tanners, potters, and weavers, who lived in the fortress, had crammed themselves inside the hall, despite the summer's heat. As a concession to comfort, the slaughtered, well-grown bull calf prepared for the feast had been cooked outside, and only when ready to be served had the servants carried it into the Hall.

I sat beside Arthur at the high table in my new gown. I'd had Cottia's daughters, the finest seamstresses in Din Cadan, make it for me out of the bolt of gold damask silk that had made a precarious seaborne journey to Din Tagel, all the way from the eastern end of the Middle Sea. Perfect for the heat of summer, it clung to me like a second skin to the waist, then widened in a sweeping skirt that barely brushed the floor.

I'd persuaded Arthur, never keen on peacocking, to make a concession to the occasion for once. To please me, he'd donned a white silk undershirt topped by an indigo tunic edged with gold embroidery and cinched by a tooled leather belt. Around his neck he still wore his dragon-headed torc, and on his head he'd set the gold circlet of his crown, nestled in the curls of his freshly washed dark hair. He'd even rid himself of his customary stubble by shaving.

Before us on the high table lay the sword, out of sight of the chattering crowd, although a few had wandered this way on arrival, trying to snatch a quick glance.

In the body of the hall, the servants dodged between the packed tables filling goblets and laying out platters of meat and side-dishes. The babble of excited noise rose to the lofty rafters and the heat pressed in on me, making me thankful the cooking fire had been lit outside.

Beside me, Merlin surveyed the hall. "The goblets are nearly all filled," he remarked, glancing past me at Arthur, on whose far side Cei and Coventina sat. "Time, I think, to make the announcement all are waiting for." He gave Cei a nod.

My big, burly brother-in-law lumbered to his feet, towering over the Hall. He didn't need to speak. Silence fell like a pall over the jammed tables.

At the head of the nearest one, Llacheu sat with his friends, eyes shining with excitement, one hand gripping the stem of his goblet. His gaze fixed on his father's face, as though no one else existed in the hall, pride radiating from him like the rays of the sun.

But where was Amhar? I searched, scanning the joyful, rosy faces and not finding him. He must have known about the sword – everyone did by now. So where was he?

Cei cleared his throat, snatching my attention back.

"I think you probably all know what I'm going to say," he said, beaming round at the sea of earnest, excited faces, all flushed with alcohol and heat. "Or if you don't, you've had your heads up your arses all day."

A chorus of laughter burst out, and a few men banged their goblets on the tables.

Cei looked at Arthur, his face as full of pride as Llacheu's. "This is the man with the big sword," he said, making a very lewd gesture that brought more gales of laughter. "You thought he was a big bloke before, but he's bloody well-endowed now."

More laughter, rising to the rafters.

"Want to see his sword?" Cei shouted above the noise.

"Get it out!" Chorused the crowd. "Show us your sword!" Their shouts could probably have been heard at the bottom of the hill. No, in Ynys Witrin.

With a wide grin, Arthur rose to his feet and held up his hand. He was a little tipsy, having knocked back several goblets of wine on an empty stomach. The shouts died away. He waited until silence settled on the hall again. "You want to see my sword?" His voice rang out across the expectant air.

"Yes!" they shouted back.

With his right hand, he seized the glittering hilt and lifted the sword, putting the blade to his lips. Briefly, he kissed it, then raised it high above his head, and shouted: "The sword of Macsen Wledig, Emperor of Rome!" His eyes shone, his face radiated joy and pride. "Excalibur! The sword of Arthur Pendragon!"

The room exploded with applause. Arthur turned to left and right, thrusting the sword higher and higher, and at last I spotted Amhar, standing at the back of the hall with two other boys, a heavy scowl on his face. The happiness slid out of my day. Why was he so angry at his father? What was wrong? I schooled my face back into a smile as Arthur sat down beside me and laid the sword on the table once more.

<hr />

THE NOISE FROM the hall crept over the wall into our chamber even though more than half the people had already staggered home, drunk. Someone was singing a haunting ballad, the chorus joined by a dozen drunken voices. They were getting maudlin now.

I stood still while Maia undid the laces down the back of my gown – an undertaking I wasn't about to let Arthur try, especially not when he was drunk. It was the only silk gown I had, and I didn't want him ruining it. As for him, he lay on his back on our bed, still wearing his boots and humming to himself, the sword on the bed beside him. He'd removed his tunic and belt.

My dress slipped off my shoulders and I stepped out of it, wearing only my silk knickers.

"You can come over here like that," Arthur called, but didn't get up.

Not likely. At least not yet. Instead, I slipped into a clean linen undershirt and, as Maia took my gown away to attend to, I brushed my teeth over the bowl of water she'd left me.

The sound of dogs quarreling carried over the wall, followed by a shout and a yelp as someone tried to separate them.

I approached the bed. He had his arms behind his head, propping it up no doubt so he'd had a better view of me undressing. How much more had he drunk? A flush colored his normally pale cheeks and his eyes held a twinkle of promise. I stood over him. "I think you're too drunk."

He smiled at me, that heart wrenchingly boyish smile he still possessed even in his mid-thirties. "You might be right." He freed one hand and touched my thigh with his fingertips, caressing the skin.

A shiver coursed through my body. I returned his smile. "Going to show me your sword, soldier?"

He chuckled and his hand went to the laces on his braccae. "I was thinking of doing just that."

I sat down on the edge of the bed and batted his hand away from his laces. "I think I might undo these for you."

He lay back again while I loosened the laces, the bulge in his braccae telling me how ready he was for this, watching, but not touching, his eyes undressing me. Shivers coursed up and down my body and a delicious ache settled in my groin. I slid my hands inside his braccae and took hold of his arousal.

A gasp escaped his lips and he arched his back for a moment.

With a smile that might have been wicked, I released him and moved down the bed to pull his boots off. His feet were bare, and freshly washed. I lowered my mouth and sucked his big toe for a moment, letting him picture what else I might do later. Another gasp that turned into a groan, his whole body stiffening under the touch of my lips and tongue.

"You're in the wrong place," he whispered.

I laughed. "And you're wearing too many clothes." I gave his braccae a tug. "I need to get these off you."

He wriggled out of them as I pulled, and in a moment his shirt joined them on the floor by the bed. Then he sat up and reached for me and I went to him.

He tugged at my linen shirt. "I don't know why you bothered to put this on. You aren't going to need it tonight. You're sleeping with a man who has the sword of an emperor."

I glanced down at his arousal. "So I can see. But it all depends on whether you can use it like an emperor, doesn't it?"

He pulled me closer, our bellies pressed together. "Want to find out?"

Silly question. I leaned forward and kissed him on the lips.

Chapter Twenty-Nine

Summer became a long, golden autumn, still with no raids from either the Saxons in the east or the Irish in the west. Instead of instilling in me a feeling of security, though, it generated an uncomfortable sense of foreboding, as though everything and everyone were holding their concerted breaths and waiting for something bad to happen.

No further news came of Cadwy making use of his extra weapons, and Arthur steadfastly refused to believe he might have gone back on his word. "We might not like each other," he said, vastly underestimating the animosity between them, "but if he's given his word, then I have to believe he won't go back on it."

Hmmm.

Merlin agreed with me. "I don't know why Arthur persists in trying to find something good in that man," he muttered to me one afternoon while we were watching the boys riding at a target on the practice grounds. Amhar had already fallen off twice and was red in the face with fury.

"People are never all one thing," I said, wondering why I was arguing for Cadwy for once, but remembering his tears when he'd discovered how he'd inadvertently poisoned the old woman who'd been his nurse, all those years ago. "I don't believe anyone can be bad through and through. But I don't believe Cadwy's changed his spots, either."

Merlin raised his eyebrows. "His spots?"

"A saying from my time. It means that once you're one way, you're unlikely to ever change." Would he have known what a leopard was? Maybe, but I wasn't going to get into a zoological discussion right now.

"What do *you* believe?" Merlin asked, narrowing his eyes against the low sun. "Do you think he meant what he said when he swore allegiance to Arthur?"

I screwed up my mouth and sighed. "I think he did. He's not stupid. He's seen how close the Irish came to Viroconium that time. He must know that if he doesn't support Arthur – or rather his position as High King – he'll lay the center of Britain open to attack. And that means Viroconium. I really do think he's still holding to his promise."

Merlin snorted in a way that indicated he wasn't so sure.

I returned my gaze to where Amhar was now back on Saeth and preparing to charge the target once more. You had to be quick when you hit it, or the weighted sack would swing round and knock you off your horse. He set his heels to Saeth's sides, and galloped toward the round wooden target. Bam. Off he went, landing spreadeagled in the dirt. Not fast enough... again.

⸻

EARLY IN THE evening about a week after my conversation with Merlin, one of our young warriors came racing up from the fortress wall-walk toward the Hall.

From my position relaxing on a stool under the porch's overhanging thatch, I watched his rapid progress in curiosity. Arthur, seated next to me polishing Excalibur's new, red-leather scabbard, stopped what he was doing and stared down the road as the young man drew nearer.

Archfedd, who'd been sitting cross-legged at her father's feet, stopped rubbing grease into her winter boots and stared as well. "Who's that coming?" she asked, her high, piping voice carrying through the still warm air.

I peered through the gloaming as the young man approached. "It looks like Mabon." My heart gave a little lurch, and my stomach knotted. Whenever someone was in haste, particularly a warrior, it never seemed to bode well.

As Mabon reached us, Arthur laid his scabbard aside and got to his feet. The young warrior's breath heaved from the exertion. Warriors have strong sword arms, but running, especially up a steep slope, doesn't come naturally to a man who's usually mounted.

"Milord," the sandy-haired young man, one of Llacheu's friends, gasped out between pants. Remembering himself, he performed a hasty bow. "Smoke spotted in the east. There's a fire burning. Thick, dark smoke. Looks like a beacon fire." The warriors who manned our early-warning beacons kept green branches ready to make their smoke more visible if they had to light their fires. It seemed they'd at last come in handy.

The young man straightened. "It was me spotted it, Milord. Just a trickle to start with, then it billowed up thick and fast. Not a hearth fire. My Watch Commander sent me straight to you."

Arthur gave him a curt nod. "Where? Show me."

Mabon moved to point between the clustered buildings, Arthur close beside him. I followed, my nervous heart banging against my ribs. Sure enough, away to the east a column of dark smoke rose straight up into the pale evening sky, there being no breeze to speak of to snatch it away.

Behind us, Archfedd laid aside her own cleaning rag and scrambled to her feet. "Can I see?" She pushed between Arthur and me. "Where is it?"

I picked her up to give her a better view, acutely aware of how heavy she'd grown of late. "There. It's telling your papa there are enemy warriors in that direction." I paused, not wanting to frighten her. "That they're attacking someone over there – a long way off."

Her hazel eyes widened. "Is it the Yellow Hairs? Are they coming here?"

I shook my head. "No. You're safe. We all are. But Papa will have to go to help whoever lit that fire. He's High King, and it's his responsibility."

Archfedd's lower lip trembled. Now she'd grown so big, I sometimes forgot how young she really was. "I don't like it when Papa has to leave us," she whispered. "I want him to stay here. With me. I need keeping safe, too. And so does he."

Was this Badon coming? Was Nennius even correct in his list of battles?

I hugged her close, her sweet-smelling hair against my cheek. "Don't worry. You're safe, and he'll be safe, as well. I know he will. I promise. Mami has special powers and knows these things."

Not really a lie.

Arthur swung away from the view of the far-off signal fire. "Go and find Merlin," he said to Mabon, before striding across our hall courtyard to where Cei was sitting on his own front step, oiling his sword. Only he, too, had stopped work when Mabon arrived, and now the sword rested on his knees as he watched his brother's purposeful approach. I followed Arthur more slowly, still holding Archfedd close.

Just inside the open doorway, Coventina and Reaghan, who'd been working together at their loom, had also stopped work to look up, an anxious frown already formed on Coventina's brow. Reaghan slid off her low stool and came to stand beside her father, one hand on his solid shoulder, her gaze on Archfedd, eyes wide.

"Trouble in the east," Arthur said. "Close. A burning beacon off toward Caer Guinntguic."

Coventina staggered to her feet, one hand to her mouth, the other steadying herself on the frame of the loom. "Oh God." It came out as a whisper, but carried through the still evening air. "I knew this summer's peace couldn't last." Her other hand clutched at the crucifix she wore around her neck. "But this late in the year?"

Reaghan's head swivelled to stare at her mother's stricken face. We all knew what the lighting of a beacon meant, and Coventina had more cause to fear it than some.

Cei rose from the stone slab he'd been sitting on and slid his shining sword home into its sheath, as Reaghan's small hand fastened onto the hem of his tunic. He stared into his brother's eyes. "It's near sunset. Do you want to set off tonight?"

Arthur held his gaze for a long moment before shaking his head. "No. First light will be soon enough. But we can't delay. I need you to go and organize the men. Let them know what's happened. I've a feeling in my bones that we'll need to take as many with us as we can. We'll leave only a skeleton force here."

Archfedd stiffened in my arms, and I hugged her closer still. Like any child here, she understood the significance of the words "skeleton force" – enough to protect us from isolatated raiders, but not enough should the full force of the Saxon army fall on the fortress. And nowhere for us to run to.

With a grim smile, Cei nodded briefly. Then he buckled his sword belt around his waist and strode off toward the barracks.

Eyes brimming with fear, Coventina met my gaze. She put a protective hand on Reaghan's ginger hair, then drew her closer, pressing her child's chubby face against her body. Reaghan put her arms around her mother's waist and held on tight.

I nodded to her, Archfedd's downy cheek to mine, conscious of a flow of fellow feeling running like a current between us.

But the difference between us was that I wasn't about to let Arthur ride off east on his own. Wherever he was bound, I'd be going too.

⟫⟫⟫⟪⟪⟪

IT TOOK THREE stories to settle Archfedd to sleep that night. Although sometimes content with Maia's tales of gods and heroes, tonight she'd wanted me and my fanciful tales of lands she'd never see. Perhaps because stories like that contained so many things that could only ever exist inside our heads, she felt they'd take her mind off the crowding fears of her everyday life. God knew, I needed that myself.

I chose the ones she liked the best – where the heroes overthrew the villains and there was a suitable "happy ever after." *Cinderella*, *The Three Little Pigs*, and *Rapunzel*: I spun them out with superfluous detail designed to bore her and send her off to sleep.

At last, it worked, and I extricated myself from her bed and left her in Maia's watchful care. Shutting the door with as little noise as possible, I retreated into our chamber. It was empty of Arthur, just as I'd expected. He had a lot to prepare for his departure in the morning.

However, with him absent, I took the opportunity to forestall him and pack my own saddlebags with what I'd need for the march and for a battle. Spare tunic and braccae, underwear of course, my own medical kit of clean bandages, honey, healing herbs, sharp needles and tough thread for stitches, and strong spirit for sterilizing.

Once packed, I stowed my bags in a corner where Arthur wouldn't see them. That done, I divested myself of the light, linen day-tunic I wore in summer, washed myself all over in the basin of water Maia had left, and brushed my teeth with the delicious combination of powdered charcoal and mint leaves. That took a bit of spitting out, as usual. However, as in the last twelve years I hadn't had the slightest problem with my teeth, it must have been working. That, and the lack of sweet things on the menu.

Outside, the sun had set, and the glorious red sky that foretold another fine day to come, had faded to darkness by the time I slid between the covers of our bed, determined to stay awake until Arthur joined me. I settled myself against the pillows, wishing I had a book to read. Zero chance of that. Hopefully the strung-out state of my nerves would keep me from nodding off.

Time moved at a snail's pace.

I'd left a single clay lamp burning, but as the minutes ticked past, the lengthening shadows in my chamber crept toward it, threatening to snuff it out. Or was that my eyelids drooping? I shook myself awake, listening out for sounds in the Hall that would tell me he'd returned.

Nothing.

My eyelids drooped again. I fought them, but down they fell, like a heavy curtain. I yawned, slipping lower in the bed, head nodding.

Chapter Thirty

I JERKED AWAKE. The clay oil lamp had gone out, sweat prickled on my skin, and the air felt hot and heavy despite the lateness in the year. My heartbeat thundered in my ears, and I strained my eyes to see, blindfolded by the cloying darkness.

A clunk. The door from the hall opened, creaking on hinges in need of oiling. Arthur padded in carrying a single tallow candle, his hand sheltering its flickering flame. The golden light threw his face into planes of light and dark, catching his eyes and making them glitter like gold.

"Arthur." The word came out on a breathy gasp from the sudden awakening.

He stopped. "Sorry. I was trying not to wake you." He kept his voice low as though afraid he might disturb someone else.

"You didn't. I had a bad dream." I kept my voice to a whisper, complicit in his effort to be silent.

He came to the bed and set the candle down on his clothes chest. "A nightmare?"

Too late, I remembered how prone everyone here was to reading too much into any kind of dream, especially before a military campaign. "Not that sort," I whispered, unable to prevent the shiver that shook my body, the sweat turning to ice on my skin. "Don't worry. I didn't see you lying dead anywhere. You've years yet to live."

I managed a small laugh, in an effort to reassure, conscious of the fact that one day he'd be riding off to battle and I would be just as certain of the opposite. Because then it would be to Camlann he'd be riding. And who was I to say how many years off that might be? Medraut was already well on his way to becoming a warrior. Time concertinaed itself inside my head and my hands gripped the covers so hard my knuckles must have whitened.

He sat on the edge of the bed beside me and put up a gentle hand to brush away a strand of hair that had escaped my braid. "Don't *you* worry, either. I don't believe in omens. You know me better than that."

Not strictly true. But if he wanted to believe that, who was I to argue? I sighed. "I tried to stay awake but failed. I think that's why I was dreaming. You know how restless sleep is when you often have the most vivid dreams."

He put his arms around me and drew me close. "You're chilled. The nights are drawing in. Maia should start putting a hot stone in your bed in the evening." His hands ran over my back. "Let me chase that bad dream away for you." His breath, smelling slightly of wine, warmed my skin.

I snuggled closer. "I want to come with you."

He froze.

I ran a hand down his spine under the soft wool of his tunic. "You need me."

One hand cupped the back of my head, his fingers in my hair. "You think?"

My face was against his throat, so I kissed his stubbly skin. Slightly salty with sweat. "I know it."

Very gently he extricated himself from my embrace, holding me at arm's length. The candlelight flickered over his face. "Is there something you know about this?"

I stared into his dark eyes, where the candlelight picked out the gold flecks and made them glow. I'd once told him that a huge battle at a place called Badon lay ahead of him. Did I really think this was it, coming now? My bones, and something else I didn't understand, but felt certain I had to listen to, told me it was.

Had some hand of fate put me here in the fifth century for this reason? To direct him to Badon? The battle whose fame would resonate down the centuries – well known fifteen hundred years after it was fought. That something other than chance had brought me back to the Dark Ages and into Arthur's life, I knew for certain. Magic. And not just Merlin's magic.

Twelve years ago, Merlin had kidnapped me from my own time to fulfill an ancient prophecy – that a woman bearing the dragon ring would help Arthur to save Britain and become the most famous king of all time. Was he about to ride out to meet that prophecy head on? Every cell in my frightened body screamed that he was.

His eyes bored into mine, and I drowned in their depths. This was the man I loved above all else, the man for whom I'd given up my life in the comfortable twenty-first century and the boyfriend I'd thought I'd spend the rest of my life with. The man I feared would die at Camlann. The man I feared would be taken from me by cruel fate.

Year by year, I'd been counting my way through his battles, the twelve the ninth-century monk Nennius had listed, interspersed with others, unknown to any chronicler, and now we seemed to have come at last to the final one on that shadowy monk's list.

And after that lay only Camlann, with all that entailed.

I swallowed. If I steered Arthur away from this, from Badon, would Camlann never happen? Would my husband die in his bed one day, an old man, with me an old woman by his side? Or would the Saxon take-over of Britain, that loomed inevitable over everything we did, happen that much quicker? Would the arrival of the English, my people, be accelerated? Tears squeezed from the corners of my eyes and trickled down my cheeks.

Did he see them fall?

"Tell me what you know," he said, his voice commanding and firm.

"I think this is Badon coming." My voice came out in a whisper, hissing through the heavy night air.

Silently, he stared at me for a minute that stretched to an eternity. At last, he spoke. "How do you know?"

I swallowed. "I-I don't *know* how I know."

His eyes bored into mine, drawing my secrets out. "Go on."

"I told you about the list." I paused, marshalling my jumbled thoughts. "The twelfth battle is Badon. Sometimes called Mount Badon. Historians think it was perhaps on a hill, a siege."

He shook his head. "I don't fight siege warfare. Never have."

"I know. We shouldn't take their word for it. They all have different theories. Not one of them knows where it truly was, or how it was fought."

"And you?" His eyes narrowed. "You think you do?"

I nodded. "My father had a theory. He took me to where he thought it took place when I was a child. Showed me the lie of the land. Explained why it could most likely have been there. Why he was convinced it had been."

His eyes flashed. "Where? Tell me, and we'll know where those Saxons are heading."

⸻

MY FATHER STANDS before me on a windy hilltop, silhouetted against a patchy sky. Clouds race high above us as I stand on all that remains of the ramparts of Liddington Castle, an Iron Age fortress on the ancient Ridgeway track. His long gray hair blows out behind him, and his lined face contorts with fanaticism. "See here, Gwennie?" He has to shout above the wind. "Come up here and you'll be able to. Give me your hand."

I take the proffered hand, and he hauls me on my still short legs to stand by his side, staring eastward. The land undulates, chalk downs stretching away almost to the Berkshire town of Newbury, while the fat gray snake of the M4 motorway thunders in the distance. Nose to tail lorries, drivers rushing through their lives at constant breakneck speed.

Here on the downs, the sense of otherworldliness presses in all around me. The soughing of the wind in the distant trees, the call of windblown larks high above our heads, the muffled chirruping of insects in the long grass. The twenty-first century feels far away, and we might be in any time.

"Look," he says, pointing a gnarled finger. "See that brow?'

I nod, the wind snatching my voice.

"That little road you can see follows the Ermin Way almost exactly. A new road set on an ancient thoroughfare. That's the road up from Silchester, once called Calleva Attrebatum, to Cirencester, which was Roman Corinium. Only, in the Dark Ages they were Caer Celemion and Caer Ceri."

I nod, fascinated as always by the stories he can weave and bring to life. "From here a lookout would see anyone coming along that road, wouldn't they?" I ask.

He beams with pride. "Quite right. Most perceptive. And this is the road that would have brought the invading Saxon army up from the Thames valley. They'd have used the old Roman roads every bit as much as the British kings. The lands were largely undrained and pretty boggy in places, not conducive to easy passage. The Roman network had already picked out the best routes to travel – why would invaders have come by any other route? Most battles for a good thousand years after the Romans left were beside Roman roads."

I nod again, proud myself to be privy to his theories, chest swelling with importance. My brother, Artie, has shown no interest in my father's work, but the mystery of it fascinates me.

"And just beyond that brow," my father says, with the air of a conjuror about to take a rabbit out of his hat, "lies a village actually called Baydon. Coincidence, or what?" He gestures around himself at the circle of the grass-covered defensive bank. "And believe it or not, this place, Liddington Castle, was once called Badbury Castle." He beams. "What other proof could anyone want that this, or somewhere close by, was the site of the famous Battle of Badon? Where Arthur defeated the Saxons under Aelle once and for all."

>>><<<

SILENCE FELL BETWEEN Arthur and me as what I'd had to tell him sunk in. His grip on my shoulders slackened and he let his hands drop. "And you think your father was right?" he asked, after a moment.

I nodded. "I do. I think I was put here for a purpose. I know you say you don't believe that prophecy, and that I said I didn't as well. But, come on. How much have I helped? Directed you to the battles you needed to be fighting?"

His brow furrowed, giving him a look of his unlovely brother for just an instant. "You think they'll be marching along the road from Caer Celemion, from the valley of the Tamesis?"

I nodded. I was doing a lot of nodding. "I do."

He shrugged.

I put a hand on his arm. "They intend to have Britain and all her kingdoms for their own. Of that I'm certain." My head twisted toward the table, where it lay hidden in the shadows. "I need a map, and I can show you the place I mean."

His tongue darted out to lick his lips. "I think I know the spot you've described. On the ridge of hills between Caer Ceri and old Spinae there's a high scarp face to the downs, facing west. Along the ancient track that follows the highest ground sit a row of old defensive forts."

"We call it the Ridgeway track in my old world."

He laughed. "It's the Ridgeway here as well. And the Roman road passes close by, following a wide valley. Where it crosses that Ridgeway path, you mean there, don't you?"

"Yes. Is the fort above it still fortified? Defendable?"

He shook his head. "Sadly not, save by a handful of men with a beacon fire. Only the shades of the old inhabitants remain, I'd imagine. And this'll please you – it's called Dinas Badan. I think your father might well have been correct."

He got up and disappeared back into the Hall, returning in a few moments with one of my carefully drawn maps in his hands. Not large, as the vellum I used, made from a single calf skin, had limited size. He fetched his candle closer. "Show me, then."

I unrolled the map, and he sat down beside me on the bed. The vellum felt fine and smooth under my fingers, the ink lines etched across it in a spidery network of roads and rivers, hills and forests, added to year by year as more information had come my way. Squares marked the towns, circles the hillforts, their names written in tiny, careful lettering. All gleaned from what I could remember of the layout of modern Britain combined with what I now knew of the once strange world around me.

But I'd made these maps with an eye to a purpose other than to ease the navigation skills of my husband and his army. With a hope in my heart that maybe, written on long-lasting vellum, one day they might be seen by future generations. With this in mind, I'd also marked on the sites of Arthur's battles, all lost to history in my old world. Wouldn't scholars love to find these.

I jabbed my finger at the center. "They'll be heading for the heartlands of Britain, and Badon is on their way. This is where the village of that name is in my time." I put my finger on the line of chalk hills that Ermin Street crossed. "And that's where you must meet them. At Badon."

He studied the map. "So." He grinned mirthlessly, teeth white in the candlelight. "I shall do just that. If it's written in your history books as the site of a great victory, then that's where I'll meet them. And I will beat them." He kissed my hair. "And it will be the battle to end all battles, just as you say." He put an arm around my shoulders, pulling me close. "Between us, Gwen, we'll write those missing history books for the people of your old world to read."

I wrapped my arms around him, his heartbeat pounding in my ear. "The Saxons will have an enormous army. This is their major push to take over Britain for themselves, and you have to stop them. But to do that you're going to need help."

"From you?"

I shook my head. "No. Not me. From the other kings." I peered up at him. "From Cerdic and from Cadwy. They're your nearest allies now. They can get help to us the quickest. You're going to need to work with both of them to bring about a lasting defeat that'll set the Saxons back for years, as you're meant to do. Cooperation's the only way."

Chapter Thirty-One

THE FIRST MESSENGER from the east arrived in the middle of the night, hot on the heels of the beacon fire. Arthur got out of bed and padded through to the Hall to receive his message in just his braccae and undershirt, and in a hurry, I wrapped myself in a blanket and followed him, the reeds underfoot prickling my bare feet.

The messenger, a slender boy hardly older than Medraut, made us a low bow and held out a crumpled roll of parchment. "Milord. 'Tis from King Cerdic."

Arthur unrolled the parchment and read it through, then passed it to me. I flicked my gaze over the spidery writing. It seemed that yesterday, the citizens of Caer Guinntguic had been treated to the terrifying sight of a huge force of Saxons marching within a mile of their city. They'd passed near enough to cause total panic amongst the inhabitants, and Cerdic had readied his warriors to ride out. But the Saxons had marched on past, as though uninterested by even so great a city as Guinntguic.

"Tell me what you yourself saw," Arthur said, fixing the boy with a firm stare. "The truth only. No hyperbole."

The boy sucked in his lips before he spoke. "'Twas as though we weren't enough for them." He shook his shaggy mane of auburn hair. "As though they were turning their noses up at us as not important."

The door of the hall opened, and Merlin hurried in. He halted a few steps back, eyes going from Arthur to the boy. I passed him the parchment to read.

"How many did you see?" Arthur asked.

The boy straightened a little as though more confident when asked about numbers. "I'd say ten keels of warriors, Milord. Reckoning's something I'm good at, being as my father's a shepherd. I can count how many sheep're in a flock in moments. Marching men're the same. I'd say four hundred, easy."

Arthur shook his head. "And yet they marched on past your walls. Leaving you untouched."

Merlin let the parchment roll back up in his hands. "A touch of loyalty for his nephew, perhaps. Maybe he thinks if he leaves Cerdic and his people unmolested, they won't feel constrained to join us."

Arthur glanced at his friend and nodded, worry at the back of his eyes. "Giving Cerdic the option to sit on the fence and do nothing, then claim he backed the winning side."

Not a comforting thought, reminding me uncomfortably of Lord Stanley at the Battle of Bosworth, waiting until he saw which way the wind was blowing before entering the battle on that usurping Henry Tudor's side. I'd always been a fan of Richard III.

Merlin found a blanket for the messenger, and we went back to bed, but it was impossible to sleep properly. I tossed and turned for some time, aware that Arthur was doing the same. Before first light the second messenger, this time from King Einion in Caer Celemion, arrived. We pulled our clothes on before going through to the hall to receive his message.

Another lightweight boy barely into his teens. This one came to us dusty and travel-weary, his eyes red-rimmed but back ramrod straight, fully aware of the importance of his mission.

All he could tell us was that a second, similarly large force of Saxons had landed on the south bank of the Tamesis, left only a small guard over their beached ships, and set off in a direction that sounded as though it would take them to meet the northbound troops from the south coast. When he'd left, late last night, the king had still held his fortified town. But who knew what the situation might be now?

"Two armies," Cei said. He'd come in a few minutes ago along with Merlin, both of them with dark circles beneath their eyes betraying their lack of sleep.

Arthur nodded, grim faced, and fixed the boy with a hard stare. "How many keels?"

The boy's gaze shifted as though uncomfortable, and his mouth opened, then closed again. "I-I don't know, Milord. I didn't see 'em for myself." He was gabbling, embarrassed about his own inadequacy, no doubt. "We had news from the farmers near the river, and the king did say as he weren't sure they could even count. One said twenty keels, another ten. A third – there was three of 'em came – said fourteen."

Forty men to a keel, so anywhere between four hundred, minus those guarding their ships, to eight hundred men had come ashore, most likely to the east of modern Reading. A daunting prospect when in all likelihood another four hundred were marching to meet them from the south. A massive force. Far more than we could fight alone, even with the advantage of being on horseback. They meant business.

Biting my lip, I glanced at Arthur, but he was bending over the map.

Seemingly unfazed, he traced the course of the Thames with his finger. "No point in heading to where they've been. We need to prepare a welcoming party where they're headed." He jabbed the site of last year's battle of Trwfrwyd, a few miles east of where the Kennet joined the Tamesis. "Here is where they'll have landed. Last year's incursion must have been them deciding where to land this year. Testing us out. Seeing what forces we could muster to counter them."

"Where is it you suggest we meet them, then?" Cei asked.

Arthur grinned, mirthlessly. "A place of our choice, not theirs. A place where we can beat them."

Cei raised his bushy ginger brows. "And where's that?" A hint of skepticism had sneaked its way into his voice.

Arthur grimaced. "That's the big question."

Badon of course. I stayed silent, watching.

Merlin pointed. "If they have as many men as we think, they'll be heading west as soon as they can, because supplies will be their problem. They'll want to take us by surprise, and strike at the heart of Britain without warning and as hard as they can." He tapped the map. "They're not fools. They'll use the old Roman roads, same as we do. Easier by far than marching across country on foot." His finger traced a line on the map. "This road here – the road between Caer Celemion and Caer Ceri. That's the one they'll take. It heads pretty much due west into the center of our power."

Just as I'd told Arthur. Comforting to know Merlin was in agreement.

Arthur nodded. "My thinking entirely. Once they muster their full force, there's no other route they could sensibly take with that many men. See here? This line of hills?" He indicated what would one day become known as the Marlborough Downs. "Right here is an old hill fort, not large and long fallen out of use, but a good place to base ourselves. My father took me there once when I was a boy."

Cei nodded. "I remember that. I was little – you were littler still. We camped within the fortress." He grinned at the memory.

Arthur drew a line with his finger, eastwards. "And from its grassy ramparts you have a view back along the road, a good three or four miles. The brow… here. My father showed us."

How apt that his father had shown him the exact same view my father had shown me. Two children with their fathers, fifteen hundred years apart. Fitting. My father would have loved to have known he'd stood in Uthyr Pendragon's very footprints.

Arthur tapped the map, further east along the Roman road. "This will be a good spot to place a lookout, with others further out, strung along the road. The Saxons will have to climb steadily uphill from the

Kennet valley. We'll have good warning of their approach."

"This fort," Merlin said. "Does it have a name?"

My turn to speak. "Dinas Badan," I said, meeting his eyes. "Badon." The name fell heavily into the room, as though from instinct others recognized its meaning.

Merlin's eyes widened, and I fixed him with a meaningful stare.

Arthur grinned, an irrepressible light kindling in his eyes – suddenly a man who knew he was on the verge of making history. "My father told me no one had lived there since long before the legions. We rode the ancient Ridgeway track together, past many wonders from that time. On the side of a hill not far north from there a huge white horse gallops, carved out of the chalk. An auspicious sign from our ancestors."

I'd been there too – the Uffington White Horse – origin unknown. I wasn't sure they'd meant it as a sign that Arthur would win at Badon, though.

He gave his head a shake as though to clear it and tapped the map again just east of where I'd marked the abandoned fort with a circle. "This will be a good place to take them. The road runs on lower lying land sandwiched between high hills, and there's still some remnants of ancient forest. The Saxons will be confident in their numbers and won't be expecting an ambush as they can know nothing of our speedy messaging system."

Straightening again, he encompassed us all with his gaze. "It's *me* they want to defeat. They think that once the High King falls, the rest of Britain will capitulate. They seek to make an example of me." He grinned again, and this time all the mirth vanished. "Of *us*."

He pulled me closer and threw an arm around my shoulders, laughing – a harsh, defiant sound. "But as well as having no idea of our messenger system, they also don't have the benefit of accurate maps, as we do, and they're riding into what for them is uncharted territory. They can have little idea what lies ahead. We'll lay a trap that'll send them running with their tails between their legs. The ones that survive, that is."

"Alone?" Cei asked. "If they join up and bring two armies against us, then we'll be outnumbered two to one." His turn to grin. "Not that I don't think every one of our men is worth ten of theirs, of course."

Arthur shook his head. "No. Not alone. I've already sent out riders. Last night as soon as we saw the signal fire and set our own. North to Viroconium, and east to Caer Guinntguic, asking for help from Cadwy and Cerdic." He pulled a rueful face. "If, that is, Cerdic decides to take our side, after having been spared by his uncle."

Cei's eyes widened. "Caer Guinntguic? Cerdic may be half Saxon, but he's half British too. And that's his father's half – the half that matters."

Arthur shot me a sideways glance. "That's what I'm counting on."

Cei kept going. "And you've asked Cadwy for help as well? Are you mad?"

With a shake of his head, Arthur removed the stone weights and rolled up the map. "No, I'm not mad. The Saxons marched on past Caer Guinntguic, and Cerdic wisely stayed within his walls and watched them do so. Why fight and die when you can live to fight another day – and win? He pledged me loyalty at the Council of Kings – the first to do so. He may have Saxon blood in his veins, but I have to trust that he'll come. And as for Cadwy, hasn't he, too, sworn to support me? When I need support?"

Cei snorted. "I trust Cerdic and his Saxon blood more than I trust Cadwy, who shares your own. He'll weigh up whether it's good for him or not, before letting a single man of his take a step on the road to meet us."

Merlin narrowed his eyes and nodded. "Swearing to send support is an entirely different thing to actually sending it."

Too true. Would Cadwy come when called? Behind my back, I crossed my fingers.

Thanks to our system of messengers with fast horses, Arthur's request for help would reach Caer Guinntguic, sixty miles away, by mid-afternoon, and Viroconium, a good hundred and sixty miles distant, within a day. But even if they set out straightaway, it could be days before we would see what support would be forthcoming. If any.

A big risk to take.

Chapter Thirty-Two

OUTSIDE THE HALL, the eastern horizon showed pink and gold, but as yet no sun had risen. In front of the stables, our men were mounting up in the chilly twilit morning, rubbing sleep from their eyes and yawning. I knew how they felt.

A few curls of smoke rose from the darkly thatched rooftops telling us some of the women were up and tending their hearths, but for the most part no one else stirred. Except for the fine-feathered cockerel who, disturbed by our noise, had strutted up to the peak of the Hall roof to rustily crow his morning greeting.

"Stupid bird," Cei muttered, grumpy at this early hour, and hurled a stone in its general direction. It missed. The cockerel fluffed himself up proudly and crowed again, as though gloating over Cei's poor aim. Arthur laughed, and even Merlin, somber-faced this morning, managed a smile.

A couple of servants led our horses out of the stables, the beasts puffing clouds of warm breath that hung like statues in the air. Arthur's was Taran, the flashy bay King Garbaniawn of Ebrauc had gifted him after Llamrei's death in battle. My Alezan, beautiful and contrary as usual, snapped at Taran in passing, ears flat back and eyes rolling her displeasure. Mind you, she'd never liked poor Llamrei either.

I took her reins from the servant and swung myself into the saddle, quickly finding my other stirrup. The servant passed me my shield and helmet, and I hooked them on the saddle horns just as the men had done. Someone had already attached my saddlebags.

A movement in the darkness of the stable doorway caught my eye. Amhar stood there, half-hidden, with his hand on the stout doorpost, brow lowered and lower-lip jutting, his eyes fixed on his father.

Arthur gathered Taran's reins and set his foot in the stirrup, ready to mount, but before he could do so, Amhar bolted toward him out of the stables and grabbed his sleeve. Arthur swung around, eyes flashing, and mouth open ready to protest.

Seeing the expression on his father's face, Amhar released the sleeve and stepped back, blanching.

Not a good time to be approaching his father.

Arthur took his foot out of the stirrup and faced Amhar, impatience written across his face and in his stance. "What is it? What d'you want? We're in a hurry."

For a moment Amhar stared at him wide-eyed, his mouth opening and shutting as though no words would come.

Arthur grunted his displeasure. "If you haven't got anything to say, then go and do something useful somewhere else." He turned back to Taran.

"Take me with you!" The words shot out of Amhar most likely faster and more loudly than he'd intended. Two spots of bright color flamed on his cheeks, but he stood his ground.

Oh no.

Arthur turned back, face dark with anger. "What? Take you with me? Into battle? Are you mad? You're not twelve years old yet." He scowled at his son. "And you're too small to fight. Go and eat your breakfast and do some growing."

Amhar staggered backwards, the color spreading across his face. Arthur turned back to Taran and didn't see him dive down one of the side alleys between the buildings, stricken. But I did.

Just for a moment, I was torn. The need to dismount and run after my child battled with my need to go with my husband to this most fateful of battles. Alezan, picking up my disquiet, fidgeted under me, impatient hooves marking time in the dirt.

Arthur settled into his saddle and without another word, spun Taran around toward the track down to the main gates.

What to do? I peered down the alleyway, but Amhar had vanished. Go or stay?

Arthur had joined Cei and Merlin at the head of our army without a backward glance for me or our son. What had he done? Knocked Amhar back yet again. Did he have no tact? The wrong time for Amhar to have tackled him, for sure, but being a father meant making time for your children, even when pressed by urgency.

For a long moment, I dithered, as the last of our warriors joined the file of riders, and the head of the column passed through the gates.

If I went after Amhar they'd leave me behind. Despite my instincts screaming at me to go to my son, dealing with his hurt feelings would have to wait. Badon was now, within days, and Arthur needed me more. But was that the right decision? Who could tell? All I knew was that I had to concentrate on Arthur.

I fell in at the rear of the column, the many unshod hooves rumbling on the cobbled road. We were off to war, ready to defend our lands.

As I forced myself to think of Badon, lying ahead with its teasing promise of victory, my insides coiled themselves tight with trepidation, not just for the coming battle but for my son.

Don't think of him. Think of Badon.

Could I trust a legend? Just because they said we were riding out to victory didn't mean any of that was true. Perhaps my presence here had already changed too much; perhaps all of us were riding to our deaths.

On top of that, the fact that we had no way of knowing if our requested reinforcements would turn up in time to support us didn't help my anxiety.

As we wound our way down Din Cadan's steep hill toward the plain, Merlin hung back to ride alongside me. "I thought you might have changed your mind," he said, glancing back up the hill toward the gatehouse.

I half shook my head, half shrugged. "I nearly did. Amhar needs me." I paused and frowned. "He needs his father."

Merlin gazed ahead at the pale expanse of the plain, dotted here and there with farms. "I saw."

In the east, the sky lightened as the sun peeked above the horizon, gilding the topmost branches of the distant forest, and long morning shadows leapt across the land.

A day for walking in autumnal woods, kicking through the fallen leaves, for taking Archfedd paddling in the stream that skirted the village, for gathering mushrooms, listening to birdsong and sitting in the sun at midday. Not a day for riding out to fight the most important battle of our lives. If I could have put this off indefinitely, I would have.

"Whatever Arthur and Amhar do, it always seems to go wrong. Amhar shouldn't have asked if he could come. He should've known he couldn't, but he asked anyway, almost as if he wanted his father to reject him." I sighed. "And Arthur should have made time for him, even if only a few minutes, to explain gently why he can't come this time. Why he needs to wait until he's older."

Merlin nodded. "You have it in a nutshell."

At the foot of the hill, the column spread out, the men talking together in low voices, as if the quiet of the dawn had soaked into them.

"When we get back," I said, "I'll try to mend their broken bridges."

Slowly, warmth crept over the plain, lifting the dew and bedecking the landscape with a golden hue that gave it the appearance of some ethereal, magical world where no danger could ever be allowed to threaten. For a while, the rhythm of Alezan's steady, springy walk lulled me into almost believing I lived in the romantic world of my imagination.

Merlin's voice brought me crashing back to my terrifying present. "He tells me you advised him where to meet the Saxons," he said, our knees knocking against each other. "That you knew which way they'd be coming."

I stared blankly for a moment and had to shake my head to clear it of the lulling, counterfeit beauty of this savage world. "Long ago my father showed me where he thought this coming battle was... will be." I squinted against the brightness of the rising sun, dazzling as the orb of fire climbed above the horizon. "He was certain his theory was correct. I've only told Arthur what my father once told me."

"That's not how he tells it," Merlin said.

I didn't answer, but looked away from him at the quiet morning unfolding around us. Over toward the Tor, a seasonal mist veiled the marshes in a cotton-wool sea that would hang about all day. Closer, the forest edge showed the foliage of early autumn tipped with gold. Stands of tawny bracken, where the fat hinds hid their youngsters in spring, encroached even onto the grazing lands. A land that should never be defiled by the barbarity of warfare.

"This is it, isn't it?" he asked. "The big one. Badon."

Behind us, the sound of many hooves, the rattle of chain mail, the clink of weapons, played a symphony of threat.

"Tell me what *you* think." Merlin said, his eyes knowing, winkling out the truth from the depths of my heart.

"If he's already told you, then you know," I said. "Why don't you tell me what you think?"

He shook his head. "I asked you first."

I hesitated, frowning some more, deep in thought and studying my hands where they gripped Alezan's reins. Then I looked up. "Something, I don't know what, tells me I'm right. We're going the right way – to the right battle site. That this will be the big one, as you called it."

Again, I hesitated, searching for how to go on. "Everything points in that direction. The arrival of a huge Saxon army, the route they're likely to take. The name of the fortress on the Ridgeway. My father's theory." I shook my head. "Something inside me is telling me this is what we have to do." I heaved a sigh. "But how could I know that? I'm not like you. I don't have the Sight."

Merlin grimaced. "You've had a strong connection with Morgana, though. She's been burrowing inside your head. Twice. Maybe more often than you think. Who knows how that could have affected you."

My eyes widened. The possibility of Morgana's influence hadn't even occurred to me. "Could she be sending me on a wild goose chase?" I asked, horrified. "Could she have made me think something that isn't true? Am I sending Arthur to the wrong place?" My voice rose in panic. The dreadful thought reared its ugly head that the only place she'd want him to go was to his death.

Merlin shrugged, seemingly unaffected by my sudden rush of terror. "Who can tell? Not I. But you. What does your *instinct* tell you? Your heart?"

I pursed my lips and frowned, considering his words with care. "That what I think is true." *But was it?* "That we're on the road to Badon. That Arthur will do what the legends say and defeat the Saxons and fulfill the prophecy I'm part of. That this is the true beginning of his golden age."

Was I only saying this because I hoped it would happen? Because the legends told me it would? If only I didn't know anything at all. Far better to be ignorant.

He smiled, as though reassured. "Then it's true." His hand touched mine. "Your instincts are correct. We ride the road to a battle that will echo down the years, and survive into your time in legend, if not in history. We ride the road of destiny."

A bit melodramatic.

I fell silent, gazing at Arthur up ahead. He and Cei were deep in conversation, their horses jogtrotting from time to time in their excitement to be riding into battle. Horses always know their riders' moods.

Alezan laid her ears back at Merlin's horse and I turned her head away, keeping a tighter rein. "Supposing my instincts aren't right?" I kept my voice low as I put into words my biggest fear.

Merlin, who appeared to have also been studying Arthur's upright back, returned his gaze to me. "You doubt yourself so much?"

I scowled. "I'm not the one with the Sight. No matter what I think – *believe* – no matter whether Morgana worming her way inside my head had anything to do with it. *You* are the one with the Sight. So, what do *you* see happening? Am I right or am I wrong? Surely you can tell me?"

He smiled again, that bloody irritating non-commital smile of his. "I've looked, but I cannot see."

Angry that he could smile and remain so calm over a matter of life and death, my hands were too heavy on the reins and Alezan, ever sensitive, danced sideways. I straightened her up. "Well, look again," I hissed at him. "What's the use of having someone with the Sight advising us, if when we need you to see, you never can?"

He sighed. "I've told you before that I have no control over what I see. I can't do it to order." He edged his horse closer. "If what you fear about Medraut is true, then this is not the battle where Arthur dies. Remember that."

I bit my lip. He had it right, but was any of what I'd told him about Medraut true? Could I rely on legends to interpret history? To tell me about a future that was really the past? Some medieval writer could have made up all of Medraut's story and he could be destined to just be a harmless, if rather unpleasant, nonentity. Nennius could have been wrong. Gildas could have been a liar, which seemed very likely given what I knew of him. Even Bede. There might never be a Camlann.

Badon, in just a few days' time, might be where Arthur died.

Chapter Thirty-Three

As we crossed the wide expanse of the grazing grounds, the lead horses of the column broke into a steady canter, and mine and Merlin's, toward the rear, followed suit. Needless to say, I'd given my saddle a thorough checking to make sure all the stitching was in perfect order. In fact, I'd done it every day since my accident. And Arthur's saddle, too. And Llacheu's, Cei's and Amhar's. No one I loved was going to have an injury caused by faulty saddlery if I could help it.

We traveled the way Roman cavalry had done, only we possessed an advantage over them. We had stirrups, thanks to me. This not only increased the maneuverability of a mounted warrior, but also made long distance riding much more comfortable. Legs didn't have to dangle, and trotting no longer needed to be avoided.

Nevertheless, we cantered a mile, rode at a walk for a mile, then got off and walked on our own two feet for another mile, which helped a lot in preventing riders' stiffness, and rested our horses and saved their backs. Although with every rider being so experienced, even the heaviest, like Cei, rode lightly in the saddle.

The second time we dismounted, Arthur came to walk his horse alongside mine, a spring in his step and a gleam of excitement in his eyes, as though whatever lay ahead might be something wonderful. *Men.* Dark Age men in particular.

The grazing lands still spread wide in all directions, a little parched from the unseasonal lack of rain, the wetlands clearly visible in their verdant hollows. Thanks to the stillness of the day, the smoke from the countless rooftops of scattered farms rose straight up in twisting columns. "I see we're not traveling via Caer Baddan," I said, waving a hand forty-five degrees to my left, northward, and deciding *not* to broach the subject of our son. "If we were, we'd be heading that way."

He nodded. "Well noticed. We haven't time to take the road. We have to get to Dinas Badan by the fastest route, and at this time of year it's faster to go across country than to use the old roads. We'll pass to the north of the plain of Sarum, avoiding the marshy bottoms."

Salisbury Plain. In my old world some of the Plain was used by the army for maneuvers, the rest of it long reclaimed as arable fields by farmers. What would it look like now, in its youth?

I found out by mid-afternoon: very little different to the grazing land around Din Cadan. Our way took us by the northern foothills of the rolling downland, some of it dotted with the raised humps of burial barrows of a long-gone people. Countless small farms nestled in the more sheltered wooded valleys, and thousands of grazing animals kept the grass nibbled short. Similar to the Salisbury Plain I knew, after all, but without the tarmac roads and marching pylons. I knew which I preferred.

Evening brought us to a place I'd once known well. Avebury.

A truly massive bank, grassed over now but once pure white chalk, encircled a well-grazed area a good three hundred and fifty yards across. Workers in the distant past had excavated an impressive ditch and thrown up the chalk to construct the outer bank. In my old world, this ditch and bank were still large, but here, without fifteen hundred years of further erosion, they must have possessed nearly their orginal dimensions.

But it was what lay inside that took my breath away as we rode through the southern entrance at the close of day. A vast, nearly complete circle of stones ran around the interior just inside the ditch. Massive rocks, taller than a mounted man, that had been somehow dragged here and set up for who knew what reason by men whose only tools were stone. Before the Iron Age, before the Bronze age even, Neolithic farmers had thought to build this enormous temple, if that was what it was. Barely any of it remained in my time, having been broken up and used for building the village that occupied the center.

Two further circles stood within the outer ring, each a good hundred yards across, and within one of them a horseshoe of larger stones reared upright. How my father would have loved to see Avebury in all its former glory.

"Built by giants," Arthur, who was riding by my side and must have seen my look of wonder, remarked. "Long before men lived here in Britain. I've seen other circles like this one. No normal man could have set these stones up." He glanced toward Merlin. "Not unless he had a powerful man of magic in his employ."

As good an explanation as I was going to get. Even in my old world, theories abounded about how primitive man had moved stones weighing several tons. If I told either of them the current ideas, they wouldn't have believed me anyway.

The sun had sunk low in the west, casting the long shadows of the stones across short grass dotted with sheep droppings. No sheep to be seen, though, which was probably lucky for them, as a bit of roast mutton would have been very attractive to our men. And me. My stomach rumbled at the distant memory of the bread and cheese I'd eaten at mid-day.

The last rays of light, blazing between the branches of the trees that clustered outside the bank, gilded the ancient stones where they stood in their timeless circle like sentinels to another world.

Arthur reined in his horse. "We'll make our camp here. It's late and this place is sheltered. A good spot to stop."

Cei gave him a doubtful look. "You're sure? This is an ancient holy place." He jerked his head at the men filing in behind us. "Not all of them will be happy with spending a night here."

With a shrug of his shoulders, Arthur dismissed their fears. "Don't the priests teach us there are no such things as spirits of past men? We're Christians now, with nothing to fear from ghosts, only our own imaginations. We make camp here."

With a resigned frown, Cei twisted in his saddle. "Dismount. We're making camp here."

A few of the nearest men exchanged nervous glances, but they were accustomed to obey, and everyone swung down from their saddles with evident relief. We must have ridden forty miles or more that day, and legs and bottoms had suffered. No one raised any objection.

"They don't like stone circles or tombs, nor even barrows." Merlin kept his voice low. "They think evil spirits dwell in them. The unquiet spirits of the people who came before us. Barrow wights and such." He grimaced. "They say human sacrifices were made here. Who knows?"

I had to admit, I wasn't keen to spend the night inside an ancient stone circle myself. The nearest stones loomed over us as we unsaddled our horses, sinister and dark, their silence threatening now the sun had vanished.

But I didn't intend to let Merlin think me a coward, or worse, as superstitious as the men. "Rubbish," I said, with more determination than I felt. "Arthur's right. This is a good place to make camp."

His wry smile told me he hadn't been fooled. Could he even be a little afraid himself?

Camp was set up quickly, horse lines organized, and the horses fed on the oats we'd brought with us. We'd watered them at the stream outside the western bank, and they'd have to do without more until the morning.

Their horses cared for, the men hurried off to search for fallen wood under the trees to the east, and several campfires soon blazed. Those men of the first watch took bread and cheese to positions at intervals along the bank, several of them carrying skins of cider.

Everyone else crowded around the fires, probably for a reason other than heat, and the smell of our dried meat bubbling with onions and barley rose into the night sky, making my mouth water. The men fell naturally into small groups, keeping close together and casting the odd furtive glance over their shoulders into the deep darkness beyond the reach of the firelight.

I couldn't help it. I did the same.

The evening darkened with startling rapidity, plunging the stones into black night for a while until the moon rose over the treetops to the northeast. I sat beside Arthur, leaning against my saddle and with my saddle blanket between my bottom and the cold ground, mopping up my thick stew with a hunk of not-so-fresh bread. I didn't care. When you're hungry almost anything tastes good, and I'd soaked the bread in the gravy to make it more palatable.

In the moonlight the enormous banks rose up around us, darker than the blue-black sky, the silhouettes of the nearest lookouts just visible. The thought of the stones, invisible behind my back, and planted there thousands of years before this day, sent a shiver down my spine. Arthur put his arm around me and drew me close. I rested my tired head on his shoulder.

"Play us a merry tune," Cei called to Gwalchmei. "Chase away the unquiet shades for us."

"There are none," Arthur growled, but not angrily, and not sounding totally convinced.

A chorus of agreement for a song echoed amongst the men, all too obviously nervous about disturbing whatever lay sleeping within these stones.

Arthur bent his head and whispered in my ear. "I don't doubt that if there are indeed any shades here, a merry tune will draw them, poor miserable creatures that they might be."

Perhaps.

Gwalchmei, slight and brown skinned, took his lyre from his saddlebags and strummed his fingers across the strings, adjusting the tuning. Silence fell over the waiting men, everyone's attention caught.

"Sing the one about the innkeeper and the whore," Cei called, and ribald shouts of encouragement filled the night air. Perhaps the dead were listening from amongst the stones. Perhaps a bawdy tune would please them.

Gwalchmei looked up from his strings, a wicked grin on his face. "Aye, I was thinking that'd be a fine one for tonight. You all know the chorus."

And so we sat there in the semi-darkness as he sang the story of a very naughty whore who tried to set up shop in an innkeeper's stables and the variety of customers she serviced, and then deprived of all their money. A lot of very explicit gestures accompanied the chorus which everyone joined in with, Arthur singing along as loudly as the next man.

Hopefully the shades were satisfied. I snuggled close, and let my eyes close.

Chapter Thirty-Four

THE NEXT DAY we reached the long-abandoned hillfort that would one day be called Liddington Castle, where it sat just above the scarp face of the downs, looking west toward the Cotswolds. The rich lowlands of Britain lay spread below the hills, the breadbasket of the island, where oats, barley and wheat grew side-by-side in small, square fields.

Flocks of sheep, tended by wary shepherds, grazed the steep slopes below the old fort, and cattle browsed the lower-lying wetlands, happy to wade hock deep to reach the choicest morsels of grass. Out of sight, some eighteen miles off, lay the tumbled ruins of Caer Ceri – modern Cirencester, and the road north to Viroconium.

Here, on the long ridge of the hills, a warm breeze blew in from across the plain, and the few hawthorn trees that had managed to take root bent eastwards out of long habit, sculpted in apparent supplication by the fiercer winds of winters past.

Only the deep ditch and towering outer bank remained of the fort. No palisading, no stonework to revet a wall-walk, no great hall and no clustered houses or barns. A few stray sheep bolted away from us – wisely – bleating plaintively at the disturbance.

We rode in through the only gateway, although calling it that was to flatter it. Just a gap in the grassy banks gave onto a wide area of about seven or eight acres – enough to feed our horses for a day or two, at least. We'd have to take them to the village sheltering at the hill's foot every day to water them and bring back water for ourselves, though. The villagers weren't going to like that much. Armies don't make for good neighbors.

Our men didn't need telling what to do. Well used to setting up marching camps, they set to with enthusiasm, unsaddling their horses and letting them roll the sweat off their backs before pegging them out on tethers to graze.

I slid down from Alezan with relief after so many hours in the saddle. Beside me, Merlin looked as pleased as me to have his feet back on the ground.

I grinned at him. "Much more of this and I'll end up bandy-legged."

This made him laugh. "There's some like that here already."

True. A quick glance around at the men provided evidence that my worries might be well-founded. More than a few of the older ones walked with the distinct gait of those who rode more than they walked on their own two feet. Clamping my legs together, just in case, I undid Alezan's girth and lifted off her saddle.

The scent of hot horse filled my nostrils. A smell I'd loved since my childhood riding lessons, and one I'd grown familiar with over the last twelve years. I plonked the saddle on the grass, and replaced her bridle with a rope halter and a long line. When I let the rope out to its full extent, she bent her knees and sank to the ground with an audible sigh, then rolled onto her back, legs in the air, rubbing the feel of saddle and rider off her coat.

I envied her. How I'd love to do the same as her to wash the grime of two-days' march off my skin and out of my hair and clothes. Fat chance of that. An army on the move is a smelly thing: hot, as it's nearly always summer when they campaign; sweaty, from having to wear thick padded tunics and heavy mailshirts; and dirty, because there's never enough water for even the smallest wash.

Once Alezan had finished rolling, I took her over to the horse lines where the men were hammering in groundpegs to tether their horses.

Merlin came over. "Give me your peg, and I'll knock it in for you. The ground's rock hard after so long without rain." He was right. The pegs were taking a lot of hammering to get them in far enough to keep the horses secure.

When he'd finished, I fastened Alezan's rope to the ring on the top, giving her a circle of grass she could spend the night grazing down to nothing. Our horses were well used to this.

I thanked him, then went in search of Arthur. Not difficult to spot. The only person standing on top of the eastern bank, his back to the fort's interior. I picked my way between the busy warriors and climbed the bank to stand beside him.

He didn't glance my way, but put out a hand and took mine. "Well," he said. "We're here. At your Badon. Now all we have to do is wait for our allies to arrive and for the enemy. Hopefully in that order, or we'll be buggered."

His rough fingers threaded between mine in that most intimate of gestures. I rubbed my thumb across the back of his hand, feeling the ridge of scar tissue from where I'd stitched his wound on the first day I'd met him. "Cadwy and Cerdic *will* come. They may not be men you like – in fact, they may be men you hate, but they're neither of them stupid."

His lips curved in a smile, but he didn't take his eyes from the distant view. "I'm not so sure about Cadwy. Many of his actions have proved him as not the smartest of men. And don't forget, he's still advised by my lovely sister."

"Even she can't want a Saxon victory here in the south that would leave the road to Viroconium open." Although now I'd said it, uncertainty assailed me. Trying to second guess what Morgana might want had never proved an easy thing.

Arthur extended his free arm and pointed. "See there, right on the brow? That's the road from Caer Celemion. Straight as an arrow.

Nearly four miles away."

I peered along the line he indicated at the view we'd both seen as children – shown by our fathers so prophetically. Trees darkened the brow – a substantial beech hanger just to the right of the road – with the land falling away behind the trees, down into a wide, sweeping valley full of small farms. The Romans had chosen the high ground for their road, following a ridge up from the Thames valley into the hills. A wise choice when so much of the lower-lying land lay wet and impassable.

"How long will it take the enemy to get here?" I asked. What I really meant was how long did we have for our reinforcements to arrive before we had to meet the enemy in battle.

He turned to face me, taking my other hand. "We can only hope they may not feel the urge to hurry. Two days to the river, perhaps. It's not an easy march. And if they've stopped to attack Caer Celemion, then that will give us more time. But they marched past Caer Guinntguic and left it untouched, so it's possible they'll do that to Caer Celemion as well. In search of greater foes and a more meaningful victory."

I moved closer to him, leaning against his chest, my face against the rough rings of his mail shirt, and he gently put his arms around me. I frowned. "I thought they'd not attacked Caer Guinntguic because of blood affinity to Cerdic?"

He shook his head. "I doubt very much that would move them to mercy. No, they're not interested in him or his small town, so near their coastal holdings. Taking that would give them small gains. Their aim must be to strike the center and strike it hard. That's why they'll be meeting with their allies from the river landings. They mean to make this a decisive victory and cripple us." He bared his teeth in a grin. "I'm in agreement on that – only it will be *my* decisive victory and not theirs."

I put my arms around him and stayed silent. If only I could be as confident. Yet doubts assaulted me from all directions: doubts that the legends I knew might turn out to be untrue; doubts that I'd already changed history and therefore Arthur's fate; doubts that whatever convictions I felt might have been false ones sent by Morgana. The weight of the world settled on my shoulders, the weight of this world, at any rate, pushing me down into the ground so hard I almost felt my feet sinking into the earth.

Arthur released me. "Come on. I'm starving. Cold rations tonight, I fear. We don't want to advertise our presence by lighting cook fires." He grabbed my hand again and ran with me down the slope of the bank, the crowd of warriors swallowing us up.

EARLY THE NEXT morning, after a chilly night's sleep, and with a thin autumn mist lying draped over the hills, Arthur led a reconnaissance party to the Roman road. With Merlin's reassurances that no imminent danger threatened, he allowed me to accompany the party, in my guise as record keeper. Nevertheless, we all went armed and armored.

We numbered twenty – Arthur, Cei, Merlin, me, and Llacheu, with the rest made up of some of our staunchest warriors. "Just in case," Arthur said, with a wink. "Merlin might be wrong."

The Ridgeway track down into the valley that bisected the long run of hills proved to have changed little in fifteen hundred years, being chalky and flinty, much as in my old world. The Roman road, the Ermin Way, clung to the northerly side of the valley bottom, heading straight as an arrow toward far off Caer Ceri.

Scrubby woodland had managed to grow here in patches, sheltered more than the high ridge. Hawthorns and juniper thickets bordered a few isolated stands of large beeches that were turning red-gold now in the evening of the year. Our chalky track became a rough path, divided into simple animal-trails, that braided its way northeast between the woodland, heading for the paved road. We followed our noses.

A Roman road is a splendid thing. Those Romans knew how to build something to last, and this road was no exception. A good six or seven paces across, its graveled surface, marred here and there by growth of weeds, stretched impressive and substantial before us. The Ermin Way. Not to be confused with Ermine *Street*, heading north from London to York, and named after a tribe of much later Saxon settlers.

The unshod hooves of our mounts made little noise on the short-cropped grass to either side of the road. A British army marches on its horses' hooves – lose one hoof to lameness, and you lose a warrior, so the stony surface was asking for trouble. Thanks to the time of year and number of grazing livestock, the roadside, although a little rutted and uneven, provided a place to let the horses canter, which we took advantage of, covering the ground at speed as we approached the beech wood on the horizon.

One of the lookouts already posted there emerged from the trees to watch our approach, and a moment later his fellow joined him, adjusting his clothing in haste as if after a toilet visit within the trees.

Our horses slowed, falling from canter into a trot and then a walk in quick succession, blowing slightly in the cold morning air, huffing pillars of moisture to be snatched away to mingle with the thin mist.

The two warriors saluted. "Nothing to report, Milord."

Arthur halted Taran. From here, the low silhouette of Dinas Badan was invisible, camouflaged by the endless sweep of the downs. No smoke to give away our position. Nothing.

Beyond the wide stand of woodland, the road rolled on, straight and true, laid out centuries before by meticulous Roman surveyors who couldn't or wouldn't use curves. It dipped into a deep hollow before rising again to a further summit a little over a mile away, where I guessed the modern village of Baydon would one day lie.

"There," Arthur said, indicating the far hill. "They'll come over that brow, following the road. We'll have good warning of their approach – I've men posted all along this road into Spinae and beyond." He glanced at Cei. "We'll have fifty men lined up here, light-horsemen armed with bows, their mailshirts under their tunics, to let the enemy think they're barely opposed and only by local chieftains."

Everyone watched and listened in silence.

"Then, behind, and out of sight, we'll have the rest of the army. I want the light-horsemen to ride forward and attack the enemy first, with arrows, but from a distance. There'll be a lot of them, and anything we can do to diminish their numbers at the start will be useful. Llacheu, you'll be in command of the mounted archers, but don't let them get close enough to be reached by Saxon throwing spears."

A grin of pure excitement slid over Llacheu's face at the responsibility. His horse, picking up on his mood, danced under him, hooves churning the ground.

Arthur moved on. "We'll tease them a little and lure them into making a charge, keeping our main force hidden. Let them think it's just a few mounted archers standing against them. They've no way of knowing we've had such early word of their arrival." He nodded to Llacheu. "After the attack, you're to retreat back to the brow and let them chase after you. They'll be seasoned warriors, all of them, but I'm banking on the thought of so small an enemy force making them break rank."

He glanced at me then back to his son. "We'll do what we always do – let them run up the hill toward us. You'll be the lure. After they've run up this hill, in battle dress, they'll be tiring just a little. That's when we'll show ourselves, tight formation, lances at the ready. If we hit them hard enough each of us can take out several men on the first charge."

"What if the farmers from Caer Celemion were right?" Merlin

asked. "What if there are twenty keels on the Tamesis banks, and eight hundred warriors joining up with those who marched up past Caer Guinntguic. That's up to twelve hundred men. More than twice our force."

Arthur nodded. "I know." His brow furrowed, probably thinking of our own four hundred. "But ours are mounted and British, and this is not the day we die."

No one said anything, but I couldn't have been the only one wondering if Cadwy and Cerdic would turn up and help even the odds.

Chapter Thirty-Five

DESPITE MY WORRIES, and, surprisingly, even before Cerdic, who had less distance to travel, Cadwy and his men arrived from Viroconium. Two tense days had passed since our own arrival, allowing our horses, who were far more relaxed than I was, to graze their way around the entire seven acres within the ringworks and up the bank as well.

The temperature at night had plummeted, and as usual, lumps abounded wherever I laid my bedroll. On top of that, I was heartily fed up with eating cold food. What I really craved was a nice cup of hot and strong black coffee with some toast and marmalade. *Fat chance.*

One of the lookouts set at intervals along the top of the bank spotted the approach of Cadwy and his army from a long way off and shouted a warning. "Dust cloud spotted! Riders from the west!"

Most of the men downed tools and crowded onto the top of the bank to look. Standing shoulder to shoulder, they had to shade their eyes against the low evening sun. I scrambled up between Arthur and Cei and copied the men, squinting to make out the distant column of riders almost invisible in the dust they were kicking up.

Amid the dust, Cadwy's army, like a long, glittering snake, moved inexorably closer. His dragon banners rippled in the breeze, and the sinking sun reflected off the metal plates on the men's helmets. It appeared Cadwy had turned out his entire army to come do Arthur's bidding.

In the six years since Arthur had made his uneasy peace with his brother, they'd only seen one another at the Council of Kings in Viroconium's huge wooden hall, and I could hardly call their relationship friendly. More that they tolerated one another now, each seeing the other as a lesser evil than the threat of foreign invasion.

At least I hoped so.

This would be the first time they'd come properly face to face other than across the wide round table. A flutter of unease in my stomach disturbed me. Could they be trusted to agree with one another? Not to fight? They were men, after all, and Dark Age kings, with all that entailed, and brothers with a lifelong history of enmity between them. Not that, if presented with Morgana, I'd be happy to bury the hatchet – unless it happened to be between her eyes.

Merlin scrambled up to stand beside us. "Well, I never thought I'd live to see the day when Cadwy did your bidding." He raised a quizzical eyebrow at Arthur. "Are you sure you didn't cast some kind of spell on him?"

Arthur grinned at his old friend. "I suppose I should take this as proof he's not the idiot I thought he was. Let's hope he's not brought my sister. We can do without her interference."

My thoughts exactly. Automatically, my hand went to the hilt of my dagger where it sat in its leather-bound scabbard on my belt.

Arthur slithered down the now not-so-grassy bank, leaving the men still watching the approach of our putative reinforcements. With one last look, I slid down as well, on my bottom half the way, and hastened after him. He stopped where we'd set up our own small camp, and began pulling on his mailshirt.

I bent and picked up my own. "You don't trust him?"

A wry laugh issued from inside his mailshirt, before his head emerged, hair tangled. "About as far as I could throw him. And you know how far that'd be, now he's got so fat. So arm yourself for battle – just in case."

Haha. Easy enough for him to have professed confidence that his brother would stick to their agreement when they were miles apart. He'd changed his tune now they were about to come face to face.

Cei joined us. "Wise decision." He gathered up his own mailshirt. "Best get yours on too, Gwen."

I wriggled into my mailshirt and fastened my sword belt as my menfolk did the same. Our warriors needed no encouragement to follow suit. In a very short space of time, we had our horses saddled and had mounted up, with helmet straps fastened and shields in place on our arms. Arthur didn't intend to leave anyone behind in camp.

Alezan danced under my tight hold, marking time with impatient hooves and swishing her tail in discontent. After two days of relative inactivity, she was ready for action, and standing around waiting didn't suit her.

Arthur must have been in the same frame of mind as Alezan. He stood in his stirrups, raising one arm in the air. "I've a mind to ride to meet our 'allies'," he called, his voice ringing out above the chink of metal and the muttering of the men. "I've never liked to wait around. Still less, meet allies unprepared. That would be the action of a fool. Follow me, men."

A resounding cheer went up from four hundred voices. Not one of the assembled warriors trusted Cadwy any more than we did, not even the men he'd reluctantly contributed to our army. Maybe those men even less, as they knew him better. Wherever our men had originated, they owed allegiance only to Arthur now.

The gateway being narrow, we had to ride out only three abreast, so I fell in behind Arthur, Merlin and Cei, and found myself beside young Drustans. As an experienced warrior now, he enjoyed a certain popularity with the ladies of Din Cadan. But the sorrow lurking in his eyes betrayed the fact that he'd never forgotten his first love, Princess Essylt of Linnuis. She was a queen, now, and long married to his ageing father in Cornubia's capital of Caer Dore, and mother to

Drustans' much younger half-brother. Perhaps those dark eyes of his, with their secret sadness, presented a tempting challenge to the ladies.

He'd had his red-brown curls cut short for battle – no man wanted an enemy to have a handle to grab – and his helmet hid what remained. The soft beauty of boyhood, that must have drawn poor Essylt to him, had hardened into the square-jawed determination of a man grown. And although he could still be called handsome, an element of frostiness clung to him preventing anyone from getting too close.

Most of the young warriors his age were already married with children, but not Drustans. I suspected he continued to hold an unquenchable candle for Essylt, even though he understood she could never legally be his. A romantic dream perhaps of a woman he'd made his ideal. A forerunner of the medieval romance tales yet to be written.

He glanced at me and touched his helmet in respect. "A battle wouldn't be a battle without you, Milady." Poor boy. I'd forced him into silence when he'd caught me in disguise, trying to ride with Arthur's men to the battle of Bassas, and he'd never forgotten how I'd blackmailed him. I'd have called him the elephant that never forgets – if he'd have known what an elephant was.

"Precisely," I said, keeping a tight hold on Alezan to prevent any of the sideswipes she was fond of making at other horses. "I'm the keeper of records now. I need to be here to see what happens. So I can write it down. And the men believe I bring them luck."

He frowned. "I don't understand the importance you put on having a written record. We've managed long enough with the bards reciting our history for us. We can go on doing that, surely?"

Trust him to find fault with anything I did.

We turned our horses north along the top of the scarp, the evening breeze, chilly with the promise of winter soon to come, blowing out our horses' manes and tails and the horsehair plumes on some of the helmets. "Bards change a story a little every time it's told," I said, with a smile. "Tell it enough times and it's not the same story it was to start with. A history written down remains the same forever – and if I am eyewitness to what I write, then in time to come, men who read my work will know it as truth."

His eyes, once so frank and innocent, narrowed. "What does it matter to us what men in time to come believe? We are in the here and now. What happens today, tomorrow, next year concerns me. Not what happened in the past. I don't think the men who follow us will have much interest in what we did. They'll be like us – concerned only with their day to day."

I smiled. "You don't know, though. And I don't mean our children, or our children's children. Nor even many generations further on. I'm writing my account for long in the future, when men will have more time on their hands and want to study the past and know what happened then for the sake of knowledge and no other reason."

"You think they will?" For a moment the eager, interested boy of twelve years ago stared back at me, fascinated by the fact that I thought people in the future would want to read about his present.

"I've written about you in my book," I said. "About your love for Essylt."

His brow furrowed and his face darkened. "You had no right to do that."

The track we followed wound downhill now, and the riders behind us had spread out, the murmur of their voices carrying to me on the breeze. "Believe me, people will want to know your story," I said.

He frowned. "A story of lost love?"

"Yes. Particularly a story like that. Much as you and your friends like to hear similar stories sung in the hall of an evening."

He gave a shrug. "Perhaps you won't see my ending. Perhaps it won't be a tale of lost love. My father is in his dotage now. It's only a matter of time before I return to rule in his stead. And Essylt will be there. Waiting for me."

My heart ached for this hopeful boy, for boy he still was, in his heart. Essylt might be there waiting for him, if he ever got there, but he could never marry her – because marriage with his father had made her legally his mother, and by law their union would be incestuous. Not that I believed he'd ever reach this point. In my old world I'd seen his grave marker and it had not named him as a king, merely as a king's son. Essylt's own son, a boy barely a year younger than Amhar, might be the one to follow old king March to the throne of Cornubia instead of Drustans. Who knew?

"I wish you well with that," I said, a bitter taste in my mouth, and spurred Alezan forward to join Arthur at the front.

We reached the valley bottom and approached the road. At the crossing point, where our Ridgeway track met the road, Arthur and Cei had our men line up in ranks, forty riders across by ten deep, spears pointing upward like the fierce bristles on a brush. Arthur and Cei stood just in front, beside Anwyll carrying our own banner – a black bear rearing up on a creamy-white background. As if to oblige, the breeze picked up and unfurled the cloth, setting the bear dancing in the air.

Merlin and I moved our horses to one side, the better, he said, for me to flee if danger threatened. But somehow, I didn't think it would. If Cadwy had come this far, he didn't mean to fight with Arthur, no matter how much he hated him, not with a huge army of Saxons on the way.

Over the brow of the western hill, Cadwy's army and standard bearers came into sight. He followed the old Roman custom, and a proportion of his army consisted of foederati, Saxon mercenaries, to whom he'd gifted land and gold, but who now considered themselves as British.

These were much like the warriors I'd met along the Wall who'd been descended from the frontier troops the Romans had posted at the Wall forts, and who'd intermarried with local girls but still passed down their golden hair through their bloodline.

However, despite the knowledge that Cadwy had come at Arthur's request, and come quickly, and my own feeling that he posed no threat, I couldn't escape the fear that he might have some trick up his sleeve. That he didn't intend to do as he'd been asked, or that he intended to twist the situation to his own benefit. Mistrust of him was well-ingrained in my heart.

We sat our horses, impassive, wary, watching the approach of this slippery king.

The wind that spread our banner soughed in the nearby treetops, rustling the autumn leaves and making the branches whisper like old gossips. Champing on their bits, our horses shifted their weight and pawed their feet as the few flies that still remained tried to bite. Men fidgetted in their saddles, and a few muttered comments under their breath to one another. Some coughed, cleared their throats and spat. Chainmail rattled, bridles jingled. Overhead a pair of buzzards wheeled on a thermal, mewing to each other like lost cats.

Cadwy didn't hurry. He'd come a long way in what must have been only three days and no doubt his men and their horses would be tired. And most likely he didn't want Arthur to think him too obliging. That would be Cadwy to a tee.

He brought his men to a halt fifty yards from our ranks, in a column ten wide, like ours. Close enough to see his ever more corpulent bulk astride a horse of similar proportions. Good living had taken its toll on Arthur's older half-brother, and although he couldn't be in more than his mid-forties, his hair, hanging in greasy curls down his back, had gone iron gray, as had his thick beard.

Beside him, his only son, Prince Custennin, a slimmer, younger version of Cadwy, but with his mother, Angharad's, pale hazel eyes, sat astride a beautiful dapple-gray horse. I'd seen this prince from afar at every Council of Kings, the last time three years ago, standing mute behind his father's seat, his sharp gaze scanning the faces of the assembled kings. However, thanks to the lack of cordiality between the two brothers, I'd never spoken with him.

I surveyed him now with interest – he must have been a few years older than Llacheu, with a neat, jaw-hugging beard and the same long aquiline nose as Arthur. Whether by chance or because he felt my scrutiny, his head turned and for a moment our eyes met. Was that a touch of surprise to see a woman in armor, pure curiosity, or just the calculated examination of a potentially wise leader? His gaze moved on before I had a chance to decide.

Nerves tingling, I glanced at Merlin, but he had his eyes fixed on Cadwy.

After a long-drawn-out moment, Arthur touched his horse with his heels and pushed him forward, halting halfway between the front ranks of the massed armies. Wise enough not to get too close to that scorpion's curling tail.

I bit my lip with fresh anxiety. We could almost be lined up for battle with each other, and yet the feeling pulsing between the rows of warriors was not one of animosity, but rather of eager expectancy.

The young prince leaned toward his father to say something, and Cadwy nodded. With a hefty kick, he urged his horse forward. It stepped out smartly across the grass despite its solid build, tossing its head. As he came level with Arthur, Cadwy hauled it to a halt, dwarfing his brother with his bulk, even though Arthur was not a small man.

They stared at one another for a pregnant moment, perhaps each weighing up the other and his intentions. Then Cadwy stretched out his great ham of a hand to Arthur, and Arthur took it. Clasping forearms, they shook.

Chapter Thirty-Six

AS WE MADE our way back up the hill to the old fortress, the two armies kept warily to their ordered ranks, with a good twenty paces between them. Merlin, Cei, and I kept our places beside Arthur at the head of the men of Dumnonia, while Custennin and an older man rode beside Cadwy in front of the men of Powys. Something familiar clung to the older man's solid, pot-bellied form and grizzled chin, itching at my memory whenever I took a sideways glance at him.

However, brimming with mistrust, I tried to keep my eyes fixed on Cadwy, far too close for me to feel safe, although probably the time for treachery had passed.

With no room, and not enough grazing, left inside the old fortress for two such large armies, and no desire from either to be setting up camp in close proximity, by sunset our warriors had moved their entire camp outside the grassy banks to the south of the fort. Cadwy's men, out of sight but not out of mind, established their own camp to the north. The two armies' trust in each other seemed as nebulous as the clouds massing overhead.

I was busy laying out our bedrolls when Arthur came striding back from the newly set up horse lines, helmet tucked under one arm, saddle wedged against his hip. Merlin and Cei hurried in his wake.

Setting his saddle on the grass, Arthur turned to Cei. "We'd best post extra guards along the run of the fort's banks. We may ostensibly be allies, but it doesn't do to place too much trust in Cadwy's better nature."

Hooray. Exactly what I'd been thinking.

"Already taken care of, Brother. But what better nature would that be, then?" Cei grinned, teeth flashing in the gathering twilight.

A snort of laughter came from Bedwyr, who'd also been sorting out his sleeping place. "I'd as soon trust a nest of vipers."

Gwalchmei put down the lyre he'd been nursing like a baby. "That goes for me, too."

Arthur gave a dismissive shrug. "He came, didn't he? A mistake to underestimate Cadwy and his intentions. He might have Saxon foederati in his ranks and a Saxon mother, but that doesn't mean he'd side with invaders."

"And what about Cerdic?" Cei grunted. "He has fewer miles to travel, and yet we've seen neither sight nor sound of him. D'you think he's already decided his own Saxon blood puts him on their side?"

"Let's eat," Merlin said, dropping to where I'd spread his blankets near to mine and Arthur's. "We need food inside us for what's coming."

Did he possess some foreknowledge of what was coming? I could never tell if he just suspected the future or had actually seen it. Might he know more than he let on? Often?

Arthur sat down, and Bedwyr took bread and cheese and smoked meat out of a bag, and uncorked a bottle of olive oil.

I sat beside my husband and broke off a hunk of the bread – hard and dry by now, but dipping it in the olive oil would soften it nicely and make it more palatable.

Arthur sliced off a hunk of cheese and passed it over. A skin of cider made the rounds, and I leaned in closer to him, trying not to think about what the next day might bring, as his arm slipped around my shoulders.

As the sky and landscape darkened, those men not on guard duty did the same as us, and overhead, the clouds kept on massing, obscuring the stars. Somewhere, a voice rose in song; a melancholy air not guaranteed to raise the spirits.

The singer had just begun a second song, more cheerful this time, when Llacheu arrived, face alight with excitement. "Father, Anwyll sent me." He made a hurried bow.

Arthur removed the arm he'd draped around my shoulders, straightening. "What for?"

"A messenger has come from the Powys camp. King Cadwy asks for a meeting with you."

My heart did a little, nervous flip as Arthur and Cei scrambled to their feet. Merlin remained seated, watching Arthur through narrowed eyes.

For a moment no one spoke, and then Arthur leaned down and caught my hand. "Come with me. I want you to hear this." He pulled me to my feet.

I dropped the bread I'd been dipping in the bowl of olive oil, no longer hungry. A mixture of apprehension and excitement curdled what I'd already swallowed, and for a moment, before I had myself under control, I feared I might vomit.

"I want you to put this meeting in your book for that posterity you're so fond of," Arthur said. "You can come too, Cei, and you, Merlin. And you, Llacheu. You'll keep Gwen safe for me."

The young warrior's eyes shone in delight at the honor of accompanying his father, even if it had been slightly tempered by being put in charge of the queen.

Merlin stood up. His eyes met mine, veiled and unreadable – a little shifty, even, but I had no time for reflection.

Cei threw down his half-eaten bread and cheese. "Could've waited till we'd eaten," he muttered, wiping his mouth on his sleeve and passing on the skin of cider from which he'd been about to take a swig. "I'll get a torch."

Still in their mailshirts, the men only needed to grab their shields and don their helmets to be battle ready. I put my own helmet on and did up the straps with shaking fingers as Cei lifted his smoky torch.

"This'll be interesting," Merlin whispered as we followed Arthur and Llacheu out of the ring of sentries in the gathering gloom of twilight. From behind us came the last verses of the cheerful song, a few shouts of encouragement, the murmur of voices. Over the empty sweep of the downs to our right, a solitary owl swooped across the dark sky, silent and ghost-like on its nightly prowl.

Cadwy stood waiting for us in the gloom. Two burly, torch-carrying warriors stood behind him, armed as we were and with wolfskins capes draped around their shoulders against the rising chill of the autumn evening. Young Custennin flanked his father on his right, with a third man taking the other side. This was the man I'd thought familiar on the ride up from the road. Now helmetless, his austere, lined face became recognizable as a man more used to pulpit than sword. Archbishop Dubricius, Cadwy's right-hand man.

Arthur halted ten yards from his brother, Cei and Merlin ranging themselves on either side of him to match the guards Cadwy had brought. Their hands rested lightly on their sword hilts.

I kept to one side, close to Llacheu, and from where I could see both Arthur and Cadwy's faces, content to watch and not participate. My importance, as a woman, was off the bottom of the scale. However, nothing would stop me from making mental notes for the next entry in my book.

"Brother," Arthur said, a slight nod of his head all that passed for a bow. He was High King, after all.

"Brother," Cadwy returned, his nod every bit as small. The thick gold circlet that served him as a crown nestled in his greasy hair, as though he'd decided we needed reminding who he was.

Arthur, bare-headed and yet a hundred times more regal, cleared his throat. "I thank you again for responding so swiftly."

Cadwy grunted. "I'm not the fool you take me for. I'm here to discuss your plan... *our* plan of action." His voice rumbled, gravelly and rough, and I'd have said he smoked sixty a day if I hadn't known that to have been impossible.

He jerked his head at where Arthur's hand rested on the ornate hilt of his sword, snug in its new scabbard. "Is that it?" A challenge edged his voice.

Custennin's gaze sharpened as he, too, stared at the sword.

Arthur glanced down, brows raised a little as though seeing Excalibur for the first time. He shrugged. "If you want to know if this is the sword of Macsen Wledig, then just ask."

Cadwy glowered, the torchlight flickering over his face making a gargoyle of him. "Well, is it?" The words hung between us.

Arthur nodded. "Yes. It is."

How did Cadwy know about the sword? The story must have percolated about Britain by some sort of osmosis. Or did he have spies within Din Cadan, just as we had spies at Viroconium?

Cadwy's fleshy upper lip curled in a sneer. "Fell into your hands, did it?"

"Something like that."

For a long minute nothing more was said, the silence crackling with tension. Cadwy's greedy, envious eyes lingered on the sword on his younger brother's hip long enough to make my heart thud painfully in my throat.

Finally, he tore his gaze away, cleared his throat and spat a wad of phlegm onto the grass. "I've more experience at this than you." His already piggy eyes narrowed to slits above his puffy cheeks. "Tell me, this army you spoke of in your message, how big is it? And do we know if it attacked King Einion at Caer Celemion? Have you had news from him?"

Arthur shook his head. "No scouts have reached us since his warning of the landings on the Tamesis. We have to assume his town's fallen. And even if it hasn't, we'll get no help from that quarter.

Sending men to us would leave him too vulnerable, being so close to occupied territory."

"And Cerdic? Has his city fallen?"

"No. They marched on past and left it unmolested. Or so his messenger said."

An uneasy silence followed.

Cadwy's beady eyes slid to Merlin's immobile face, perhaps hoping he'd learn more from Arthur's advisers than from the king himself. "You are certain of this?"

Merlin regarded him from stony eyes. Like me.

Arthur nodded. "We are. Aelle and his men landed on the south coast – the messenger didn't say where – and marched north. He seems to have passed within a couple of miles of Caer Guinntguic, but he left them be. Whether because he feels he has bigger eels to fry, or because he's Cerdic's uncle, I doubt we'll ever know. Possibly a mix of both."

Dubricius frowned. "Have you asked him to send men?" Too much fine living had filled out his mailshirt, stretching it tight over his potbelly, and a double chin rested on his chest, obscuring his neck. Nevertheless, he had a look of toughness about him beneath the fat. This was a time when churchmen could easily double as warriors. Just as Bishop Germanus had done sixty years ago when he'd led the famous Alleluiah Victory.

"I have," Arthur said. "And asked them to meet us here. We've had no reply as yet."

"You think he'll come?" Cadwy asked, unable to stop his lip curling again. He was himself half Saxon but seemed to have chosen to forget that. Nobody reminded him.

Grim faced, Arthur nodded. "I do. He swore loyalty to me, to the position of High King. He will come."

Beside me, Llacheu fidgeted as though in disagreement. If only my scanty knowledge of Badon had been more specific, I might have felt less like him. Good thing someone was feeling confident.

"Those two heathen armies will have combined by now and be headed west," Dubricius said, rather stating the obvious.

Arthur shot him a frown. "They'll be following the Caer Ceri road. Why else are we waiting here if not to cut them off and halt their advance?"

I itched to make a comment, but restrained myself. With difficulty.

Cadwy, as tall as Arthur but twice as wide, his natural bulk enhanced by a well-padded mailshirt and the huge bearskin he wore as a cloak, grunted. "You're sure of that?"

"As sure as I can be," Arthur said, with a nod in Merlin's direction. "I have my seer's advice on this."

Not strictly true, but if he wanted to hide where he'd got his information, then that was fine with me. The less I had to do with Cadwy, the better.

Cadwy snorted like a bull about to charge. His very being was more bull-like than human – he'd have been great at playing the Minotaur... or a bad-tempered version of Hagrid.

I'd never have marked him and Arthur as brothers. Or even half-brothers. Now Cadwy's hair had gone gray, not even their coloring hinted at consanguinity. His face, red and shiny with sweat, had puffed up so much his eyes peered out from folds of sagging skin, and broken veins threaded his overblown cheeks.

His piggy eyes slid sideways once again to stare at Merlin. "I notice you have your necromancer with you." His upper lip curled in a sneer yet again. "You think he knows, then? Sees them coming?"

Arthur nodded. "He does. I have it from reliable sources that my information is correct."

How I hoped he, and I, were right on that.

He set his hands on his hips. "And if you didn't believe it yourself, you wouldn't be here. I take it Morgana saw their coming as well." Not a question. A statement.

Cadwy's fat lips parted in a grin. Time had not been kind to his dentition. "She did." He barked a laugh, harsh and coarse. "Told me not to come. Told me to leave you to your fate, then take your empty seat at the Council of Kings."

I edged closer, the better to see Arthur's reaction, already in my head composing how I'd write this in my book.

Llacheu's hand on my arm held me back. "Not too close," he whispered.

Arthur let his gaze run from his brother's dusty boots to his face. "Then why *did* you come?"

The air between the two brothers tingled as the tension rose. I wouldn't have been surprised to find my hair standing on end, from all the electricity buzzing back and forth.

Cadwy cleared his throat and spat copiously on the ground once more. "Because for once, she has it wrong." He showed his alarming teeth again. "I could have done what she wanted – let you ride out against the Saxon host alone… and fall. But if I did that, how long would it be before they came knocking on the doors of Viroconium? I'm not a fool." He wiped his hand across his mouth and laughed again, this time with true amusement. "She wasn't pleased about *that*, I can tell you."

I had the feeling he'd enjoyed refusing his sister. What kind of relationship did they have that he was glad to get one over on her? Maybe not so close as I'd always assumed.

All around us the shadows had crept closer as the night drew in, the sky in the west darkening as the light pursued the vanished sun over the horizon. The torches blazed and sparks floated skywards.

Arthur laughed as well. "I'd have liked to have seen her face when you told her 'no'." For just a moment, a hint of camaraderie existed between the two estranged brothers, a suggestion of what might have been possible… once.

Cadwy's gaze shifted to Merlin. "Don't you ever tell *your* dog 'no' then?"

Not a muscle moved on Merlin's face, but a wave of pure hostility emanated from him that nearly sent me reeling. Cadwy gave no sign he'd noticed, though. Thick-skinned, that one.

Arthur was silent a moment. "My counsellor always gives me sound advice," he finally said. "I never ignore his words, because I know wisdom feeds them."

Camaraderie dispensed with.

Cadwy laughed again, spit bubbles forming at the corner of his overly-wet mouth. "So you say. I won't argue with you on that one. But enough of how we had our warnings. Now, tell me what precautions you've taken."

Arthur, who must have had to make a hasty change to his previous plan of battle now we had our reinforcements, pointed east, unfazed and calm. "Lookouts along the road, every mile or so. Watching for the Saxon advance party. If one fails, the next will surely not. I've posted them right down into the valley of the Kennet, to where the old town of Spinae sits on the riverbank. And some up in the hills to either side, as well, although I'm certain they'll take the road."

"Wise move." Cadwy shifted his considerable weight as though uncomfortable with standing. "And I presume you've decided where we should face the enemy when they come?"

Arthur nodded. "The road from Caer Celemion makes a steady climb from the Kennet Valley and follows a ridge of high ground this way. It's mostly clear to either side, with only grazing land, some heath, and small farmsteads, with pockets of woodland but very little forest. Nowhere there to conceal our forces and stage a surprise attack."

He pointed into the darkness. "But in daylight, if you look east from here, you'll see a distant brow with a good-sized beech hanger stretching into the valley to the south. The road passes that way, dips down steeply, then rises again onto a long hill. There's more than enough woodland to give cover to at least half our force."

"Just half?" Cadwy's eyes narrowed.

"Yes. Half. The other half will meet them on the road, facing them full on. We'll lure them forward and let them charge. Then the hidden warriors in the woodland will ride in from the side in tight formation to flank them. Bows first, then lances."

Cadwy rubbed his greasy beard. "And what of Cerdic? What part will he play – if he comes?" He frowned. "If, that is, he doesn't get here and decide to take his uncle's side."

An awkward silence bristled. Yes. Where was Cerdic? I badly wanted to know. Surely he'd had enough time to march here by now?

Arthur broke the silence. "I'd hoped to station his men to the north, to make a two-pronged flanking attack on both sides of the Saxon army."

I glanced at Cei, but he remained impassive, his eyes fixed on his brother.

Cadwy shifted his weight again and rolled his shoulders. Probably stiff after his long forced march. "Without him, do we have enough men to defeat the Saxons?"

The words hung in the cold night air.

I wanted to shout "Yes, you'll win" but I couldn't very well, and besides which, I had no idea if Cerdic was meant to be here or not. I pressed my lips together and schooled myself to silence. This was a meeting of kings – of men – and the opinion of a woman, even if she were a queen, was not wanted. Even if it irked me to stay silent, right now I had to conform.

Arthur shrugged. "The honest answer is that I don't know. We haven't seen the Saxon force, or counted them. Their numbers are just hearsay. But they'll be on foot, and we have cavalry, and that's already an advantage. And our men are better disciplined than theirs. Another advantage."

He rubbed his chin, heavy with five days growth of beard. "If we were facing a Roman legion, then we would have little chance. They'd lock their shields in testudo and even our strongest cavalry charge would be unlikely to budge them."

A grin revealed Arthur's teeth, gleaming white in the darkness that had so quickly become total. "But they're not the legions, thank God and all the gods. When they see us, with what they'll think is so small a force, let's hope they won't be able to resist charging. And when they charge, they'll lose any advantage they have in numbers. Because we'll be on horseback, and they won't. And we have mounted archers."

Cadwy grinned back, as mirthlessly as Arthur. "Good plan, Little Brother. It may well work." He sighed. "But it would be better were Cerdic and his men here to boost our numbers." He gave a disgusted snort. "You still think he'll come to fight his fellow countrymen? That he's on his way?"

Arthur compressed his lips before answering. "Cerdic once declared that he was British now. His father was British, and the crown he now wears is British, as are many of his men. I believe he will come."

Cadwy nodded. "Let's hope you're right." He sighed again and rubbed a hand across his eyes. "I'm for my bed now. Hard ground or not, I'll sleep well tonight after three days in the saddle. This is further than I've ridden in years. I bid you goodnight." He turned away, his men falling in behind him like a pair of over-muscled pit bull terriers, with Dubricius a fat Labrador and Custennin a watchful hound, and they vanished into the darkness.

"Humph," Merlin muttered. "Cerdic better bloody well had come."

Chapter Thirty-Seven

I WOKE SHORTLY after sunrise to find the warm body that had been lying next to mine, Arthur's, had vacated the bed and left my back chilly. I pulled our blankets, speckled with dew, closer around myself and tried closing my eyes again, but sleep refused to return. The ground felt hard and lumpy as rock, the cold was eating through the blankets, and I needed a pee. Annoyed, I sat up and pushed the covers back.

The clouds of yesterday had thinned. High overhead, almost invisible against the brightening sky, a late-season skylark sang its bubbling chorus. Knuckling sleep from my eyes, I peered around at our camp. Most of the men were already sitting in groups to breakfast on hard bread, cheese, and onions, washed down with cider or ale.

My stomach rumbled, but oh, how I longed for a slice of toast and marmalade and a strong cup of coffee. Not for the first time. Was I getting too old for traipsing after the army?

As I hadn't undressed the night before, nor even kicked off my boots before snuggling down in Arthur's embrace, all I had to do was stand up and stretch; a state of being with both advantages and disadvantages. On silent feet, I padded through the camp to where Cei had very kindly organized the construction of a small, roofless shelter specifically for my use. The men had to use any old spot for their toileting, but I had a hole in the ground to squat over, out of the sight of curious eyes.

That over, and scratching a scalp made itchy through a pressing need to be washed, I went in search of my husband. No sign of him, nor Cei, but I came upon Merlin by the rows of tethered horses. Most of them stood with a back leg crooked and heads down, sleeping as the sun rose higher and warmed their backs. Perhaps somewhere to the east it was already shining on the ranks of our approaching enemy. Alezan pricked her ears when she spotted me, and a throaty nicker rumbled from her throat.

I gave her the nub of hard black bread I'd kept in my pocket from last night, and her soft nose nuzzled it from my outstretched palm with relish. Which was more than I felt for it. That longing for food I could never have resurfaced at the thought of what awaited me instead.

"Not hungry?" Merlin asked, running his hand along his mare's back. Like any horseman the world over, he would be checking for lumps, sore spots or rubbed areas. A horse's back is vulnerable, and without a good back, as without good feet, the horse is lost. And the warrior must walk and fight on foot, like a Saxon.

I shook my head. "I have an unbearable longing for something hot."

He laughed. "Same here. One of the problems of campaigning is the lack of good food. Or rather, the same cold food over and over again until it's stale and moldy."

I ran my hand down Alezan's forehead and rubbed her nose, feeling the downiness of her growing winter coat. She lipped at my hand, probably hoping for some other tidbit. "Do you know where Arthur is?"

He jerked his head eastward. "Ridden out before first light to take a second look at the lie of the land, now we're sure of our reinforcements."

"Sure of them? Has Cerdic arrived?" I scanned the camp in hope of seeing strange warriors, but nothing had changed. Just clusters of our own warriors grouped as though they had fires to gather around, talking together in low voices. Some in the horse lines like us, brushing down their mounts.

Merlin shook his head. "Not yet. Give him time. I think he'll come."

Well, if Merlin thought he would, that was good enough for me.

I peered eastward myself, but from where I stood, only the brow of the hill showed against the skyline, dotted with a few stunted hawthorn bushes. "Who did Arthur go with?"

Merlin wrinkled his nose. "With ten of our men and ten of Cadwy's – and Cadwy himself. He wanted to see the land he's to be fighting on. Understandable, I suppose."

My heart gave a lurch of uncertainty. No matter how I tried, I couldn't bring myself to trust Cadwy, and the thought of Arthur riding off with him sent a shiver down my back that I couldn't disguise. Even if he did have ten of his own men with him.

Merlin must have noticed. "Don't worry. I see no danger in him doing that."

I forced a smile. "I would have liked to have gone with them. The better to be able to describe it in my book."

He turned away from his horse, one hand still resting on its quarters. "I've seen no danger for him with Cadwy, and I've seen the Saxons drawing close now. But you *know*, don't you?" He fixed me with a penetrating stare. "You know about this battle. What does your future tell us about it?"

Damn him.

I rubbed Alezan's long ears, soft between my fingers. "Nothing. That's the trouble. Nothing at all except idle gossip and romantic invention."

He raised his eyebrows, waiting.

"All right. That Arthur slew nine-hundred-and-sixty men all by himself in the battle." I laughed. "An impossible feat."

Merlin eyed me speculatively for a long moment before nodding gravely. "Indeed. I hope that even with two armies, the Saxons won't have that many men at their disposal." He glanced at our own men. "Let's hope not, anyway."

<hr />

ARTHUR AND CADWY returned at a gallop halfway through a morning that had been growing steadily more overcast as heavy dark clouds massed in the west. Shouts went up from our lookouts to warn us, and a moment later the bunch of horsemen broached the rise, their horses' hooves kicking a shower of clods of dirt up behind them.

Half veered off to the far side of the hillfort, Cadwy at their head, while Arthur and his warriors galloped into the center of our camp. Over in the horse lines every single mount swung round on their tether, heads up, ears pricked, sensing the excitement of their fellows and quivering like bowstrings.

Even as he wrenched his horse to a standstill, Arthur was shouting to our men. "To horse. All of you. Saxon horde sighted coming up from the River Kennet. They may be on foot, but we've not a moment to spare."

I'd been grooming Alezan, something both she and I enjoyed, and that I'd hoped would steady my nerves. I dropped my brush and ran to where my belongings lay. All around me, men rushed in every direction, pulling on mailshirts, grabbing saddles and hurrying to their horses. Ordered chaos reigned. Everyone knew what they were doing, even me.

I wriggled into my mailshirt as quickly as possible and fastened my sword belt around my waist, having to concentrate to steady the shake that had taken my fingers. To my right, I spotted Llacheu stringing his bow, and with a lurch of fear remembered his planned role. He slung his full quiver over his shoulder and heaved his saddle up, his eyes meeting mine.

I took a moment to stare, taking in everything about him from his close-cropped head down to his booted feet. Was I afraid I'd never see him alive again? An icy shiver ran down my spine.

He grinned. Every inch a warrior, but still with the frank eyes of the boy I loved. Eyes not unlike those of his cousin Rhiwallon.

My fear rose like a sickness in my belly. I swallowed bile, pushing thoughts of dead Rhiwallon out of my head with difficulty. This was not some exercise. This was war, and Llacheu had the role of cannon fodder, even in the days before the invention of such a weapon. "Take care," I gasped, finding it hard to catch my breath. "Don't play the hero. Promise me. Don't get too close."

He grinned again, his smile so achingly like his father's. "Don't worry. I know what I'm doing."

Rhiwallon had probably felt the same.

I wanted to grab him and hold him tight and never let him go, but I couldn't. This was a man's world, and all men, from the lowliest swineherd to the king himself, saw their role as fighters, defenders, champions of the rest of us. And despite my armor and weapons, I was firmly in the category of 'the rest of us'.

Wedging his saddle against his hip, Llacheu hastened away to find his horse.

I watched him go, rooted to the ground while the chaotic order raged around me, an island of stillness amongst the maelstrom. Self-doubt arose unbidden. *Badon.* We were marching to Badon. Had I chosen right? Was this really to be the battle from the history books? Was I helping to write them?

"Get your helmet and saddle and hurry up." Merlin, shouting, grabbed my arm and gave me a tug. "This way. We have to make haste."

Snatched back into the here and now, the shouts of men battered my ears. I bent and grabbed my helmet by its straps. Merlin shoved my bridle into my hands. "You're to come with me."

He carried both our saddles, one wedged against each hip. At the horse lines the mood had stayed with our beasts, and none of them seemed keen to stand quietly while we readied them. Alezan danced on her long rope, hooves churning up the short-nibbled turf, and Merlin had to hold her still while I saddled her with too much haste, my fingers clumsy on the straps from fear.

Further up the line, some of the men had mounted already, and were weighing lances in one hand while holding their excited horses' reins tightly in the other.

With difficulty, Merlin got a bridle onto an impatient Alezan for me, despite her excited head-tossing, then gave me a leg up into the saddle. Before I'd settled and found my stirrups, she whirled around, snorting, tossing her head some more, her tail whipping back and forth. She would have sent Merlin flying had he not dodged out of her way. She wasn't a war horse, but today she thought she was.

I set both hands on the reins and shoved my feet into my stirrups, whispering sweet nothings to her that she completely ignored. My own heart beat a rapid tattoo against my mailshirt, trying in vain to break out.

Low overhead, a flight of crows twisted on the rising wind, their backs bent, ragged wings outspread. Thunder rumbled in the distance. Did the birds sense the coming weather or the coming battle? Or both? Were they here like gory camp-followers to predate upon the casualties of war? Already?

Merlin shortened his horse's reins in an effort to hold her still, but even so, she swung around and he had to spring into the saddle instead of using his stirrup to mount. He held her tight as his feet groped for his stirrups, and her nostrils flared as she snorted.

In the center of our now ravaged camp a forest of lances protruded from the ground like quills on a porcupine, amid the detritus of three days inactivity strewn across the grass.

At a canter, Merlin seized one of the lances and swung it up, turning his horse on a sixpence and riding back to me.

My anxious eyes scanned the seething mass of riders, almost every man mounted now, the forest of lances transforming fast into a sparse copse. Where was Arthur?

If only he'd still had Llamrei, who with her gleaming white coat had been so easy to spot. I searched in desperation for his bay, spotted the banner held aloft again by Anwyll, found Cei's red-head, helmetless and shining like a fiery beacon, but no Arthur.

Thunder rumbled again, closer this time, and a wind came whipping in from across the plain. The clouds on the western horizon had darkened to a threatening slate gray.

A shout rang out above the clamor of voices, the squealing of horses, and the whistle of the wind as it blew across the summit of the hill. "To me. In ranks. Archers to the front."

There he was. Astride his bright bay, his white shield on his arm with the rampant black bear rearing up across it, rallying his men.

Beside him, the slight figure of Gwalchmei raised the battle horn to his lips and blew three short sharp blasts. Like magic, the chaos of churning riders formed into ranks of ready warriors behind their king. I'd seen all this before, many times, both in practice and in action, but the alacrity with which they accomplished it never ceased to amaze me.

What a splendid sight they made.

The banner, held aloft by Anwyll, snapped out in the obliging wind, allowing the black bear that was Arthur's sigil to shimmer with life. Rank after rank of well-oiled mailshirts shimmered like the scales on a slippery trout. Helmets glittered, and lances bristled upright.

"We're to keep to the rear," Merlin said, close beside me. "Whatever happens, you're to stay with me. We're to join Cadwy's army and wait out of sight in the woodland."

I nodded, unable to find words, as a churning lump of emotion welled inside me. Pride had its home there, but beside it, other things jostled for position. Foremost rose the thought that not all these brave men lined up in front of us would be returning. Some, perhaps many, were riding out to die.

Not cleanly or mercifully, but perhaps the way Cei's son Rhiwallon had died, sobbing for their mothers with their insides hanging out. A cold lump of fear settled in my belly. Even if Badon turned out as the legends said, and this became the victory I longed for, we, the victors, would not really be the winners at all.

Chapter Thirty-Eight

THE QUIET OF the day was not really quiet at all. Half a dozen buzzards rode the turbulent air overhead, circling in the slate-gray sky and surveying us with the air of interested spectators, their mewling, plaintive calls snatched away by the rising wind.

Hidden within the sheltering woodland, our restive horses snorted and fidgeted, and that same wind rattled the branches, making the leaves chatter like long forgotten, angry ghosts. The first drops of rain pattered on our helmets.

Bridles jangled and saddles creaked, but any rider who had to speak kept his voice to the lowest of murmurs. The noisy wind and our own silence were our friends.

Merlin and I, with half a dozen men of Dumnonia to guard us, waited behind the backmost rank of Cadwy's Powys warriors. It had been a case of let me come or leave me behind at Dinas Badan, both unsafe options according to Arthur. Having me close by, despite being ostensibly in Cadwy's charge, had narrowly won.

Merlin had helped my cause by taking Arthur aside to point out that the only safe place, *if* you could have called it that, from which to watch the battle would be the beech woodland that darkened the southern slopes of the ridge. Where Cadwy was to have his men stationed.

So here we were, eight Dumnonians behind four hundred men of Powys. If I hadn't been so worried about the outcome of the battle, I'd have felt a sight more disquiet about that slippery eel's proximity. But it seemed Cadwy, too, had other things on his mind. He hadn't so much as glanced at us from his position alongside Custennin and Dubricius, just behind the archers.

I couldn't say the same for young Custennin, though. Several times, as we'd ridden here, I'd caught his thoughtful gaze on me and seen it snatched away as though he were anxious to disguise his curiosity.

I had no such qualms and studied him with interest. Although cursed with the heavy brow and fleshy lips of his father, he'd grown into an altogether more attractive specimen, with more than a hint of Arthur about him – not unlike his cousin Llacheu. Probably as big a hit with the ladies of Viroconium as Llacheu was with the girls of Din Cadan.

Now, though, as we waited inside the woods, all I could see of him was the top of the plumed helmet that distinguished him from his father's warriors in their less splendid headgear.

These men now lined up ten deep in front of us, although not Dumnonians, presented a ferocious front. Solid men on solid, well-muscled horses. Unshaven faces, harsh with battle lust, glared from beneath their helmets, their eyes ablaze, jaws set, and large hands fisted around the shafts of lances.

Just inside the woodland edge, the front line, as the designated light cavalry, had their bows at the ready, arrows already nocked. Between them and us ranged the lines of heavy cavalry, as ordered as it was possible to be while squeezed into the irregularity of the woodland, their lances bristling skyward, ready to form the second wave.

I swiped a scattering of raindrops from my face, and Alezan swished her tail in discontent. We'd been waiting for over an hour now, hidden between the trunks of this friendly beech wood, far enough back that no light should catch the metallic glint of our armor and betray our presence. Between us and the out-of-sight road, a quarter of a mile or more away, stretched open grazing, empty now of the sheep and shepherds who'd fled the moment they laid eyes on us.

At least the trees gave some shelter from the rain.

To our left, the woodland thickened where the road ran up the hill. There, the main force of Arthur's warriors stood waiting on the road, hidden by the brow and trees from the view of anyone approaching from the east.

How I longed to be able to see, to watch over my husband and keep him safe. The itch welling up in me grated in my stomach, heart, and mind, making my whole body quiver with fearful anticipation.

I tried to picture what was happening.

Llacheu would have his band of forty archers ready, strung across the road and out to either side of it – the only warriors the approaching Saxons would see. They'd hidden their mail shirts under their tunics, the better to look like local farmers, not king's warriors, and rode helmetless at Llacheu's own suggestion. Farm boys possessed bows, not plated helmets.

As yet, all seemed quiet and peaceful. The last scout had arrived not half an hour ago to warn Arthur that the Saxon army was nearly upon us. A rider had come to share the news with Cadwy, and this in turn had filtered back through the ranks as fast as water down a drain.

All we knew, though, was that the Saxon army, vaguely described as huge in number, was drawing ever closer. However, as not many men could count above twenty, any estimate of army size was to be considered unreliable.

My position behind the men restricted my view, but I knew better than to try to move. Not that I could have even if I'd wanted to, as, in a fit of zealous overprotectiveness, my guards had surrounded me and Merlin. Rows of horses' bums, men's backs, and lances pointing skyward were all I could see between the bulky bodies of my escort.

I'd managed to take a good look at the lie of the land on the ride to the woodland, marking out the proximity of the road to the north and, in my head, the escape routes to the south. Who knew if I might need that knowledge before the day was done? Best to be prepared for every eventuality, despite my hope that the outcome of today's battle would be as I expected.

Hard, now, to picture this countryside as it would one day be – with rolling arable fields made huge for combine harvesters, a motorway, and pylons striding across the domesticated panorama. Here, small, earth-bank-surrounded fields were the norm, and apart from the stony ribbon of the Roman road, all other routes were dirt tracks, some nothing more than narrow deertrods.

I took my feet out of my stirrups to stretch legs that ached from doing nothing, pointing my toes and wiggling my feet. Nothing I could do about my nerves, though.

With nowhere else to look but up, I peered through the wildly swaying, rust-red foliage toward an ever-darkening sky. All around me, dead leaves fell in a silent rain, to join the rustling carpet under our horses' hooves.

Thunder rumbled again, closer now, and a stronger wind whipped the branches into a frenzy. The leaves fell more thickly, and Alezan stamped in agitation, no better at being patient than I was.

Merlin shifted his weight in the saddle as though he, too, was stiff from inactivity. "A storm's brewing," he muttered, as though he thought perhaps I hadn't noticed.

He'd confined his long hair in a single braid, and his helmet strap hung unfastened on his shoulder. A frown darkened his brow.

I managed a nod and the briefest of smiles. "It's heading our way."

His horse fidgeted under the too-tight hold he had on his reins. Was he as nervous as I was? Did we have reason to be, despite my belief, not nearly so strong now and rapidly diminishing, that this would be a victory for Arthur?

I had to think of something else or I'd go mad.

Was this an ambush we were staging? I'd never participated in one before. Been ambushed, yes, but never been on the giving end. The waiting, new to me, itched my very soul. My innards had coiled themselves into an anticipatory ball and refused to unravel. If only the battle would begin. If only it were over, which would be better. If only we were home safely with it existing as just a bad memory.

Up by the road, Cadwy had posted a scout, hidden in bushes and armed with a copper mirror. Now suddenly a flash of light arced across the slope, once, twice, three times, before it died.

The Saxons had come into view, but not from here, for me.

My stomach did a convulsive flip, and I gripped Alezan's mane so tight between my fingers she tossed her head and stamped. A hissing murmur of excitement ran through the ranks of Cadwy's men like a Mexican wave.

Another rumble of thunder. Much closer, this time.

If only I could see Arthur. But from here I might as well have been blind. Llacheu must be waiting in full view of the Saxons, with his small force of light archers on their fast horses, bows at the ready. How must he be feeling? Like me? Or did men not feel the nerves that knotted my insides before every battle?

Wait, was that thunder to the east as well?

Merlin stood in his stirrups to make himself taller and put his reins into one hand, gazing east.

Anxious and excited at the same time, I did the same. Between the silvery tree trunks, the distant brow of the hill that formed our horizon, and that one day would mark the edge of the village of Baydon, bristled suddenly with marching men. Ten wide, row upon row appeared like a tidal bore, their heavy boots mimicking the rumble of distant thunder.

I sat down hard on my saddle, jolting Alezan who laid her ears back. How many could there be? The fear that the farmer who'd guessed at twenty keels ashore in the Thames had been right, or had even underestimated, gripped my heart, and my breath seemed to have stopped.

Every battle I witnessed seemed more brutal than the last, and my knowledge of the previous ones only made dread of the one to come worse. I forced the air out of my lungs and heaved in a breath, my knuckles white on Alezan's reins.

Like the deep rumble of surf on a beach, the sound of marching boots on the road echoed through the chill air. Footsoldiers every one of them, many of them in mailshirts and with round metal helmets that caught what light there was and flashed like precursors of the promised lightning.

Impossible to see as yet, but they'd be armed with long swords, wicked, double-edged axes, and spears. And beneath their helmets they'd have yellow hair and drooping mustaches. I'd seen enough Saxons in my time to know their harsh faces would match those of our own men for determination and ferocity, and that they'd fight as though they had nothing to lose and all to gain.

The road dipped steeply, dropping out of sight from where we stood, before starting its climb toward Llacheu and his archers.

I glanced at Merlin in desperation. "I need to see what's happening."

He grimaced, annoyingly calm. "Don't we all."

A shout rose from the Saxon ranks, guttural and gleeful, carrying across to our sheltering woodland. Had they spotted Llacheu and his men lined up on the brow? The frustration of not being able to see gnawed at me.

Every Powys horse champed at the bit, or stamped impatient feet, picking up the nervous tension and battle lust of the waiting warriors.

My mouth had gone so dry, I couldn't swallow.

Merlin put out a hand and caught my arm. "Here they come." His eyes were closed. How could he know?

A shiver of electricity ran up my arm from where his hand gripped it, and for a moment an image flashed into my head. A horse's ears, a view down the road toward the charging Saxon army, a hand that wasn't mine holding a bow and arrow. And then the electricity and the image were gone.

I stared at Merlin, my mouth hanging open.

In front of us the warriors of Powys tightened their grip on their weapons. Their backs straightened, every man and horse poised for action.

But I ignored them. They didn't matter. What had just happened? What had I seen?

From beyond the brow, completely hidden from us, the strident call of a battle horn carried on the wind. Once, twice, three times. And thunder, rumbling overhead with a sinister threat.

I couldn't drag my gaze away from Merlin.

From the front, Cadwy's voice carried, barely audible above the rattle of the rising wind in the branches. "Not yet," he growled.

Alezan danced beneath me, eager for the off, and I had to give her my attention, even though all I wanted to do was demand of Merlin what he'd done. He snatched his hand back to better control his own mount, and I tightened my reins.

Two flashes of light from the signaler on the brow.

Words rippled back from man to man, reaching us in moments.

"They've taken the bait."

"They're charging."

"Hold your horses, men."

"Wait for the signal."

"Archers only first. Rest of you stay hidden."

From where I stood, the only thing I could see was the tail end of the Saxon column vanishing rapidly into the dip as though in a run, but still holding formation. What was the front end doing? More war horns sounded.

If only I could see.

Merlin. He could show me.

"Let them get halfway up the hill," Cadwy shouted, all need for silence gone. The Saxons wouldn't hear him now. "Wait for my order."

At least he didn't seem to have any treachery planned. At the back of my mind a tiny nub of doubt had been festering that he might do the thing we feared Cerdic might do – and come down on the side of his mother's people.

Shouts rose in the distance, snatched by the wind. Were they from Llacheu's men or from Saxons stuck with arrows? I couldn't tell.

The archers in our front line were having great trouble keeping their eager horses under control.

Time ticked past, so slowly I wanted to scream. More shouts, the familiar sounds of battle, made worse by the howl of the wind and not being able to see. Or was that better? I couldn't tell. More strident battle horns. The light flashed on the brow again.

"Archers away!" Cadwy shouted.

They shot forward like the hare out of the trap at a greyhound race, galloping full tilt toward the unseen road, silent but for the thud of hooves on turf.

"I need to see," I hissed at Merlin, as the rows of men in front of us fought to keep their horses under control, and Alezan swung around in pirouettes worthy of an Olympic dressage horse. "You need to show me."

He shook his head, brow furrowed in irritation, but eyes flashing with the excitement any warrior feels before a battle. My guards mirrored his expression, their horses prancing on the spot in their eagerness to join in.

Was Llacheu safe? I looked wildly to right and left, but my guards were keeping close around me. Merlin must have guessed my thought. He reached out and caught Alezan's rein near her bit. "No. Stay here where you're safe." He knew me all too well.

"Then show me," I hissed, my voice rising. "Show me again what you can see."

From up on the hill came the sound of British war horns.

I put my reins into one hand and grabbed Merlin's arm. "Show me!"

At the front, Cadwy raised his voice in a shout. "Forward in close formation. Spread out to doubles. Charge!"

His war horns sounded, loud and close. Thunder crashed overhead in the boiling clouds. The gloom of semi-darkness filled the beech wood as the branches whipped and screamed. I yanked Alezan's head to turn her in a circle, away from the warriors.

As for them, all they needed to do was release the hold they had on the tightly coiled springs that were their mounts. Like the start of the Grand National, the horses leapt forward straight from halt to gallop. Their riders, howling war cries at the tops of their voices, fighting to keep their side-by-side formation, thundered across the turf toward the unseen left flank of the enemy, the line widening as the riders spread out.

For a minute I had to concentrate on preventing Alezan from joining them.

Chapter Thirty-Nine

EVEN WITH BOTH hands on Alezan's reins, I struggled to prevent her from galloping after Cadwy's charging cavalry. She snaked her head down, yanking me forward to get more rein, but I jammed my legs forward and hauled her back up then turned her in a circle, keeping her head facing away from the road. Cold rain scalded my face. Beside me, Merlin and our guards were having the same trouble. Horses, being herd animals, have an instinct to stay together, especially if some of them go galloping off.

"Hold hard!" Merlin shouted, as one of our guards lost his fight, and his horse galloped after Cadwy's cavalry. "Look to the Queen."

I fought Alezan to a halt, her head up, ears pricked, and body quivering with tension. The smell of hot, excited horse rose around us in a fug.

From having been sightless at the rear, now we had an unimpeded view of the approach to the battlefield and of Cadwy's cavalry as they disappeared over the brow of the hill. More thunder crashed overhead, and lightning lit the dark sky, drowning out the sounds of battle.

Merlin brought his horse in beside me. "Back inside the wood. We don't want to be seen."

I glared at him. "I need to see this battle. He's my *husband*. And I *know* you can show me. You have to."

For a moment, confusion filled his eyes, swiftly followed by realization. "You *saw*?"

I nodded. "I did. I saw Llacheu's men preparing to attack. Just for a moment, when you touched me."

He reached out and grabbed Alezan's right rein. "Back inside the wood then. Get out of sight, and I'll try again. Come on." He had to shout above the noise of the wind and rain.

With our guards, we plunged between the smooth beech trunks, back to where we'd originally been standing. Low branches thick with turning leaves blocked our view, rattling in the wind, and the force of the rain lessened.

"Make a circle around the Queen," Merlin snapped at the five remaining men. "Not you. Get to the forest edge, and watch out for Saxons coming our way. Now." The fifth rider spun his horse back to the northern boundary of our wood.

Four riders couldn't make much of a circle, but they did their best.

Impatient, desperate even, I caught Merlin's wrist, my nails digging into the flesh. "Show me now, before it's too late."

He compressed his lips. "I don't know if it'll work a second time…"

I scowled. "Well, try." The words shot out like bullets from a gun.

Alezan's hooves paced time in the leaf mold, but I didn't release Merlin's wrist.

Heaving in a deep breath, Merlin set his teeth over his lower lip for a moment. "Trying is all I can do. You know how little control I have over my gifts. Be patient."

I let go.

His chin dropped to his chest, and his eyes closed. His restless horse, as though influenced by her rider's sudden change, stood quiet, head down.

I stared, unable to drag my gaze away.

Merlin's shoulders rose and fell as his breathing slowed, their movement almost hypnotic.

Every cell in my body quivered with anticipation and need.

Our guards, wary and afraid of anything that might be magic, turned their heads away. Their swift, secretive fingers made the sign against the evil eye.

I waited, my heartbeat counting the seconds.

Time stretched out. Thunder rolled again, followed by a jagged streak of lightning almost overhead. We were at the eye of the storm.

Merlin's left hand shot out and closed around my right forearm. "Shut your eyes." His voice, almost unrecognizable, had lowered to a hiss.

I obeyed. The rain began to fall more heavily, and the wind lashed the still leafy branches. Water ran off my helmet and down my neck.

Darkness behind my eyelids. My own breathing loud in my ears.

I concentrated on the touch of his hand on my arm. His warmth radiated through my tunic, blossoming until a real heat threatened to sear my skin.

Sound came to me first, battering its way through the darkness. Horses screamed, men shouted, weapons clashed, and thunder rolled. So loud and so real my eyes almost flicked open in terror that the battle had somehow found its way into our wood, and we'd been surrounded.

Then came smell. Blood. Shit. Sweat. Wet horses. Wet men. A stench of sulfur that might have been from the raging storm.

I opened my eyes. Lightning fissured the black clouds, sending jagged bolts to strike the earth like the wrath of God himself. Rain tumbled down. The dark clouds that had made a dim twilight of the day blazed with a strobing light, as beneath the storm the battle raged.

Chaos. Men fought pressed up against one another. Shoulder to shoulder, face to face. Saxons, or they might have been our men, unhorsed, fell under the hooves of our cavalry, trampled into the wet ground. Impossible to tell who was who.

Shouts – "For Dumnonia!" –whose voice was that? Battle horns – sounding for which side? Screams of the dying. The harsh cries of the circling carrion birds. The crash of lightning, the drum of rain, the stink of death.

A horse's brown ears lay flat against her head in front of me. She struck out with her front hooves as she'd been trained, then kicked out with both back legs, jerking me in the saddle. As good, or better, a weapon as a lance, but more use at close quarters. I had no lance. Instead, a glittering sword flashed in my hands, the damascene blade slick with blood.

Excalibur.

I was inside Arthur's head. With Merlin.

The shock almost threw me out, but I scrabbled back inside, and Arthur's primal exhilaration surged through my body. No fear, so I had none, either. We were as one, more so than at any time in our lives together, closer than even the act of sex could make us. Did he know I was here, seeing through his eyes?

My fingers – his gloved fingers – gripped the sword hilt. Excalibur scythed through the air, biting into a Saxon neck. Blood fountained, splattering onto Taran's coat and my leg. Arthur – my hand under his, in his, with his? – wrenched Excalibur free, and with him I kicked his horse on. Instead of the normal revulsion and nausea, all I felt was exultation.

The Saxon leader. Arthur knew him, so I did too. His name leapt into my head. Aelle. Cerdic's uncle. A giant of a man, but small compared to a mounted warrior.

My sword arm buzzed with heat in every muscle as I slashed to right and left, leaning down to drive my weapon into a throat, to lop off a head, to beat back an attacker.

Deep in the melée, I saw no further than the men around me. My men.

Someone slashed at my leg – Arthur's bad leg – and warm wetness ran down my thigh. But it was nothing. I swung my horse, she reared, deadly hooves striking out. The sound of the man's head caving in was like the splitting of a log with an axe. Got him.

My hand went to my leg for a moment. Just a scratch, and no pain as yet. That would come later.

The part of us that was me wanted to look for Cei, and Llacheu and the other men I knew and loved, but what linked me with Arthur kept me shackled inside his head, in his body, seeing only what he saw. A sea of enemy warriors, our cavalry amongst them. The clash of weapons. The red of blood. The dead underfoot, trampled into the sparse downland soil.

Something made me turn my head, water running into my eyes. His head. We turned together. On the edge of the melée, a rider knocked an arrow to his bow, setting it to his shoulder in one swift movement. For the smallest morsel of a second our eyes met across the maelstrom of battle.

Then a hammer-blow impacted my left shoulder, swinging me round and almost knocking me off my horse. Only the four steadying horns kept me in the saddle as I lost my stirrups.

My link with Arthur shimmered and I felt him being pulled away from me. I looked down. An arrow shaft, white feathered, protruded from between the close coupled rings of my mailshirt. Blood darkened the rings.

Horror, mine alone, not his, shivered through me, as pain did the same to Arthur.

Our link severed. I recoiled into my own body in the woods, the battle left behind.

My eyes snapped open, wide and terrified. They met Merlin's.

"He's not dead." Merlin's whisper came so low I almost didn't hear it. "Wounded but not dead." The look in his eyes did nothing to reassure me.

Tears streamed down my cheeks. "I lost him." My words came out on a gasp, as low as Merlin's. "I lost him." I dropped my reins and clutched his hands in mine. "Oh God. I felt it happen. He's hurt. I felt his pain. An arrow…" With all the connotations that brought.

Merlin grasped my hands. "He'll be all right. I know he will."

How could he know? My husband was hurt. Badly. I snatched my hands back and stared toward the unseen battle.

From the trees beyond the brow, a flock of crows soared into the air in a flurry of dirty-washing wings, and overhead those buzzards wheeled in greedy anticipation, ignoring the rain. Thunder rolled again, further off, and the leaden rain hammered down harder.

I swung around on Merlin. "How can you be sure?" My voice rose in panic. "I need to see him." My heart, that had already been racing, sped up even more, as though it might come leaping out of my dry, constricted throat.

Alezan stuck her head in the air, eyes rolling wildly, and I had to grab her reins. She wanted to be a part of this, to gallop with her fellows. The urge to let her do so rose up strong in me. A firm hand came down over mine on the reins.

I looked into Merlin's anxious face. "No," he said, voice harsh. "Arthur would never allow it. And neither will I. You stay here with me. It's my job to keep you safe."

Almost as though something had transmitted itself from his hand, through mine and into Alezan, she settled, ears twitched upright, but no longer itching to gallop into the fray. And the yearning left me too. I heaved a huge breath, finding I'd been holding it too long.

"That's right," Merlin said, more gently now. "Your place is to watch and record what you see. For posterity. And you can't do that if you're lying dead on the battlefield."

"What if Arthur is?" I snapped. "What do I write then?"

Merlin bit his lip. "He won't be. This is not the day he dies."

Every hair on my body stood on end. Did Merlin know that day? Was it fast approaching? I wanted so much to ask him what he knew.

Instead, I pulled my hand away from his. "Don't you wish you too could fight? Be part of this battle that will go down in history and legend?"

He pulled a rueful face and shook his head. "My duty is to do as my lord bids."

"And wait," I said, unable to keep the bitterness out of my voice.

He nodded. "And wait."

With nothing to see; that was how we waited. Blind, but not deaf. The thunder moved away, but didn't take the rain with it, and the constant drumming dimmed the noise of battle. The trees, with their late autumn gowns already depleted by the vicious wind, gave us little shelter.

I drew my cloak closer around me and pulled up my wet hood over my helmet, but it made little difference. My leather braccae kept some of the rain out, but water pooled on my saddle, and my tunic soaked up the rain like blotting paper. The rain mingled with the tears I couldn't staunch.

Where was Cerdic when we needed him? Where was that two-faced bastard? He'd taken the knee to Arthur and vowed to be his man, and yet he wasn't here. We'd sent for him, a mere sixty miles off, and he hadn't come. Hatred bubbled within me, hot and vibrant and all-consuming.

Time inched past. The rain kept falling. The thunder and lightning retreated.

Gradually the battle must have been inching our way, until at last we could see the fighting on the brow of the hill. Dead and dying men fell to the soaking grass. A few crawled our way, perhaps thinking to find a safe hiding place within our woodland. They didn't reach us.

Where was Arthur? I scanned the seething maelstrom of men but didn't find him. Nor Cei, nor Llacheu, nor anyone I knew. Every man's face was dark with blood – theirs or their enemies'. Like some Dantéesque inferno.

The battle had been raging for an eternity when my sharp ears caught a distant sound carrying on the wind. I grabbed Merlin's arm afresh, voice rising in a mixture of panic and excitement. "What's that? Did you hear it?"

He cocked his head on one side, like a dog, listening, and the four men surrounding us did the same. The sound came again.

Merlin's face lit up. "That's a horn. A war horn. From the south. Not one of ours. This way."

Spinning our horses around, all six of us crashed through the trees toward the south, away from the battle. The wood wasn't deep. As we burst out onto open ground, the warhorn sounded again. I pulled Alezan to a halt and stared, open mouthed, as relief washed over me. Galloping across the wide, rainwashed valley came Cerdic and his men. A fresh army.

"Let's hope they've decided they're on our side," Merlin said.

My hand went to my mouth. Might they not be? Might this be why they'd left it so late? Could Cerdic have chosen to join his uncle's men? Cold fear closed around my heart and my knees went so weak I had to grab Alezan's neck to stay in the saddle.

Chapter Forty

CERDIC AND HIS army didn't pause, but swept past us around the eastern end of our beech woodland, hooves thundering on the turf, kicking up clods of dirt, their chainmail glittering. Their angry, insistent warhorn sounded again.

Merlin reached out a hand to steady me. "Back." We swung our horses around once more and urged them into the woodland, guards in hot pursuit. Branches whipped my face, but I didn't care. On the far edge, I wrenched Alezan to a halt in time to see Cerdic's forces fall upon the battle.

Time stood still.

For one long and terrible moment I thought they'd joined the fight against Arthur and Cadwy and that we were doomed. That Badon would not be the British victory of legend. That I'd changed too much, and history had chosen to follow a different path.

"Yes!" Merlin punched the air. "He's chosen us."

Now we had the advantage, surely.

But the Saxons were nothing if not determined, and the fighting continued, inching back toward the road and out of our sight as our forces gained ground, propelled by Cerdic's fresh onslaught. I could still see nothing, nor tell which warriors were ours. There was a lot to be said for different colored uniforms.

I itched to follow, but Merlin held me back. Sensibly. What good could I have done? A lot of harm, most likely.

Slowly, as the rain at last began to lessen, the battle shifted over the brow. Were the Saxons in retreat? Did we at last have them beaten? Oh, how I longed to know.

And what about Arthur with that arrow in his shoulder? Unable to do anything, I pushed my fear for him away, but with little success. All I could think of was that terrible thud as the arrow had pierced his mailshirt and flesh. And the pain that had severed my link with him.

The conflict might have been out of sight, but the battle noises carried, the terrible death noises I dreaded – the noises I would hear forever in my nightmares.

If only I could see what was going on. Not for my book. No, that was forgotten. For Arthur.

Alezan, alert to my anxiety, refused to stand still, instead pacing and tossing her head, her tail switching back and forth.

"Can't we ride closer?" I begged Merlin, at last. "I can't stand not knowing much longer." I swallowed the lump that wouldn't leave my throat. "Almost as much as I hate to see it." Hysteria lurked close by.

He shook his head. "Too dangerous."

I sucked in my lips, groping for something, anything. "Can you look again? See? I mean… can you use the Sight to tell us… to tell me… if Arthur lives?" Just saying the words brought tears to my eyes and the urge to sob swept over me. I dug my nails into my palms and fought for self-control. "Can you? For me?"

This time I didn't want him to share. Didn't want to see if he found Arthur… dead. Didn't want to even think about it. Yet did. The gnawing at my insides brought bile into my mouth. I spat and spat again.

Merlin licked lips which were probably as dry as mine, indecision in his dark eyes.

"Please," I whispered, my voice dry with fear and tears streaking my cheeks. "Please, Merlin."

He nodded. "All right. For you. But I warn you – it probably won't work a second time."

Should I watch? Or look away? My fear of what he'd find made me lower my eyes to the horns of my saddle, where my icy fingers clutched the reins.

Something told me he'd closed his eyes. I took a sideways peek. He had. His thin face had a tension about it for a moment, before it relaxed, and his shoulders shuddered and sank.

Silence pressed in. The wind that had been harrying us all day died, and the branches hung motionless above us as though we'd stepped out of the real world. The very air pressed in thick around me. Alezan's ears flicked back and forth. She snorted. Dead leaves rustled, suddenly loud.

"He lives," Merlin said, his voice barely above a whisper. "He is wounded, as you saw, but he lives."

Thank God. I choked back a sob of relief. "And Cei?"

Silence.

Breath held, I waited.

"He lives."

I heaved a sigh. One more. "Llacheu?"

An even longer silence. My heart knocked against my ribs and my mouth went sawdust-dry.

"He lives."

Another sob escaped me, bitten back. I dug my nails into my hands, staring down at them and willing the tears not to fall. "And...Cadwy?"

Silence. "Do you care?"

Did I? No. But his death might mean change for the better. "Does he live?"

He shrugged. "I see him lying broken on the battlefield."

How strange. I'd expected to be glad. I wasn't. I'd hated Cadwy for so long, and now he might be gone. Why did I feel sad? Because he was not just a feared enemy, a man not to be trusted. He was a human being with a wife and son, with feelings, who I'd seen distraught over the accidental death of a servant. No one is just bad with no good in him. We're all a mix of both.

Merlin grunted, as though in pain himself. "We have the victory." His breathing came harsh and loud. "The Saxons have ceded defeat. The battle ends." He sounded as though he'd been running. "The Saxon army has retreated."

I waited for him to go on, eyes still firmly on my hands, the relief that had flooded through me on hearing Arthur lived ebbing. Even if he had survived, others, who would never return to their wives and families, had not.

"Many lie dead." Merlin's voice broke. He choked on his words. "Blood soaks the ground. Men, horses. Crows settle. Tearing at flesh." He fought to get the words out from between teeth that must have been clenched. "Heads, arms, legs. Truly a battle to be proud of." Was that bitterness in his voice?

Did he see the futility of all this, as I did? He wasn't the Merlin of legend, no old wizard in a long gown, but a man with the Sight who happened to be a warrior too. And yet, there was about him something else. A knowing. A compassion. A sense that he saw further than the rest. Did he, perhaps, see that one day it would be the Saxons who would take over this island? Did he know I came from a world shaped by them?

Out of the corner of my eye I caught his movement as he shook himself. I turned my head and began to breathe more regularly. "Can we go? I need to be with him."

He frowned, his head tilted to one side, listening again, like a dog. "I think so. But if I tell you to ride away, you must do so without question. At a gallop." He straightened. "However, I'm fairly sure it's safe to go. And Arthur will want to know you're safe as much as you wanted to know he was." He shortened his reins. "I'll lead. Keep close, and we'll take it in a walk. Give them even more time." He beckoned to the guards who fell in on either side of us, eyeing him askance. Rarely did he give any evidence of his well-hidden powers. This would make a tale to tell around the hearth to their families.

We rode up the gentle slope to the road, through the sudden quiet of the afternoon. Only it wasn't really quiet, any more than it had been while we'd lain in wait for the Saxons.

The storm had passed, leaving the land rainwashed but not clean. Never clean. The dead dotted the slope where they'd crawled or rolled, and already the carrion birds had settled. Crows carked raucously as they competed for the choicest morsels, pecking at the soft flesh of faces. The buzzards I'd seen circling descended for the feast, bold enough to ignore us as we rode past.

A few of the still-living moaned for help, weak-voiced and piteous. I averted my gaze, guilt for not stopping to help them almost overwhelming. Some could have been our own men, but the blood and dirt of battle hid that from me. That was my feeble excuse.

Determination to see for myself that Arthur still lived overrode everything. These men would have to wait.

Closer to the road, the dead lay everywhere, scattered across the ancient, graveled surface, sprawled in the still-deep ditches to either side, spreadeagled on what had once been close-cropped green grass but now was black with blood.

The sickly, iron-rich stench of their blood mingled with the stink of excrement, a hand over my nose not enough to keep it out. I fought the old urge to vomit.

But I couldn't drag my horrified eyes away. Just as Merlin had said, severed limbs and hacked bodies lay in tangled jumbles where they'd fallen. Already their humanity had vanished – they lay like broken marionettes, tumbled, forgotten, unreal, their unquiet souls fled.

More crows settled in swarms like flies, eager for the feast. The not-quite-dead batted feeble arms to fend them off – crows make no discrimination between the living and the dead.

The inclination to vomit receded at last. Twelve years had hardened me. The innocent librarian who'd tumbled back in time had long ago become a warrior queen.

Horses lay gutted and twitching, legs broken, intestines hanging out, squealing and groaning in pain, and our men hastened to finish them off. The men's filthy, blood-smeared faces showed their horror at doing this. A horse was more than just transport to them, more than just a servant. A horse was their friend, their partner, dearer to many of them than their wives. How much must it hurt to have to kill them?

But they weren't just finishing off the horses. Their swift, sharp knives slit the throats of the wounded enemy, as well. Gurgles and cries filled my ears, drowning the moans for help. Even a warrior, when mortally wounded, becomes a child again, calling for his mother.

I tore my eyes away and set my gaze between Alezan's sharply pricked ears, fixed on Merlin's back. The fear that if I looked to left or right, I would find one of my dear friends lying dead, or worse, not yet dead, threatened to overwhelm me. Alezan stepped daintily over the bodies, unfazed by the sight and stench of death. She'd seen it before enough times. She knew death as well as I did.

The battle was well and truly over.

Our men had gathered on the far side of the ridge. Many had dismounted. We approached with caution, my eyes scanning the blood-spattered faces of the exhausted warriors, searching for my loved ones.

A man lay on the ground in the center of the group, half propped against his dead horse. Cadwy. His thick legs sprawled akimbo, his bulky body, soaked in blood, slumped like a lumpy sack. But he wasn't dead. His small, malevolent eyes peered out from between the folds of gray flesh that sagged on his face.

Arthur was on his knees beside him, with Custennin. Both of them had discarded their helmets, their hair plastered to their heads with sweat. I couldn't miss the arrow still in Arthur's shoulder, the white fletching on the shaft stained with blood, the point protruding from his back.

Merlin dismounted, and I, too, slithered to the ground. My knees gave way as the world spun for a moment, and I had to hang onto one of the horns on Alezan's saddle or I'd have sunk to the churned mud. My heart wasn't so much hammering as doing uneven leaping bounds in its efforts to emerge from my throat. Merlin slid a much-needed supporting hand under my elbow as I drew a steadying breath.

"Arthur." His name came out weaker than I'd expected, but he heard and turned his head, a little awkwardly as though doing so pained him.

"Gwen."

I shook off Merlin's hand and took the half dozen steps to reach Arthur's side. Custennin didn't move, but Cadwy's piggy eyes blinked up at me, as if he were struggling to focus.

I went down on my knees on the wet, trampled ground beside Arthur. Were those tears in his eyes? Did he, despite their years of emnity, care about his brother?

Cadwy's lips moved. "The Ring Maiden sees my end." Just a whisper.

On an impulse I put out my hand and took his. If his wife couldn't hold it as he died, then I could do it for her, and perhaps offer him some comfort.

The ghost of a smile brushed his blueing lips. "You chose the right brother."

I nodded, and took Arthur's hand as well, linking them.

Arthur grunted. "You did the right thing at the end," he said. "And you will be remembered for it."

Cadwy snorted, his face contorting in a grimace. "Make sure it's not your end as well." His eyes went to the arrow shaft.

"Just a scratch," Arthur said. "Just a scratch."

Cadwy's eyes flicked to his son's face. I followed his gaze.

He licked his lips. "You'll be a better king than me," he whispered. "Look after your mother for me."

Custennin, pale-faced and filthy, swallowed. "I promise, Father."

Cadwy's eyes began to glaze. Under my hand, his went slack, and a sigh bubbled from his lips with a trickle of blood. His head lolled to one side, jaw slack.

Custennin swallowed again. No mere prince now, but a king. Dried blood masked his face, but apart from that he showed no sign of injury. He released his father's hand, and got to his feet. Leaning on me, Arthur did the same, his face beneath the dirt nearly as pale as his dead brother's.

The urge to make Arthur sit down while I looked after him welled up inside me, but I didn't move. He couldn't afford to show any sign of weakness in front of another king. Just because Custennin was not his father didn't mean he harbored no desire to annex Dumnonia to Powys once again.

I kept my arm linked through Arthur's in unobtrusive support in case he staggered.

My anxious gaze slid over the crowd, picking out my loved ones, my relief rising at the sight of each familiar face: Cei, Llacheu, Bedwyr, Drustans, Gwalchmei, Anwyll. And Cerdic.

Arthur straightened, with a grimace of not-so-well-disguised pain, and held out his bloody right hand to Custennin. The young man took it, clasping forearms in a manly shake that brought another grimace. Then Arthur, teeth gritted, raised his nephew's arm. "King Custennin," he shouted, with perhaps less strength than usual. "God save King Custennin."

Chapter Forty-One

ALL AROUND US men raised their voices – the warriors of Powys of course, cheering Custennin, their new king, but also our men of Dumnonia, and Cerdic's men from Caer Guinntguic. With gusto, Cerdic joined the chorus of cheers, his face alight with what might well have been a sense of belonging.

How hard must it have been for him, brought up at a foreign court, to take up his father's crown and try to rule a kingdom of predominantly hostile subjects. A sudden sense of bonding rose unexpectedly in my heart. Like me, he'd been a stranger to his people. Like me, he'd had to win them over. But for him it must have been ten times harder.

Arthur released Custennin's arm and took a couple of unsteady steps back, face drawn. Bedwyr was by his side in a moment, a hand slipping under his right elbow. "Leave this," he muttered, keeping his voice low. "You need to come with me and let me get that arrow out."

"I'll help." I followed Bedwyr as he forcibly escorted Arthur away from the center of activity, leaving the body of his brother and the celebrations of the new king behind us. How ephemeral was kingship that Custennin could be cheered with his father's last breath still hanging in the air? Would Arthur's men do that when he was gone? A shiver wracked my whole body, and I hurried my footsteps.

After a dozen wary paces, Arthur halted. His wound must be jarring with every step he took, the numbness adrenalin would have provided dissipating. With awkward precision, he turned to face me, almost as though he'd not noticed me until now. "Gwen." His tone was apologetic. Pulling free of Bedwyr's hold, he gingerly put his hand to his shoulder, taking care not to touch the arrow. "It's nothing. Bedwyr will get it out." He managed a faint and not-at-all convincing grin.

"It's an arrow," I said, my voice wobbling despite a heroic effort to keep it steady. "I'm not an idiot. I know how bad that is." Images of the wounds removing an arrow could cause kept flashing through my mind, impossible to chase away.

Bedwyr caught Arthur's elbow again. "This way. I need to get it out."

Arthur shook his head, wincing. "I have to organize a new camp. What to do with the prisoners. Set up lookouts."

I met Bedwyr's anxious gaze. "Cei can do that," I said. "You know he can. Do as Bedwyr says. Please."

For answer, the sound of Cei's raised voice rose behind us, shouting orders. He didn't need telling he was in command for the time being.

Arthur's failed effort to shrug made him screw his face up in pain. "Very well. Get it out and bandaged up and get me back where I belong."

Where he belonged was in a hospital bed after a proper, sterile, surgical removal of this arrow, but that wasn't going to be happening any time soon.

"This way," Bedwyr ordered. Where the trees crowded the roadside, two of our younger warriors, his apprentices, stood holding his horse and their own, all three laden with heavy saddlebags that would be full of wound dressings and medicines. As the nearest thing to a doctor we had, Bedwyr had come prepared.

He rummaged in the copious saddlebags and came out with a small saw.

Arthur managed a chuckle. "Which bit of me are you thinking of amputating?"

Bedwyr shook his head, face serious. "Sit down." He indicated the hump of a dead horse. "You'll need to. I need to get this out as quickly as possible and make sure no dirt was carried in with it. No bits of your clothing."

Oh God. I hadn't thought of that. Not only did we have to face digging out an arrow, but also the possibility the wound was already infected. Hadn't Richard the Lionheart died from an arrow wound? I wouldn't think about it.

With only a cursory glance, Arthur sat down on the horse's flank, setting his feet apart and his hands on his knees. "Get on with it."

Bedwyr pursed his lips. "Better take a swig of this." He handed Arthur a flask from a pouch on his hip. He eyed his friend. "On second thought, better have it all."

Arthur needed no encouraging. He put his head back and drained the flask.

"What shall I do?" I asked, trying to instil in my voice some hint of capability and confidence. The very day I'd met Arthur, all those years ago, I'd treated his wounded hand, and been able to do so with perfect equanimity, save for the worry that if he died from the wound I might well have been blamed. He'd meant nothing to me then. Twelve years had wrought a huge difference to my feelings.

Bedwyr glanced at me out of anxious eyes. "Do you think you can hold him steady?"

I set my teeth and nodded. No ambulances here. It wasn't a matter of choice – I had to.

He grunted. "Then get behind him, brace your knee against his back and take hold of his shoulders."

Swallowing my fear, I did as I was told, stepping over the spear lodged in the dead horse's belly to stand between its legs, my shins pressed against its cooling skin.

The arrowhead had come right through Arthur's shoulder to stick out between the broken links of his mailshirt on the far side. When I took hold of him, he grunted in pain, but I knew better than to let go and have to try again. Best to be firm the first time. I put my knee against the small of his back, bracing myself, compressing my lips in a hard, determined line.

Merlin and Llacheu approached, no doubt having left the organizing to Cei.

"Father?" Llacheu's voice wavered as he stared at his stricken father out of wide, frightened eyes, suddenly a boy again.

"It's nothing," Arthur repeated the lie. "Let Bedwyr do his job."

Merlin put a restraining hand on Llacheu's arm, perhaps in comfort. "He knows what he's doing."

Disregarding this not quite glowing reference, and without a glance at either of them, Bedwyr took the saw and laid it against the shaft of the arrow close to where it stuck out of Arthur's chest.

Merlin laid a gentle hand on my shoulder. "Let me do this."

I shook my head. "No. I have this. But thank you."

He stepped back to stand beside Llacheu, who'd gone as pale as his father. The boy's Adam's apple bobbed as he swallowed several times. Like me, he'd seen enough of battles, deaths and wounds before, but it's different when the wounded person is someone you love. And every one of us was acutely conscious of how any wound in these dangerous times of no antiseptics or anaesthetics could prove fatal.

Bedwyr began to saw. Under my hands, Arthur's body quivered, and he gripped his knees. Bedwyr didn't slow. "Best to get it done quickly," he muttered. "Lucky it's a bodkin and not a barbed arrowhead."

The saw worked back and forth. Arthur's knuckles whitened and the tension in his body twanged. At last, the arrow shaft snapped off, close to Arthur's chest, with less than half an inch left showing.

Bedwyr let it fall to the ground. "I'm going to pull it through from behind," he muttered, half to Arthur, half to me, Merlin, and Llacheu. "That's the only way. If I try it from this side the arrowhead could come off inside the wound and be hard to get out. He's lucky it went right through and missed his shoulder blade."

"I am here, you know," Arthur said, through gritted teeth. "Get on with it before I change my mind and decide to keep it."

The pulling of an arrow shaft through a body is the most terrible thing to see. Well, it was the most terrible thing I'd seen, because it was being done to the man I loved. Bedwyr had a special tool he gripped the arrow with, close to Arthur's shoulder and just below the long, vicious looking head. Bedwyr heaved on that arrow, while Arthur sat, rigid with pain, and this time both Merlin and Llacheu, with their greater strength, had to hold him still in place of me.

It didn't want to come. A puncture wound from a long, thin, bodkin-headed arrow is like quicksand. What goes in, doesn't want to come out. The flesh has been torn and damaged, but it's hanging on tight, sucking onto the intruding weapon and not wanting to let go. Bedwyr had to twist the shaft to loosen it, as Arthur sat stonily silent, his face paper-white.

At last, with a horrible sucking noise, it slid out of the wound with a gush of blood.

If I'd had anything to eat that day, I'd have been sick on the spot. The blood, my wounded husband, the lack of food, my rising thirst – all contributed to a wave of dizziness that sent me staggering.

Arthur must have felt much the same. He swayed where he was sitting, and his eyes rolled up in his head. Bedwyr threw the damaged arrow aside. "Quick, while he's fainting, get his mailshirt off."

He, Merlin, and Llacheu had that shirt off in a moment, followed by his wet and blood-soaked, padded tunic. The rain hadn't reached his undershirt, but they pulled that off too, keeping him propped upright on the horse's flank as they did so. Bright blood ran down both his chest and back from the wound, but not so vigorously as it had when Bedwyr extracted the arrow.

"Let me see his clothing." Bedwyr examined both tunic and undershirt, squinting myopically at the hole the arrow had made, while I held my breath. "It's all there." He grinned. "Nothing carried into the wound as far as I can see."

Arthur's eyes opened, unfocused and bleary. "It's bloody freezing," he muttered, wrapping his right arm across his torso. Balmy autumn had given way to early winter in one short day. Was he in shock? All I knew about that was that you had to keep the patient warm and it could kill as swiftly as a wound.

"I'll be quick as I can," Bedwyr snapped, glancing up at me. "There's a blanket roll behind my saddle. Get it to wrap around him. We have to keep him warm."

Glad of something to do, I unfastened the blanket and unrolled it, eyes fixed on Arthur's face.

"Hold him still." With calm efficiency, Bedwyr tipped spirits into the wound on both sides, eliciting a bitten off cry of pain from Arthur. Then he scooped honey from an earthenware jar and packed it into the wound, pushing it in as far as it would go. The only antiseptic ointment available.

Two large, clean linen pads went on next. With gentle fingers he applied one to the entry wound in Arthur's chest, turning to me with expectant eyes. "Can you hold this in place?"

I did, as he covered the exit wound in his back in the same way. What was in the shoulder? More than you think, was all I knew. This wound was high – just beneath his collarbone. Hopefully it had avoided damaging anything important. At least he wasn't coughing blood, so it hadn't touched a lung.

Arthur briefly raised his eyes and shot me a weak smile, which I returned. While Merlin and Llacheu kept Arthur upright, Bedwyr wrapped bandages around his chest and shoulder, finally fastening the end in place with a copper pin.

I draped the blanket around Arthur's shoulders and pulled it tight in front of him to keep the warmth inside.

His good hand came up to hold it firm. Drawing a shallow breath, he forced himself up straight, looking past me at Merlin. "Done. Find me my horse."

"No riding until tomorrow," Bedwyr said, his tone firm.

Arthur arched an eyebrow at him. "I need my horse. The men must see I'm recovered." He set his hand on my shoulder and leaning heavily on me, got to his feet. The blanket fell away. "Clothes and my horse. Now."

A pregnant silence ensued.

I could see his point. This was an age when the strongest man ruled. He didn't want to appear weakened in any way. But I could also see Bedwyr's. The arrow might have come away cleanly and missed anything vital, but that was nonetheless a nasty wound. I licked my lips.

I was saved from having to speak by Cei's hasty arrival.

"I've had the men set up camp in the beechwood here on the brow," Cei said, gesturing to the woodland behind us. "It's a bit drier. A few have ridden back to bring what we left behind at the fort. Custennin's organizing his men to do the same. The prisoners we've taken will keep – they're securely under guard. The survivors have fled, but not that far. Onto the far hill where they can see us, and we can see them. We've got both their leaders here in chains, and they don't look like they want to leave without them."

Arthur nodded, then winced. "I need to speak with Aelle and whatever their other general… king… commander is called."

"Octha," Llacheu said. "Cerdic told me."

"Not today," Bedwyr snapped.

Cei nodded. "They can stew overnight. We've enough guards to keep them safe. Their runaways won't dare attack for fear we'll kill their leaders. I've posted lookouts in all directions."

Arthur grimaced. "As you say." He glanced at Bedwyr. "Best go and attend to our other wounded. But before you go, do you have any poppy syrup? This burns like a red-hot poker in my shoulder." He managed an unconvincing chuckle. "Didn't hurt a bit when it happened."

Bedwyr took a vial from his bag.

Arthur stretched out his hand, but Bedwyr handed it to me. "Half now, half to get him some sleep tonight. It's strong stuff. Easy to overdose. You keep it."

He passed me a cup. "That's the right size dose for someone his size. No more."

I measured out the liquid and Arthur swallowed it down greedily, grimacing at the bitterness. I stowed the empty cup and the vial in the small bag that hung from my belt.

"Now," Cei said, "let's get you to the woods."

"On my horse and in clothes," Arthur said.

Bedwyr heaved a sigh. "On your horse, then. You're going to regret putting clothes on, though."

Chapter Forty-Two

Someone had lit a fire. Well, quite a few someones had lit fires, taking advantage of the amount of fallen wood within the sheltering trees. And to my relief it had at last stopped raining. The damp woodland twinkled as though a handful of flaming stars had fallen from the now crisp, clear sky, and columns of smoke curled up between the silvery tree trunks to twist between the sweeping branches.

Those men who weren't on guard duty watching over the prisoners, or on watch around the outskirts of our camp, had gathered around the fires, and an air of conviviality adhered to everyone: the conviviality and relief of still being alive after such a battle; the awareness of life coursing through their veins; the buoyancy of stress departing.

Skins of cider passed from hand to hand, and actual hot food, even if it was just dried meat and onions boiled up in cider, filled the holes in every belly. Fresh meat from any of the dead horses could have made a tasty stew, but that would have been like eating one of their friends. One of *our* friends.

Whether it was forced conviviality, I couldn't be sure. Perhaps just the determination of warriors not to allow the loss of brothers and comrades to spoil their victory. In the morning they'd be digging graves for our dead and burning the corpses of our lost horses, but tonight they were refusing to think of that.

Arthur had already declared that we'd be leaving the enemy dead for them to deal with themselves.

I sat with my front toasty warm, and my back chilly, as is normal around a fire at the end of autumn, dipping my hard bread into the hot, meaty broth to soften it, then sucking on the soggy pulp. Delicious.

Whatever would my friends say about my diet? They'd wonder how I got by without salad vegetables and fruit in winter. Without potatoes, tomatoes, pumpkins, aubergines, tea, coffee, oranges… the list of things I sometimes missed, and they'd be horrified to do without, had no end. Chocolate. Maybe that most of all. Now I tried to bring that memory to life, I couldn't remember what it had tasted like. Oh well…

Arthur sat beside me, in a clean undershirt and tunic and with his thick cloak wrapped close around his shoulders. His left arm rested in the sling Bedwyr had insisted he wore.

He'd taken a dish of the stew Gwalchmei had cooked, but most of it still sat in the bowl untouched, and he'd not taken a bite from his bread. Unsurprisingly. Even with the help of the poppy syrup, which I could see was making him sleepy already, he'd have no appetite when in so much pain.

He caught me looking at him and managed a smile. "Not hungry."

I took the bowl from where he had it cupped awkwardly in his left hand. "Want some help?"

He shook his head. "I'll have some more of what Bedwyr has in that flask, though." The strong spirit Bedwyr had given him so he could take the arrow out, distilled from our cider. Like the Breton *Eau de Vie*.

I glanced across at Bedwyr, who shook his head. "Not if you want poppy syrup before you sleep. The two don't mix well."

Arthur sighed. "I'm thinking the time to sleep can't come soon enough." He nodded to Gwalchmei. "How about a rousing song to mark our victory? We could all do with one of those."

Gwalchmei set down his empty wooden bowl, and reached behind him for his lyre. But before he could even start to tune it, a figure loomed out of the gloom.

I stared. Custennin. Unattended by any warriors.

Silence fell around our fire. Custennin's men, as well as Cerdic's, had camped cheek by jowl with ours now Cadwy was no more, but for the young man to have come boldly into our camp by himself, unguarded, surprised me. A daring, or perhaps a trusting, move.

"Good evening," he said, halting a pace back from the circle, the firelight that flickered over his face revealing a hint of awkwardness. He was hardly any older than Llacheu, after all.

Wordless tension fizzled between the seated men. This was Cadwy's son, and no one was about to forget it.

Arthur, drawing himself up straighter and tucking his left arm out of sight beneath his cloak, nodded a welcome. "Come. Sit down and join us. You're welcome at our fire."

On the fallen log on the far side of Arthur, Merlin shuffled along, and Custennin took the seat of honor beside his uncle with due dignity, settling himself and stretching out his long legs toward the fire.

A silence settled between us, all of the men wary and curious, eyes fixed on the newcomer. The new young king of Powys. Cei spoke first. "Cider?" he asked, passing the skin to Custennin.

The young man's heavy-browed face softened into a smile, washing away the look of his surly father and replacing it with more than a suggestion of Arthur. Maybe Cadwy had looked like this as a young man. "Thank you."

He took a swig from the skin, and passed it to Arthur, who, under Bedwyr's reproving gaze, waved it on to me. With no such restrictions, I took a big restorative gulp of the rough, apple-flavoured liquid.

The skin made the circuit of the watchful men – ending at Llacheu, empty. He tossed it to the ground and searched behind himself for another. One thing we weren't short of was alcohol.

Gwalchmei fingered the strings of his lyre, twiddling with the tuning. One of the men threw another log onto the fire, and sparks spiralled up into the darkness, heading for the stars.

"Don't let me stop you," Custennin said, waving a hand at Gwalchmei. "I only came to see how my uncle was. I've seen for myself now, and I'd like to hear a rousing battle song, if you have one."

He didn't seem all that bothered that his father had just died. Nothing like Cei when Rhiwallon had been slain. But then, Custennin had become a king through his father's death, so maybe that saw off any sorrow he might have felt. And Cadwy hadn't exactly been the lovable sort.

Arthur, pale-faced, managed a grin. "Yes. Get on with it, Gwalchmei. Give us your best." He was sitting straighter, probably to disguise from Custennin the pain he was in. I watched him closely.

Gwalchmei finished tuning his lyre and plucked a few rippling notes. He began to sing.

I only half listened to the words, letting the tune roll over me in waves. I'd heard the song before, many times, around the hearth fire in the hall at Din Cadan. A story of long ago, of a great victory fought in the north against the Picts by a king called Cunedda. A wise move by Gwalchmei, to have chosen one of Arthur's and Custennin's own ancestors.

I kept a wary eye on Arthur. Custennin had leaned in toward him, and Arthur was talking in a low voice, hushed and earnest, under cover of the song. I strained my ears but couldn't catch their words.

Around the fire, everyone but Arthur and Custennin, and me, joined in with the rousing chorus, their voices rising skyward with the glowing sparks from the fire. I'd long ago learned that past battles were somehow not so devastating to view in hindsight. Maybe, one day, someone would sing a song about Badon, and make it as stirring as this one. But as far as I knew, it would become lost in time and no longer exist in the distant twenty-first century.

The song came to a rousing end, with all the Picts lying dead on the bloody battlefield and the ancient king victorious.

Custennin clasped forearms with Arthur once again, and got back to his feet. "Thank you for your hospitality, my Lord."

>>><<<

MERLIN AND I made a bed for Arthur close to the fire, despite him telling us not to fuss. A drift of dead beech leaves served to insulate the bottom blanket, but nevertheless, the cold, hard ground would fight its way through. Not that I wasn't used by now to sleeping on the ground. Dark Age queens needed to be tough. But for Arthur, lying down wasn't easy. Eventually, I got him settled lying on his right side, but it was clear he wasn't comfortable, even with the remains of the poppy syrup inside him.

I spooned against his back in an effort to keep him warm, my left arm around his waist and my face close enough to the back of his head that he'd feel my breath on his neck.

For a while, he lay still, and so did I, afraid to move and jiggle his wound, but his breathing betrayed that sleep hadn't come to him.

I moved my mouth a little closer to his ear. "How is it?" I whispered, not wanting to be overheard. Although anyone would have had a job doing so with Cei snoring not far away.

"How d'you think?" he muttered.

"Isn't the poppy syrup working?"

He shifted a little. "I don't think you gave me enough."

I tightened my hold around his waist. "Now you see why Bedwyr put me in charge of it. If you'd had it, you'd have taken an overdose."

He fell silent for a few minutes, but I could tell he was nowhere near sleeping, even though he must have been exhausted.

"Can I do anything?" I whispered.

He grunted. "Find me the man that shot me. I'd like to insert my spear where the sun doesn't shine."

Back in my old world, if anyone had expressed this desire, I'd have taken it with an enormous pinch of salt and laughed. Here, in the savage Dark Ages, I didn't. Doing just that to Arthur's assailant didn't seem an unlikely revenge. The most disturbing thing was that I wanted to do it too. The twenty-first century seemed a long way off.

I stroked his right hand. "He's probably amongst the Saxon dead."

He shifted again, and his body stiffened as though a shock of pain had shafted through him. "I doubt it." The words came out between gritted teeth. "He wasn't a Saxon."

My turn to stiffen. "What?" My voice rose in alarm, and I fought to control it. "Who was he then?" An indignant hiss this time.

"Didn't you see the arrow?" He grunted in pain. "Fletched with white feathers. Powys. An arrow from Powys."

"No-o," I stretched the word out in a gasp of shock. "It can't have been." I paused, uncertainty washing over me. "Can it?"

"Well, it was. Go and look at the Saxon arrows if you want proof. They fletch them with goose feathers. Gray goose feathers with a paler cock feather. These were white with the cock one a light brown. From young swans on the Sabrina river. By Viroconium." He drew an unsteady breath. "I should know. I used those arrows myself as a boy. One of my friends was the son of my father's fletcher. They pride themselves on the whiteness."

My eyes might well have been starting from my head. "You think the man who did this is still alive? Amongst Custennin's men?" I fought to keep my voice under control, my head twisting to peer over my shoulder into the dark woods at my back. Might he be out there now, aiming to finish what he'd started? Sneaking past our lookouts?

"Most likely."

"What will we do?" I bit my lip. "Why didn't you tell Cei and Merlin?"

He sighed. "And ruin what could be a good alliance with Custennin? He's not his father. Nor his aunt. We made a pact tonight, while everyone else was singing. I don't want to risk offending him at the very start of his reign over something he had nothing to do with."

The impulse to shake some sense into him burgeoned. Only his wound stayed my hand. "But it might have been Custennin who organized it. My God, he came to see you tonight to see if you were dying and his plan had worked."

His head moved in the smallest of shakes. Perhaps all he could manage without causing himself more pain. "No. It wasn't him. I'd swear it. And I doubt it was Cadwy, either. This has the mark of Morgana stamped all over it."

Morgana. Why hadn't I thought of her straightaway? Because she was miles away and hadn't traveled with Cadwy's army. But that didn't mean she'd not planted her own men within it. What kind of a relationship did Custennin have with his aunt? Might Morgana's star be on the wane now he was king? I bloody hoped so. "Are we safe? Can her man get us here?"

"Not here," Arthur murmured, sounding sleepy at last. "Too many guards. You don't think I'd let the men of Powys camp beside us without Cei setting up a row of guards between us, do you? If my would-be assassin wasn't killed in the battle, he won't get through tonight. And he failed. I'm not dead. He might well have already fled rather than reporting back to Morgana that he's let her down and her plan has failed – again."

I nodded, but something still puzzled me. "But now Cadwy, her candidate, is dead, who could she want to put on the High King's throne?"

"Not Custennin," Arthur whispered, more sleepy still. "Her brat by Merlin. That's who."

A girl. And a girl with power, at that. I shivered. I wouldn't have wanted to be in Custennin's shoes when Morgana decided it was time her daughter should take the reins of government.

Chapter Forty-Three

THE MORNING BROUGHT clear skies and a world washed clean by the storm's downpour, but the ground remained wet and mired where the battle had taken place. With it came the digging of graves and the burial of our dead.

Cei set the prisoners to work on the grave-digging. As he pointed out to Arthur, "Why have a dog and bark yourself?" Thirty or so big Saxons, shirtless and filthy, labored on the churned-up grassland beside the road. A dozen of our heavily armed warriors watched over them, as they hacked their way through the thin soil and chalky bedrock with pickaxes and shovels. Despite the downpour, the rain hadn't penetrated far below the surface, and the soil was nearly as difficult to dig as the chalk.

Declaring himself recovered, which wasn't true, Arthur told Cei firmly that neither of the commanders should be submitted to humiliation. "I want to make some sort of treaty with them, not turn them into worse enemies," he said, standing by the still smoking remains of last night's campfire. His face remained ashy-pale, and he had his left arm hidden under his cloak, but at least he'd eaten.

After breakfast, Bedwyr had given him another dose of the poppy syrup – smaller this time, to Arthur's disgust. "Too much, too often is bad for you," Bedwyr cautioned. "I've seen men take just a few doses too many and then crave for it like mad men. Best not to get to that state. This dose has to last you all day."

Addiction. The hidden danger of the poppy seed concoction hadn't even occurred to me. Wasn't it morphine in poppy seeds? A strong painkiller indeed, but one that had done a lot to raise Arthur's mood.

Cei scowled at being told to go more easily on the captured Saxon leaders, as perhaps he'd been looking forward to subjugating them. He still bore a grudge for Rhiwallon's terrible death. However, he did as he was told, and the two leaders were not made to dig with their men.

The Saxon warriors proved good workers, and as the sun climbed high into the still clear sky and warmed the chilly earth, our dead took up their new residence. With the heathen Saxons looking on, hostile expressions on their rebellious, dirt-streaked faces, Dubricius said our Christian words over the grave, and the earth was piled back into place. Only a long, low mound of freshly turned soil, flints and chalk, grizzled like the hair on Cadwy's head, marked the spot where our heroes lay.

The dead of Badon. What wouldn't modern archaeologists give to discover this battle's burial ground? Hidden from them by fields of wheat and barley, sleeping beneath the surface with no trace of the mound left to betray their last resting place.

Cadwy's body had not joined our dead in their earthy bed. Custennin had other plans for his father's burial. "I'm taking him back with me to Viroconium," he declared. "To bury alongside my grandfather. Where one day I, too, intend to lie, waiting for the Day of Judgement. My mother and aunt will want to oversee his funeral."

Queen Angharad, that mousy, shadowy figure I'd only ever glimpsed lurking silently in the background at Viroconium, and whom Cadwy had once volunteered to put aside so he could marry me. Hard to imagine she'd be all that sad about her husband's demise. And as for Morgana, she might see it as one step closer to the throne for her and her daughter. Nimuë.

But there was no time to dwell on the consequences of Cadwy's death for those in Viroconium. With our dead buried, the prisoners needed dealing with. Publicly. As soon as the dead were buried, Cei organized our triple force into a formidable reception committee. All three armies lined up on foot in a wide semi-circle, bridging the road just outside the woodland, with the fresh burial mound to our left.

On the brow of the far hill, a mile away along the road, the remnants of the once huge Saxon army still lurked, assembled in some order, but not advancing. Watching us. Hopefully our prisoners served as hostage to their behavior, although even that was doubtful. But we did at least have their two chief commanders, alive and in chains.

At the center of the semi-circle, Arthur, Merlin and I stood waiting for Custennin and Cerdic. That Arthur was a little high on the effects of the poppy syrup seemed obvious, but Merlin was either ignoring it or hadn't noticed.

Arthur, his good hand resting on Excalibur's hilt, nodded toward the far hillside and the disorderly ranks of the beaten Saxons. "All it needs is for some ambitious captain to decide they no longer require their original commanders to lead the two armies, and they'll be charging toward us again for round two." He kept his voice low.

Merlin nodded. "The sooner we sort this out, the better." Like Arthur, he'd come without his mailshirt, although not for the same reason, but his sword hung on one hip with a fierce dagger on the other. Every inch as fierce a warrior as my husband.

Custennin arrived first, flanked by Dubricius, both in full battle gear. "My Lord." He bowed to Arthur, and Dubricius did the same. Arthur returned their bow, a little stiffly. I could have curtsied, only that would have looked very odd in tunic and braccae. I contented myself with a bow, and Custennin took his place to our left.

From amongst the group of prisoners, Cei and a detachment of our warriors singled out Aelle and Octha, his fellow commander, to usher them forward, their hands bound in front of them.

Where was Cerdic? Did he not relish dealing with his uncle? He was making a habit of turning up late.

Even as this thought crossed my mind, Cerdic made his entrance at the head of half a dozen warriors, also dressed for battle. His gaze fixed on Aelle as he took his place beside Arthur, the warriors falling in behind him. No bowing from him. Not this time.

Despite Cerdic having chosen to support us in the battle, I couldn't help but feel the nagging doubt that his loyalties might still be divided. Aelle was the man at whose court he'd been brought up, after all. Although, in common with many dynasties throughout history, having blood ties didn't mean you had to like your relatives.

In the ranks of Dumnonia, weapons rattled as hands went to sword hilts. This half Saxon king might have been sitting at the round table with all our British kings for years, but that didn't mean our men trusted him. Especially not when he didn't bow to their High King. Not that I did, either.

Some of our warriors stood to either side of Aelle and Octha, not touching, but swords drawn and poised for action should it be required.

I stared at the two Saxons, fascinated, committing them to memory for my book. I wanted to be able to describe them in every detail for history.

Someone had stripped them of more than just their armor, and they stood before us in linen undershirts and braccae, their feet bare and dirty in the cold mud. Like their men.

A gray stubble covered Aelle's scalp but for a short tail at the back, and his drooping, yellow mustache held strands of white that betrayed his age. A huge man, he had wide-shoulders and a barrel-chest, with hammy forearms and muscular, knotted calves. But his large, square-jawed face held no impotent rage at defeat, but rather a calm dignity that surprised me. Not what I'd been expecting.

Octha, a younger man, was more classic, history-book Saxon. Nearly as big as Aelle, he had long, dirty-blonde hair, a blonde mustache and a deep, indented scar running down the center of his forehead and onto his nose that would have made Harry Potter's scar look like a scratch. He, too, despite his fearsome disfigurement, had a look of quiet dignity about him.

When you've always seen someone as the enemy, as a sort of faceless, unmet threat, meeting them for the first time can be illuminating. These were not the bogeymen of fireside tales used to frighten children into behaving, the classic villains with no redeeming features. These were human beings with feelings just like mine.

Arthur turned to Cerdic. "Will you translate for us, please?"

Cerdic, keeping his face expressionless, nodded. How difficult must this be for him? How hard had it been to choose whose side to take? Perhaps the blood of a British father called to him more than the Saxon blood his mother had imparted. Perhaps his British born people at Caer Guinntguic had swayed him our way. Would his army have obeyed him had he sided with the Saxons?

Aelle's blue-gray eyes, icy as the northern waters he and his men navigated, came to rest on Cerdic, his face as expressionless as his nephew's. What was he thinking? My hand went unbidden to rest on the hilt of my sword. Not that I would have needed to do much had the Saxon chosen to launch a weaponless attack. Our men would have cut him down before ever he reached Arthur.

Whatever Cerdic felt, the air between him and his uncle crackled with tension.

Arthur drew in a breath. "First of all, I have a question. This is Aelle? You're sure?"

Cerdic nodded, face suddenly grim. "Aye. It is. I'd know him anywhere. As you know, my mother and I lived at his court in Ceint after my father died. I saw him often."

Calm dignity flown, Aelle shot a furious glare at Cerdic, who stood his ground admirably under the sort of look that would have flattened a lesser man. Beneath Aelle's graying mustache, his upper lip curled in disdain, his opinion of a nephew who'd chosen the other side clearly marked across his face.

Up close, lines made by sun and wind, and perhaps by smiling, corrugated his weather-worn skin, and eyes full of venom for his nephew stared from beneath his bushy brows. I didn't really blame him for this. He'd no doubt expected Cerdic to take his side, especially as he'd had his troops bypass Caer Guinntguic.

"So, this is the self-styled King of the South Saxons," Arthur said, his voice icy cold. He glanced at Cerdic. "Tell him who *I* am."

Cerdic spoke a few unintelligible words, that one day in the distant future would morph to become modern English, no doubt. But right now, I could no more understand them than I could have done Swahili. Which meant we had no way of verifying what Cerdic said to his uncle.

Aelle lowered his head like a bull about to charge, his nostrils flared, and the men on either side of him took hold of his upper arms. Perhaps due to our choice of interpreter. But he didn't struggle. Instead, he barked a few sharp, guttural sentences back to his nephew.

Cerdic faltered, discomposure flashing across his face for a moment.

"Well?" Arthur asked. "What does he say?"

"That he is Bretwalda – king of Britain. That this is his land and his people's." Cerdic hesitated. "That I am a traitor to my people, and to him…"

That did sound as though he were telling us everything. Hopefully.

Arthur smiled. "He dares to claim kingship when he stands before me as my prisoner? Tell him I didn't take him for a fool, but that is what he seems to be."

More words passed between nephew and uncle. Merlin edged up beside me, and I moved a step closer to him, finding reassurance in his presence.

"He says to tell you that you may call this land your own, that you may throw him in irons or kill him, but that one day, soon, it will be his, his sons' and his grandsons' for the taking." Cerdic had the grace to look apologetic.

However, a cold wave washed over me from head to foot, as every hair on my body stood on end, alert to these prophetic words. I glanced at Merlin, as my heart did acrobatic leaps, but his face remained impassive. Had he not seen this coming? Had he no idea that right here we burned the last dying light of Britain before the birth of an England that would extinguish it forever?

I swallowed the lump in my throat.

Arthur shook his head. "Tell him that whatever he thinks the future may hold, right now, this is my land, and my people's land. That we are prepared to defend it to whatever end might lie ahead."

He waited while Cerdic translated for him. Aelle's face darkened as he listened to the words. He opened his mouth to speak, but Arthur held up a commanding hand.

"You are my prisoners. Your army has fled. They lurk a mile away, waiting to bury their dead." He paused, eyes boring into Aelle's. "Waiting for us to execute our prisoners. No doubt they want to give you a good send off." His eyes glittered dangerously. "By rights, I should execute you all, here and now, on this very spot." He gave a nod to Cerdic who swiftly put the words into Aelle's tongue.

The two Saxon leaders glared at Arthur from between their captors, but a shred of their initial dignity had returned. Maybe they thought to make martyrs of themselves, and die with honor.

Arthur's right hand fingered Excalibur's hilt again, as though he'd like to draw it and perform the executions himself, perhaps. "But I am not a man who likes to kill for the sake of killing," he said. "And I do not want to kill you." He nodded to Cerdic, who, a puzzled look on his face, translated. He'd probably been expecting a beheading.

Arthur met Cerdic's gaze. "Cerdic of Caer Guinntguic and I have fought on opposite sides in the past, but at our Council of Kings he paid me homage as High King. And I accepted his allegiance. Today he has proven beyond doubt that his word is his bond. In defending our lands against you, he has become a true British king."

He paused, and for a moment his eyes slid sideways to me, before he stared once more at Aelle, as though willing that man to understand his words without translation. "But Britain is a wide land. A land where men might bring up families, till fields, raise cattle and sheep, and prosper. You Saxons already have lands of your own in the east. Lands granted to you by dead kings and that I do not wish to dispute. Lands your people have held for generations. Lands where you live side-by-side with British farmers, marrying their young women, in peace. I do not wish to drive you from those lands. I do not dispute your hard-won right to be there."

He glanced at Cerdic, who translated quickly, while Aelle and Octha listened, puzzled frowns settling on their heavy brows.

When Cerdic finished speaking, Arthur went on. "I have fought against your people all my life – as a prince beside my father, as Dux of Britain, King of Dumnonia and now as High King. Rivers of blood have flowed, and the dead are without number."

He threw out his right hand to encompass the piles of Saxon corpses still lying in the dirt. "This carnage can go on for as long as you wish. We, the British, are united in our cause. You do not fight one kingdom – you fight all of us. We will not let you steal our lands. If you continue your aggression, we will take the fight into your lands and to the doorsteps of your houses. We'll burn your farms so your wives and children will starve in winter. We'll maim your warriors so they cannot fight or till the land. We'll destroy your ships and set them blazing on the water. You will regret not making a peace with me here today."

He paused and Cerdic translated.

Aelle and Octha exchanged glances but remained silent. What were they thinking?

Arthur waited a few moments before he continued, letting the silence stretch out. No one moved. Everyone was listening. At last, he spoke. "But I don't want that. I, as victor, would have it that we call a truce. That you and I agree to a peace between our people. That this battle, here today, shall mark the end of all hostility. That we shall learn to live, if not together then side-by-side, in peace." He turned his hand palm uppermost, almost in supplication. "What say you?"

Cerdic translated.

For a long moment, Aelle regarded Arthur through narrowed eyes. What was going through his head? Perhaps that a fool stood before him who had his enemy in his power yet wanted to strike a deal. Perhaps that what Arthur suggested was reasonable and wise. Who knew?

Then, without taking his eyes from Arthur, he spoke to Cerdic again.

We waited. I schooled my face to calmness, mirroring my husband's.

Cerdic's eyes moved from Arthur to Aelle, then back again. "My uncle says that you speak wise words. He is not young anymore. He says he's not a fool, either. You defeated two armies here, and you drew not only upon your own forces, but upon mine – and although he calls me traitor to my mother's people, he acknowledges the power you have that brought me to your side." He cleared his throat. "He will make a treaty with you, one Bretwalda to another." He paused. "Bretwalda is to him and his people what High King is to yours… to ours."

Arthur nodded. "As he is Bretwalda, can I trust that he speaks for all his people? That if we agree today, and we make a treaty together, it will encompass every Saxon, every Angle, every Jute who seeks to call our islands home? That all hostilities will cease, that his people will remain in what have become their ancestral lands here in Britain, and not bring battle to the west? Because if they go against him, then I will rain down my revenge, starting with him in Ceint."

A quick exchange of words flashed between Cerdic and his uncle.

"My uncle says that if he gives his word today, no man will dare gainsay it. He is their Bretwalda – what he says is law."

Arthur nodded again. "And no more keels from across the German Sea, seeking to steal new lands for themselves. That must be guaranteed. If any come, then they are to be accommodated in the lands already Saxon. No further expansion. If he can give his word to that, then I, too, will give my word that the British people will not offer aggression to their Saxon neighbors. I am High King. My word is also law. The other kings will do as I say."

He heaved a deep breath, shifting as though uncomfortable, which wasn't at all surprising, all things considered. "I myself wish for peace, not constant warfare. I wish for rich harvests and good hunting, for food and wealth for my people." He paused. "And I wish that for Aelle's people, too."

"My uncle says he, too, wishes the same for his people."

Arthur and Aelle stared into one another's eyes. Gray blue met dark brown. I held my breath. This was what the legends said. That after Badon, peace would come. Had I had a hand in making it happen? Was I truly what the prophecy had said – the woman who would make Arthur great? Who perhaps had already done so?

Arthur stepped away from Custennin and Cerdic, up to where Aelle stood between his two guards. He held out his right hand.

Aelle looked down at it. His own were still tied in front of him. He held them out, and Arthur nodded to Cei, who stepped forward and sliced through the tight bonds. They fell to the ground unnoticed. Was this setting a tiger free amongst us? Could we trust this man?

Time ticked past. The silence seemed to lengthen. Overhead a buzzard mewed.

Aelle studied Arthur's face for a moment, before reaching out and clasping his forearm, as Arthur's hand clasped his. Handfasted, they stood for a moment, regarding one another warily, perhaps each suspecting the other of being some sleeping predator with some trick up his sleeve.

"You and your men are free to go," Arthur said. "To bury your dead and perform whatever rituals you require for their passage to the next world. My men will not prevent you leaving. I have no wish to be your enemy. You shall have your arms and armor back." He glanced down at Aelle's dirty feet. "And your boots."

Cerdic translated. For another long moment Aelle hung onto Arthur's arm, before releasing his hold, and stepping back.

Arthur held up his hand to the warriors surrounding the prisoners. "Stand down. Fetch them their belongings."

Our men shuffled back, muttering their displeasure – they'd seen the Saxon belongings as rightful booty. Their weapons barely wavered, distrust written across their suspicious faces. An enemy does not become an ally with a few easily spoken words.

The Saxon arms and armor were brought out. The men pulled on any boots they could find, and grabbed their mailshirts and weapons as though afraid we'd change our minds. I didn't blame them. A lot of our warriors looked as though they resented Arthur's amnesty. They shuffled closer as the Saxons gathered their belongings.

Arthur held up his right hand. "Let them pass. We have agreed a peace. They may leave. After we have left, they may return to bury their dead. Unmolested."

With reluctance, our warriors retreated, still gripping their weapons, their eyes never leaving their ex-prisoners. They, in their turn, clearly had no wish to turn their backs on their heavily armed captors, and with Aelle and Octha amongst them, shuffled backwards away from us.

"Tell him he has my word my men will not attack his," Arthur said to Cerdic. "Or they will feel my wrath. It's peace I brokered here today, not war."

Cerdic raised his voice as the Saxons retreated en masse. With more space between them and us, they half-turned and continued more quickly, while keeping a wary eye on our men.

Arthur turned back to Custennin and Cerdic. "Let us break camp. We'll leave them to bury their dead and head back to Dinas Badan. He grinned, clearly still on the high of the poppy syrup. "And we'll station plenty of lookouts – their leader might have agreed to peace, but that doesn't mean his men will feel the same, as yet."

He turned to me, lowering his voice. "Will this suit your book, d'you think? Is this the battle you told me about?"

Chapter Forty-Four

THE GOOD WEATHER of the day after the battle lulled us into a false sense of security. The following day, unrelenting rain sleeted down, with no respite even when we made our soggy camp in a wooded valley not far from Stonehenge.

A lone farmhouse squatted there, dismal and gray on the edge of a beech wood. A wall of piled up flints encircled a small roundhouse with a conical roof of blackened thatch and a few tumbledown sheds and animal pens. Smoke hung snagged between the trees in dirty shreds.

At the edge of the wood, pigs fled squealing at the sight of us, as well they might. We were hungry, and roast pork would have been tasty. The chickens were not so lucky.

I swung down from my saddle into wet mud with a squelch, and beside me, Merlin did the same. Arthur leaned his hands on his saddle horns and stayed put.

Bedwyr came tramping over. "This rain is ridiculous. I'm winkling these farmers out and commandeering their house." He shot an anxious glance up at Arthur. "Not just for you. There's a good few other wounded men I want to see inside out of this rain."

Arthur nodded, water dripping down his face from his soaking hair. His skin had a disturbing gray look about it that sent a shiver of fear down my back. I'd been so busy being glad Badon had turned out as I'd predicted, I'd almost forgotten to worry about possible infection of his wound.

"I'll go," Cei said, swinging his leg over the front of his saddle and sliding down from his horse. Mud spattered. "You get the wounded all together. I'll see them dry tonight."

Hanging onto Alezan's reins with one hand, I put the other on Arthur's knee, cold and wet under my touch. "Stay there a minute, until Cei gets back."

Water had traveled down my legs into my boots. I couldn't tell if my feet were cold and wet from that or from the mud seeping through my boot seams.

Under the dark thatch lurked a low door of silvered wood. Cei bent beneath the meager shelter and hammered on it with determination.

Nothing.

Cei hammered again. "Open up in the name of the High King, lest you want me to set light to your house."

I swiped my wet hair out of my eyes, glad of a cloak made of oiled wool that had kept at least some of the rain off. What a contrast to our rain-free journey on the way *to* Badon.

The door opened a crack. Cei jammed his booted foot into it and gave it a shove. "Since when do you keep your king standing out here in the rain? Get out of my way."

Once, I might have protested at his attitude, but I had a wet, wounded husband to care for, and he came first.

Cei disappeared from view. In a moment he was back. "Plenty of room here for our wounded. Fetch them in."

Merlin and I got Arthur down from his horse, under protest. "I'm fine," he complained. "Stop treating me like I'm not." But he swayed alarmingly. Coping with pain can exhaust you faster than anything. Merlin grabbed his elbow, but Arthur shook him off. "I can do this. Let me be."

Men and their egos.

Luckily it wasn't far to the roundhouse. As Bedwyr got the rest of our wounded off their horses, and Llacheu organized the remainder of our men, I walked with Arthur to the door. With difficulty he bent his head and ducked inside, me, Cei and Merlin close behind.

A fire smoldered in the center of the gloomy interior, providing the only light, and above our heads a fug of smoke hung under the conical roof. The men had to stoop to avoid inhaling it. Around the walls, the available space, that seemed bigger now we were in here, had been divided up by low wicker walls – some holding beds, some used as storage.

The farmer, a short-legged, burly-bodied man, stood back to one side, glaring at us from under a shaggy mane of grizzled brown hair, and caterpillar-thick eyebrows. His family crouched around the fire, eyes wide, mouths hanging open, fear written clearly across every face: an old woman with thin, white hair stained yellow by the smoke and the sunken, softly wrinkled features of the toothless; a younger woman with a naked baby at her breast; two adolescent boys; and three small, half-clothed children of indeterminate sex.

Arthur and Merlin's presence dominated the space, towering over the seated people and the farmer. Cei, unfazed by any notion of waiting to be offered, jerked his head toward the door. "Out, all of you. You're sleeping in one of your sheds tonight. This is your High King, and I'm requisitioning this house for him and our wounded."

The people stared at us, uncomprehending for a moment, as though he'd spoken a foreign language. A few glances shot between the adults. Their gazes slid to our weapons. They weren't stupid. The woman with the baby got to her feet from the log she'd been using as a seat, pulling a shawl around her child.

"Not you," Cei said. "We're not animals. You and the baby can stay."

Her eyes widened in fear. Not unnaturally. Soldiers weren't known for kindness to women, after all. Not even the soldiers of her own High King.

The farmer took a step forward, but Merlin held up his hand. The farmer bristled. "My wife's a good girl, m'lord." His voice shook. "Don't hurt her. Please."

Merlin frowned, perhaps realizing what the man feared. "She'll be safe. You have my word. We want your house for our wounded. None of us are interested in your woman. Except not to let her and your child catch cold. The rest of you will have to manage in one of your sheds. If our men aren't already in them. Now go."

The woman remained standing, while the children, shooting terrified glances at the three enormous warriors who'd invaded their home, grabbed their cloaks and a few hunks of bread and hurried out after their father. The old woman, hobbling on arthritic hips, was last to rise, drawing a shabby cloak about her scrawny shoulders.

Merlin stopped her at the door. "You may stay as well."

She shot him a venomous look that held no thanks, but hobbled back to stand beside the woman and the baby. After a moment or so, they sat back down next to one another, both of them regarding us from beneath suspicious brows, mouths set in sullen sulks.

Cei tossed firewood from one of the alcoves onto the fire, and fresh flames leapt, illuminating the gloomy house. "Let's get some warmth in here to dry us out."

I steered Arthur to the fireside. "Sit down."

With a sigh of relief, he sank down on one of the low logs encircling the firepit, stretching out his wet legs toward the flames. I'd have to get those braccae off him before too long.

I sat down beside him, relishing the warmth and being out of the rain, and wishing this was Din Cadan already. A long ride stretched before us in the morning, with no prospect of the rain letting up. Late summer that had stretched on into autumn had at a stroke become early winter.

Unfastening the pin that held my cloak, I shrugged it off. Silently, the young woman handed her baby to the old crone and, taking my cloak, hung it from a hook where the roof sloped down to meet the low wall. With soft footsteps, she returned to Arthur and her gentle fingers unfastened the fibula that held his cloak in place. Had she realized he was wounded? His cloak joined mine where hopefully they would dry overnight.

I took a better look at her. The bearing of the six children we'd seen had aged her, putting gray hairs amongst the rich auburn, but once she must have been a pretty girl and was probably younger than me. Wide, gray eyes the color of a rainy day, no longer so frightened, peeked from beneath thick eyelashes, and her mouth had a sweet-natured turn to it. Life couldn't have been easy for her, but she'd made the best of it.

A large earthenware pot sat at the edge of the fire, steam rising from it. She gave it a stir with a wooden spoon and eyed Arthur. "I've stew if you'd like some, M'lord. Put some color in yer cheeks." Yes. She'd noticed.

Arthur sighed and shifted his weight, steam rising from his wet braccae. "Thank you."

She got to her feet and ladled the stew into a wooden bowl. More a sort of pottage, a few bits of meat sat in a mess of swollen grains and onions. But it was hot. She handed Arthur the bowl, and a hunk of black bread, then filled one for me.

On a gust of windy rain, the door opened, and Bedwyr ushered in our half a dozen wounded. The woman's eyes widened at the sight of so many warriors in her house, but she took it in her stride and handed me a bowl of the savory smelling stew.

The old woman, cradling the baby, seemed to be enjoying the much fiercer heat now being thrown out by the fire. We were probably burning their hardwon winter's supply, but right now, I didn't care. The farmer and his two older sons would just have to cut more.

Arthur scooped up some of the food with his bread and took a bite. At least he was eating now, but was that rain or sweat on his forehead? I felt it. Hot.

With an impatient gesture he shook me off. "Just a little fever. To be expected after an injury. I'm fine." He scooped in more food. "Look, I'm eating, so I must be." He gave me a lopsided grin, then switched his attention to the woman. "It's good. What's your name?"

Those lovely gray eyes widened in renewed fear, but she was made of stern stuff. "Raewyn, M'lord."

The old woman cleared her throat and spat onto the ground in front of the fire, shooting her daughter-in-law a venomous look. Presumably she disapproved of consorting with anyone but their own family, and probably especially not with passing soldiers, whatever side they were on.

Arthur smiled. "Thank you, Raewyn. My men and I appreciate your hospitality. I know it's enforced, and I'm sorry for that, but we have wounded men who need a night out of the rain." He touched his shoulder where blood had leaked through from his dressings. "Myself included."

She bobbed a rough bow to him, and gave the stewpot a stir. The old lady, scowling, stuck a gnarled and grimy finger into the fretful baby's mouth for it to suck on. Yuck.

"He be hungry," the old crone grumbled. "As I be."

Our wounded settled themselves around the fire, their clothes steaming. Raewyn hung all their cloaks near ours, and dished out the remaining stew, scraping the bottom of the pot. The old woman, with a disgusted snort at losing her own dinner, hawked and spat again, and, minus its tasty finger, the baby set up a mewling cry.

Under the interested gaze of our men, Raewyn gathered up the baby and retired to one of the alcoves to feed him, and I finally relaxed enough to try the food as well. Tastier than I'd expected from its bland appearance, the heat revitalized me. I scraped my bowl as well as the next man, and Cei produced a skin of cider that did the rounds. Bedwyr handed it to the old woman, who smacked her lips and took a long pull that dribbled down her wrinkled chin. The man beside her had to wrest the skin from bony claws that didn't want to give it up.

Bedwyr sat on the log nearest to Arthur, "I'll need to look at your shoulder, I'm afraid." He sounded apologetic, as well he might have been.

Arthur sighed, the sheen of sweat on his face shining in the firelight. "If you must."

Oh, for a shirt that buttoned down the front. For buttons, actually. Now, there was something I could introduce. How useful would buttons be for things like flies on braccae? How useful would flies be, full stop. I chided myself for not having thought of them before. We had a craftsman at Din Cadan who carved in bone – I'd get him to make me some buttons for my next gown. The only drawback would be learning how to hand stitch a buttonhole, and sewing was not my favorite pastime.

Merlin and Bedwyr edged Arthur's tunic and undershirt off as carefully as they could with minimum movement to his shoulder, but even so, he winced in pain. His shoulder would have stiffened up no end. The bandages, stained with blood and difficult to pry apart, came off. I held my breath, and Arthur's hand, as Bedwyr peeled back the pads covering the two wounds. Underneath, the flesh around the small exit and entry holes looked inflamed and red, but no pus showed. Bedwyr sniffed both wounds, probing gently with practised fingers.

"Well?" Arthur asked, through clenched teeth.

"Smells clean," Bedwyr muttered. Then, seeing my anxious face, "Natural for all this inflammation after such a severe wound. And for the fever. I've an infusion of Feverfew for him to take tonight, instead of poppy syrup. He's had enough of that already."

Arthur grunted. "Talk to me, not her. It's my shoulder you're discussing. And I've not gone deaf."

The old woman gave a loud snort. "Comfrey's what 'e needs on that."

Bedwyr turned his head, eyes eager. "You have some?"

She sucked her flaccid lips in over empty gums, as though she were gurning. "I might have."

Bedwyr glanced toward the closed door to outside. "Fresh?" The thick thatch had muted the sound of the falling rain, but no doubt it hadn't stopped.

She shook her sparsely covered head. "Already made into a salve." She waggled a bony finger at him. "By these hands."

Not a great recommendation. "These hands" were ingrained with dirt, the nails broken and blackened.

"May my healer use it?" Arthur asked, ignoring the potential threat. "Not just for me. My men, as well, would find it helpful." He gave her his most winning smile, which to my knowledge had never failed to work on a woman of any age.

Even with its owner unshaven, pale-faced, and sweaty, the smile worked its magic yet again. The old woman bridled like a coy teenager, and levered herself to her feet, no doubt stiff from sitting for so long.

Bedwyr sprang up and hurried to her side, supporting her to a shelf tacked lopsidedly onto one of the rafters. A row of small, covered pots adorned it. She took one down, lifted the lid, sniffed, and handed it to Bedwyr. He sniffed as well, and his nose wrinkled, to be followed with a smile. "Thank you, Old Mother."

From over on one of the beds, the baby noisily suckling, Raewyn grunted. "She be a healer born."

Bedwyr helped the old woman back to her place by the fire and pressed the cider skin into her clutching hands. "For you, in exchange."

With a cackle of glee – she'd have made an excellent witch in Macbeth – she uncorked it and took a long draught, the cider running down her chin.

Bedwyr took the seat beside Arthur and took the lid off the pot. The salve inside was a faint green, which at least looked as though it might be clean. Bedwyr scooped some out and applied it liberally to Arthur's wound.

The pain must have been excruciating. Arthur's hands fisted on his lap, and I covered them with mine as Bedwyr managed to poke some of the salve inside the hole the arrow had left, where it could do the most good. A trickle of fresh blood ran down Arthur's chest. Then clean bandages went back on, and the sling, and Bedwyr moved on to attend to our other wounded.

For a minute or two Arthur sat rigid, breathing steadily, as though waiting for the pain to subside. Eventually, he turned his hands over and clasped mine, our fingers intertwining. "I've not really had the time to appreciate our victory," he said. "Nor to acknowledge that you were correct in everything you told me."

I leaned toward him, resting my forehead on his bare shoulder – his good shoulder. "I didn't foresee that you'd be wounded, though." My thumb caressed the back of his hand. "You're not out of the woods yet."

He nodded. "I'm all right, really. You don't need to worry."

I kissed his shoulder. "You've got a fever."

"It'll pass. With most wounds you get a fever. For a day or two."

Ridiculously, I was beginning to feel aroused. We were surrounded by people – our men and the two farm women, and yet the power Arthur had over me came creeping up. My skin tingled, a warm feeling developed somewhere south of my navel, and all I wanted to do was take him in my arms and kiss his hurts away. And maybe a little more.

He chuckled. Did he suspect?

"You know what's the right way to celebrate a victory such as this?" he whispered.

He did suspect, or we were so in tune we were thinking the same thing.

I nodded. "I do. But not while you're in pain, and certainly not in public. You'll have to wait to celebrate when we're back home. When you no longer have a fever."

He grinned, a touch of his old self returning. "I can have a kiss, though, can't I?"

I released his hand and touched his cheek, his short beard bristly under my fingers. "You can."

I turned his face toward me. Our lips touched, tongues meeting. The kiss deepened, and so did the urge to do something more than kiss.

A ragged cheer from the men disturbed us.

Our lips parted and I caught Bedwyr's gaze. He stuck his thumb up in that age old gesture. I had to laugh.

"Want a bit of privacy?" Merlin asked, with a wide grin. A sudden conviction that he, like me, was thinking Arthur on the road to recovery, rose inside my head. I returned his grin.

Chapter Forty-Five

WE RODE UP the track to Din Cadan's main gates two days later. The rain had lessened somewhat, but nevertheless the trek back across country, instead of by the road, had been unpleasant and difficult, and only taken from the necessity to get our wounded home as quickly as possible.

The problem with riding across country in the Dark Ages, as I'd very early on discovered, was the sheer wetness of the land. In a time before drainage existed, except perhaps in its most rudimentary form, by the tail-end of the year, every valley had begun to turn marshy, and only the higher ground remained passable.

Rivers, that in my old world had run along narrow channels with high banks, here spread out to more than twice, or even three times, the width they'd one day have, sometimes with multiple, braided channels. Shallower and easier to ford in good weather, but surrounded by wetlands for the larger part of the year.

There turned out to be a lot more valleys between Salisbury Plain and Din Cadan than I remembered, and the storm, followed by the nonstop heavy rain, had started them off well toward their winter goal of impassability. We had to take a lot of detours.

For victorious warriors returning, we made a rather sorry sight as our column wound its way up toward the main gates in the gloom of a gathering wintry dusk. The rain had stopped for a while, but cloaks aren't like coats, and they don't stay nicely buttoned up and cozy. You have to keep rearranging them and pulling them close about you, and the wind does spiteful things like snatching them away. They keep the worst off your back, but your front isn't so lucky.

Cold and miserable, I couldn't have been happier to see the double gates swing open in welcome.

The guards on duty on the tower above the gates gave us a rousing cheer as we rode beneath them.

A sharp-eyed lookout must have spotted our approach at a distance, because, despite the persistent drizzle and the rapid onset of night, most of the people of the fortress had turned out to line the road up to the stables and Great Hall. Old men with long white hair leaned on sticks. Grizzled warriors stood between the womenfolk, who ranged from pretty teenagers to wizened old crones, while boys not yet old enough to ride to war gazed on in envy. Little children raced about, impervious to the mud underfoot and getting in everyone's way.

"Dumnonia!" Shouts rose above the hum of voices.

"Long live our great High King!"

"The Luck of Arthur!" Hands reached out to touch my legs as I passed. As I leaned down to brush fingertips with my people, a warm glow of belonging surged through me. By my side, Arthur, his reins held loosely in his left hand, did the same.

Our people. My people. They'd been that for a long time now, but the thought never ceased to amaze me, bringing a tear to my eye.

My tired spirits rose with every cry of welcome and every hand I touched. Alezan pricked her ears and picked up her feet with renewed vigor instead of plodding up the roadway, as the shouts of praise showered upon us.

Arthur had sent news of our victory on ahead by fast riders, so everyone knew we'd won. Easy to be carried away by the atmosphere of rejoicing. If I tried hard not to think of those who weren't returning, I could almost find it in me to think the battle, and my part in causing it, worth it.

But not quite.

Young girls, some of them wives already, ran beside our horses, laughing up at their sweethearts, promise written across their open, pink-cheeked faces. But what about the wives and sweethearts of the dead? The young men buried out beside that lonely woodland, their grave marked only by an earthen mound, that all too soon would grass over, sink and be forgotten. They were not rejoicing.

Amongst the happy faces lurked the heartbroken, turning away with tears in their eyes. Some clutched fatherless babies to their breasts, some wept for sons they'd never see again. When I looked at them, my spirits sank once more, and I couldn't find it in me to be happy.

Our young apprentice warriors ran up the road with us to the stables, ready to help with the horses. Amongst their eager, excited, and openly envious faces I searched for Amhar's, but didn't find him.

A few torches already burned in brackets on the outside wall of the open-fronted stable block, swiftly ushering in the night. The familiar smell of dung and ammonia, and the whinnying from the horses already in occupation, welcomed us home.

Cei leapt off his horse, his head switching from side to side like a hound scenting the air. "It's good to be home. Where's my wife?" He thrust his horse's reins at a boy. "Coventina!" His bellow was enough to shake the foundations of the building.

"Cei!" She came running, elbowing her way through the press of people and horses, Reaghan following behind her like the bobbing tender of a great sailing ship.

Cei swept her up into his arms – no mean feat given her size, and planted a long kiss on her lips. Reaghan hung onto his arm, jumping up and down in impatience. "Papa! Papa!"

Over their heads I scanned the crowd for Amhar and still didn't find him.

Arthur swung his right leg over the pommel of his saddle and slid to the ground. Only a small wince betrayed how much his left shoulder must still be paining him, although it was healing remarkably well. He held out his good arm to me, and I slid down from Alezan into his embrace, glad to feel him holding me close for a short moment.

Two boys took our horses. Someone other than us could tend to them this evening. I slipped my arm around Arthur's waist as the older men who'd remained to guard Din Cadan slapped him on the back and shouted their congratulations, making him wince time after time.

"Well done, lad."

"Dumnonia rules!"

"That showed the Yellow Haired bastards."

In my old world, if I'd ever stopped to think about it, or discussed it with my father, we'd imagined King Arthur would be a noble king, distant from his people, divided from them by his status and birth.

This was something different. If only my father could see. Maybe he could? Arthur wore his kingliness like a familiar cloak, but one he could shrug off whenever it suited him. He knew his people by name, from the oldest retired warrior down to the smallest baby. And they loved him for it. What king in my old world could you slap on the back like this as though he was a friend you'd met in the local pub? What king could you laugh and joke with even if you were just the pigboy?

But he was mine before he was theirs. I caught his hand and tugged him with me toward the Great Hall. All around us, the mill of people churned, warriors and horses mixed up with the welcoming party, men kissing women, fathers greeting wives while their children clamored for attention, a few babies wailing.

A small rocket hurtled into me, arms outstretched to encompass us both, her chestnut head buried between us, two fat plaits hanging down her back.

"Archfedd!" I wrapped my free arm around her.

"Mami, Papa." Her voice came muffled from amongst our thick, damp cloaks, her fingers hooked on like limpets. "You're back!"

To stop Arthur trying to pick her up, I heaved her into my arms and hugged her close. "We're back safely, just as I said we would be. Where's your brother?"

Arthur tousled the top of her head, meeting my eyes above it. "It's good to be home."

"Amhar's being grumpy," Archfedd muttered, lower lip jutting. "Again." She heaved a sigh and leaned away. "He keeps being mean. He... he said you weren't coming home. Maia said to take no notice... but he's my brother, and I don't like it." A wet kiss landed on my cheek. "Maia said it was just boys, but Llawfrodedd's not like that. He's nice, and kind, and I like him. He said to take no notice as well. But it's so hard. I was scared he was right." She held her arms out to Arthur.

He reached for her, but I shook my head. "Papa's hurt his shoulder and can't go lifting you up at the moment. And you're getting too heavy for me, so I'll have to put you down." I plonked her on her own two feet. Had she grown since we left? Surely not in hardly more than a week. Maybe I'd just forgotten how heavy she'd become.

She grabbed a hand from each of us, tugging, unfortunately, Arthur's left hand.

I pried her free. "Not that hand. Swap over." With her between us, we walked up to the hall, where Maia waited in the gathering gloom, under the overhanging thatch. I hugged my maid to me with a fierce joy at seeing her familiar face again, and she put her thin arms around me.

But where was Amhar?

Once inside the well-lit hall, and with the turmoil shut outside in the descending dark, I turned to Maia. "I could do with a bath. Can you organize hot water to our chamber? We won't ask for the bath house at this time of day. It'd take too long to heat that much water, and I'd like my bath now, not at midnight."

As my maid, she'd not have to do anything so lowly as fetch water herself but would be able to boss some lesser servants about and make them do it, which she'd enjoy.

I glanced at Arthur, who was unbuckling his sword belt. "And take Archfedd for me. She can dine with us in the Hall tonight. She'll need sprucing up and putting in her best dress to honor her father." I passed Archfedd's sweaty little hand into Maia's firm grasp. "Go with Maia, my darling, and let Papa and me take our baths." I patted her head. "Off you go now."

Eyes bright with the promise of dining in the Hall with us, Archfedd departed with surprising obedience, and a moment later I heard Maia shouting for servants to bring hot water to the king's chamber. I'd give them a few minutes to sort that out.

The bright lights in the Hall dazzled after the gloom of the late evening. A fire glowed in the central pit, with several cauldrons bubbling in the embers and sending enticing smells wafting through the smoky air. My mouth watered in anticipation.

Arthur laid his sword and belt on the nearest trestle table and turned to me. "Alone at last." He held out his arms.

I stepped into them, mailshirt to mailshirt, and he hugged me close, resting his cheek against my hair. For a long minute, we stood like that, just holding one another. A kind of lethargy crept over me, as the tension in my limbs began to dissipate, and relief at being safely home, with Badon over and done with, poured itself over me in a warm wave of happiness.

The only bug in the bed was Amhar and his continued absence.

Maybe Arthur hadn't noticed.

The doors opened and old Cottia entered. Gray and shrunken now, and only half the woman I'd met on the first day of my life in the fifth century, she still liked to keep busy about the Hall. "Arthur!" Her wrinkled face broke into a wide smile, and she bypassed the bubbling cauldrons to shuffle up the hall on arthriticky legs to greet us.

Arthur, ever the diplomat where she was concerned, released me and allowed her to fold him to her still squashy bosom. The top of her head only reached his chin so this wasn't too suffocating.

When she finally let him go, I gave her a hug as well, finding I felt nearly as glad to see her as I had Maia. She wasn't as fond of me as she was Arthur, in fact, she nurtured a touch of jealousy, but submitted to the embrace with a good grace, even going so far as to pat me on the back.

"Come along," she tutted, unable to say anything without a tut. "Let's get you into yer chamber and outta these nasty mailshirts. The pair o' you."

Chapter Forty-Six

THE COALS IN the brazier glowed, the air above them shimmering with heat. Someone had lit oil lamps and set them in the recesses around the wall, and a warm golden glow bathed our entire chamber. By the brazier, the rugs covering the flagstones had been rolled back to make enough clear space for the wooden bath. Just as well, as water was slopping out over the edge to form wet puddles on the flags while Arthur and I attempted to share it.

A small bathtub in the first place, where I couldn't even stretch my legs out if I was in it on my own, we'd opted to stand up and soap ourselves off. Not that the soap was the nice lathery sort I'd once been used to, but I didn't care. This close to my naked husband, I had other things on my mind. The soft lamplight played across his body, highlighting the taut muscles and long limbs, making a man of bronze out of him. With no mirror available, I hoped it had done the same for me, camouflaging the marks childbearing had left.

Arthur clearly had other things on his mind as well. "I don't think I can bend over," he said, fingertips touching his shoulder. "I don't want to set my wound bleeding again..." His bandages were still in place, and had managed to stay dry so far.

What a fibber, but I'd play along, gladly.

Already clean and perched on the hard edge of the bathtub, I squeezed the natural sponge I was holding, an item that had traveled an almost unimaginable distance to get to my hand, and peeked at him through my eyelashes, in what I intended to be a coquettish and flirty manner. "I can wash you… if you like…" But which bit should I leave till last if I wanted a completely clean husband?

A slow grin spread over his face. "If you don't mind…"

I began at his feet and worked slowly upward. "Of course," I teased. "If you're likely to set your wound bleeding again, perhaps you'd best rest it for a few more days. You know – no *exertions*."

From over the wall in the hall came the scraping of the tables being pulled across the paving slabs for our celebratory meal. A woman shouted crossly – Cottia most likely.

He chuckled. "What I have in mind doesn't require much use of my shoulder."

I rubbed soap over the knotted scar on his thigh, where he'd been stabbed all those years ago, and moved higher. "How clean do you want to be?"

His stomach muscles, in front of my nose, tightened. "Very." And his voice rose a note or two as I leaned forward and brushed my lips over his lower belly in a provocative kiss. He was definitely in the mood. I sponged his torso in long, languorous movements, guaranteed to provoke him further.

With a stifled groan, he reached out and caught me by the shoulders, pulling me to my feet. "It's no good. I have to kiss you."

I offered no protest, lifting my face to meet his, and his mouth came down on mine, hungry and demanding. I kissed him back, our tongues entwining, wrestling, eager for each other, and for an instant, I remembered the very first time he'd kissed me. In Viroconium, after he'd defeated Cadwy and managed to hang onto the kingdom his father had left him in his will. A kiss as passionate as this one.

Unlike that time, where after the exhuberant kiss he'd let me go, this time he pulled me closer, both arms encircling my naked body, pressing me against him. Between us, his arousal throbbed against my belly, hard and insistent. Oh, how I wanted him. Right now.

A knock came on the door from the hall.

With great reluctance he released me, laughter bubbling up, and we grabbed the towels Maia had left.

I glanced down at the definite tenting of his towel. "You'd better hide that before you answer the door. It might be Cottia and you'll shock her."

"Damn it." He laughed again, joyful and carefree, a sound I loved and didn't hear often enough. "I can't while you're standing there naked. Go somewhere I can't see you, and cover yourself up."

I scuttled to the bed with my towel wrapped around me, and perched on the edge, demure and innocent.

Arthur, shooting me a knowing and somewhat reproachful look, called out, "Enter."

Merlin came in, clean and tidy in fresh tunic and braccae, wet hair slicked back from his face. "Everyone's coming into the Hall now. We've broken out a couple of casks of the Falernian wine you've been saving." He looked Arthur up and down and a slow smile spread over his face, before he quickly wiped it away. "I'll go and wait outside." He glanced at me. "Don't be long. We can't start without either of you."

I fought to suppress the giggle that was trying to burst out. How much more obvious could we have been? Poor Merlin. Always the gooseberry.

As soon as the door shut behind him, Arthur came over to the bed, dropping his unwanted towel to the floor. He stopped in front of me. Merlin's interruption didn't seem to have affected his desire for me one bit.

I raised my eyes, my gaze hovering for a minute on his arousal. I heaved a sigh. "You're going to have to wait. And so am I." I rubbed my chin. "And before you kiss me again, you need a shave. If you're quick, you can have one before we go in for dinner. Put on your braccae, and I'll call Maia in to help with my gown and hair."

He adopted the sulky expression of a small boy told he can't have sweets. "What if I can't wait?"

I eyed his tempting physical state with a certain amount of longing. "Well, you're going to have to. We both are. Our people come first... don't they?"

He sighed. "I suppose so. But just for once I wish they didn't." He reached out a hand and gave me a gentle push back onto the bed. "I can be quick?"

Just what a girl wants to hear.

I snorted as my towel slipped and he pulled it loose. "That's not nearly as attractive a proposition as you think it is, you know. Quickness."

"You want me, too."

I chuckled. "I know. But not quickly. You seem to have forgotten I'm a woman. I want you to take your time, not go at it as fast as you can so you can get to your dinner." I tugged my towel back up, not very successfully.

He inclined his head like a puppy listening to its master, a habit he had when he wanted something badly. "You'll enjoy it. I promise." He lowered himself down on top of me, pushing my legs apart with an insistent knee. "You know you want this." His weight coming onto his injured shoulder made him wince. Good. Served him right. Only I did want him too... badly.

He twitched my towel down again.

"That does it," I said, abandoning my towel and wriggling out from under him, stark naked. "I'm not having you risk more damage to that shoulder. So no, you'll have to wait. No quickies for you tonight."

I bent over his clothes chest and lifted the lid. Untidy as usual. Maia spent a lot of time folding his clothes and layering them with the dried lavender that kept away fleas and lice, but every time he needed something clean, he upended everything. I rummaged for clean braccae suitable for a celebration.

Unrepentant, he came and stood behind me, pressing himself against my bare bottom, warm and beguiling and very hard. "This feels good." Hot hands slid around to my breasts, and my treacherous body thrummed with desire. For a moment, I almost gave in, as he pulled my body against his, but the rising chatter of arriving warriors and their womenfolk carried over the wall. Much as we both wanted this, we'd have to wait.

I turned around and thrust the braccae into his hands. "Put these on."

Chapter Forty-Seven

It felt as though everyone in the fortress had crammed themselves into the Great Hall, which would have been impossible. People sat jammed shoulder to shoulder, and someone had dragged in extra tables. The flames of the hearth fire leapt toward the sooty rafters, and a dozen torches flared on the pillars that supported the roof, all contributing to the fug of smoky heat.

Old and young, men and women, all had come together to celebrate our soon-to-be famous victory. It seemed every person had turned out in their best clothes – shades of red, blue, mustard, green and brown – a muted rainbow of color. Women had donned their finest jewelry, as I had. Girls' hair hung loose and shining to their waists, as mine did, and a few of the older women had piled theirs up in curls after the Roman style.

At the high table, Arthur sat, clean-shaven now, with just the odd cut from his overly hasty ablutions, in his dark tunic and braccae, a stately crow amongst a medley of would-be birds of paradise. His only concessions to ornamentation were the heavily embroidered gold edging to neck, sleeves and hem of his tunic, the golden torc about his neck, and the circlet set in his dark hair.

He certainly scrubbed up well. I couldn't take my eyes off him, but that was nothing new. Whatever it was he possessed, it clung about him now in a cloak of noble kingliness, drawing every eye in the hall. Gone was the playful lover of earlier, and in his place sat a regal warrior king, gazing benevolently at his gathered people. Beside him, as his warrior queen, I sat up straighter, conscious of the gaze of so many people resting on me. No comfortable slouching for a queen.

Archfedd, in her best dress, which to judge by its tightness needed replacing, sat on my right, her round face pink-cheeked and bright with excitement at being allowed to dine in the Hall for once. Another concession had been made, and Reaghan sat at her side, her shining eyes mirroring her best friend's.

Servants carried the food from table to table. They'd served the high table first, of course, and a plate of sliced venison sat in front of me – with a sauce of onions and wine. This was accompanied by leeks and the customary cabbage, this time cooked with apples and raisins imported from the eastern end of the Middle Sea, like my sponge and the Falernian. A king's hall eats well.

Cei, Coventina, and Merlin sat beyond Arthur, with Llacheu at the far end of the high table. His likeness to his father struck me once again, and as I watched him, a proud smile slipped across my face. A son to be proud of, for not just Arthur but for me as well.

From nowhere a shiver ran down my back. If I'd been in my own world, I'd have said someone was walking over my grave, and laughed it off. But here, my instinct for being more wary had me searching the Hall for whatever had raised my hackles.

Underneath the table, Arthur's hand caressed my thigh, the heat of his touch radiating out and settling in my groin, an ache I longed to satisfy. I covered his hand with mine, and kept on scanning the crowded tables.

At the shadowy far end of the hall, the young apprentice warriors had all crowded together at one long table, sideways on to the rest of the hall. Something about them drew my attention, but I couldn't work out what.

Under my curious gaze, they raised their goblets to one another, shouting with laughter at something one of them must have said.

Probably some crude joke – boys that age aren't renowned for their wit.

All but one of them. Amhar's cold stare was fixed on me, icy enough to freeze the leaping hearth fire between us.

If I hadn't been already seated, that stare might have sent me reeling backward. As it was, my free hand went to my mouth before I could stop myself, to stifle a sharp gasp of shock.

Why was he staring at me with so much venom in his eyes? How could an eleven-year-old boy look at me, his mother, with such hatred? With an enormous effort, I pulled myself together, gathering my shocked wits, and forced a nervous smile.

He looked away, turning his back with determination. The boy beside him sloshed cider into his beaker, and Amhar raised it to his lips.

I glanced sideways at Arthur, the heat of his hand on my thigh suddenly suffocating. Could Amhar have seen me looking at Llacheu? Was that jealousy I'd surprised on his face? Could he be *jealous* of his half-brother? For a few moments I struggled with a wave of guilt that somehow, I'd let him see something that had so upset him.

A servant slid more meat onto my plate before I could wave him away. Arthur and Cei laughed together on my left, oblivious to the cold dread that had settled in my heart. A dread born not just from the natural upset at my son's expression, but from my knowledge of the future that suddenly weighed on me like heavy pigs of lead, pressing me down.

Amhar's back remained angry and stiff as he held out his goblet for more cider.

I looked down at my food. Food for which I now had no appetite at all.

In an attempt to watch my son covertly, I picked at the meat. Another servant refilled my goblet, and I took a long gulp, letting the rich amber wine run down my throat. Arthur had been saving it for just such a special occasion, but the pleasure of it had deserted me.

I glanced along the table. The same servant filled the goblets of Arthur, Cei, Coventina, Merlin... and Llacheu.

For the first time, I wondered if Arthur was honouring his oldest son, his bastard, more than he should be. I loved Llacheu like a son myself, not caring that another woman had birthed him, nor that he was illegitimate, but Amhar was my own child. Somehow, without our noticing, he'd reached the age where he'd soon be a man, ready to fight as a warrior beside his father and brother. That he already felt a kind of jealousy for his cousin Medraut had been apparent for some time, but I'd never expected to find him nurturing the same feelings for Llacheu, the kind big brother he'd always looked up to.

Arthur's hand squeezed my thigh, and all I wanted to do was shake him off. The desire of earlier had evaporated like morning mist in the hot sun.

Laughter, joyful and drunken for the most part, rose to the rafters, too loud, too merry.

Scarcely three days after the battle, the men seemed yet again to have put behind them the deaths of their comrades, the suffering they'd seen, the violence they'd had a part in.

I'd seen it all before, many times, but tonight their ability to forget made me want to shout and scream at them that battles were terrible, and how with their friends lying cold and dead, we shouldn't be celebrating like this.

But I couldn't. I had to remember they lived in a time where the obligation to defend their king loomed large, that danger lay in the most unexpected of places in their everyday lives, and that all of them knew they might *die* at any moment. Living like that, how could I expect them to dwell on the losses in their lives? Their behavior didn't mean their comrades were forgotten. Rhiwallon was not and never would be. But it did mean that once mourned, the lost were put away, life went on, and grief was kept private and muted.

Maybe there was no other way to cope.

I watched their faces as they downed their wine and cider, their celebrations a bit too loud, a bit too enthusiastic, as though they thought that by doing so, they'd still the unquiet ghosts of the dead who huddled in the shadowy corners of the Hall.

A sobering thought.

Arthur leaned toward me. "I wish this was all done with." He smiled. "I want you to myself."

I forced a smile, but the pleasure had vanished from my heart. I groped for some way to rebuild the barriers we'd so inadvertently set up between our son and us. "Do you think you might include Amhar tonight? Single him out from his fellows?" I bit my lip. "I think he's feeling rather forgotten."

Arthur shrugged. "What for? He didn't do anything. He's just a boy, learning his trade. He'll have to wait his turn to win battle honors."

Sometimes my husband could be far too obtuse. "I know all that," I said, struggling to be patient. "But he's our son. He's your heir. He should be here on the high table with us. With his brother and sister."

Arthur frowned. He'd had rather a lot to drink, and for a moment he stared unfocused at me. "Llacheu won his place on the high table through his own valor. He was at the battle, leading the attack. Amhar did nothing."

I grit my teeth. This was like wading through treacle. "I know what Llacheu did. But Archfedd is here, and Reaghan. They didn't do any fighting and nor did Coventina." I paused. "And I might have been there, but I didn't fight."

He sighed. "Archfedd is a princess. She sits here for that reason. And you are my queen. And Coventina is Cei's wife."

"Amhar is a prince. So why isn't he here?"

This made Arthur scowl. "He would have been here if he'd come to greet us with his sister on our return. Where was he then? Skulking with his friends in the barracks, drinking, gambling? Who knows? But he wasn't at the Hall to welcome us."

The knuckles of the hand gripping the stem of his goblet whitened. "If he's not interested in us, then why should I single him out for any honor?" He glanced at Llacheu who was talking loudly to Merlin, a chicken leg in one hand and his goblet of wine in the other. "He needs to follow Llacheu's example more closely."

Oh, for crying out loud.

Was he stupid? The urge to grab him by the shoulders – yes, his bad shoulder as well – seized me. I hung onto my rapidly unraveling patience with difficulty. "You've managed to sideline Amhar once this year already by singling out Medraut and making it seem like a reward." I kept my voice as low as possible, acutely aware of the part I'd played in that. "And now he's down there with his friends thinking you've ignored him again."

Why hadn't I thought of this beforehand and asked Arthur, in private, to include our son at the high table? Because I'd been too busy wanting Arthur to make love to me. Because I'd been thinking of myself. Big mistake when you're a parent – bigger still when you're a queen.

Arthur could scowl with the best of them. His brows lowered over his eyes even further, and he removed his hand from my thigh. A bad sign. "Maybe if he were a little more like Llacheu and Medraut, he might find himself treated like the warrior he wants to be."

"That's not really fair. He's just a child. They're both older than him. How can he compete?'

On my right, Archfedd and Reaghan, who'd been allowed a little watered wine, were giggling with gay abandon, tipsy, no doubt. At least one member of our family was happy. Down in the center of the hall a juggler was tossing apples into the air.

"He'll be twelve soon," Arthur said, his voice hardening. "He needs to grow up and stop behaving like a sulky child. Don't think I haven't noticed, because I have." He jerked his head down the hall toward the bottom table. "I saw the look he gave you. For that alone he deserves a whipping."

Oh no.

"That was my fault," I gabbled. "He saw me looking at Llacheu. I couldn't help it. I was thinking how much like you he is." And how proud I was of him. Had that been written across my face for all to see?

Arthur put his hand on mine where it lay beside my plate, his grip iron-hard. "And Amhar isn't?" Just three words, but they held so much. Was he really raising that now? After so long? I struggled to steady my breath, panting as though I'd been running.

What was I doing? Everything I said was sinking me deeper into a mire of my own making. Somehow, I'd turned a joyful celebration into a fight between me and Arthur, and not a fight I wanted to conduct in public.

I pulled my hand away from his. "I feel a little unwell. The heat in here's too much for me. I need to retire to our chamber." Before he could stop me, I'd pushed my seat back from the table and risen to my feet. "Goodnight." I kissed him lightly on the cheek.

He made no move to detain me. At least he had the sense not to cause a scene in public. I turned away, and at the far end of the hall saw Amhar's dark head turn to watch me leave.

Chapter Forty-Eight

I DIDN'T SLEEP. The partition wall, which didn't reach the roof, did nothing to diminish the shouting, singing, the fights over scraps between hounds, the music rising to the rafters, and the intermittent banging of goblets or knife hilts on tables.

After Maia had unlaced my gown and I'd had a quick wash and brushed my teeth, I climbed into bed and pulled the covers over my head, but even that didn't keep out the noise. And of course, my overactive brain wouldn't let me sleep, either.

Everything I'd ever known about King Arthur, almost all of it learned from my father, spun around inside my brain as if it were a tumble dryer on fast spin, making my head ache. It was widely believed that no son of Arthur had inherited his role in Britain.

When Gildas had written his moany rant some time in the mid-sixth century, he'd mentioned no heir to Arthur. Although Gildas, if I was honest, had only written about five kings, and all of them he'd labeled as bad. So maybe Amhar would be a good king, and go on to rule after Arthur's death – or removal to Avalon, if you believed that nonsense.

Having to think about Arthur's death, the proximity of which was another thing weighing heavily in my heart now Badon was behind us, cut me to the quick. But I couldn't avoid it for much longer – one day soon it would be coming.

I rolled onto my other side, my back to the noise in the Hall.

The fact that I'd never heard of any of Arthur's sons meant nothing. My father might well have known of them. It didn't mean they hadn't existed, as they clearly had – or even that they'd died before Arthur himself did. That last thought renewed the shivers down my spine. I pushed it away with determination. It didn't bear thinking about. Oh, how I wished I could talk to Dad. He'd have known. Although the thought of knowing didn't give me any comfort.

I rolled over again and pulled one of my pillows over my head. The racket persisted. Everyone in the hall must be getting very drunk. When the fighting began, fueled, no doubt, by an excess of alcohol, I groaned and clamped my hands over my ears. Shouts followed, amongst which I recognized Cei's voice, and after a bit the noise died down. No doubt the troublemakers had been evicted.

I must have dozed off for a while because a crash woke me. A couple of the oil lamps were still burning in their alcoves, and by their light I made out Arthur's shape, standing one of our chairs back up again, one hand rubbing his shin. Unaware he was being watched, he leaned heavily on the table, his head drooping between his shoulders, motionless for a long minute. Not enough light for me to make out his expression, but his body language told me more.

He was drunk. I hadn't seen him like this for a long time, and it usually only happened when he felt particularly emotional about something. I lay still, watching from half beneath the covers on our bed.

He straightened up, running the fingers of one hand through his shaggy hair, pushing it back from his face. A gesture of despair.

Why? What was wrong? Did he feel something of what I'd been feeling all evening?

Without moving from the table, he began peeling off his clothes. His belt hit the table-top with an audible clunk from the heavy buckle. His boots went skidding across the floor as he kicked them off. He hauled off his tunic and linen undershirt as though they'd burned his skin, dropping them to the floor from where no doubt Maia would pick them up tomorrow.

In just his braccae, he padded to the bench, where a large earthenware bowl always stood. Maia had replenished it with clean water after I'd had my wash, but it would be cold by now. Water splashed, drops catching the dim light of the fading lamps and sparkling like diamonds. He paused, head hanging again, hands resting heavily on either side of the bowl. Then he dunked his entire head in the cold water. He must be very drunk to need to do that.

Lifting his head, he gave it a shake, wet hair sending a spray of water that made the nearest oil lamp hiss. Then, with careful precision, he brushed his teeth, spitting the bits of powdered charcoal and dried mint leaves out into a small bowl – the forerunner of a spittoon, perhaps.

Beyond the wall, silence had fallen, interspersed with snoring. Arthur's shoulders rose and a deep sigh carried to me.

Weaving a not too straight line, he headed for our bed. I stiffened, watching through eyes open only a slit, wary of what he might have in mind. I was in no mood for sex, and he was in no state for it. But I needn't have worried. Without bothering to remove his braccae, he flopped down on top of the covers on his side of our wide bed, letting the air escape his lungs in another long sigh.

I lay still, as a mixture of thoughts and feelings whirled in my head. Part of me wanted to reach out to him and pull him close, to hold him against my breasts and never let him go. But another part, with perhaps a louder voice, told me he was being unreasonable, that he wasn't being a good father, and I shouldn't pander to him.

I stayed still.

From beyond the wall, the sound of snoring increased, like that of a nasally congested pig. Someone who'd been too drunk to make it home – or possibly one of the hounds.

From his quick breathing, I could tell Arthur wasn't sleeping.

I tried to make my own sound natural.

"Gwen?"

A fail on that then. "Yes?"

"Are you awake?"

Despite myself a smile curved my mouth. "Clearly."

A long silence. Maybe he was dozing off. After all that alcohol he ought to be.

No, he wasn't. "What have I done wrong?" His voice sounded uncertain, confused, perhaps regretful.

I bit my lip. I'd been with my modern-day boyfriend, Nathan, for such a short time compared with the years I'd been with Arthur. We'd not had children. I'd worked with them in the library, but nothing had prepared me for being the mother of a budding warrior, a mixture of a rebellious prince and a jealous child going off the rails. I had no idea how I'd have coped with this in my world.

He turned onto his side to face me. "Am I a bad father?"

This was so close to what I'd been thinking, I caught my breath loud enough for him to hear.

Another long silence. I tried to marshall my thoughts. I was tired, hungry as I'd not eaten much, and my head ached. Not a good condition for a deep conversation.

"It's hard being a parent," I whispered, conscious of the fact that if I could hear the snoring next door, there might be someone there who might overhear my words.

One of the surviving oil lamps guttered and went out, casting one side of the chamber into darkness.

His head moved as he nodded. "I know."

"I didn't ever think it would be easy," I went on. "I've seen enough naughty children in my old world, and here. But I think here the difference is they grow up so quickly. Too quickly. They're not children as long as they are in my old world. Amhar's not quite twelve, yet, but he's well into his training to become a warrior – already part of a man's world."

I felt him stiffen. "As I was."

My turn to nod, even though in the gloom he probably couldn't see my reaction. "Yes. Like you. But he's not you. And he's not Llacheu, nor Medraut either. He's himself. And in many ways, he's still just a little boy. A child. One thing I've learned is that children grow up at different rates. Not every boy will be ready to be a warrior at the same age." I paused. "As young as you were."

"I do know that."

"But you don't let *him* know that. You don't show him any patience. He thinks you love Llacheu and Medraut more than him because they can do more. He believes you think they're better. He's your heir, which should make him feel loved and wanted and important. But I don't think it does. I think he feels he's constantly having to catch up because he's the youngest."

"I do try."

Not very hard.

I sighed. "I know you do. You're a good father to Archfedd. She adores you. But she's a girl, and it's different for fathers and sons."

Oh, for a book on the psychology of parenting. There'd be plenty on the shelves in the library where I once worked.

I wriggled around onto my side, so I was facing him. The light from the one still-burning lamp illuminated his face.

"I suppose," he whispered, "that I didn't have such a good relationship with my father either. He preferred my sisters. And Cadwy. Or so I thought."

I seized upon this like a drowning man would have done a straw. "Yes. You're right, and you mustn't let history repeat itself. This is just like your situation as a boy. Only Llacheu isn't Cadwy, and he loves Amhar, not hates him. They shouldn't be rivals for your affection. You mustn't let Amhar see it that way."

He nodded. Despite the toothbrushing, his breath reeked of alcohol. "I'm sorry, Gwen. I love all my children, but perhaps I expect the most from Amhar. Perhaps I expect too much." He paused, the light from that single lamp highlighting a glimmer of moisture in his eyes. "He's my heir. I sometimes forget his age." He moved closer, wincing as he leaned on his bad shoulder. "I need him to learn that you only gain respect from your deeds. That you don't inherit respect – you have to win it for yourself. If he's ever going to make a strong king, he needs to learn that."

I reached out and stroked his cheek. "I see both sides from where I'm sitting. I see you wanting a strong, capable son by your side. You've got Llacheu and that pleases you, and he's a wonderful son I love as my own. But you've another son who can't quite make it yet, but who desperately wants to. He longs to be like Llacheu, and have you, and me, look at him with eyes full of pride."

A lump was forming in my throat. "But he can't do that yet. He wants to be big and strong like Llacheu... and Medraut. He wants the other boys to look up to him, but they're all older and bigger. But above all he wants you to notice him and show your pride." I hesitated. "That wouldn't be so hard, would it?"

Silence for a few long moments. His eyes closed.

I waited.

He opened his eyes. "I *am* proud of him."

I pulled him closer. "Then show it." I leaned forward and kissed him gently on the lips. "Show him you love him better than the others. Llacheu's old enough to understand. He won't be jealous, I promise."

He nodded. "I'll try."

But were we already too late?

To be continued in *The Road to Avalon*

If you want to follow Fil and read more of her books then you can find her on the following social media sites and on her website where you can sign up for her mailing list. She loves to chat with her readers.

filreid.com
facebook.com/filreidauthor
twitter.com/Filreidauthor
instagram.com/fjrflicka

Author's Notes

Thank you for reading my book. I'm hoping you've read books one to four, as well, and will go on and read the final book when it comes out in November – *The Road to Avalon*. I've loved writing this series and was very sad to get to the end of it. However, a reliving of the pleasure of the writing returns as each book comes out and reviews start to come in. So, if you have read and enjoyed my book, it would warm my heart if you were to leave me a review. Thank you.

I do almost all my research from books, online and with in-person visits to the sites I write about. Someone recently commented that they thought I'd clearly visited all the places I describe, and they were right. Not just so I can better write about them, but because they fascinate me, as does everything remotely Arthurian. And everything historical as well. Oddly, I didn't like the history A level I did at school, as that was so dry and dusty and boring. What I like about history is being able to get hands on, to stand right on the spot where I've visualised my characters standing, and to be able to craft a narrative that's as believable as possible due to my research.

This is the fifth book in my series about Gwen and Arthur, and in this one, the penultimate chapter of their story, we finally reach the last of Nennius's twelve battles. I've built my timeline roughly around them. It's doubtful they're historically accurate in any way, but they're well-known enough for me to want to use them. And Badon is the final one of the twelve, so I've been looking forward to getting there. And of course, there's Excalibur in this book as well.

I've steered clear of including too much of the "romance" stories of the later Middle Ages, but I wanted to include a few bits and pieces that are strongly associated with the Arthurian canon. One of them was Merlin, of course, and another is Arthur's swords. Not everyone knows that the sword in the stone was a different sword to Excalibur. Arthur supposedly broke the sword in the stone and was thus presented with Excalibur by the Lady of the Lake. I've tried to incorporate this legend and make it as realistic as I can without any mysterious arms truly sticking out of a lake. I hope you've liked my version of events.

The characters in all the books are as closely based on real people as is possible considering the 1500-year time gap. I sourced the names of most of the kings from genealogical king lists that are, of course, not that reliable, but the names fitted in well with my time period. The kingdoms really existed, Roman Britain having divided up into lots of self-governed small areas after the legions departed, and, as archaeology progresses, we are beginning to discover that a lot of the old Roman towns did continue on throughout the fifth and into the sixth century.

Several people have remarked that they didn't know Arthur had children. Well, he did, and all the children mentioned in these books "existed" if you can call it that, in legend if in no other way. And they have 'endings' to their stories that you'll find out in book six. I've particularly enjoyed using some of the lesser-known Arthurian legends. For Arthur's companions, I've stuck with the ones thought to be his earliest, and thus perhaps best attested, as genuine – Cei, Gwalchmei, Bedwyr, Medraut, and even Llawfrodedd whose name you might think you've never heard before. Well, he has a smidgen of a legend of his own, but don't go searching or it might spoil book six for you.

Two of my favourite Arthurian sites are Glastonbury Tor and South Cadbury Castle (Din Cadan). The former always swarms with tourists, so in actual fact, Gwen would have found it almost impossible to scatter her father's ashes alone in book one, but the second is much quieter. It's only about ten miles distant from Glastonbury, a route that's crossed by something called Arthur's Hunting Path or The Hunter's Causeway, where, if you stand at midnight on Christmas Eve, you'll see him and his ghostly men ride past with their hounds, off hunting.

South Cadbury has been associated with Camelot (whose etymology suggests Camulodonum – Colchester – in the East of Britain, and is entirely late medieval in its origin) for a long time. John Leland, in 1542, first wrote about this association, but it's likely it existed locally long before he committed it to paper. This was followed by William Camden (1551 – 1623) who wrote:

"…and taketh him a rill neere which is Camalet, a steepe hill and hard to get up: on the top whereof are to bee seene expresse tokens of a decayed Castle with triple rampires of earth cast up, enclosing within it many acres of ground, and there appeare about the hill five or six ditches, so steepe that a man shall sooner slide downe than goe downe. The inhabitants name it King Arthur's Palace…"

This hilltop fortress, thought until then to be exclusively Iron Age, was excavated in the 1960s by Leslie Alcock, who discovered it had been massively refortified at exactly the right time for the leader who organised it to have been Arthur. Whoever he was, he was lord of the biggest fortified hilltop in Britain, so he had to have wielded enormous power. I was lucky enough, aged about nine, to visit South Cadbury in the final year of excavation, taken by my parents. I have to admit to having been slightly disappointed in it back then, as at that point all I knew of King Arthur was gleaned from Disney's *The Sword in the Stone* and the musical *Camelot*. Nowadays I feel quite differently and it's one of my favourite Arthurian sites to visit.

To return to Badon. No one knows where any of Arthur's battles were fought, nor if they really existed. Badon, though, is mentioned not just by Nennius but also by Gildas in his *De Excidio Britanniae* (a moan about the kings in or around the 540s so after Arthur's death) and in the *Annales Cambriae* (the Welsh Annals), which also mention

Camlann, Arthur's final, fateful battle. But whether these mentions were added in much later, no one knows, and Gildas rather meanly never mentions Arthur by name, instead implying (a little ambiguously I must point out) that it was Ambrosius who won at Badon, despite him having to be an ancient graybeard if he did.

Because none of the battle sites are anything more than conjecture, I've been able to choose relatively freely where to set them. Hence, the Battle of the City of the Legion in book four being in York rather than Chester or Caerleon. There are a good few choices for Badon, but my personal favorite happens to be not far from where I live. Liddington Castle, a hillfort lying on the Ridgeway, an ancient chalkland track, above the village of Badbury. A hillfort that used to be called Badbury itself. Just below the fort, the Roman road of Ermin Street, running from Silchester in the east to Cirencester in the West (both Roman towns) crosses the Ridgeway. And if you head back a few miles further East, that Roman road runs right through the village of Baydon. You can see why I chose this location for the battle now, can't you? I was lucky enough to be able to go up there and stand where the armies in my books were, to plan out the battle and see what they could see from where they stood. A great help to a writer, and I hope it shows in my version of the battle.

That's enough in the way of explanations. I could go on forever talking about Arthurian legend and history, so I need to stop myself right here. Thank you so much for reading this. I hope you've enjoyed my books and will go on and read the final instalment – The Road to Avalon – in which all the loose ends get tied up. It's out in the last week of November.

And don't forget to join my mailing list on my website.

Fil Reid
5th August 2023

Acknowledgements

I'd like to thank everyone who has helped me even in the smallest way with the writing of this book – with the writing of the whole series in fact. First of all, my husband, Patrick, who listened to each book as I read it aloud to him looking for errors and made lots of suggestions. He's also been my walking encyclopedia of reference as he's the cleverest and best-read person I know. In particular, he knows a lot about wildlife, so if I ever want the call of a bird in the background, he can tell me which to mention. He's been a support to me in many other ways as well, which I won't go into here. If it wasn't for Patrick, I'd never have got these books written.

Then, of course, my publisher, Kathryn Le Veque at Dragonblade in the US. She gave me the opportunity to enter their annual competition and win a three-book contract, which has now extended to the next three in the series and more books next year. Thank you so much for this opportunity. At Dragonblade I'd like to mention my wonderful editor, Amelia Hester, Shawn Morrison and Natalie Sowa, as well as the talented Dar Albert, their cover designer for the amazing covers she's given my books. I love them. Thanks also to my agent, Susan Yearwood, and my PA, Dee Foster, for all the work they've done.

About the Author

After a varied life that's included working with horses where Downton Abbey is filmed, riding racehorses, running her own riding school, owning a sheep farm and running a holiday business in France, Fil now lives on a widebeam canal boat on the Kennet and Avon Canal in Southern England.

She has a long-suffering husband, a rescue dog from Romania called Bella, a cat she found as a kitten abandoned in a gorse bush, five children and six grandchildren.

She once saw a ghost in a churchyard, and when she lived in Wales there was a panther living near her farm that ate some of her sheep. In England there are no indigenous big cats.

She has Asperger's Syndrome and her obsessions include horses and King Arthur. Her historical romantic fiction and children's fantasy adventures centre around Arthurian legends, and her pony stories about her other love. She speaks fluent French after living there for ten years, and in her spare time looks after her allotment, makes clothes and dolls for her granddaughters, embroiders and knits. In between visiting the settings for her books.

Social Media links:
Website – filreid.com
Facebook – facebook.com/Fil-Reid-Author-101905545548054
Twitter – @FJReidauthor

Made in the USA
Middletown, DE
15 September 2023